THE
MOVEMENT

AYISHA MALIK

REVIEW

First published in 2022 by
HEADLINE REVIEW
An imprint of HEADLINE PUBLISHING GROUP

1

Cataloguing in Publication Data is available from the British Library

ISBN 978 1 4722 7931 6 (Hardback)
ISBN 978 1 4722 9833 1 (Trade paperback)

Typeset in 11.5 / 16pt Dante MT Std by Jouve (UK), Milton Keynes

Printed and bound in Great Britain by Clays Ltd, Elcograf S.p.A.

HEADLINE PUBLISHING GROUP
An Hachette UK Company
Carmelite House
50 Victoria Embankment
London EC4Y 0DZ

www.headline.co.uk
www.hachette.co.uk

THE
MOVEMENT

By Ayisha Malik

Sofia Khan novels:

Sofia Khan is Not Obliged
The Other Half of Happiness
Sofia Khan and the Baby Blues (*Quick Reads short story*)

This Green and Pleasant Land
The Movement

For younger readers:

Seven Sisters
Mansfield Park

To my bulbul, Shaista Chishty, for being the voice inside my head.

And to Eli Dryden, for being the voice outside it.

Table of Contents

PART ONE

THE CALAMITY
May 2021

I have suffered so long from an inclination to tell people to shut the fuck up that I've finally decided to take my own advice. I have decided to shut the fuck up.

A revolutionary notion.

What's become the purpose of words anyway?

My conviction has collapsed under the weight of verbosity. The need to know. Be known. The self-reverence! The push notifications, emails, Whatsapps, phone calls, texts . . . It's all muted the better part of my own mutable person. I can barely hear my own voice. The world's always been falling apart, but that's not to say I should fall apart with it. There's no excuse for that sort of behaviour.

A lack of priority is how we – I – got into this fucking mess.

I've nothing new to say. Has anyone?

'Beware the Barrenness of a Busy Life.'

Yours,
Sara Javed
May 2021

P.S: I will not be writing opinion pieces about this.

Sara Javed had tried to tolerate people but the age of fervour and passion hadn't aroused in her an equal zeal. In that sense she was out of fashion. Sara had undergone a protracted period of struggling before going silent, alleviated, marginally, by the noise-cancelling headphones she'd felt compelled to purchase four years ago. She would wear them on book tours, author dinners, even at home, as she became increasingly popular and therefore subjected to an equally increasing demand for *opinions*. She had tried to conjure indignation, when the occasion called for it, but it generally only lasted for a few hours, and some tweets.

Sara's watery engagement with most things made the letter her publisher, Penelope Pembrooke, was reading now, under the domed ceiling of the Royal Literature Arts Club, all the more galling.

'Are you fucking kidding me?' exclaimed Penelope, tugging at her sequinned dress.

'I just got the email as the taxi pulled up,' said Katarazyna Nowak.

'Is that it?' Penelope scrolled up and down Kat's phone, expecting her, as Sara's publicist, to have more information on this unprecedented turn of events. 'What does she mean she's decided to *"shut the fuck up"*?'

'She's taken some sort of vow. Of silence.'

'*Silence?*'

'So much of what she's been saying over the past year's making sense now,' said Kat, gravely. 'She was becoming a little—'

'*Difficult*—'

'Tired.'

'Of *what* exactly? Her sales. Awards? *Her rising success?*'

'People choose to take control in all sorts of ways. It might be good PR-wise,' Kat added. '*Silence amid noise.*'

'There's a time and place for this kind of thing,' exclaimed Penelope who did not think in copy.

'She just had enough of . . .' Kat gestured at the hall with its marble floors, waiters in white tuxes offering wine and canapés. *People*. Their constant chattering. 'You know . . . the absurdity of it all.'

Someone in a group by the reception doors guffawed.

'"Words, words, words," she'd say, in that exasperated tone.'

'*Words* are her job,' retorted Penelope. 'She has a prize to accept!' *The prize.*

Her eyes darted around as people streamed into the hall in all their finery.

Penelope had been tipped off that Sara was going to win tonight's award. It was supposed to be one of the most illustrious nights of Sara's career. And, by default, Penelope's too.

'Darling!' Penelope pushed the phone into Kat's hands and air-kissed a passing literary agent.

'I've got everything crossed for Sara,' said the agent. 'Especially after all that nonsense last year. Mountain out of a molehill.'

Penelope nodded. The way Sara's words had been twisted by a minority during the Victoria Park Book Festival debacle, damaging a nature that was already predisposed to self-doubt . . . The public were impossible sometimes.

Penelope spent the following ten minutes being wished luck or told emphatically that the tide was turning – no one explained towards what. Sara's publisher's belief in her was about to pay-off in front of two hundred members of the industry's elite.

Kat tried ringing Sara again. Nothing. 'I'll draft a press release.'

Professionally speaking, this was going to be a PR ball-ache for Kat, yet she couldn't help but admire that Sara had put her money where her mouth was. Literally.

'She's gone through a lot the past year,' continued Kat. 'And silence *is* a virtue.'

Penelope stared at her. As if virtue was a necessary aspect of success!

(Virtue-signalling stood a much better chance.)

'*Shit.* I'll have to accept the prize on her behalf.' She grabbed Kat's phone, cutting and pasting Sara's words to suit her own speech.

(The line between editing and erasure wasn't that fine.)

'Who said "*Beware the Barrenness of a Busy Life*"?' muttered Penelope.

'Socrates. Sara quotes it all the time.'

'Oh, yes. With that look. As if you've been dodging your taxes.'

What would people think? The effrontery of winning the Mildred Aitken Award and not turning up. Had Sara forgotten the first four years of her career in which she'd sold a total of five thousand and fifty-nine copies of her three books – across all formats. But Penelope believed that Sara had *things* to say. Was Sara often hesitant when it came to voicing them? *Yes.* Did Penelope wish Sara could be more categorical in her opinions? *Of course.* It'd save people having to think too deeply about what Sara meant.

'Hi.'

Roxy Hussain stood beside Penelope.

Of all her needy authors, here was Roxy, stoker of the Victoria Park fire, dressed in a tailored red suit. A sharp note in the sea of black gowns and tuxedos. Penelope leant forward and dutifully air-kissed her on both cheeks.

'Sorry I haven't got back to you yet about your new book proposal.' If one could call it that. 'It's been so busy with—'

'Sara's shortlisting,' Roxy finished.

Sara's protégé and friend, Roxy, had initially delivered on the promise Penelope had sensed when Sara first introduced them. Roxy's debut, a controversial memoir, had become a bestseller and had stayed in the charts for two full weeks; it was in the end of year press round-ups, a sure sign of success. She had been listed as 'One-to-Watch' in two major magazines. Only that was three years ago now, and one could only watch for so long.

'I haven't seen Sara.' Roxy looked about the room. 'I'm on a table with, ugh, *Aadhi Sathar.*'

Kat eyed Roxy with decided coolness.

Aadhi Sathar! Oh, he'd enjoy Sara's silence enormously. Another thing about which to *opine*. 'Let's set up a meeting,' said Penelope. 'You had some *interesting* thoughts . . .'

Kat watched as Roxy walked away. 'Being a one-hit-wonder would serve her right for the way she treated Sara after Victoria Park. As for Aadhi, he can—'

'*Pen!*—'

Penelope looked up at the approaching publisher, arms outstretched.

Kat forced a smile.

'—You must be *so* proud of Sara.'

Roxy Hussain took a deep breath as she walked towards her table, where sat one of the country's most acerbic and thus, naturally, sought-after cultural critics.

'Aadhi Sathar?' said Roxy as she stopped beside him.

Aadhi who had been talking to his neighbour looked up.

Roxy swapped her place-card, a few chairs away, for the one next to Aadhi and sat down, waiting for similar recognition. She was a bestselling author, after all. 'I enjoyed your most recent piece in *The Telegram* . . .' As a minority woman forging her way through an unjust world, *what* you read mattered just as much as *where* you read it, and so she added, 'Surprisingly.' She offered a smile to counter the intended bite.

'Oh,' replied Aadhi. 'Thank you. I suppose.'

His piece had been about the farcical nature of book awards. Despite two long-listings and one shortlisting, Roxy's memoir had not won any awards, and so she was inclined to agree with him.

'Sorry, you are . . .?'

Roxy felt the inevitable flattening of self at the slight. Surely as one of the few women of colour in the literary world, alongside Sara, her name should be etched in his brain. So what if she had only written – and deleted – two-thousand-and-fifty-three words in the last three years?

(It hadn't yet occurred to her that being a writer meant telling more than just one story. That it centred around others, not the self.)

'I wrote *An Unveiling*—'

Pause.

'—My *bestselling* memoir—'

Aadhi arched an eyebrow.

'—about growing up gay in a Muslim household.'

'Ah,' Aadhi gave a vague smile, then turned back to his neighbour.

Aadhi's inability to place her had displaced her entirely. But she knew his type of brown man. Fawning over old, white male authors just to feel important. Well, fuck him. The arrogant, self-satisfied, uninquisitive . . .

Deflated, Roxy looked around the hall filled with white faces, with its low, tastefully lit chandeliers and elaborate, floral centrepieces. She was here because she deserved to be. She hadn't written about her struggles just to be snubbed by the likes of him. She'd left her family home, broken ties with her parents, even her sister, Halimah, in order to live her Truth. She'd worked as a waitress before she got a job in a bookstore, and then she'd met Sara Javed. A brown Muslim woman. Finally someone who would actually understand the daily literary battles.

Roxy had to remind herself that *An Unveiling* had also inspired conversation! And when there was public agitation over the title of the book, considering Roxy had never worn a headscarf, she was duly contrite. She had subsequently written a piece about the influence of Sales & Marketing and the boxing in of marginalised authors. She'd toured bookshops, appeared on panels, spoken to people with similar personal struggles, was invited to important cultural events. She would live her life in service to others.

(Self-deception often felt heroic.)

But when Roxy began to speak to Sara about 'changing the narrative', Sara's eyes would glaze over, as if she were bored. Surely her role model, confidante and fellow woman of colour should have had more to say than 'hmmm', in expressionless acquiescence.

The unfortunate truth, however, was that after scrolling through Halimah's latest Instagram posts, Sara was the one person Roxy wanted to speak to. She could see from her sister's photos that their mother had lost weight. That her dad's usually kind face looked terribly drawn. Had Roxy living her Truth stripped her parents of the ability to live theirs?

Roxy looked around for Sara. Why wasn't she here already, basking in her literary glory?

How fleeting that fame had been for Roxy.

How significantly extended for Sara.

People were taking their seats in the main hall, ready for the speeches to begin.

'It won't do,' muttered Penelope to Kat. She had fought her first husband and cancer and won, while raising two reasonably turned-out children, and coping with an increasingly vague mother. She wouldn't be beaten by *this*.

'Sara owes it to herself and the people who've fought to get her here. Whether she likes it or not, her *voice* matters. So, go and get her.'

'Bu—'

'Now.'

A hush descended as people turned to look at something. Some*one*.

Slowly, walking through a sea of sartorial opulence, wearing just jeans and a sweatshirt and a look of defiant conviction, was the reason for all of Penelope's current panic and acute frustration.

Sara Javed.

Roxy stood up for a better view past the candelabras. *What was Sara wearing?* She was walking towards her own table, head bent low, in *Puma* trainers. Honestly, Sara was so often lost in her own head she didn't care what she might be doing outside it.

Aadhi stood up next to Roxy. 'What a spectacle.'

He had a face that looked as if it were unused to laughter. Another reason, Roxy recalled, that Sara would purse her lips every time the man's name was mentioned.

'Being mirthless is so bloody one-dimensional,' she would say, claiming

11

there was laughter to be had in everything. 'I guess I should be amused by the shit reviews he's given my books.'

Aadhi's words finally registered with Roxy. 'What do you mean, *spectacle*?'

'This need for attention,' he replied.

Roxy felt maddened that Sara, as usual, had got it all for herself.

Her heart quickened as the lights dimmed and a spot-lit Lauren Berger, presenting the award, appeared on stage. News cameras flashed. People at their tables were Live Instagramming, Tweeting. Sara didn't seem right. She looked *serene*.

In her fucking jeans and sweatshirt.

A year ago Roxy would have wished nothing but for Sara to win this prize. But now it would be an *affront*. Sara seemed to have forgotten *who she was*. And if she won, it would break Roxy's belief that words mattered. Words which were her passion and livelihood. Through which Roxy could understand and had been understood.

She felt her face flush, indignation rise.

'The judges apologise for looking exhausted,' began Lauren Berger. 'It's what happens when you lie awake at night, having to decide on a winner from such a staggering list. But in the end, there can only be one—'

Sara was looking at the ground, hands resting on her lap.

'—And so, it is with great honour that I announce the winner of this year's Mildred Aitken Award is . . .'

Roxy's stomach turned. How could Sara look so calm?

Lauren gripped the award, smiled. '*The Stories We Told Ourselves* by Sara Javed.'

What the fuck?

Roxy's disbelief was disturbed by the applause that erupted at the announcement.

How could this be happening?

Flashes from cameras, journalists clamouring forward as Sara looked up from where she sat. Expressionless. Motionless. Kat whispered in Sara's ear. Penelope Pembrooke jumped up, clapping, her smile strained.

Why wasn't Sara moving?

The applause went on.

And on.

And on.

Finally, Sara stood up. She looked irritated. People seemed confused by her reticence as she walked slowly towards the stage, mounting the steps. Lauren, in her four-inch heels, loomed over Sara, as she handed her the coveted award, looking equally confused by Sara's reaction.

Sara was finally holding on to what, Roxy knew, had been her dream. She looked so out of place, standing calmly in front of the mic and yet, strangely, as if this is where she belonged. What genetic strand had she inherited that eluded Roxy?

Roxy waited for Sara to speak. Attempted to stop herself from throwing over the damn centrepiece at how *unfair* it was.

The audience waited.

Sara looked back at the crowd, a panicked expression crossing her face.

Roxy could now hear the indeterminate noises of the room. The tapping of phones. Muffled voices out in the hall. Why wouldn't she speak?

Then Penelope swept into view. She grabbed the award from Sara, pulled her into a hug.

Sara, without acknowledging her, pulled away, and walked off the stage.

Aadhi Sathar, commentator, respected reviewer, filmmaker and advocate for taking responsibility for one's actions, watched on, bemused. The award winner was now sitting back at her table, looking altogether idiotic in her casual attire. The levels to which some people stooped in order to get attention: the world was filled with this type of pseudo-revolutionary. But there would always be an audience for it, as exemplified by the way in which the room now buzzed with curiosity.

He hadn't meant to come to today's ceremony. Unless he was a nominee, he tended to avoid such events: he found the small talk diminishing. But he had been startled awake at 2 a.m., with a cavernous loneliness which he couldn't shake. The quiet horror of recent months, of witnessing his father's descent into dementia, of entering his own unlit flat, alone, at the end of each day, compounded Aadhi's fear of one day being erased from people's memory and history altogether.

Although Sara Javed, silently getting on stage, in her jeans and trainers, confirmed Aadhi's conviction that the world and its people were inherently stupid.

He should have stayed home.

'What an extraordinary honour—' A flustered Penelope Pembrooke looked out on to the perplexed crowd. '—Through her literary career, Sara Javed, author of such critically acclaimed novels as *Woman in Waiting* and *Rule-makers*, has challenged the reader to interrogate intentions, question perception. Sara's far too modest, but as her editor, I have come to thoroughly admire the way she's drawn upon her culture and experiences and brought it to her writing.'

Aadhi groaned. He felt Roxy – *Rukhsana* – glance at him. Of course he had recognised her. But she was everything he despised. Someone who watered down her Muslim identity on one hand, but used it to her advantage to tell her story on the other – so typical of her generation.

'*The Stories We Told Ourselves*,' Penelope motored on, 'is a beautiful, heartfelt, funny and brutal . . .'

Aadhi noticed Sara rubbing her forehead; she looked agitated.

'. . . This book compels us to reveal who we are to ourselves. Compels society to . . .' Penelope struggled. '. . . to think about the choices we make.' She cleared her throat. 'But Sara has always captured the mood of a nation. Anyway, I know you're all wondering about mine and Sara's award relay . . . Ha-ha. In an inspiring move, Sara, who never fails to surprise, has taken . . . a vow of silence. She will not communicate with anyone in any form.'

The audience shuffled about on their seats, a sea of heads turning towards Sara. Cameras flashed. Sara looked determinedly at the ground.

14

Roxy started an Instagram Live feed.

'Do you know her?' Aadhi asked Roxy.

'Oh, I know her.'

All tiresome people knew each other. Then he recalled there'd been some sort of spat between them at a literary festival. He couldn't remember what it had been about. Something ridiculous. He leant forward, watching as Roxy zoomed in on Sara's face, flushed and impenetrable. And he found himself staring at Javed through Roxy's lens, caught between inherent cynicism and something *possibly* interesting.

'The world seems to have got so loud that, and I quote Sara,' continued Penelope, "I can barely hear my own voice".'

The room rippled at the seemingly familiar sentiment. Aadhi scoffed.

'Let's all raise a glass to her incredible win here tonight and her noble endeavour. Sara, may you find your voice—'

Sara's head shot up. For the first time, she looked angry.

'—And may we all *"Beware the Barrenness of a Busy Life"*.'

These words passed like a current through the audience, each mind scanning its regular pastimes. Books and yoga. Activism and navel-gazing. Baking and boxsets. Where exactly did barrenness lie?

'Give me a *fucking* break,' Aadhi muttered.

Penelope descended from the stage and tried to hand the award to Sara, but Sara stood up abruptly. The audience waited for Sara to accept it so they could duly applaud. But she looked at the tall, triangular marker of her struggles and success, still in Penelope's hand, as if she didn't know what it was doing there. Everyone watched, waited, hooked. Then, Sara Javed merely shook her head and backed away.

The murmurs rose.

Aadhi sat in stunned silence. This should be one of the greatest moments of an author's career, yet Javed seemed desperate to escape it.

He noticed Roxy looking at Sara in similar disbelief. Appalled.

A camera flashed in Sara's face and then she pushed through the clamour and strode – practically ran – out of the hall, leaving behind a speechless audience.

Aadhi found himself staring after her. This woman, a writer, feminist – if her books were anything to go by – was *voluntarily* abandoning attention and accolade. Rejecting her award and everything writers – *people* – hold sacred and triumphant.

Their very own voice.

BRAVE NEW WORLD

One Year Later . . .

THE FINAL COUNTDOWN

Matthew Barker, creator of *The Nonrhetorical Forum* Blog, May 2022
3.2M Followers

During a year of unprecedented change the controversial case of Grace Jenkin,s and custody of her son, hovers over our national psyche. Non-Verbalism has forced us to reprioritise individualism. Who knew that there was another way to live? So at odds with what we thought we wanted, which ended up being something we needed. But we must not pretend there haven't been grave repercussions. Or that this government has behaved with anything other than incompetence, splitting this country into factions. Our political leaders should have been judged in court, not Grace Jenkins – a black, single, working mother (defending herself against, might I add, her son's father, whose white, privileged background has afforded him advantages that can't be ignored in the whole case).

The urgent Global Unity Summit – for which we *still* await its outcome – has us on edge. The flip-flopping, the nation-wide unrest . . . Will the Prime Minister listen to the people? And if so, *which* people? We cannot go back, but that does not mean we will move forward.

Everyone has a story about the financial and emotional impact of Non-Verbalism. Stories about finding meaning. Peace in a world that favours war. If Non-Verbalism, and Grace Jenkins, has brought home anything, it is that actions speak louder than words.

I am a lettered, permanent Non-Verbal, but I urge everyone not to let this government polarise us further; to communicate, using whatever means necessary, with friends and family, local communities, gather your neighbours and your conviction.*

When we move forward in our bid for freedom, Verbal or Non-Verbal, we *must* move as one.

* *(A link on the latest Non-Verbal communications software is available on this blog's homepage.)*
To subscribe to the freshest takes on world affairs click *here.*

Aadhi was irritated and it wasn't even 9 a.m. He was running late, his morning ritual of repeating his bank account number, his favourite literary quotes, the birthdays of his friends and family – an obsession correlating to his father's pronounced decline into dementia – holding him up somewhat.

Aadhi prided himself on being the sort to *not suffer fools gladly*, which might account for why he often didn't feel glad, especially over this last twelve months. Aged forty-three, his professional life had possibly passed its peak – as had his personal life – and the gnawing sense of an imminent downward trajectory had given him insomnia. The several awards he'd received for his journalism and documentaries hadn't seemed to make up for the gap left by his past failed relationships. With each passing year, his ex-girlfriend had become increasingly extraordinary in his memory. After five years, the pedestal on which she now stood may as well have been in high heaven. A suitable situation considering the hell from which he viewed her now happily married life, mostly from behind his desk as he sped towards the next deadline.

Aadhi often observed the ease with which people seemed to find life-long, or at least temporary, happiness in another, and so he was forced to consider that perhaps the fault lay in *him*.

A sobering notion.

His existential worry was now punctuated with other, more pressing matters: bloody Matthew Barker of *The Nonrhetorical Forum* espousing impractical idealism, the incompetent government's inability to make a decision to tell the nation *the plan*. Freedom of choice was all very well but only if people actually understood the impact of their choices.

Aadhi sighed.

He noted his sighs, today, were spread far and wide. Even among

Non-Verbals whose queue here in the coffee shop was longer than usual. Aadhi had places to be, news to deliver about the documentary, the project he had been working towards this entire, foolish, life-changing year. Sometimes the documentary felt like the culmination of his entire career. His anticipation blurred against the wait for the announcement of the Global Summit's resolution. Lives would change – only no one was sure whose.

In that sense, there was equality in agitation.

Aadhi checked online for news, but there were no updates since he'd last checked, 36 seconds ago.

The Non-Verbal barista smiled with pointed patience at the gentleman who flicked through the iPad menu. Another unnecessary complication of silent lives. Aadhi let out a more audible sigh. Non-Verbals turned towards him. A few stared until the realisation crept upon them as to who he was. They looked away in pronounced disdain. Collective censure to those who were outspoken about the fact that words still mattered.

Aadhi had never signed up to be a poster-boy for Verbalism, but principles came at a price.

A disgruntled voice emerged. 'We're not allowed to sigh anymore?'

Aadhi turned to see a man, looming large.

Everyone now looked at The Man Who Dared To Speak Without Being Spoken To.

'This is why we're in this state,' he added. 'Thanks to *your* kind—'

Non-Verbals shuffled their feet.

'—Why should *we* suffer in silence because of *your* choices?' he demanded.

As if Verbals suffered anything in silence, the Non-Verbals' scoffs seemed to suggest.

Aadhi wished that Verbals could stop these sorts of outbursts, placing external blame on, clearly, an internal issue. It did not help the cause.

'My kids no longer speak to me,' the man continued, face reddening. 'My wife's left me. And it's because of *you*.' He stepped towards the Non-Verbals' queue, jabbing his finger at them.

Aadhi got ready to intercede.

'Excuse me, sir.' A barista walked up to the man, clearing his throat. 'This is an inclusive café. Please quieten down or . . . or, we'll *have* to ask you to leave.'

'Are you saying I'm a Non-Verbalphobe just because I don't agree with them?' the man exclaimed, so loud Aadhi stepped between him and barista. '*Even you're on their side?*'

The man was demonstrating his civil liberty as a Verbal! But even the illusion of liberty was under attack. He would not be treated this way! He walked out, slamming the door behind him.

Throats were cleared. A Verbal stepped forward. 'People like him – they're just a minority,' she murmured to the Non-Verbals. 'We are with you.'

A Non-Verbal put his hand on his heart by way of thanks. Aadhi used to think it was quite dignified. Until the gesture became a binary statement of either acceptance or rejection for a way of life. The Verbal woman looked sensible enough, but there was no accounting for the way one thought. And yet . . . He quelled his own ideas before they rose. He must.

'Our ethos is respect for each other's way of life.' The barista attempted a smile as he bowed in front of both queues, shooting a grateful nod in Aadhi's direction. 'I'll be practising Non-Verbalism between 9 and 12, but if you have any issues my colleague will be verbal for that duration. Just check our badges.'

Who are we without words! Aadhi wanted to shout.

The doors that had slammed in his face a year ago, after his appearance on *The Great Debate*, made Aadhi wonder what sort of professional foundation he had built for it to give way so easily. He had then refused to give Non-Verbalism more attention. If you gave something space, it grew to occupy it, eventually consuming it. Until of course he was forced to reconsider his verbal choices in a world that was silencing itself. To rail against Non-Verbalism became a matter of survival as well as principle.

He chose not to think about which came first.

The sheer irresponsibility of it had evoked in Aadhi a passion surpassing most he felt in life. But despite the opinion pieces, interviews and TV appearances, nothing could stop this tidal wave of silence from flooding the globe. Sara Javed's singular act at the Mildred Aitkin Award ceremony, one year ago, had spread, mutated, and infected the masses with varying forms of silence.

What would happen if speaking became obsolete? There were social structures in place for a reason. And they were crumbling under silence.

His father, and people like him, didn't need the added difficulty of nurses' and doctors' silence in the face of mental decline. The comfort of a kind voice. What had become of the Hippocratic oath?

They were experiencing the worst global recession for generations, yet people were holding on to silence as a salvation, refusing to see the destruction it wrought. 'Down with Capitalism' was a noble thought, but thoughts did not sustain life. Not in a practical sense.

Revolution was a misdirection.

Then there was Grace Jenkins. Aadhi wasn't sure if he was repelled by her story or in quiet awe of her. It had been rare, in recent years, to see someone hold on to such literal, silent conviction. Despite what she risked losing.

A light flashed above the Verbal counter.

'An Americano and one flat white,' said Aadhi.

The server checked his watch, took off his badge and replaced it: *Non-Verbal.*

Aadhi glanced at the wall behind the counter. *Beware the Barrenness of a Busy Life.* The Socratic quote hung above Sara Javed's letter that had been enlarged and framed, an homage to the woman whose single action had imposed itself upon the world's conscience and changed the way it lived. There were even mugs to prove it. Available for sale with the Socratic quote stamped on it in bold, black letters. Also available in white. Both were being offered at a 15% discount.

Six months ago Aadhi would have stalked out of the café to find a place that refused to capitulate to popular opinion and which only served Verbals. But – and here he couldn't lie – he *was* finding it harder to muster the same indignation he'd felt at the beginning. It worried him that doubt could leak into the crevices of certainty.

'How do you feel about what Grace Jenkins' has done?' he asked his Non-Verbal server. 'You're probably too young to have a child of your own. Do you support her? Given what we know about the child's needs.'

The server shook his head emphatically.

'Why not?' Aadhi asked. 'She's Non-Verbal and proud.'

He raised his eyebrows as if Grace had no right to call herself Non-Verbal.

'I thought you were all meant to stick together?' Aadhi persevered.

The server pushed the two coffees towards Aadhi, *have a shit day*, impressed upon his face.

Someone followed Aadhi out and grabbed his arm.

'I'll tell you something about Grace Jenkins—'

It was a woman, in her early forties maybe, Tory Burch shoes and Silver Cross stroller.

'—no mother in their right mind would be so hideous. What Jenkins has done is practically child abuse,' she proclaimed. 'You're that journalist, aren't you?'

He nodded.

'I organise a mothers' club and have a Facebook following of over forty-thousand women, globally, and growing – who all feel the same about this. *Motherhood* unifies us.'

People walking by turned towards them. They were speaking too loudly, in public. It was quite improper. Tory Burch Mum reached into her puffer vest, pulling out a business card which she offered him.

Aadhi took it: *Mothers for Justice*. 'What do you hope to achieve?'

'To make sure that eventually that child – *every* child – gets what's best for them.'

Aadhi believed in gender equality to such an extent that he was often accused of misogyny. He held this woman in almost as much contempt as he held the father of Grace Jenkins' son.

'You must have a solution, since you have such a strong opinion. Are you offering to take her child in?'

Tory Burch Mum stared at him in surprise. 'You're just another one of those spineless *liberals*,' she announced before stalking off.

'I take offence to that,' he called after her. 'I hate liberals.'

He carried on towards Granary Square, past a series of TV billboards erected around King's Place. 'Silence can change your life' on a loop, along with a Zen proverb: 'When you speak, it is silent. When you are silent it speaks.' Then an advert for a new Silent Room opening in Fitzroy Square. These bloody Non-Verbal moralists with their high ideals loved to ignore the privilege of silence. He knew that for many activists, adopting Non-Verbalism was their attempt to promote equality – if people didn't have an equal voice, then silence was solidarity. Yet these same people paid £70 an hour for a room, alone, to perform their Non-Verbalism.

He remembered when silent afternoons had been introduced in his niece's primary school, a mere three months after Non-Verbalism had begun to spread.

She was five.

He had to admit though, he had noticed an improvement in his niece's ADHD. It created yet another crack in his conviction.

But silence leant itself too much to disorder. Workplaces being forced to accommodate Non-Verbal employees who cited – in writing, of course – their civil right to silence, threatening legal challenges to employers. Aadhi knew the stories of people demanding employers reform their hiring process to be inclusive of Non-Verbals . . . and wasn't the revelation about who was *really* being discriminated against something? Hate crimes against Non-Verbals had almost tripled in the past three months; even lawyers banding together in certain fields to accommodate Non-Verbalism.

And how did such changes *better* society? How could anyone justify it in the face of a flailing economy – people, having bought into this lie of silence, had stopped buying into the lie of material happiness. Emergency services had to re-evaluate protocol due to silent patients: in extreme cases – in which a minority of Non-Verbals had, like Sara Javed, eschewed the written form entirely – DNRs couldn't be signed.

As for criminals, only four weeks ago, because of Grace Jenkins, an official precedent had been set that could make practising Non-Verbalism a contempt of court, and sentencing had since become more severe. Verbals were dismayed at the so-called Non-Verbal Justice Warriors' continued silence. According to NVs who still communicated in writing – known annoyingly as lettered NVs – silence was a means to dismantle the criminal justice system. It would finally be revealed as an outmoded structure, and eventually evolve into a rehabilitative system. Yes, a price would be paid, but for the greater good. A greater freedom.

Stupidity had no limits.

But this had happened so suddenly that governments weren't equipped to handle the changes. There was the natural crushing of the unnatural lifestyle choice in countries like North Korea and Russia. (One would've assumed that silence in certain places would be welcome. But when people in authority asked questions, they demanded answers.) The subcontinent was apparently experiencing a spiritual re-awakening. And when elections were stolen, instead of riots on the streets, there were floods of silent protestors, serene in the face of tyranny.

The first time a mass silent protest happened the world's media had been mesmerised. The feet that stamped the earth in rhythmic unison, the fists that pumped the muted air. The tens of thousands that sat outside the governmental building until they were dragged away by police. And then *that* woman. Aadhi had forgotten her name, but not the image. A policeman grabbing her arm with such force. Instead of pulling away, she had stepped up to him. Her nose almost touching his. Her face raised in pure defiance. At any other time, this image would have provoked a thousand conversations. There had been some commentary, until it was agreed that to talk about a woman, who had moved people without a word, was wrong.

The conversation was shut down.

Instead, her face had been graffitied on walls in cities, towns and villages around the world.

'Silence is Power.'

One only had to look at the image to understand this. It was thus made available to purchase via online retailers across the globe.

Swathes of people in countries like the US and UK embraced Non-Verbalism with as much verve as they'd embraced veganism and avocado on toast.

Aadhi reached Granary Square. A marquee was erected in the middle, urging Verbals and Non-Verbals to come together in peace. People sat in circles, passers-by hovering on the edges.

As Aadhi looked on at the scene he wondered if both sides' principles and convictions were wavering. The factions that had been formed this past year seemed to have dissolved in the past few weeks. Rumours of what the government might mandate, what leaders might say, after all the lies, had not just unsettled people, it had enraged Non-Verbals and Verbals alike. A mutual feeling that no one had anticipated.

A leaflet was thrust into Aadhi's unwilling spare hand.

We demand the government say NO to silence.

Or perhaps not.

It was a group of silent, anti-silence protestors. The masks around their mouths labelled, 'Your silence will not protect you.'

Aadhi sat down on one of the stone benches in the square and set down the coffees. The sun shone through blossom trees, casting shade and light on the marquees and stalls. The bright, late spring day charged with the quiet hustle of opinion. The students were standing in solidarity, Verbals and Non-Verbals in groups bonded by placards and resolve. There was muttering, often the case in public spaces now, both out of respect for Non-Verbals, but also, Aadhi supposed, so NV-curious Verbals could get a taste of what quiet felt like. He never denied it had merits.

Aadhi had tried to make sense of the world shedding the skin of its verbal traditions. Everything he believed in – the power of words, the need to stand up and be counted as one who had not just partaken in life, but actively shaped it – all seemed to shift into something inexpressible.

What did he actually want the government's position or the Global Summit's conclusion to be, when it finally made this announcement?

28

How civil would civilisation be if either Verbals or Non-Verbals had to live in direct conflict with their beliefs? The documentary seemed to stand in its own space, elucidating a time that people still hadn't managed to get their head around.

Aadhi got out his laptop, balancing it on his knees as he opened up the interview files he'd created. He clicked on *Grace Jenkins*. How long could she hide from the inevitable? What would happen to her and her son? He rubbed his eyes, then checked Sara Javed's Twitter page. Nothing new since her tweet in May 2021:

This time I will not apologise.

💬 27.3M   ⬆ 46.1M   ♡ 57.3M

Her following had hit 125 million people, but he'd clicked on several of these accounts and there was hardly any activity on them.

(This particular chamber now only echoed with Verbals' opinions.)

'*Idiots*,' he muttered. Devotedly following someone who *admitted* they have nothing to say.

'Talking to yourself is actually permitted by some Non-Verbals,' came a familiar voice.

He looked up to see Roxy Hussain, hovering over him.

Aadhi handed her a coffee. 'You're all dolled up.'

'Don't say *dolled*,' said Roxy. 'I have another date with Lauren. She's *way* out of my league. But I'm interesting now, so . . .'

Aadhi wasn't afraid to admit when he had been wrong. He believed it to be a redeeming feature. Over the course of the year, since the awards ceremony and its ensuing chaos, he'd been forced to reassess his swift judgement of Roxy.

That night, after everyone had watched Sara Javed march out of the hall, the room had stilled. Penelope Pembrooke had sliced through the bewildered silence by putting herself in front of the cameras to respond to questions.

Aadhi had noticed Roxy, standing and watching. "Tell me more about this book you wrote,' he had asked. But she had swept out in apparent pursuit of Sara. Aadhi had followed.

He had found her perched on a bench outside the gate of St James' Park. People meandered up and down the road. Cars honked. A homeless person sat by the dumpsters.

'It's not often I give people a chance to talk about their book and they walk away,' Aadhi had said and Roxy had looked up, surprised to see him.

'Did you manage to catch up with her?'

'Didn't do me much good.' She looked so miserable that Aadhi had found himself offering to buy her a drink.

'What did you want to say to her?' he had asked, minutes later, as they sat in Henry's Café Bar.

It took her about two-and-a-half minutes to speak.

Roxy relayed that she had made the mistake of looking at her estranged sister's Instagram before the ceremony and it had made her cry.

It had made her want her friend Sara.

'But there I was, all on my own. In my lonely flat, by my lonely self.'

Aadhi was generally sparing in offering empathy, but this struck a personal chord. For obvious reasons.

'My parents' reaction was nothing compared to Halimah's when I'd been caught kissing a girl in the park. They're simple, you know? But I had expected more from my sister. She couldn't forgive me for going against whatever "*religious teachings—*" Roxy had paused and emitted a rather guttural sound. 'I mean, sorry, but there's this thing called compassion. I didn't abandon my faith. But it wasn't just that. It was hurting our parents. She began to watch my every move,' added Roxy. 'Not so much little sister as fucking big brother.'

Eventually Roxy had demanded her parents' respect and acceptance of her sexuality. This was her fundamental human right. Her parents, panicked about Roxy's soul and their social circle, pleaded for her to respect *their* tradition and values. This was *their* fundamental human right.

Somehow two rights had made a wrong.

'Why did you want to speak to Sara though?' he asked.

'I know what some people – mostly white, obviously – have said about Victoria Park. How I, and people like me, overreacted. But the truth is, by then Sara was my only family. The brilliant, talented, indifferent Sara-fucking-Javed.' Roxy shook her head, clearly recollecting the event. 'She had this disregard for writers like me. Climbed the ladder and then took it away. Refused to see the difficulties we face once she'd overcome them herself. I still needed her though. She just didn't need me. Sara Javed doesn't need anyone.'

Aadhi had looked at his watch at least three times during this story. There was nothing unique, at that time, to warrant further investigation.

Now, in Granary Square, a full year later, they were surrounded by evidence of the fallout from Sara's one act of protest.

'How does Lauren feel about you compromising your principles and still working with someone like me?' Aadhi asked, one eye on the billboards in case of a flash announcement.

'What? A right-wing twat?' Roxy joked. 'Some things are bigger than principles.'

It hadn't been long before Aadhi had recognised Roxy as the type who suffered for her art. This was bad enough, but to suffer for art that she hadn't been able to recreate since her first and to-date-only success which, having skimmed the first chapter of her book, Aadhi felt was probably for the best, seemed to be an acute kind of injustice to her.

(Seeking justice was a core part of Roxy's social identity. It was on her Instagram profile.)

It had been a rude awakening for Aadhi when people had begun to disregard *his* views. The messages he received after his appearance on *The Great Debate* last year after Javed's vow of silence, lambasting him for the way he raised his voice, disrespecting his fellow panellist, a person who had served the education system for over thirty years, had been quietening. He was used to trolls and racist threats, but this was something new. Until he came across Roxy Hussain's message. She'd suggested they join forces against the surge of Non-Verbalism. He had ignored her. A collaboration? With a foetus! He hadn't strived for two decades just to kowtow to a one-hit wonder writer with such a personal agenda against Sara.

Then Roxy had messaged him again. She had insight into Sara Javed like no one else, she said. If he wanted to lead the charge that would counter Non-Verbalism, as did she, he *needed* her. But Aadhi would not compromise his journalistic integrity. So, he ignored her again.

Roxy persisted, somehow getting hold of his personal email address. He'd ignored that too. Until she showed up at his office.

She had heard about his documentary on the grapevine. That he had failed to find anyone interested in one that projected the negative impact of Non-Verbalism on institutions and society. Even though economists, some of whom were his close friends, were warning against it. Bringing the enigma that was Sara Javed into it, according to Roxy, and interweaving the personal with the political while driving his message home, was *exactly* what people would want.

'Everyone's made Sara out to be a messiah,' she had commented. 'As if giving up one's voice is the answer. When they understand that Sara doesn't give a shit about others, then *maybe* things will change.' Roxy had looked him in the eye. 'And we'll have been the ones to do it.'

Roxy Hussain, whatever her shortcomings, knew how to break a person down.

Something he could admire, at least.

'This documentary's more important than ever,' she said now. 'It's the only thing that has any meaning among the madness.'

He and Roxy *had* created something important out of the quiet chaos. And had it not been for her, their documentary would've been no different to many others now vying for attention.

The Movement that Has Silenced Us and the Woman Behind it.

He was overcome with a sudden fondness for Roxy. It was quite surprising.

'—And the interviews we've got,' she continued. '*The* interview we've got. Just imagine how you'll feel when your dad watches it.'

Aadhi had imagined what his dad's reaction would be more often than not. And for sentimental reasons, to which Aadhi wasn't often prone, he wondered whether his father watching this documentary – one that could bring some semblance of normality back to the world – might, even for a moment, bring his father fully back to him.

'I got an email from Day Break Productions this morning.' Aadhi attempted to control his satisfaction, but he wasn't made of stone.

Roxy grabbed his arm.

'They loved it,' he said eventually, trying not to laugh at Roxy's animated expression.

'*What.*'

'The final interview nailed it.'

'*How did you not lead with that?*'

'I couldn't resist. Plus, I'm trying to stay objective. Day Break loved the personal Sara content. No one else has that. They want it finished ASAP though, considering how fast things are moving.'

'We've got most of it already,' said Roxy. 'This is it, isn't it? *This* is the moment. For us both?'

Aadhi's intensity of feeling sprawled into an unknown yet optimistic future. He had forgotten that these pivotal moments still existed. Oh, the loneliness still came, but he could not deny that no matter how much he condemned Non-Verbalism, it had wrought opportunity. Roxy was a keen reminder. She threw her arms around him.

When Roxy reached for her phone, he shook his head. 'No, no. Don't go announcing anything on social media. Execute some patience.'

'*Patience,*' she exclaimed, forcing heads to turn. 'Majority opinion will have to turn against Non-Verbalism once people watch this. Sara's not a messiah, she's just—'

'Human.'

'That's no excuse,' replied Roxy.

'One question: what's the line between professionalism and respecting someone's personal decision?' Aadhi wouldn't consider himself as one who suffered for his art, but he had an especial distaste for opportunism. Despite having benefitted from it.

'Big picture, Aadhs.' Roxy gestured towards the Non-Verbal volunteers handing out leaflets. 'It's about claiming back our *voice*.'

She was right, of course. Plus, despite the crowdfunding Roxy had successfully done, Aadhi had invested all his money in this project, even taking out a second mortgage. They'd later been approached by Day Break Productions. Aadhi and Roxy had pitched their reveal-all documentary about the woman behind the movement and the real-time material they had, recording the unfolding of one of history's most significant moments. Day Break did not hesitate in optioning the documentary for a considerable sum. Aadhi had never wanted anyone to interfere with his artistic vision, but they needed the injection of cash, so, he and Roxy had agreed that it was the sensible thing to do.

Now they were on the brink of completion, Day Break was exercising their option in collaboration with Pixie Entertainment, the most popular global streaming channel. It was a remarkable feat for Aadhi and Roxy.

Aadhi hesitated before asking Roxy, 'Do you miss her?'

'I miss what she *stood* for. Until she stood for nothing . . . You still believe that silence can strip someone of their rights, don't you?' added Roxy.

'We're on the same team here.'

(Which was so often a fundamental factor in being united.)

'I get what she's been through. But she should've handl—.' Roxy broke off as an alert appeared on the live billboard above the square. Aadhi almost spilled his coffee. People looked up.

'It's *happening*.' Roxy started her Instagram Live . . .

Slowly, people emerged from the marquee. The silent, anti-silence protestors removed their masks.

BREAKING NEWS:
Prime Minister to address the nation about The Silent Movement.
Action to be taken by global leaders to tackle the problem that has
polarised world.
Live 7pm GMT tonight. All Channels.

The collective took a deep breath.

Someone called out, '*Finally.*'

Bodies shuffled away in haste.

Aadhi looked at his watch: in nine hours there'd be some sort of decision.

'What are they going to do, Aadhs? . . . I feel sick.'

Aadhi's discomfort was visceral. 'I don't know,' he whispered.

It was the climax everyone had been waiting for. The familiar quiet of inevitability hung in the hushed air. Leaders around the world would be addressing their nations. Aadhi's indignation was suffused with an emotion he could no longer deny.

Doubt.

Roxy was already scrolling on her phone.

#WheresSara was trending again.

'She abandoned everyone who trusted her.' Roxy's fingers were almost white as she gripped her phone. Sara, the instigator and abdicator, had only ever thought of herself.

Aadhi's resolution strengthened. Moving forward demanded focus and conviction. Their documentary would play its part in ending the disease of silence altogether.

(Such were the hopes of true artists.)

'*Oh.*' Roxy showed Aadhi a new email on her phone, its subject line: 'Help'.

'Who's Zainab Aalam?' he asked.

'I don't know.'

He read the email again.

I'm reaching out to you because I've seen you on television. Please help Zainab Aalam. I believe that you'll *want* to.

She's in trouble. And Non-Verbalism's made things much worse for her . . .

'Weird. But look, we have enough material and we need to finalise things *quick*,' said Roxy.

'Don't you want to know more?'

'*Obviously*, but . . . there's no time for more stories. The PM's talking *tonight*. We have what we need, Aadhs . . . *Come on.*'

Aadhi wavered. Time's essence couldn't be denied. But what advice would his dad give?

'No,' he said, finally. 'There's *always* time for another story.'

PART TWO

PART TWO

LAMENTATIONS

Sara

London, 2010

Sara Javed sat at the kitchen table, in her one-bedroom flat in south London. She refreshed her in-box. Again.

The rest of the nation was glued to their TV.

At every general election, Sara would remember her dad and stepmother, Lily Javed, nee DeSouza, back in 1983, watching their black-and-white television, looking sickened by the government that was holding so firmly on to power. Her dad had gripped Lily's hand.

It had been affecting.

Now, Sara glanced at Henry, sitting in the adjoining room, watching the news on their HD screen.

'Shitshow,' said Henry through a mouthful of masticated Cornflakes. 'Baby, it's 8 a.m. Post-election. Don't publishing types start their day at twelve?'

'I'm trying optimism,' Sara replied. 'It's less lazy as a concept.'

She made a note in her A5 notebook: *Cynicism = lazy?*

'And the cheers that erupt in Sunderland . . .'

'Can you turn the volume down?' she asked. 'The news makes it feel like everything's falling apart.'

'It's a hung parliament,' Henry replied. 'You're a writer – isn't this all material?'

'*Writers* get published.'

Sara's mobile rang. She glanced at the screen before answering. 'Hi, Dad.'

'Have you heard back?'

'No,' she said.

'Only a matter of time.'

'How do you know?' she asked. 'Maybe the publisher was just being polite when she asked to see my opening chapters. People say things at book parties all the time. And I had organised very good canapés at that launch.' She paused. 'What if all these hours . . . *years* of writing amount to nothing?'

'What do I always tell you?'

'*People lacking in effort are lacking in character.*'

'You can lack anything, but character . . . Are you watching the news?'

'It could've been worse.'

'*Could've been worse* is the verbal dr—'

'—drug that leads to apathy. Yes, Dad.'

Sara scribbled:

Am I apathetic? Discuss. With self. Not Henry.

'—Is *he* there?'

Sara glanced at her boyfriend, milk on his chin. '*He* says "hi".'

Her dad grunted. 'What does Lily think about the results?'

'Why don't you phone her and ask?' asked Sara. 'Cut out the middle man.'

'What was the point in me raising you?'

'You made a terrible mistake, obviously.'

'I know she will be as upset,' her dad added. 'Just because we're not married anymore doesn't mean I don't know her—'

Sara leant back and listened to her dad's favourite refrain: the immigrant narrative with his education from Pakistan that didn't translate – among other things – in England.

'And I had you in my arms,' he said. 'Even as a baby you didn't cry, and there was a lot to cry about.'

'Thanks, Dad.'

'People said, *you are a single Pakistani man, you can't raise your brother's daughter alone.* And what did I say?'

'*Fuck you,*' replied Sara, impersonating her dad's baritone. 'You've always been accomplished at swearing.' Her dad wasn't apathetic. Another reason to adore him. And he *was* her dad. Sara's biological father had died on the way to the hospital while her mother's own life flashed before her eyes, trying to push Sara into the world.

Sara, in that sense, felt she was born in the remit of death.

Her biological mother didn't have the same capacity to care for a child as she had to birth one. Being young and beautiful, it wasn't long before men were vying for her hand in marriage. It would have done her mother some credit, according to her dad, had she struggled with her decision to hand Sara over to him. So Afzal Javed told the family he would take his niece to England to seek a better life. The crossing of a continent made his widely acknowledged eccentricity seem fiscally reasonable.

He had arrived in London with Sara in the late seventies and, within a year, had fallen in love with Lily. They had met at the London Buddhist Centre in Bethnal Green. Afzal noticed Lily's polished brogues. *Out of place.* A sentiment he recognised.

He had asked Lily for the time.

'Afzal Javed?' she had repeated, when he told her his name. 'Isn't that Muslim?'

'Yes. Are you surprised?'

'A little, considering where we are. But then, I'm one to talk.' She gestured towards her tailored jacket and skirt. 'My very middle-class family think I'm learning French.'

'You're a Buddhist?'

'No, just interested. You?'

'I call myself a practising Non-Muslim.'

'Sorry?'

'You can only call yourself Muslim when you have let go of your ego. Buddhists are very good at that. We should learn from everyone.'

'. . . Well, it was nice to meet you.'

'Did I say something wrong?'

She had turned away, now she turned back. *'Practising Non-Muslim?* I live with enough pretension.'

Afzal had laughed.

Lily had smiled.

That was the beginning.

Lily had the demeanour of a middle-class woman living in Chelsea but, Afzal argued, a Punjabi spirit. Rejected by her family for wanting the wrong man, she had been determined to forge a future with Afzal with little else but affection and a dependent baby. Lily had fallen in love with Afzal because he was funny and romantic. She'd fallen in love with Sara because it was easy to expend emotions on a life born into tragedy. The marriage hadn't lasted, but their passion for learning and change was as generational as the trauma.

'How's that idiot of hers?' Sara's dad asked.

'Martin? He gardens with their grandkids mostly. He's shit at it though.'

'What kind of a monster likes geraniums?' Afzal then sighed, getting back to the matter at hand. 'Another opportunity gone with this government. Twenty years and it always comes full-circle.'

This felt poignant to Sara.

'The email will come,' her dad said. 'And with it, things you haven't even imagined. That's how God works.'

Sara didn't have quite the same beliefs as her dad, but if there was a higher power governing the mystery of life, she wouldn't be surprised.

'Right. I need to get goat's brains from the butchers,' added her dad. 'I'm making *maghas*. Your father's favourite. I will think about him today.'

As would Sara since Afzal mentioned him, but not too much. It felt remiss to consider she had a dad other than the one who brought her up.

She told Afzal she loved him, then broke off to refresh her in-box again.

'Will I have to get a job in recruitment?' she muttered, deflated.

'No,' Henry responded, who worked at Simmons' Advertising Agency. Today he had to secure a client selling cat litter. 'You being a part-timer makes me feel needed.'

Sara's nerves tensed. Being needed made her uncomfortable. And to feel *in need* was surely undignified. She could never tell Henry this or they'd have to go to couple's therapy.

(Her independent spirit was something Henry liked in theory. Like cycling.)

Henry kissed her before he left for work. 'I love you, you're brilliant.'

'I hope you're not this delusional at work.'

Henry waited, brows raised.

'I love you too.'

It was Sara's day off from BookBait, the bookshop where she worked, so, to distract herself, she made a coffee and stood by the window of her flat, staring down the residential street. Witnessing others' lives, shifting from singledom into couples and procreating, made her wonder whether her set-up with Henry had all the makings of a cliché.

To love is to be tethered. Can one soar in such a state?

The seemingly unconsidered way in which her birth mother had given her away diluted Sara's sense of self. A reasonable sentiment without a reasonable outlet. Her emotional understanding had come from the characters she read about. The Isabelle Archers and Bathsheba Everdenes. The Antoinette Cosways and Esther Greenwoods. Stories offered the possibility that she wasn't captive to her past; that the only real cages were the ones we built for ourselves.

(That wouldn't last.)

She often paced the flat when she was alone, speaking out loud the interaction she would have with her birth mother if she met her. It was always from a point of having succeeded in her literary career – at becoming *someone* – showing her mother that Sara had been worthy of her love.

At 11.20 a.m. Sara got out the journal which she kept hidden in a shoe box, under a pair of four-inch stilettos which she hardly wore.

M,

I want to speak to you about what it means to wait. An eternal stagnation. Emotional vacuum, in fact, grappling for something that might not materialise. That's what you feel like. You are, through biological fact, a part of me. Nothing sentimental there. It seems stupid that waiting for this email is like waiting for you . . . it's not logical. But life doesn't often follow logic. Even I don't often follow logic. I follow feeling – when it finally (belatedly) arises. Perhaps I got that from you.
   It's not like I don't know my flaws.

At 4.30 p.m. Sara received an email from publisher, Penelope Pembrooke.

At 7.30 p.m. Henry came home and Sara told him the publisher wanted a meeting.

That night, just when they were about to make celebratory love, Sara looked up at Henry, trying to recognise what she was feeling.

'What?' Henry's hand cupped over her breast; his breath was laboured.

'I feel quite alive,' she said.

'*Quite?*' he replied, eyebrows raised.

'Well, let's not get carried away.' She laughed as she pulled him down on to their bed, caught up in the passion of life's potential.

Grace

Calais, 2010

Grace Jenkins had a knack for emotional redirection, and this time it involved a geographical change. She had been a volunteer for the past three months in Calais where refugee camps were being bulldozed. She and a group of people had managed to take over a warehouse from a concerned citizen to handle the donations coming in. All of which prevented Grace having to sift through the chaos of her own mind. A skill she'd been forced to develop at a young age.

As with every morning since her arrival, she stood outside the warehouse, in her mud-soaked wellies, raincoat and hi-vis, icy rain spitting from the heavens. Grace rubbed her hands together for warmth and gathered the temporary volunteers into their daily circle of inspiration.

Several volunteers were poised to take pictures to upload to their Facebook.

Perhaps with a quote about serving humanity.

It garnered more likes.

'I know news of the re-election isn't what we wanted.' Grace looked at her bedraggled team.

A permanent volunteer walked passed, a tumble-dryer strapped to his back like a baby. 'Clearly we're all feeling its weight,' she added.

The new volunteers laughed. The more seasoned ones checked their watches.

Grace would have to work harder to energise them.

'Just remember that even though it feels shit when nothing seems to change; standing here in the cold and rain, *you* are playing your part.

'People aren't being given their basic human right to shelter,' she exclaimed.

Volunteers booed.

'—Being here – no matter why,' Grace looked at David Hodgkin, pointedly, 'shows that things *can* change. And that *we* are on the right side of history.'

There was applause. Someone whooped.

'That's the spirit,' Grace approved. 'And guys, please stop making out behind the shoe store. There are cameras.'

She saw David smile before she announced which volunteers were on which duty and dispersed the circle.

'You haven't changed your mind then?' David asked as Grace checked her to-do list.

'I'm not about to let you write a profile piece about me just because we slept together, Hodgkin.'

'Technically, it's about the escalating refugee crisis, but you make it more interesting.'

She tried not to laugh. 'Don't be full of shit.'

'What can I say? You're photogenic.'

She turned, intending to do her first task, counting the medical supplies. And her blessings. Something her mother always reminded her about, which was rich, considering.

'Come on,' said David, holding her arm.

'Just because I made a mistake last night, doesn't mean I'll make another one.'

'Wasn't it worth it?' he whispered.

Grace attempted to ground her heart as firmly as her feet. Her capacity to love unreservedly had always been her shortcoming. She had sought it, like a frenzied being desperate to live. This time was no different.

'Yeah, for *you*,' she replied. 'Managing to sleep with a twenty-two-year old.'

48

David smiled. A twinkle in his eye. 'A conquest.'

'*Twat.*'

He leant into her, so sure of himself. Grace's disgust for him was diluted by his desire for her. A shameful consequence of her own insecurities.

'It wasn't just about sex.'

He was right. She had cried in his arms, and the memory of it brought about a fresh need to weep for displaying such weakness. Her emotionally chaotic state was a result of talking about the loss of her dad. So, Grace had slipped and fallen into a night of passion.

'Let me come over tonight,' he said. 'Another memory for the bank.'

It was the type of habit which seemed to have formed a part of her character. How could she battle her own person? Wasn't fighting the broken world enough?

And perhaps this time it would be different?

(That fateful hope with which mistakes were relived.)

Grace took a step towards him. 'Make sure no one sees you.'

Zainab

Lahore, 2010

Zainab Aalam spoke to her British husband-to-be, Kashif Taufiq, with a better command of English than most of the UK's inhabitants. It was a part of her attraction for Kashif. Born and raised in Lahore, Zainab had a Master's in Maths and Economics from the Lahore University of Management Sciences, and a predilection for both Urdu and English literature. It exemplified her well-rounded sensibilities. (Aged twenty-three, she was also ripe for baby-bearing, and without, according to her soon-to-be mother-in-law, the incessant expectations of the Pakistani–British women, with their ambition and romantic aspirations.)

When Zainab walked down the aisle of the air-conditioned Defence Marquee and Event Complex, Kashif stood on the decorated stage, trans-fixed by, he had told her, one of the most beautiful women he'd ever met. And he had met plenty.

Even among the fairy-lights, which might dim a bride's attire, Zainab was a vision in a red *lengha*, embroidered with antique gold, studded with sparkling diamantes.

No one at the wedding could have imagined that the bespectacled, bookish Zainab would one day evoke such aesthetic pleasure. Several years of being considered plain and boring – at university she didn't care about make-up and boys – she didn't have the conceit that was often syn-onymous with beauty.

Zainab glanced at Kashif as she approached the stage and tried not to smile too widely. She was marrying someone her family had suggested, whom she *wanted* to marry. Kashif was respectful, masculine, family-orientated.

She had held back speaking to him about how much she loved maths and literature. Instead she had listened to him. She was a woman who learnt from her mistakes. A boy at university had once approached her in the library – she had begun to wear lenses, left her hair loose – the slow shedding of her former self. She had got so excited about Mirza Ghalib's poetry, Austen's wit, Grisham's ability to thrill, that he had looked confused.

'You study maths, no?' he asked, eventually.

She smiled keenly and launched into her research of Fermat's Last Theorem.

The boy said goodbye and never spoke to her again. It made her wonder about her curious, excitable nature that produced such a flurry of words – that they weren't always what others wanted to hear. The deflation she felt subsequent to that conversation had been as keen as her initial enthusiasm. Her mother had told her that a husband would love her for her brain *and* beauty. Watching Bollywood films fortified Zainab's idea that love prevailed. But after that incident, she had to rethink the part she played in it.

'Do you read?' she had asked Kashif, carefully, when they first met.

He shook his head. 'But we can read together. For the rest of our lives.'

Now, Kashif's family and his friend from Glasgow, Suleiman, greeted her. For a moment Suleiman caught her eye. She turned away, blushing at his obvious admiration. Men could do with taking the habit of lowering their gaze more seriously. Kashif, as was his right, continued to stare. She held *his* gaze, experiencing the power of her own beauty with pleasure.

Zainab would eventually get a spousal visa and move to Glasgow. It could take anything from six months to a few years. Keen as she was to start married life, she felt the weight of saying goodbye to a part of who she was. To the students she taught. She always felt such pride at each graduation. The fierce opinions the students held, the aspirations they had – she would pray for the fulfilment of these daily. And to the girls she'd say: *Of course you must go abroad and study.* Her own parents had urged her to go to MIT, but Zainab, not wanting to leave them behind, decided against it. So, as was her nature, she ensured that her students should not live with such regret.

And of course, the wait for the visa would give her enough time to finish her teaching term so that her students weren't deserted in the middle of exams. Zainab was the sort of woman who kept promises.

Sitting next to her husband on stage, decorated with flowers, surrounded by four hundred members of their closest friends and family, Zainab felt the hope and cumulation of romantic notions swell within her. She had abided by duty, which had aligned with her dreams. It had made her a successful daughter. A successful sister.

To all intents and purposes, she was a successful woman.

That night, in their hotel room, Kashif put his hand on her leg and she felt a swarm of emotions, nerves not being the least.

'I've waited so long for this,' he whispered.

She had little experience in love, but plenty of aspirations for it. Her knowledge of sex was limited to the innuendos bandied about by her students at which her face still reddened profusely. Her married sister had merely said: 'It'll hurt like hell.'

But Zainab didn't fear pain if it was anything like the pleasure of her husband's touch. He told her to take off her clothes, to which she complied, feeling so aroused she touched herself.

'Lie down.' He unbuttoned his sherwani. 'No. The other way.'

He switched on the television behind her. She glanced back – expecting something romantic, like Bollywood songs. Instead she saw what she could only describe as two men forcing themselves on a woman. She looked at her husband now pressed down on her, all her desire dispelled.

'What is this?'

He stroked her face. 'It's how men like it.'

Unfortunately, Zainab had no point of reference to refute him. 'Can you switch it off?'

He put his hand gently on her neck, glanced back at the screen. 'Don't you want me?'

'Of course,' she reassured him. 'But—'

He put his finger over her lips. 'You'll enjoy it. I promise.'

Then instead of removing his finger, he clamped his hand over her mouth, as he looked up at the screen.

The pain hadn't mingled with pleasure. It had been piercing – a trauma so acute it would take her years to understand why any woman would voluntarily undergo such a violation. How she had ever longed for it. He had called her names she blushed to remember; her confusion, along with Kashif's hand over her mouth, rendered her silent. The only thing she could do was pray to God that it would soon be over. The two minutes and twenty-three seconds stretched out for Zainab like the inimitable darkness of her future.

Eventually, Kashif collapsed on his back, grabbing the remote to switch off the television. Zainab gripped the side of the bed, as if holding on to the vestiges of her own person.

'Oh,' said Kashif, getting up.

She covered her naked body with the bed sheet, her head thumping.

He got a small box from the bedside table. 'I was meant to give it to you earlier.'

It was the traditional gift a husband gave his wife before they consummated their marriage. Her hands were shaking. Kashif took one and kissed it.

'I like it like that. It won't hurt as much next time,' he said. 'Open the present.'

Zainab could barely see the gold earrings through her tears.

What just happened?

He slid his hand between her legs.

'God, you're beautiful.'

She had to beat down the bile, the misplaced hope, the disconnection

53

between the fiction she had read and the reality that had transpired. Was *this* love? Zainab would have to reconfigure her hopes – *herself* – so far removed from the ideas she had cultivated over the course of her so far innocent life.

May 2021

Press Announcement from Pembrooke Publishing

For immediate release

Sara Javed's Vow of Silence

In a bold move, bestselling author and winner of the 2021 Mildred Aitken Award, Sara Javed, has relinquished communication in both spoken and written form.

Her vow of silence and decision to hand back the award shows Javed's pure and tireless pursuit of truth in her writing, and her principle that unspoken words matter as much as ones spoken. As her proud publisher of ten years we fully support Sara in her endeavour.

Penelope Pembrooke says:

'Sara Javed's silence is an inspiration considering the times we live in, where everyone speaks but no one listens. We hope Sara's act of protest and her brave decision to hand back her prize, will promote reflection – and, ultimately, action – about who we want to be as individuals, as a culture, and even as a nation.'

May 2021
Pembrooke Publishing is a feminist imprint, amplifying women's voices.

★

Mad scenes @ArtsClub @MildredAitkenAwards. @Sara_Javed vow of silence & rejecting award is artistic revolution! Dismantling status quo by shutting the fuck up?? #STFUisthenewblack

💬 21   ⬆ 125   ♡ 3,217

Used to be fan of #SaraJaved until #VictoriaPark. Now she rejects award that so few brown women have opp to win! IT'S TIME TO AMPLIFY VOICES FFS #notinmyname #wewillnotbesilenced

💬 12   ⬆ 123   ♡ 547

That's one way to deal with writers' block. STFU. #Sarajaved

💬 8   ⬆ 106   ♡ 219

Sara

London, May 2021

Storming out of her own awards ceremony was ungracious at best, but it was a little late for grace.

The looks, the flashing cameras. The aggrandising of Sara's choice to go silent was embarrassing. She hadn't planned to reject the award like that, but how could she, in good conscience, have accepted it, considering everything?

Jesus she almost cried out, spinning around in the alleyway, ready to hit whoever had grabbed her shoulder.

'*It's me,*' said Kat.

Sara rested her noise-cancelling headphones around her neck. She now heard the traffic from Piccadilly, people's voices, the hustle of London. The light from the streetlamps, at the end of the alleyway, was a beckoning call. She stared at her friend, publicist and one of perhaps four people whom she still liked. Who hopefully still liked her.

'You could've told me,' said Kat. 'I could've helped. And you realise how much harder you've made my job? What does all this *mean?*'

Silence.

It was quite awkward practice.

Eventually, Sara pulled Kat into a hug, hoping she appeared as sorry as she felt. She had told Kat about her mum once on a book tour. It had been relayed to her as an aside. Sara hadn't even looked at Kat as they sat in the back of the cab. She immediately wished she hadn't said anything, the silence so oppressive. Then Kat said: 'Well. That's shit.'

Sara had appreciated it.

Now she wanted to tell Kat that consistently biting back her own bewilderment about people, what they expected of her, what she expected of herself, had silenced her; that it was an escape from the world, to work in tandem with a confrontation of who she was. The unfolding of recent events in her life made that necessary. One could not escape oneself, especially if one didn't know who one was.

Sara had centred her life around *one* goal . . . What, after all, had it meant?

Of course, saying all this would rather defeat the point.

'Penelope's going to make your letter public.'

The letter could've been more thoughtful, but Sara had written it in passionate haste. That would have repercussions.

As passion often did.

'Are you OK? Is it about Victoria Park?' continued Kat. 'Or is it about . . . your mum?'

Sara could feel the prickle of tears. She could not slip into speech out of guilt – even among friends. Life required mastery over *something*.

'This is *everything* you wanted—'

Overcoming desire is the first hurdle.

'—Do you understand what this might do to everything you've worked for?'

The fear of loss shouldn't deter one from action.

Before Sara could pull her friend into another hug, she glimpsed Roxy, striding down the alley towards them.

No. Roxy could talk herself into a breathless stupor, but Sara would *not* listen.

'*Sara*,' Roxy called out.

Sara hurried away, towards the light at the other end of the alleyway.

'*I want to talk.*'

Sara put on her headphones and lost herself in the crowd.

Her silence was an act of self-preservation. And to preserve herself she would have to strive towards that one thing that despite the (slow) success and (mounting) accolade, the (increased) book sales and (recurring) awards, had eluded her.

Taking out her phone, she tapped the Twitter app. *A final message.*

This time I will not apologise.

💬 0   ⬆ 0   ♡ 0

She would strive towards peace.

A Not-So Silent Cry for Attention

Aadhi Sathar, *The Telegram*, May 2021

This month in the obscure and absurd is Sara Javed, bestselling author, who has decided to abandon words. Entirely. Setting personal opinion aside about why her perceived verbal artistry has any impact at all, Javed's act of so-called protest is meticulously timed. Having been subjected to some criticism after her appearance at Victoria Park Book Festival in Oct 2020 (there's nothing like a difference of opinion to inspire a torrent of tweets), Javed's reputation in certain circles has been called into question. One can imagine the author of Rule-makers *frantically flipping through the pages of her own titles, looking for guidance, only to discover the best form of self-help is to retreat. The idea is noble, which makes its mockery even more provocative. Perhaps silence is Javed's belated way of showing penance to her critics for her vocal faux-pas. I'd like her less if that's true. But the positioning of her in publishing (much to her critics' chagrin) as a pioneer feeds into the illusion that people have the capacity for originality.*

PR stunts are a way of life and I suppose Javed should have an equal stake in the game, but a stunt by any other name would smell as pungent.

Aadhi Sathar is a writer, journalist, social commentator and filmmaker.
His book, *False Fiction*, is out now. Buy online <u>here</u>.

Grace

Manchester, May 2021

The memory with David, which was meant to have been for the bank, became too realistic a part of Grace's life. It had her ask herself, 'What if I hadn't kept the baby?' Sometimes, in her bleakest moment, the thought crossed her mind still. But she looked on this as a fault in herself, rather than her boy.

Eleven years after her brush with fate in Calais, Grace was still in search of an ideal self. She had been born into humble means, living on an estate in Longsight, Manchester, avoiding the tropes expected of girls like her (drugs, etc.). Despite her high intellect, her grades were average. She had a special disregard for authority and spent too much time railing against the education system, rather than getting an education; falling in love with boys who found her opinions a hindrance to getting sex. When she did give into her need for another body to be close to hers, she found herself swiftly forgotten. Yet, unable, herself, to so easily forget.

She began volunteering at the local homeless shelter after one such heartbreak and found it so cathartic that it became her drug of choice. Grace chose to excel in this environment, which was familiar, rather than fail in an academic one that might lead to something unknown.

One day, aged sixteen, and considering life's many injustices, Grace wrote a letter of complaint to the education board for whitewashing the reality of colonialism. Her form teacher, aware of Grace's home situation, told her: 'Save yourself, and you'll be better able to save others. You're too exceptional to be getting average results.'

That Grace was anything other than ordinary had never occurred to her. But she wanted to live up to the *idea* of being exceptional. It ignited in her a will to pull herself out of her social and mental poverty.

She prepared better for exams while still volunteering. Her part-time job at the Costcutter helped to pay the bills while her father paid the rent. Her mother, Dede, flitted in and out of their home, consuming more than just food, until she vanished, without explanation, when Grace was about to take her GCSEs.

Grace was resolved to be everything that her mother wasn't. She got her degree in Law, interning at Dean & Dean's for experience in human rights, working part-time for The Red Cross, saving money by living at home. When her father died a year after she had graduated, he left her a 'pot of money for my pot of gold'. It wasn't much, but it was clear he had sacrificed living his own life so that Grace might have a better one.

She was alone at the funeral. Her boyfriend at the time didn't find it necessary to attend. And there was no way of letting her mother know.

Grief and another heartbreak had fused into overwhelming loneliness – the empty home, the lack of family, made Grace yearn for *some* sort of belonging. The refugee crisis fell in line with her personal one. Who better to help the displaced than a person who had so much experience in it?

And if it hadn't been for her pregnancy, perhaps Grace wouldn't now be a practising divorce solicitor – prying people apart from their children and belongings for the modest sum of £250 per hour. Perhaps she wouldn't be wearing tailored Reiss suits, living in a top-floor flat, overlooking Salford Quays.

Perhaps she would still be giving speeches to strangers, trying to reduce their dependency on Wi-Fi, and focusing on a world outside their own. She could not abide people congratulating her on her voluntary work when she knew the people she claimed to help were, in actual fact, helping her.

Now Grace sat in her corner office, at her mahogany desk, on the ninth floor of Albert, Smith and Canon's Law's Georgian building on Kings Street. The view of its bustle behind her high-ceilinged windows. She kept glancing towards the picture of her mother and her nine-year-old son, Benji, taken last year. His arm wrapped around Dede's neck, smile radiant.

People left. That was the way of things. But Dede had outdone even herself in the art of abandonment.

Being alone, for Grace, was cyclical.

Her phone pinged.

Her own Wi-Fi dependent life.

Google Alerts

Pembrooke Publishing's Statement on Sara Javed's **Silence**
. . . has **muted** the better part of my own mutable person – I can barely hear my own **voice**.

Grace had set-up notifications for words like _mute, voice, silence_. She recognised Javed's name, which she had seen on book covers on the tables in Waterstones.

She clicked on the letter, laughing at its opening line, heart sinking as she read on, indignation simmering that a woman chose silence, that she _had_ a choice.

Taking for granted that one form of communication that Grace agonised over.

. . . but a crisis needs the right sort of attention. A lack of priority is how we – I – got into this fucking mess.

Grace swallowed the lump in her throat.

Her sense of achievement, which had jumped from escaping familial shackles to altruism, to corporate servitude, was now tied up with how often she could get Benji to interact with her in any verbal – and, thus, to

63

her mind, meaningful – way. The shadow of her mother's absence continued to stretch and bend in the trajectory of their lives.

Her boss, Graham, entered her office. 'Can we talk?'

Had he been watching her through the glass door?

'About?'

'That night.'

Last week had been a mix of the crowded bar, the exhilaration of having won an important case, the closeness of Graham as he spoke into her ear over the music. Surely the babysitter could stay with Benji a little longer? Surely Grace was allowed one night off?

'Another drink?' Graham had asked. 'We're celebrating. Boss's orders.'

'Throw your weight around elsewhere.'

He laughed. 'What if I don't want to?'

Grace had tried to ignore the way he'd hover in her office, giving her the latest gossip. Sitting with her after hours, going over cases. He had leant over her once: she had held her breath.

'Grace . . .' He took her by the hand and they weaved through the suited crowd, until they found a quiet corner.

'I wanted to say you're doing brilliantly. Your passion and grit—'

'Are you selling me something?' she asked.

'*You*,' he replied. 'To yourself.'

'So make me a partner.'

'Are you always this impatient?'

She stared at him. 'I know what I want.'

He took her chin, lifting her face. It had been years since someone's touch had made her feel this way: on the brink of falling.

'What *do* you want?'

No more repeats.

'Well?' he'd asked.

'Everything.'

Now, sat in her pristine office, the messiness of that night of freedom was stark and shameful. Her fury was with herself. For having felt the euphoria when he gripped her wrists and whispered in her ear.

'It was unprofessional,' Grace replied.

She shuddered. She might drive a Lexus, own a Nespresso machine and Le Crueset diningware, but she was still the same woman in wellies in the pouring Calais rain, falling into the possibility of love.

'Don't worry. I won't report you for sexual harassment.'

'*Grace.*'

Love had always been a disturbance and she refused to enter into its emotional negotiations anymore. A personal repression that made her feel in charge. Impenetrable, so to speak.

'Listen,' Graham continued. 'I know Harold's promotion was a blow, but I managed to get here . . .'

'*You* are a beacon of optimism,' Grace said with derisive laughter. As if Graham, growing up with his family's various holiday homes, could understand Grace's past. 'A strong black man in a position of power.'

'You know, you're impossible sometimes.' He walked out of her office.

Of course she was.

That's why she was alone. The alternative – that she was inherently unlovable – felt far too personal and it was best to keep away from that sort of thing.

She was still trying to reason that her harshness was for the best when her phone rang.

'Ms Jenkins, it's Benji's school. He needs to be collected.'

Grace sighed. How would it feel to not have to speak to anyone? Not to have to *therap* disgruntled husbands and wives, deal with Harold-shaped prejudices and daily microaggressions at work . . . Not to have *incessant* teacher meetings.

To join her son in his all-encompassing silence.

For a moment it felt like a liberation.

She reread Javed's letter, reminding herself that she was no victim.

She was a warrior.

★

Grace watched Benji buckle his seat in the car outside the school. 'You can't just *throw* things at kids who are mean.'

Benji's teacher had just explained that a truck hurled at a child's head could have serious repercussions.

'It took ages to get you integrated into that class . . . *Look at me so I know you're listening.*' She knew she shouldn't shout, but *Jesus.*

Grace put up both hands and counted down with her fingers. By the time she had reached one, Benji would know her anger had subsided.

'No comics for you all month,' she added.

Considering their latest upheaval, courtesy of her absent-again mother, Grace should've been more forgiving. Benji's look was blank. One that made her wonder whether – guiltily, and just for a second – who was there?

Of course, she *knew* her son.

She had sought every possible means to understand why Benji was unable, or unwilling, to speak. Specialists had said that his cognitive development was below average but all those verbally loaded tests – of course it seemed that way. Her son's social anxiety seemed to prevent him from saying a word. With an aching heart, she had watched him flounder as other children thrived, waited for his first words, which had turned into a lifelong anticipation. She joined online forums, tried various types of therapy, tried to pinpoint anything she might've done that rendered her boy Non-Verbal. Every day, any hope that Benji would speak dwindled.

Grace got into the driver's seat, recalling Javed's letter.

What's become of the purpose of words, anyway?

'You've lived your life without them, haven't you? Words,' Grace said to Benji from the rear-view mirror.

He stared back at her.

'Can you give me a thumbs up?'

He put his head down, barely raising his thumb.

Each day brought its own heartbreak. She had failed her son. Benji's silence wasn't only an accusation. It was its very own proof.

★

Grace put Benji to bed. She wanted to press him to her like she used to when he was a baby and repeat all the promises she had made when she had felt equal to the task: *I will give you an extraordinary life.*

But the theory of happiness, it seemed, was circumstance dependent.

She dialled her mum's number as she loaded the dishwasher. 'It's me. *Again.* I don't even know why I'm calling anymore. *Where are you?*'

Grace couldn't sleep. She was surprised at how much she missed her mother – how hard it was to function without her.

She reread Javed's letter on her phone before clicking on another link.

'*Woman in Waiting*,' she whispered, an ironic laugh escaping her as she pressed the 'buy' button for Javed's debut.

She started reading it straight away on her Kindle. Ten years ago she'd have labelled it as navel-gazing bullshit. But time had its impact.

She had almost finished the book by the time she had to get Benji ready for school the next morning. The character's descent into madness, the restorative act of her creating her own language had gripped Grace in a manner she found both disturbing and familiar. She hadn't managed to know her son through verbal communication. What if she could know him through its opposite?

As she made their breakfast, she dismissed the thought. Benji ate his Marmite on toast while she responded to several work emails.

It would be ridiculous to just *stop* speaking. Wouldn't it?

But after she'd dropped Benji to school, watched him wave in resignation, she looked back at her life: the daily grind of talking, talking, talking. Finding the right words, slipping up; expecting words, receiving the wrong ones; fighting with other people, *for* other people. And here she was, still without peace. She had never, until today, considered that Benji might actually benefit from *her* silence.

The world's always been falling apart, but that's not to say I should fall apart with it.

Grace realised that she *was* falling apart. Perhaps she had been for several years, precariously stitched together by the thread of her mother finally being by her side and her focus on work. One thread had unravelled entirely and her professional one . . . wasn't it just a distraction from a fraying life?

She stood outside her office building and called Benji's doctor.

'What if I went silent?' she asked.

'Sorry?'

'What if I stopped speaking, too?'

'Ms Jenkins, you'd be enabling him.'

'Ten years of everything else hasn't helped,' muttered Grace as she put the phone down.

She made an emergency appointment with Benji's therapist, asking the same question. He referred her to the speech and developmental leader, who said it would do no good. What was Grace hoping to achieve?

But this was about understanding her son's world and maybe, by default, her place within it. To find that motherly connection, which was meant to be instantaneous. What else was life but a constant need to connect? Grace had spent years now expecting something to shift within her, to finding that elusive feeling of contentment. It struck her, vividly in that moment, that nothing had changed but that something *must*.

Grace Googled Sara again and found her on the cover of some book magazines.

Sara Javed Rejects Mildred Aitken Award and Words.

It had been years since Grace had felt the bloom of inspiration. Javed's letter was a reminder that change *was* possible.

That evening she sat Benji down.

'It's just you and me now, kid, isn't it?'

He nodded, vaguely.

'Who's to say what's right? Your gran's left us, but we have each other, don't we? And, you know I love you? That *everything* I do is for you?'

Benji looked confused.

'Right?'

He nodded.

She gave a small laugh at his worried face, before holding it in her hands. 'You and me? We're going to be OK.'

In the end, to explain herself felt too exhausting, too at odds with the desire which had gripped her. It would simply dilute and distract. Sometimes one had to contain a thing to maintain its force.

The following morning, both Grace and Benji faced the world together, in unified silence.

Unedited footage: *The Movement That Silenced Us and the Woman Behind It*

Roxy Hussain: Author
Sara Javed's former friend and mentee
Anti-Non-Verbal Activist

Aadhi: Did you feel professionally jealous of Sara?
Roxy: I was her *biggest* fan. A woman of her background, writing about structural injustices and interrogating them through a lens we don't see often enough was inspiring and important. We all want to be seen, right? Some get seen in literature and film more than others.
Aadhi: Why is Sara's silence so problematic for you?
Roxy: Because women like me have always been told our voices don't matter. We're never given the same opportunities; we're talked-over when we are - I'm fed up of our complexities being distilled and made palatable for public consumption. Now, by taking words away, we're being robbed of the very thing that helps make our complexities *known*. More lost opportunities.
Aadhi: What about the opportunities that have opened up for you through the growth of Non-Verbalism?
Roxy: What? 'Opportunities' so that I can finally be *heard*? To be asked something other than: 'where are you really from?' Do you know what that's like?

Aadhi: I'm familiar with the question.

Roxy: Try being a woman, on top of it. It's exhausting.

Pause.

Aadhi: Speaking of which, I'm going to take a break.

Zainab

Glasgow, May 2021

Zainab Aalam sat at the breakfast table, alone, to finish rereading *Woman in Waiting* by Sara Javed.

This time I will not apologise.

The author's silence struck Zainab as bold yet disappointing.

As she turned the last page, she let out a quiet sob. Reality and fiction had morphed and for three hundred and forty-three pages Zainab's mind had trod an emotionally potent, but neutral state. Her knotted brain – and heart – had loosened.

Zainab heard the toilet flush.

It was 7 a.m. and her mother-in-law was in the bathroom. Kashif would be next. Her father-in-law last.

Zainab began to prepare breakfast, as she had done every day since she moved to Glasgow eight years ago. Her mother-in-law came into the kitchen and checked the hob, if all the plates and glasses had been laid out.

'Don't put sugar in your uncle's chai today,' said Naz. The health of the men in Naz's life was a measure of her success as matriarch.

Zainab complied.

Kashif came and sat at the table, looking at the morning's offerings. He was followed by her father-in-law, Iqbal.

'You look tired,' said Naz to Kashif.

'I didn't sleep very well.'

'You leave the window open; you'll catch a cold.'

Kashif squeezed his mum's hand.

Tea and juice were slurped, chatter about the garden fence needing fixing, the dinner party that weekend, the multiple reasons for Kashif's lack of sleep.

'Where is the sugar in this tea?' Iqbal asked.

'The doctor said you must cut your intake,' Naz replied.

Iqbal looked into his cup, dejected.

Kashif bit into his toast.

Zainab imagined him choking. Naz exclaiming, *my son, my son*, shouting at Iqbal to *call the police. Do I have to tell you* everything?

Zainab offered Kashif another slice.

Once finished, he loaded his plates into the dishwasher.

'Zainab will do that,' said Naz. 'She starts work late today.'

'Just call me the ideal husband,' replied Kashif, with the smile of a man who had borne the twists of life and fate with nobility. He was the type of husband who recalled regularly the times he'd done the dishes and made the bed. A man who'd hardly brought up the fact that his wife was barren.

Kashif had stopped watching pornography once they were ready to conceive though the sex was hardly less humiliating. It wouldn't be proper. The sanctity of uncreated life somehow having precedence over the one in existence.

Zainab often wondered if her infertility was God's way of punishing Kashif over his disregard for her body. If so, why must she suffer in the process?

When no child arrived, Kashif had the right to look for another wife. (He had reflected on the matter for weeks. Sometimes it still crawled into his thoughts. But he had quietened his family's suggestions because he understood duty. He faced Zainab's barrenness, stoically, turning, instead, to his local imam for guidance.)

After Kashif left for work, Zainab listened to Naz in the living room, speaking to one of her friends.

'Yes, she's still teaching in the mosque . . . Without children how can you pass your time? Once she has citizenship, who knows—?'

Silence.

Zainab's education and cultural sensibilities had only proved important in theory. The family thought it much more becoming for a woman to teach children at their local mosque.

The screen on Zainab's phone flashed.

'Hello,' she whispered.

'Meet me.'

Zainab's heart thumped.

'Make an excuse.'

She paused. 'OK.'

'The usual place?'

'Yes.'

She told Naz she was going to get a birthday present for a friend. Instead she drove to Kelvingrove Park. The gallery housed a Dali painting that she once went to see. Since then she returned regularly to look at *Christ the Redeemer*. No one else in the family was concerned about things like the art of expression.

She was standing in front of the painting, asking God for guidance. Peace. Though she had little right to ask Him for anything, considering.

'There are other paintings here, you know,' came a voice.

Zainab continued to look at the painting. 'What are our sacrifices in comparison?'

'Even prophets made mistakes,' replied Suleiman. He lowered his voice and leant into her. 'I wanted to see you.'

Her heartbeat quickened. She tried to focus on Christ. To bear children was to nurture but also to correct things. That was now a lost opportunity. Even if her marriage had been made up of affection and respect, it wouldn't have replaced the hollowed part of the very essence of womanhood. Perhaps she would've borne it stoically too if it weren't for the looks of pity she received at her own physical incompetence. Kashif's pain was the byproduct of her body's malfunction. A victim of her inhospitable womb.

'Kashif's going to finish applying for your naturalisation.'

She turned towards Suleiman.

'I've finally talked him into it,' he said. '*This* is your home.'

She wanted to kiss him. But not in a place that housed relics of the past. Not when he was the one with whom she'd mapped out a future. Three years ago now, Zainab had started the process for naturalisation in the UK, found the lawyers, collated the paperwork, but Kashif would make excuses about the lawyers she chose being too expensive. He should check the paperwork; he was busy; what was the hurry? His mother would make remarks about wives leaving their husbands after receiving citizenship. Zainab was allowed to work, Kashif had bought her a car, and with it independence. What if Zainab took that independence too far?

Naz liked to remind Kashif that his wife's confidence in her own beauty and mind should be tempered with a reality check as to the condition of her womb.

'It's God's will,' Kashif would often reply. 'And she's a good wife, isn't she?'

'With such a husband, she should be.'

But after their break in the Hebrides together two months ago, Kashif had been cold. Why would he do something to make Zainab's life easier now?

'I don't understand,' she said.

'He mentioned the argument you had when you went away. I just suggested that maybe, if he stopped withholding your citizenship, you'd be more open.'

'Suleiman—'

'I know, but Zainu, haven't you suffered enough? They treat you like a servant.'

Suleiman assumed hers was a story of generic subjugation.

(He was sufficiently in love with her to not need details).

She suspected he might kill Kashif if he knew the truth. Or worse.

He wouldn't understand at all.

Zainab steadied herself. She had spent ten years gathering the pieces of who she was – the wife, daughter, daughter-in-law – holding on to the belief that she existed outside of these roles. That she was a being in her own right.

She would no longer be a *woman in waiting.*

After a decade of living a muted life, that being was finally going to come into existence.

Unedited footage: *The Movement That Silenced Us and the Woman Behind It*
Roxy Hussain

Aadhi: OK, let's start again.

Roxy: No one knew Sara like I did. Both sides of her.

Aadhi: Tell me about the other side.

Roxy: The truth is, Sara was - *is* - broken in ways she won't admit, which could be freeing to so many. As well as herself.

Aadhi: Broken in what way?

Roxy: She found it hard to admit just how much being abandoned by her mother affected her. I'm all for privacy but she has a platform. This comes with a responsibility. We cannot shirk these. Especially when considering how many marginalised women don't have the same opportunities.

Aadhi: How had your relationship evolved after the publication of your memoir, *An Unveiling*?

Roxy: Ironically, in many ways, Sara inspired me to write the book - a personal and painful reflection on sexuality and oppression in family dynamics. I thought Sara would be proud of that. But she began to have contempt for everything and, well, that seemed to correlate with my book's increasing success. She used to be a compassionate listener . . . And then one day, it was like, I'd share a thought, and she'd look at me, unmoved . . . She'd stopped paying attention to women in our field. Stopped amplifying their voices. She'd stopped saying *anything*.

People should be held accountable for their words *and* their silence.

ANOMALIES

Sara

London, 2011

M,

I had a dream you were waiting for me in the reception of my publisher's building. You came to wish me luck. Sometimes I wonder, when you looked at your new family, whether you thought about me. I like to think you have sleepless nights. Then the opposite idea surfaces and I realise you probably don't think about me at all.

But you turn up in my dreams. To wish me luck, of all things! As if that's what I need, and not a mother.

Anyway, there's no use in wishing dreams into a reality. It is action that does that.

PS. I would still like your luck.

Sara tapped her feet, nervously. She had handed in the first draft of *Woman in Waiting*, which now sat on her publisher Penelope's desk.

'I like to ask all my authors,' began Penelope. 'What do you want? From your career.' She paused. 'What *inspired* you?'

Sara had always felt that writing helped to recycle life's momentum, giving it a new quality altogether. Perhaps her books could soothe readers the way they had soothed her when she was growing up. But she was not prepared to go into the particulars of death, rejection and adoption. Sara could have told Penelope about her dad's emotional collapse after Lily had left when Sara was twelve. The jobs she had to take, as soon as it was legally allowed, to keep them afloat because her dad had been unable to hold on to one. Writing had begun as a catharsis and metamorphosised into a dream. But trying to extract sympathy was unbecoming. The words clung like shame in her throat. Sara, privately, wanted to shape her story as one of success against the odds, under the guardianship of a man who had loved her when no one else did.

'Sara?'

'Oh. Sorry.' She was prone to tuning out. 'What do I want from my writing career?'

She *must* say the right thing.

'The same thing I want from life?' she replied with a small laugh.

'So, *everything?*' Penelope's laugh was louder.

'Yes. Sales, awards. *Everything.*'

'Which awards do you see yourself winning?'

Sara paused. Forced herself to translate her most private thoughts into words. 'There's only one that means everything.' The Mildred Aitken Award, with prize money of thirty thousand pounds and unsurpassed professional respectability, was the thing to strive for.

Sara imagined herself, on stage, accepting the award to rapturous applause. Her father unspeakably proud. She would then find her mother. Tell her everything she'd achieved. Her mother's regret would be the dramatic arc before Sara's life's resolution. Sara would have written her way into significance.

'These things are extremely competitive,' said Penelope. 'But let's focus on your book . . .' She rested her hand on Sara's manuscript. 'It is *beautiful.*'

Sara's heart raced. Possibilities abounded.

'You have *so* much to say,' Penelope continued, as Millie and John from Publicity and Marketing entered.

Sara smiled, uncertainly.

'The novel's so much about language and feminism—' began Millie.

'Female friendship—'

'Familial discord—'

Sara swallowed hard. 'Thank you.'

'Could you send me a biog of your background?' said Millie. 'Experiences that informed your book?'

Sara thought that the point of stories was that they were rooted in nothing but their own existence. She needed Henry. He'd know what to say.

'Experiences?' repeated Sara. 'They're all quite average.'

There was an uncomfortable pause. Being average was never a winning feature. And if one were average, well . . .

'I'll do everything possible to prevent people from finding that out,' added Sara.

There was some laughter.

'Now, I've got some editorial notes here,' said Penelope after Millie and John had left.

Sara's anxiety mingled with the newfound thrill of the potential for change. The way you could, with a book, deconstruct something that seemed to be built from nothing, and put it together again.

M – your good luck, such as it was, worked.

Love,
S

Grace

Manchester, 2011

Grace sat opposite David in the Costa in Leeds, and told him that she was having a baby.

'Who's the father?' he asked.

She should've thrown the coffee in his face.

Her decision to keep the baby, conceived during their four-night stay in a hostel in Calais, was partly based on the belief that though she belonged to no one, her baby would belong to her. She imagined her baby growing up, saying '*Mama*', the school dances and graduations. She refused to listen to friends who said she was too young, too unaware of the strains of motherhood to go through with it. To have an abortion, she was advised, would be the kindest thing she could do.

But Grace's compassion never did extend to herself.

She had wrung her hands all the way to see David, flitting between scenarios that ranged from raising a baby alone, penniless, to living with him in a semi-detached in Deansgate. And a rescue dog.

She needn't have taught herself to hope.

Grace felt her face burn. 'It's *yours*.'

'Right. Shit. Of course. Are you keeping it?'

'What do *you* think?'

He paused. 'There are options.'

'Are you serious?'

'I can't tell you what to do, but . . . this wasn't in my plan.'

She supposed he had no desire to be associated with someone whose background was so wholly different to his.

She never contacted him again.

Her labour had been one of lost love in that sense. The way that time and the pain seemed to expand and contract, pulsating as if on the verge of eruption, had Grace wishing for *a* mother – someone who understood what her body was doing to her – if not her own. When Benji was finally born, his whimpers evoked in Grace a love so desperate and aching, filled with a tsunami of panic to get things right. She kissed him again and again until the nurses had to take him away.

Grace's resolve, unfortunately, hadn't prepared her for the cacophony of cries and tears (often her own), nappies and formula in her one-bedroom flat, still in Longsight. Sometimes she sat in the dark, Benji finally asleep in her arms, embracing and fearing the silence in equal measure.

Three weeks into motherhood Grace's phone rang. She dived for it, but too late.

Benji woke up.

She picked him up, his cries a sledgehammer to her sanity.

'Hello.'

'Grace?'

That a voice could bring Grace out of this moment was as surprising as the voice itself. Grace paused. Harangued by her son's inability to sleep, and her mother's timing.

'Listen to those lungs.'

'How did you find out?' Benji finally latched on to her nipple. 'It's been seven years.' Her voice almost cracked. She could not reconcile such resentment and relief.

Dede Jenkins never considered that motherhood meant forgoing her inclinations in favour of Grace's needs. A young Grace would say things to her father, like: 'Sophie and her mum go bowling on weekends.'

Her dad would reply: 'Try to understand. Everyone's different.'

And shouldn't differences be tolerated?

It was only when Grace was older and wiser that she understood the necessary boundaries of compassion. Duty surpassed individualism and Grace was determined never to allow her mother back into her life.

'Mother's intuition,' replied Dede now.

Benji, distracted by outside noise, yanked Grace's nipple from his mouth. '*Ow*. One minute.'

'Sore breasts?' asked Dede. 'Are they hot?'

'Yes.'

'Mastitis probably. Try massaging the area while feeding. Hot pack before and cold pack after.'

Grace felt the tears well. She looked at Benji, sapping from her both will and reason. Would she forever have to do everything alone? She began to sob.

Dede remained silent.

'Why are you calling me now?' Grace asked between sobs. 'After Dad. After everything?'

'Oh, baby, I'm sorry. I messed up. I messed up bad.'

Benji let out another wail.

When Grace let Dede back into her life, they both knew that it had not been an act of compassion. But desperation.

Zainab

Lahore, 2011

Zainab's mother waited for the gaggle of giggling cousins to leave the bedroom.

'Your father's nieces are the silliest girls in Lahore,' she said, shutting the door, eventually smiling at Zainab.

'You can put on more lipstick. You're a wife now.' She handed Zainab a shade of red.

Kashif was returning to Pakistan for two weeks, after a year away. Zainab's spousal visa hadn't yet come through and everyone understood that a man had needs. It was assumed that Zainab was keen to meet them.

'He's a very good man,' said her mother.

A feeling was pushing itself to the surface of Zainab's mouth, trying to formulate into words.

'*Ammi*, I . . .'

It failed.

Her mum cupped Zainab's chin in her hand. 'What? You can talk to me.'

But one could only talk about a thing one understood.

'Nothing. This lipstick's too bright.'

'Allah gave us a good daughter and He's rewarded you with a good husband. Be thankful for all the blessings,' she added.

Zainab *was* a dutiful daughter.

And so she reasoned that what happened must have been natural, even

87

if it didn't feel it. Sex might just be a degradation of the female body, and a woman must learn to enjoy it.

When Kashif arrived, he had brought Suleiman, his friend from university, with him again. Upon seeing her husband, a knot in Zainab's stomach crawled all the way to her chest.

'Salamalaikum,' Suleiman greeted Zainab, while Kashif embraced her father.

She noticed Suleiman's stare. Her face burned. She was *not* an object to be ogled.

'Auntie.' Kashif spoke to Zainab's mum as they sat in their ornate dining room. 'We need to find a wife for Suleiman, too.'

'We don't all expect to be as lucky as you,' said Suleiman, glancing at Zainab.

Everyone laughed, but Zainab felt oppressed. When Suleiman asked her to pass the salad, she did so without looking at him.

After dinner, they got up to go into the living room. She caught Suleiman's eye and looked away in barely concealed disdain.

'Have I offended you?' he whispered, the rest of the party ahead of them. They stood behind the glass doors of the dining room.

'It's improper to stare at a married woman. At *any* woman.'

His face reddened. 'Bhabi . . .' He addressed her as his sister-in-law.

She waited for him to deny it.

'I was—'

'*What?*'

'I was wondering why you looked so sad,' he replied, eventually.

Zainab, caught between embarrassment that a stranger should notice something her family didn't, and contempt at his audacity replied: 'Don't presume to know how someone feels.'

She was about to walk away, when he added, 'I'm sorry. But I don't think it's presumption.'

Zainab observed Kashif all evening, smiling readily, standing up when Zainab did. The looks of envy from her family, pride from her mother, all leant themselves to self-distrust.

That night, when everyone had gone to bed, and she was alone with Kashif, Zainab's journey of mistrust began again, Suleiman's words playing in her mind, over and over.

The following morning, when Suleiman attempted a smile, she did not look away.

May 2021

Famous YouTuber's Vow of Silence

Priya Patel, *Hollywood Weekly*, May 2021

Mimi Munkin, LA-based YouTube sensation, declared on TikTok her inten-tion to take a vow of silence. Inspired by a writer she admires, Munkin added: 'Modern women are juggling motherhood, careers, the home, and being told that we should be doing it all, looking perfect. I'm blessed, but guys, I'm exhausted. Peace begins with yourself. And I don't ever want to disappoint my fans by not being true to my inner Mimi. We have to change ourselves before we can change the world . . .' The video has had over 3.6 million views, and counting.

Follow Priya on <u>Twitter</u> and <u>Instagram</u>

Unedited footage: *The Movement That Silenced Us and the Woman Behind It*

Henry Green: Screenwriter
Sara Javed's husband.
Non-Verbal

Roxy: We really want to understand who Sara was before the movement, so it'd be good to start with how you met her.

Henry: It was fourteen, fifteen years ago now. I was in a bar in Clapham. She was sitting at a table on her own even though the place was packed. There were plenty of attractive women there, but I guess her seeming so preoccupied, all alone, she stood out. I walked past her to use the toilet and some guy was asking if he could buy her a drink.

She had looked around, surprised, as if he might be talking to someone else.

Henry laughs.

She's unapologetic but there was always something slightly awkward about her too. It was endearing.

Roxy: Unapologetic how?

Henry: She said to the guy: 'Are *you* sure *you* want to do that? I'm both boring and get bored very easily.'

When he walked away, I turned to her and told her I felt sorry for the poor sod.

'*I was saving him the trouble of small talk.*' Those were her exact words.

So I replied that maybe he liked trouble. According to her, he'd come to the wrong place. And then, this part I remember clearly, she got out her notebook and scribbled something. She seemed to have forgotten I was there.

I hovered until she'd finished. I'm not sure why. She picked up her notebook and went to leave.

'*Is that a hit list?*' I asked her.

She told me I was lucky she didn't know my name. That's when I asked for the notebook. She held it to her chest. I promised that I wouldn't give it to the police, and I could tell she was amused. Then she handed it over. I flipped to the back page and wrote my name and number.

She looked at it and laughed.

She has a great laugh. It made the fact that she told me she wouldn't call a lot easier.

It didn't matter, because I replied: '*Yes, you will.*'

I don't think she was used to men being that forward. I don't think I'd ever been that cocky - we were so young - but I guess that's the point. Someone, from somewhere, brings something new out in you. It's the surprise of it that makes you want more.

And Sara always wants more.

Sara

London, May 2021

Sara was sitting on the floor, in the middle of the bare living room, when Henry thrust his phone in her face: *The Standard Issue: Mimi Munkin Takes Back Her Voice by Giving it Up.*

Sara grabbed the phone before skimming the article.

What the actual fuck?

'What the actual fuck,' said Henry.

Mimi Munkin – as vacuous as she was popular – promoted spiritual well-being from her apartment on Malibu Beach, Instagramming mantras alongside a photo of herself on the beach doing a headstand with lotus legs, the sun illuminating her dermabrased face. She highlighted stretch-marks on her tanned skin with the hashtag #bodypositivity, which had won her the accolade of being a feminist, as well as a modelling contract. It was misfortune enough to be liked by her, but this was taking it too far.

Henry stood over Sara, hands on his hips.

'I know things have been hard . . . but it's been *two weeks*, you haven't said a word and now Mimi Munkin's seems to be following your example,' he said, clearly bewildered. 'You went to your awards ceremony *without me*. In a *sweatshirt and trainers*. You snubbed everyone I thought mattered to you. *And* we have no furniture. How long is this meant to go on?'

As long as we both shall live.

Sara took a deep breath. She had been sitting in the same spot for two hours. Stillness of mind began with stillness of body. That's what she'd read once.

'I've been there for you every step of the way and now *I* need *you* . . . Yours isn't the only career.'

Sara quietly scoffed.

'What? What was that?'

Or perhaps not so quietly.

It was much like talking to a child, she supposed. It gave her a sadistic satisfaction. Three months after Sara had fallen in love with Henry's attentiveness, his ability to know something about almost everything – and relay them in run-on sentences – he mentioned that he found her variety of straight-talk offensive.

'What, exactly, am I offending?' she'd asked, part-defensive, part-curious.

'Just, people have feelings.'

'What are they?' She widened her eyes in mock horror.

Henry had laughed. 'We could all stand to be more compassionate, couldn't we? And passionate,' he whispered, leaning into her.

'*Passion?*'

'I'll teach you about it . . .'

Then they had kissed. It hadn't felt like it had with previous boyfriends, whose hearts she was always sorry to break. Her thoughts, never quite present in the moment, had felt anchored to her body when Henry touched her. Sara, still in her twenties then, believed herself to be deficient in many things, and wondered, maybe *this* is the person meant to understand me.

She might finally come to understand herself.

That had been the point.

Fifteen years later, she recognised that she never should have put such expectation upon him. And was thus no closer to achieving her initial point.

When the doorbell rang, Henry went to answer it. Sara could hear her dad and Lily's voices. Henry had obviously called them, always in need of assistance. Afzal and Lily walked in. If Sara squinted, they might be thirty-five years younger: brave and brilliant – defying expectations. Sara remembered hearing their laughter when she'd be reading in her room. She would watch them through the banisters as they listened to Leonard Cohen, dancing in the living room.

'Just *look* at what I'm dealing with.' Henry gestured at the empty room. 'I didn't say a thing when she started emptying her wardrobe. All those dresses. Gone. Shoes she'd loved? Dumped in a charity bin. And *then* she gets rid of the mural she loved. After that, well . . . see for yourselves. What am I meant to *do*?'

Sara felt a twinge of guilt.

'I never thought success would change you.'

The guilt promptly disappeared. Sara was ready to tell her husband that perhaps he should consider that her success changed *him*. That she stopped taking him to events because he'd started saying things like:

'How can you stand such pretention?'

'All this fawning over you is so disingenuous.'

'You'd think that books saved the world the way this lot talk.'

Words, words, words.

Noise, noise, noise.

'Many spiritual traditions are steeped in silence,' said Afzal now.

'Dad, *please* . . .' Henry sighed, failing to notice Afzal's look of disdain. Afzal had never sanctioned Henry calling him 'Dad': it was just another source of Henry-related irritation.

'Is that what this is?' Henry asked Sara. 'Are you *finding yourself*? I get that but . . .'

Sara looked pointedly at her dad.

'My daughter isn't that prosaic.'

'OK, everyone,' Lily interjected. 'Sara, don't you think we deserve an explanation? We're worried. Afzal, *say* something.'

'People who do things out of the norm are the most interesting,' he replied.

Lily moved closer to Afzal, lowering her voice: 'She's *unhappy*.'

'Of course she's unhappy,' he replied, serious, pensive. 'But all grief is an opening towards something.'

95

Sara felt the tears well.

Henry let out an exasperated sigh. He often said that Afzal's affection for Sara surpassed the obligatory unconditional love of a parent, that Lily's continued membership in the family was excessive. He hadn't ever understood the pains it had taken a twelve-year-old Sara to bring Lily back into their lives after she'd left six months before. Even at that age, Sara understood that Afzal would not function the same without Lily. So Sara had called her daily to keep her in their lives, bridging gaps through conversation.

'This is just Sara finding new ways to be aggressive,' said Henry.

There were, it seemed, many ways to argue.

As they turned away from Sara, quarrelling, she watched, removed, yet still the centre of contention. If she didn't speak, then others would speak for her. That had its own sense of liberation; learning to detach herself from the opinions of those closest to her. If she could master that, surely she'd master life?

'—I think that's a bit unfair,' accused Henry. 'Especially considering that I've said *nothing* about the fact we're not having children.'

Sara's stomach contracted. A noticeable absence of hunger for mother-hood. She had thought this *need* to correct past wrongs via procreation was a little heavy-handed, but Henry had reacted as if she was renouncing the role for which her body had been formed.

The doorbell rang. This time Jyoti walked in. 'I'm glad you called. Afzal, Lily.' Jyoti nodded towards them.

Sara wasn't sure if she was annoyed at Henry for calling her friend or relieved.

They had met on a panel at a literature festival in Wales. Sara was promoting *A Woman in Waiting* and Jyoti's third book, *Mixed Brown Bag*, about being a single mother and activist had proven just as successful as her first book, *Rise Again*, a manifesto of womanhood in the twenty-first century.

Jyoti's was a voice to which Sara often listened with admiration and a latent feeling of self-loathing for not having achieved enough in her own life.

Recently, though, Sara hadn't been moved by anything Jyoti said. Her delivery had evolved, her syntax refined, but *the content* hadn't changed. Still, a hoard of young women hung upon Jyoti's every word, unable to distinguish between ideological consistency and monotony. Even before Sara had won her award, she was bemused by her own increasing followers. She had scrambled through notebooks, skimmed through her publications, only to find that she had also been guilty of a languishing verbosity.

It had been a formative blow.

Jyoti scanned the room, commanding attention by virtue of her flaming red hair. 'Could you at least get some chairs?' Then she looked at Sara, her tone softening. '*What* is going on?'

Sara's non-response seemed to irritate Jyoti.

'Just *look* at Munkin's Instagram. She hasn't even mentioned you. Not by name.' Jyoti showed Sara her iPhone.

There was the quote 'Beware the Barrenness of a Busy Life', Munkin's reason for silence below it, garnering hundreds of thousands of likes and comments even as she watched.

This is amazing. I once did a talk in school about silence and people are still talking about it.
Never herd of Javed, but you are an inspiration.
People have issues.
You are beautiful, inside and out.

The whole thing made Sara's point: eventually your words would be taken out of your own hands. But she was in search of a space she could be transformed, not transfixed. Her lack of reaction seemed to irritate Jyoti further. '*Years* women have fought to have a voice and you're *giving yours up.*'

'Exactly,' said Henry. 'Where's your feminism?'

This felt like a lot of pressure for a woman.

'We used to believe in all the same things and now,' Jyoti continued. 'I don't even know you.'

Sara's heart sank. Connection boiled down to common beliefs in the end. It felt so *artless*. She wanted to be alone in the sanctuary of her home. To reimagine her life in solitude. To reckon with herself before reckoning with the world.

'Christ,' came Henry's voice. 'Another fucking celebrity's gone silent . . .'

Mimi Munkin's Silence Inspires Followers

Susan Colby, *The Snuff*, May 2021

Mimi Munkin's silence of two weeks has inspired thousands to follow in her footsteps. Munkin's fans have been adopting silence with the hashtag #nolongerbarren, which is trending internationally, as a means for rejecting the deluge of social expectations put upon women, and, as Munkin put in a written statement, 'fertilising the inner voice.' The hashtag is related to Socrates' quote in a letter that Munkin read, which moved her to take a vow of silence: 'Beware the Barrenness of a Busy Life.'

Susan is a freelancer writing for @HashtagPress @Liberati and more.

Subscribe to our online mag *The Snuff.*

Grace

Manchester, May 2021

Grace read her newsfeed, indignant, leaning against the steel kitchen counter.

Fertilising the inner voice.

She clicked on Munkin's #nolongerbarren Instagram page. Soft-focus images of Munkin looking pensive in white trousers and pastel jumpers. Staring out of a window at crashing waves. Playing with a puppy. Mimi Munkin's life was still *and* full.

Hashtag silence.

Hashtag no-longer-barren.

'*Do Not Let The Parameters of Language Confine You.*'

Grace picked up her Kindle and searched 'parameter' in *Woman in Waiting*.

'*She had let the parameters of language confine her . . .*'

Grace shook her head at the obvious plagiarism before she caught Benji staring. He offered her his glass of water. He did this much more often now – held her hand, gave her a hug. The first time he sat and put his arm around her since her silence, she had to stop herself from bursting into tears. Had he forgiven her for driving his grandmother away, if that's how he saw it? For giving no explanation as to why Dede disappeared three months ago?

Grace pointed to Benji, the glass and then herself, pretending to cradle something: *You're babying me.*

He brought out his arms as if to say, *What are my choices?* She could see him as a teenager, and for a moment she felt that if she stayed like this, allowed him verbal space, there might be a future in which he *would* talk.

Grace had not informed Benji's teacher about her Non-Verbal decision. She had never gone more than a few weeks without speaking to Ms Palmer about Benji's progress, but no one seemed to have noticed yet. She had stopped his speech therapy. Grace's awareness of how these sessions must have felt for Benji were now somewhat raised. She had always found them uncomfortable but had never fully understood why. Now, she was beginning to see it as enforced speech.

Surely her Non-Verbalism was a more organic approach for Benji?

She did wonder whether it was necessary to omit words entirely – knocking on Benji's door to let him know dinner was ready, asking for help in shops through mime, everything imbued with the irksome task of communicating without speech. Calls from friends had dwindled to the point where the lack of words felt tantamount to a lack of existence.

The mutterings at work had been audible. By the end of Grace's first week of silence, the partners had called her into a meeting.

'Is this a protest over Harold's promotion?' asked named partner, Andy Canon, who was sitting next to Graham.

Harold! If only!

Grace shook her head and placed a piece of paper in front of Andy. She had enough savings to last her and Benji a while, but to lose this job would be to relinquish stability, to witness people's perplexity . . .

She must not crumble under the weight of expectation.

'Who *is* Sara Javed?' said Andy, looking at the letter. 'And what's she got to do with you?'

Graham looked concerned. Grace had thought about typing her own letter, for a sense of professionalism, but either way she would probably seem ridiculous.

'Grace,' said Graham. 'You're an asset to us in every way—'

'But what exactly do you want to achieve?' interrupted Andy.

Silence was something her boss would never comprehend in his verbose life. One of summer barbeques and winter holidays, funded by an exemplary profession, which engendered both awe and envy (and one day, in the near future, a premature heart attack).

Then there was Graham calling her an *asset*. Almost stripping Grace of her humanity. And hadn't humanity, helping people, been the single thing that motivated her? Necessity had morphed her into something she would have railed against ten years ago. Motherhood had made her desperate. Worse, it had made her generic.

Grace was now rejecting this hamster wheel of trying to buy happiness because perhaps she was ready to understand from where its opposite stemmed.

Such introspection would make most uncomfortable.

When she indicated that she wouldn't take leave, after more meetings, emails, they eventually came to an agreement and Grace left the office permanently without further fuss.

The goodbye with Graham had involved regret and a lingering look. What would it be like to not smell his scent when he leant over her?

She thought perhaps he'd drop her an email. A WhatsApp.

Nothing.

There was no turning back.

Grace opened the coffee shop door. She pulled at Benji's hand so that he looked her way and gave a wide smile.

'Hi, what can I get you?'

Grace showed the barista her phone in which she'd typed: *coffee and carrot cake, please*. The barista glanced at her, uncertain.

'And young man, for you?' she asked Benji.

He shook his head.

Benji licked the icing off his cake and emptied the contents of his puzzle box at their table. He looked at the empty seat next to Grace, of course missing Dede who would always do puzzles with him. Grace kissed the top of his head. Empty words could be as deceptive as empty spaces.

'Excuse me?'

Grace looked up at the barista.

'I'm sorry, but . . . I had another customer come in and do the same –
well, she used her My Fitness Pal App, but are you doing that Mimi
Munkin thing?'

Mimi Munkin.

The insidiousness of misinformation never ceased to surprise her. Then
her phone rang.

Unknown number.

It could be her mother. Should Grace speak? Break a rule for a woman
who had no regard for them?

'. . . Hello?' came a man's voice, eventually. *'Hello?* Can you hear me?'
Grace gripped the phone. She looked at Benji, piecing together the jigsaw.
'Grace? It's me . . .'

David.

'What is going on. *Hello?'*
Grace, it turned out, couldn't have spoken even if she wanted.

From: D.Hodgkin312
To: Grace.Jenkins55
Subject: Hello

Grace,

It's been a while, hasn't it? I tried calling you but no one spoke.
Maybe I had the wrong number.

I know this is out of the blue. I've been thinking about you for a long
time. I just haven't had the courage to contact you.

There's a lot I want to say, but face-to-face. I want to meet you.

I want to know about our son.

Yours,
David

IVIEW NEWEST RELEASE

A PIXY ORIGINAL SERIES

Showing Now

Mimi Munkin: Muted

125,000 ratings
3.7* average

Social media influencer Mimi Munkin turns reality TV star in this revealing look at her vow of silence. An empowering must-watch for anyone who wants to know how to quieten the world's noise.

Click <u>here</u> *to discover Mimi Munkin's collaboration with* CleanBeauty's *new line of cosmetics* Ssshhh.

Zainab

Glasgow, June 2021

Zainab drank her evening tea with her in-laws in their sparse living room. It looked as bleak as Zainab often felt with its linoleum flooring, grey sofas and magnolia walls. Quite different from her home in Lahore, which had a marble staircase and two columns erected at the entrance. The walls there were replete with family photos.

She'd once suggested redecorating.

Kashif had agreed.

His mother had not.

'Hashtag, *"No Longer Barren"*? said Kashif now, flicking through *The Herald*. 'Turning silence into a celebrity fad.'

The television flickered in the background. Kashif's face flushed with indignation.

She looked at him, confused. He hadn't touched her in over a week and she wasn't sure what had caused the lull. Especially since the sex had been particularly humiliating after their trip to the Hebrides.

On their last day in Skye, Zainab had found herself on the cliff's edge, looking towards the Highlands. The scaling cliffs, the tumultuous nature of the sea had invoked in Zainab a rare case of belonging. Nature was meant to bring one closer to God and, unfortunately, Zainab had the urge to pray.

Kashif had been watching her. 'Let's head back.'

'I'll stay.'

'If you go missing, they'll think I killed you,' he said, half-laughing.

She stared ahead.

'Why are you always so serious?'

Solitude and silence was too much to ask. To bask in the safety of her own insignificance amid the magnanimity of creation; to feel at peace with her own obscurity.

'Sometimes I feel . . .' He paused. 'We have no children but I'm *still* here. It doesn't seem to matter to you though. The things I've done.'

A gust of wind whipped her hair around her face.

She let out a laugh. '*The things you've done.*'

Zainab turned to walk away. He grabbed her arm.

'I give you everything and all I get is your silence. Even in bed you're—'

'What, Kashif?'

'You just . . . *lie* there.'

The wind picked up, gulls cried in the background.

'I like to get it over with.'

He tightened his grip.

'This is what you like doing, isn't it?' She had held his gaze.

'Fine. Walk back alone.'

He had left her, standing in her sought obscurity, at one with the elements, feeling the power of her own reserve.

When they returned to Glasgow, Kashif reminded her about the rights he had over her body. But since Suleiman said Kashif would finalise her naturalisation application, she'd noticed her husband looking at her differently. Sometimes, he almost seemed worried.

'*Goray*,' said Iqbal now, reading the headline about influencer Munkin's silence as Kashif flung the paper on the coffee table. 'Only white people do things like this.'

'The author who actually started it is Pakistani,' commented Zainab.

She'd usually stay quiet, but the hashtag had brought tears to her eyes. It was one of the few times she'd seen the word *barren* used in relation to something other than her womb.

'*Mimi Munkin.* Just the *name.*' Kashif shook his head and switched on

The Great Debate. Munkin's silence had people in a flurry of arguments about why it was gaining popularity so quickly. 'Let's see what holier-than-thou Aadhi Sathar has to say.'

Naz, in the meantime, began reading out the side effects of too much sugar to Kashif.

Zainab leant forward as Aadhi Sathar spoke.

'Don't be fooled by Munkins' series. This originated with one woman, author Sara Javed. Yes, the world has its problems but using silence as a form of protest is not the answer.

'They might be a minority now, but we have – what? – fifteen secondary teachers, including Michael Smith here, adopting silence.'

Aadhi Sathar looked at his fellow panellist who typed something that came up on a large screen for all to read.

I've come here to support an idea that I, and some of my colleagues, feel is significant. We've found we can learn so much from silence. A way to listen and change things.

Aadhi looked perplexed.

'How on earth can we put an emphasis on education on one hand and allow the people in charge to disregard the rules?'

'You needn't raise your voice.'

'God, look at his face,' said Kashif, watching the presenter admonish Aadhi.

'I apologise. But just take supply chains . . . how will import and export be affected if there's no communication? What next?'

The presenter chuckled. *'I don't think we need to worry about it taking over. Michael has something to add.'*

Non-Verbals aren't anarchists . . .

'Non-Verbal? Are we going to act as if this is a thing now?' interrupted Aadhi.

'Please, you've had your chance to speak.'

Why do the rules Aadhi speaks of never apply to those in positions of power? We've been given the illusion of having a voice – but when was the last time we were truly heard? Silence, for me right now, is power because it is shattering that illusion and I am in control.

There was some applause from the audience.

'This is the most absurd argument I've heard—'

'Aadhi, I have to ask you to lower your voice.'

'No. No. What happens when people who have been historically oppressed are forced to go silent?'

'Aren't you being parano—'

'If something becomes popular, it never remains a choice. It becomes a reason to be shunned if you don't follow the herd. If we keep going this way – with teachers like Michael irresponsibly spouting personal ideals without thinking about the consequences – then damage will be done.'

You're shouting about it as if silence is contagious . . .

'I'm not – I'm not shouting. But if history teaches us anything it's that ideas are contagious. If we don't nip this – thing – in the bud. Then we are in for a whole lot of trouble, and you know what? People who support silence will deserve what they get.'

Zainab and the family watched Aadhi Sathar, red in the face, continuing his tirade, as Michael Smith looked on calmly. Almost in pity. Even the audience didn't seem to know what to do, until, quite dramatically, Aadhi Sathar unhooked his mic from his lapel, throwing it down, before storming off.

'The imam at the mosque talked about Munkin today,' said Kashif, who seemed captivated by Aadhi's televised loss of control.

Zainab felt it took a sensitivity of spirit to deliver a sermon on a Hollywood celebrity without commenting on their being hell-bound. Iqbal switched the channel to *Muted*.

On the screen, Mimi sat in the middle of her private yoga studio, meditating.

'You know all these quotes on her social media have been taken from Sara Javed's work?' added Kashif, gulping his tea.

Zainab wondered what would happen if it went down the wrong way as a voice-over narrated: *Mimi's mom and stepdad have arrived to talk about their daughter's silence.*

Munkin came out of her studio, hugging her mum, as if bearing the burden of a difficult but necessary choice.

'The imam's sermon was about reflection,' continued Kashif.

'All this mosque-going will turn you into a fundamentalist,' murmured his father, transfixed by the onscreen Mimi Munkin. 'How do you get these subtitles on?'

'*Honey, have you seen your influence?*' said Mimi's mother to her, grasping her hands. '*Women are saying* no *by saying nothing at all! You gave them permission to say* – enough.'

'The brothers at the mosque love the idea,' added Kashif.

Iqbal leant forward, brows furrowed, trying to listen to the documentary.

'Media and TV is a corruption,' added Naz. 'Everything is OK in moderation bu—'

'Oh-ho,' interrupted Iqbal. 'Let us be corrupted.'

Zainab's mother-in-law stared at her husband, as if about to say something. She didn't.

Zainab sat and listened to the inanities of their speech – once Kashif applied for her naturalisation, she would no longer have to bear it.

Perhaps silence could be as victorious as it was vicious.

Unedited footage: *The Movement . . .*

Glenda Hill: Journalist
Colleague and friend of the first openly Non-Verbal
journalist, Joanna Marks
Verbal

Aadhi: Can you tell me why Joanna Marks, someone who's always spoken up about women's rights, has chosen to go silent?
Glenda: She's always been controversial, but what eventually happened with Mimi Munkin forced her to look into Javed. She'd heard of Sara but, owing to recent events, she became a little obsessed. She read the letter, of course. Said it was ridiculous. But she read Javed's books, interviews, and was taken by her sheer audacity. Jo's been fighting for free speech her entire career. It's one of the reasons why when I told her I'd been approached for this interview, she nodded her assent. She's fed up of all these sensibilities stifling debate under the guise of liberalism. *Mono-liberalism* as she calls it. And she saw you on *The Great Debate* . . . which, well . . . what could get an influential man so riled, she wondered?

Javed's letter is a big, old - excuse me - *fuck you* to everyone who dictates what should or shouldn't be said. Joanna's silence has been calculated. She

110

told friends, colleagues, family, convincing people that this was the ultimate form of protest.

Aadhi: Why?

Glenda: Because it hasn't been done before. Her public statement, declaring it on Twitter, practising it day to day, garnered a lot of support. For all the hatred she faces she has a lot of loyal followers, women – and men – who are inspired by her principles and compassion.

Aadhi: But isn't that exactly what Jo's adversaries, who disagree with her politics, want? For her to stop talking?

Glenda: Oh, absolutely. They thought that *they* had silenced her. Cleared the way so there's one less person to challenge their views. And they loved it. But Jo urged her supporters not to respond to any vitriol. Her very own high-moral road. Nothing agitates moralists more than others taking a higher moral road.

Now it feels as if these very people, the ones who revelled in her silence, are waiting for her to break it. Jo said that people's egos feed on having something to rail against, but she's no longer giving them the opportunity. Can you see how Verbals' arguments are already floundering? Jo's silence is quietening toxic narratives.

And look around you – her success in declaring and maintaining her silence is having a knock-on effect.

THE FOLLOWING

Sara

London, 2013

Sara glanced up from checking her Twitter notifications for new follow-ers, which had increased suitably since the publication of *Woman in Waiting*. This, unfortunately, was not reflected in today's live audience in the bookshop. It was her first literary event and a total of seven people had turned up, one of whom was Henry, giving her a thumbs up, another, her father, sitting next to Henry, and looking annoyed with him already.

Sara had been checking Twitter to distract herself from the primary humiliation of such a sparse audience, and to save herself from the second one of the chairperson being late.

She found herself going to the Notes section on her phone:

M – where are you, where are you, where are you?

What was wrong with her? It was one thing to write letters to the mother who abandoned her, another to relay it in a stream of conscious-ness on her iPhone. She deleted it.

Sara's debut was about a character who creates her own language because she doesn't feel understood, or able to understand, the world around her. With each new word, knowledge of her native English dissi-pates as her mental health improves. By the end no one can understand her, but she understands herself, which was the point. Penelope called it odd but beautifully brave, showcasing Sara's imaginative powers, as well as her ability to pick apart the human condition.

Unfortunately, the main character was a woman of colour, so the book probably wouldn't sell. It had, however, garnered generous critical acclaim, the likes of:

'Unsettling.'

'Bold.'

'A feminist tour-de-force.'

Sara hadn't intended for the book to be any of these things.

(Intention, she would come to understand, hardly mattered.)

The only negative media piece had been by lauded critic Aadhi Sathar. Sara had always thought he sounded like a Grade A twat with his literary snobbery and opinions.

Understandably, she wanted his rave review.

His words were etched in her brain: *'Javed's prose is engaging, but ultimately,* A Woman in Waiting *is a pseudo-literary work, claiming a feminist angle without reflection on the linguist traditions of patriarchal structures.'*

Linguistic traditions?

Patriarchal structures?

She wasn't an academic!

Penelope said the review was unnecessarily scathing. It had been a month since its publication, but Sara still shuddered. She had spent days rereading her book, looking for proof of her own shallowness and had, unfortunately, found it in every line. Had the critical acclaim been because of the novelty of the main character being a woman of colour? Like Sara was herself?

Devastated, Sara had emailed Penelope to tell her she could never write again. A stranger – a well-respected critic! – had read beneath the surface of her own clichés. How could she face the blank page again?

All thoughts of her mother were forgotten in the tumult of lost nerves.

Penelope spent an hour disabusing Sara of the idea that she was a hack. But, often, when Henry was asleep, she'd Google Aadhi Sathar. Check his verified Twitter following of 46,000. The documentaries he'd produced and conservative ideals he espoused.

Fuck that guy.

Only, today's turnout gave credence to his opinion.

'Sorry,' said her publicist, bringing Sara back to her current predicament. 'They did a bad job of advertising.'

She should be relieved there were only seven people. What if she said the wrong thing? Or worse, her words meant nothing? Her desperation to succeed was equal only to the horror of what succeeding might mean.

Sara observed a young woman in the front in a white polo-neck, hair wrapped in a floral turban, hoop earrings. Such enviable poise, pen and notepad in hand. Sara would *have* to say something to warrant being noted.

The chairperson finally arrived. Sara forgot about the trembling of her hands the more she talked about her novel, her character's layers of discontent that spiralled into what the chair called a heart-breaking ending.

'I don't believe in happy endings,' Sara replied, noticing Henry roll his eyes and smile.

Eventually, Sara had talked herself into believing in her book again.

The young woman in the front put her hand up.

'When I read your book—'

Beads of sweat formed on Sara's upper lip. Her need for validation at that moment felt debilitating. *Fucking Aadhi Sathar.*

'—it changed the way I think.'

Sara's smile was wide (and, some might say, captivating). At the end of the session, the woman came and took Sara's hand.

'Sorry I got carried away. Just . . . as a brown Muslim woman, *thank you*. I finally felt *heard*.'

Sara wasn't sure about the etiquette of claiming one's hand back from a stranger. Or what her brownness should have to do with anything.

'Thank *you* for asking questions,' Sara replied. 'Things could've got awkward.'

'I'm Roxy, by the way. It's short for Rukhsana. I think I might be your biggest fan.'

Sara laughed. 'It's not a big pool.'

'Well, brown women always have to work harder,' she paused. 'I can't believe there aren't more people here. *Your book* . . .'

So involved was this young woman's admiration it bordered on the sycophantic. A reprehensible characteristic, generally speaking, but not in that moment.

Sara didn't let go of Roxy's hand. She gripped it harder.

Grace

Manchester, 2013

To become indispensable was its own kind of manipulation. Grace's mother had swept back into her life after that phone call with such focused energy that Grace had to reconfigure all she knew about Dede. There'd been no acknowledgement of past grievances, no talk of Grace's father who her mum had betrayed, in more ways than one.

The past didn't stack up against what Grace had witnessed for the past two years: the tidy flat, her mother soothing Benji while Grace took a nap, dinner made so that Grace ate proper meals. There was such precision in Dede's actions that the memory of her haphazardness felt like a mis-remembrance. Grace's dad would be on a late shift and Dede would be out so Grace would make herself a peanut butter sandwich for dinner. Her mum would saunter into Grace's bedroom later, and kiss her on the cheek, smelling of alcohol: 'Don't tell your father, OK? No man is a woman's keeper.'

'What will you eat if there's nothing in your fridge?' Dede said now, as she stocked it up.

'How much do I owe you?'

Dede had pushed Grace's offering away. 'Just let me do this.'

'You can't afford it.'

'No, but I'll manage. *We'll* manage.'

Grace's mother talked about the hardship of making a clean living, staying sober (three-and-a-half years now), having regrets, but she was vague about what these were.

'Get the baby's father to pull his finger out,' Dede added. 'Be a man.'

'I'm not asking him for a penny.'

'Who was he?'

'A mistake.'

Dede stroked Benji's chubby cheek. She couldn't seem to take her eyes off him. Grace felt a yearning for something which she thought she had outlived.

'Most men are,' replied Dede. 'Baby, how long will you work as a receptionist in a law office? You have a duty to use that brain God's given. Do something with your degree and *make money*. For your family. Benji's older now. I'm here and I think it's time. We might both save something.'

The cost of success meant renouncing past resentments for Grace. She'd retrain in family law.

Grace discovered the inevitability of interdependence because Benji had changed everything. In that sense, life would beget life.

Zainab

Glasgow, 2013

Upon Zainab's arrival to Glasgow, almost two years ago now, there had been dinner parties, consisting of gifts and prayers. Such a couple, such beauty.

Such promise.

Three months later, Zainab had her first miscarriage.

On the phone, between Zainab's sobs, her mum had told her to keep faith. 'God always provides.' What this provision might be was anyone's guess.

The second miscarriage meant the couple's promise was more precarious. Spiritual counsellors were sought, medical specialists seen. The former suggested prayer. The latter eventually concluded that Zainab would probably never carry a baby to term, although, they should keep trying.

In both cases, leaflets were handed out.

By the third and latest miscarriage, one just had to be grateful for one's health.

The ghost of Zainab's body now haunted her. She wanted to be home in Pakistan again. Feel the comfort of her mother's arms. The physicality of loss was compounded by the way her emotions would hook themselves to a thought, digging into what felt like disintegrating flesh.

She'd often wake up and imagine that Kashif had died in his sleep, which was the only time she felt alive. Her imaginings hadn't manifested into a reality and the subsequent numbness had its own spiritual repercussions.

Time was universally acknowledged to be a healer though, and there were still chores to do. Shopping and preparations for dinner parties, like tonight.

The women sat in a different room to the men. Zainab's mother-in-law was in the kitchen. The wives paused when Zainab entered, pretending not to notice her cascading hair and flawless skin. The curves of her body.

Tahera, leader of the wife-pack, observed Zainab without any qualms. She was also from Pakistan and so it was expected that the two would get on especially well. Kashif had insisted Zainab mingle. He described other women as having a 'good sense of humour', by which, Zainab presumed, he meant women who were amused by his jokes.

'Zainab, *please* stop Auntie Naz from any Islamic lecture,' said Tahera. 'I've already had the Taliban in my house once. Honestly, men fuck who they want and then want us to be virginal wives.'

'*Tahera*,' exclaimed a wife.

'Oho, that was my first husband,' added Tahera. 'The second I had to draw diagrams of a woman's body parts.

'Third time's the charm, ladies.'

'I'd better help Auntie in the kitchen,' said Zainab.

'That Tahera . . .' said Naz. 'Three children and *still* so loud.'

Tahera followed Zainab and helped her load the dishwasher. 'You're too beautiful to handle dirty dishes. Not the only thing that'll be dirty tonight,' she whispered, nudging Zainab playfully. 'Are you OK?'

The wives' incessant talk of sex and babies had become a point of nausea. Zainab nodded, convincing enough to belie the fact that she'd like to take the dishes and smash them all against the wall.

'I don't want to hear that men are never in the kitchen,' came Kashif's voice. He entered with Suleiman.

'Imagine knowing where it is,' said Tahera. She met his gaze with the same audacity as she seemed to meet everything. 'Let's hope you have a son with your sense of direction.'

Kashif didn't seem to notice the irony in Tahera's voice. Suleiman laughed.

No one outside the family knew about the miscarriages.

Zainab felt the tears well up. She had read about steely women with agency, warrior women in Islam who led battalions into war. And here was Zainab, weakened by words.

'Great food, *bhabi*,' said Suleiman, setting the empty bowls on the counter.

She couldn't bear the kindness in his tone. She tried to keep the tears in, but one would fall upon her soft skin.

'Zainab?' Suleiman whispered, leaning into her.

'Right, everyone,' he declared, finally turning around. 'The men will make the tea.

'Modern times, Auntie-*ji*,' he added, before Naz could say anything. He turned back to Zainab.

(The small veins in her eyes were pink enough to warrant empathy, not so pink to undermine her beauty. A combination that even the most moral of men could not have resisted.)

The following day Suleiman showed up outside the mosque where Zainab taught. They stared at one another, only this time, she did not look away.

He walked towards a side street. She followed.

He checked the area for local spies. 'Let's sit in the car.'

Zainab barely hesitated before opening the passenger door, settling herself in.

'Kashif told me. About the . . . *you know*. I'm so sorry.'

She really shouldn't be here, but his look of concern felt necessary to Zainab. As necessary as her serenity possibly felt to him.

'And then Tahera . . . she can be a lot. You know her mum wanted me to marry her?'

Zainab looked at him as he let out a laugh.

'It's true. But she's, well . . . you know when something's not right.' He paused, adding quietly. '*And* when it is.'

'I should go,' said Zainab, but he put his hand on her arm so gently, she stopped.

He lifted his hand to her face, stroking her cheek. Somewhere between their altercation three years ago in Pakistan and now, Zainab had found that Suleiman brought a lightness to any given situation and it reminded her of who she used to be. Even so, she was surprised that she didn't flinch when he touched her. Instead, she felt her body stir. She did not move his hand away. And it had been enough to know, the ghost of her body still had the capacity to be moved.

The Many Voices of Non-Verbalism

Amy Wang, *The Ward*, July 2021

The story of Xiang Mei from Macau has many people around the world ask-
ing: might silence finally bring change? News of the growth of Non-Verbalism
in the West reached China and seemed to have moved Mei to mobilise the Falun
Gong, a religious organisation that was declared illegal in 1999. Hundreds of
thousands of Falun Gong practitioners are estimated to have been imprisoned,
subjected to psychological abuse, torture, and coercive methods of thought
reform by Chinese authorities. They had united in taping their mouths, mask-
ing their eyes and plugging their ears to highlight their persecution in China.
This was met with swift retribution from the government, which is reported to
have increased the number of re-education camps for members of the Falun
Gong and other religious minorities. This act of silent protest was caught on
camera by Austrian anthropologist, Emilja Bauer, who uploaded the video on
TikTok, which went viral. It has gone on to inspire minorities from around the
world to do the same in the past two weeks; Christians, Muslims, Hindus,
Atheists, the LGBTQIA+ community, have been adopting the stance to hostile
governmental reaction. Groups have been spearheading ways to impact power
structures for years and it is not the first time for silent protests to take place in
China. It has come at considerable human cost. However, there is a prevalent
hope amid the violence protestors are facing, given the global emergence of
Non-Verbalism, that their combined, even collective, silence will continue to
cross borders and speak louder than words.

For ongoing updates click <u>here</u>.

★

OMG Munkin's a HACK. Lied about being Non-Verbal just to get a show. Fuck celebrities. Fuck privilege. I STAN SARA.

💬 73   ⬆ 2,365   ♡ 5,899

LMAO people around the world literally being killed protesting their right to just BE. and yall arguing over #Munkin #Worldminorities #seenoevilhearnoevilspeaknoevil

💬 36   ⬆ 17   ♡ 67

Unedited: *The Movement* . . .

Jamila Jenna: Journalist
Author of The Ward *article,* 'The Problem with Mimi Munkin'
Verbal

Aadhi: Your article about *Muted,* being, I quote, *an affront to creativity and the real woman behind the movement* has gone viral. It's quite a scathing account of ways in which people of colour have been historically sidelined, and the danger of industries paying lip service to diversity, while in substance changing nothing.

Jamila: Listen - Munkin, a white, blonde, cisgendered woman became the poster girl for an action and an idea inspired by a *brown* writer. It's just *one* example of how, despite success, a woman of colour's idea can be monetised for a white woman's gain. Just look at Munkins' Instagram, plagiarising Sara Javed's work. Why does it take a celebrity to endorse an act of protest for it to have merit? And why is it only after discovering she'd been lying about being a Non-Verbal that we're having this discussion?

Aadhi: How do you feel about Javed's continued silence in light of the controversy?

Jamila: It would be a good time for Sara to speak out.

Aadhi: Do you find it frustrating?

127

Jamila: That's hardly the point. Her Non-Verbalism highlights structural hypocrisies, but it's the *structure* we need to focus on. Why should one woman be forced to take responsibility for a systemic problem?

Aadhi: Your piece has been polarising. Have you watched *Muted*?

Jamila: Absolutely not. Munkin's show is an affront to *every* creative from an under-represented background whose pioneering has been co-opted by a white counterpart. This kind of self-involved behaviour is compounded by the structures that give privileged people opportunities without any sense of a wider responsibility. There has to be a limit to levels of self-promotion.

   Pause.

Jamila: Quick question: Will links to my article be featured in the documentary?

Sara

London, July 2021

Sara and Henry stared at the television screen. A photo of Mimi Munkin in a short, black dress with netting around the hem, chandelier earrings and hot pink purse, posing on a red carpet. There, right next to her was an image of Sara in her Nike sweatshirt and ripped jeans. She was on stage, holding the Mildred Aitken Award, looking out into what seemed an abyss. The unassuming, admirable author – because how many would dare to turn up to an awards event in jeans? – whose act of Non-Verbalism, it was now being reported, Munkin had appropriated.

Henry murmured '*Fuck*' as another breaking news banner emerged.

—People taking voluntary vows of silence around the globe—

Sara checked outside the window of their flat, where a small crowd had gathered on her doorstep, carrying placards:

'*Stand with Sara*'

Penelope's name flashed on her phone. Given the circumstances, she had little choice but to answer.

'Sara. *Sara?*'

Sara heard a presenter's voice coming from the other end of her mobile. She suspected Penelope had put her phone by the speaker.

'The discovery that Mimi Munkin co-opted and faked Non-Verbalism in order to sign a reality show has led to the cancellation of Muted. *Munkin has been forced off Instagram on which she had 6.4 million followers. The once much-loved star has had to move home due to death threats.*

'#KeepingSara – a hashtag highlighting support for the author and demonstrating users' Non-Verbalism in solidarity – has been trending on Twitter. British Prime Minister Harold Fernsby is due to hold talks with European leaders and the US President about the rise of Non-Verbalism across their countries.'

'Did you hear that?' Penelope could barely contain her excitement. 'Kat's been checking your Twitter and Munkin tagged you in an official apology, along with your letter. It's gone *viral.*'

Sara couldn't take her eyes off the news as the world was frantically attempting to catch its own stillness.

'Your book sales have spiked dramatically in the overnight reports,' added Penelope. 'Though I've half a mind to sue Munkin. You must be livid.'

It hardly mattered – people seemed to be feeling enough on Sara's behalf. As for her books sales, she was too preoccupied with what was unfolding around her to interrogate whether they still mattered.

'They're beginning to call it a *movement.*'

Who were *they*? And what, exactly, was being *moved*?

'Now, how long do you plan to do this Non-Verbalism?' asked Penelope. 'There's just the small matter of the next book . . . Of course, you can't be rushed. But you're now at the epicentre of this thing.'

Sara let out a groan. She didn't want to be the epicentre of anything.

100.8 billion people have lived and died. We are all, ultimately, peripheral.

'Hello? Right, anyway . . . I'm here in case you decide to email or however you choose to communicate.' Penelope paused. 'Because in the end, you are communicating *something.*

'This is a unique opportunity and it's my job as your editor, and, I hope, your friend, to tell you not to let this moment pass you by.'

Penelope hung up.

Sara had wanted to ask what exactly she was meant to do with this moment. Catch it, or catch up with it? Or had she already moved too far past it? *What the fuck was happening?*

'This is insane,' said Henry. 'I mean, *look*.'

He gestured at the TV. A woman in a grey suit appeared on screen.

'*"Political events have polarised people across the globe," according to Amber Green, a social scientist from Durham. "If no one's listening, why speak?"*

'*The President of the United States had his own take on Non-Verbalism—*'

The camera cut to the United States' leader, pointing his finger in the air, leaning forward into the mic.

'*And let me tell you . . . good. It's great. Some people* should *shut up. Am I right? Yeah. You agree, don't you?*'

There was riotous applause from his audience.

Henry switched channels.

'*There have been studies claiming the health benefits of silence. According to Dr Katherine Tang, Non-Verbals can expect: lower blood pressure, a boost in the body's immune system, and to benefit brain chemistry by growing new cells. It's too soon to tell if this is connected but we've seen a 6% dip in the past 40 days in GP visits.*'

Another flick of the remote.

'*A signed letter from Hollywood celebrities has collected over four hundred signatures denouncing Munkin and Muted as "pure and exploitative cultural appropriation".*'

The camera showed a clip of Chris Taylor – Hollywood heartthrob and recent activist.

'As a white cis-gendered male, I acknowledge all my privileges. I'm choosing Non-Verbalism in solidarity with all those who have historically been silenced . . .'

This time Sara grabbed the remote.

'We're joined in Liverpool by Edna and her husband, Bill. A postman on the verge of retirement, he is a semi-permanent Non-Verbal, a form of Non-Verbalism in which a certain number of hours of speech are allocated per day or week, as desired. SP Non-Verbals often still use the written form, but this may change as Non-Verbal variants are developed.

'Edna, what inspired your husband?'

Edna and Bill sat, hand-in-hand, joined by a readily made-up teenage girl.

'Our granddaughter, Lucy here, was watching Muted, before it got cancelled, when Bill came home. He doesn't usually like all these reality shows – but he's been fed up of everyone and their empty buzzwords for a while. He watched the show. "She's got a point," he said. "Blonde bimbo from California has a point!"'

'And how do you both communicate now?'

'We've been married for fifty years! But those hours he does talk are precious to us.'

Sara hadn't logged into her email for months.

How could she *not* check her in-box with all these unravelling reports? Eventually she scrolled down her messages, scanning the subject lines:

You're my Hero!

YOU'RE NO ALLY.

BBC World Service Interview Request

Who the fuck do you think you are??

Hello! Magazine

CNN Network

Writing Mentor?

TV Panel Request: Whose Words Are They Anyway?
Attention seeking bitch. I'm coming for you.

Each subject line demanding her attention was a pellet to her fraying silent nerves.

Then she saw a familiar name. *Aadhi Sathar.* Henry looked over her shoulder.

'*CN-fucking-N.*'

She closed her laptop. *What the hell did he want?*

'Sara,' Henry said. 'It's *CNN*, the BBC. It's the whole damn *world.*'

I know, she wanted to exclaim.

Sara had long ago deleted social media apps from her phone, refused to go online. But the world didn't have a delete button. It seemed to be in the process of resetting itself entirely.

'Don't you have *anything* to say?' He paused hopefully. Then, 'All couples have their problems, huh?'

The very aspect of him used to be a consolation. Now she wasn't sure why.

'Who am *I* in all this? . . . I've been asked for a meeting about my theatre script. Suddenly people are interested in me. Guess that's thanks to you,' he said. 'What kind of a person does that make me? Taking meetings because of my wife?'

It makes you lucky, Henry.

This script had been in progress for two years. She had read some pages, helped Henry to focus and refine until he'd finally said their 'artistic vision' was different.

She picked up her tote bag.

'Where are you going?'

'I *need* you,' he said, standing in the hallway.

Either it was Henry's shortcoming for not having understood Sara or hers for having expected it. She wasn't sure who was more unreasonable. But in that moment, her needs trumped Henry's. She opened the door and left.

'I can't fucking believe you—'

She slipped on her headphones, muffling Henry's voice. It was less successful in muffling her guilt.

As she opened the door a modest, but earnest crowd, cheered. For *her.*

Sara almost stepped back and shut the door again.

Two people came forward, each placing a hand on their chest. She supposed it was to show their support. Sara tried to nod and smile as she pushed past them. Overwhelmed by the unexpected din, she ran towards the bus stop and leapt on the first bus that came, checking that no one had jumped on behind her. Several stops later she got off at Finsbury Park.

Considering the circumstance, she had to take a few minutes to focus.

It was a muggy day, the sky overcast. As she walked through the park, she found herself staring at people, wondering who was or wasn't now silent. Inside, watching the news, checking her in-box, it felt like the world had changed, but outside the shift was imperceptible. It must be a storm in a media teacup. And then she stopped to stare at a banner sprawled across the gate of the park:

Beware the Barrenness of a Busy Life – Sara Javed.

The sign and misattribution was, somehow, more alarming than Mimi Munkin or the US President. It could have been made by any one of these people surrounding her.

People who were taking pictures of it.

What was wrong with them?

Eventually someone stood next to her to contemplate the banner too. Sara felt their gaze rest on her.

'You're . . . *Sara Javed,*' she saw them mouth.

Did no one hold the sanctity of noise-cancelling headphones dear anymore?

Sara walked off as quickly as possible, glancing over her shoulder to see the person taking photos of her. She broke into a run again and carried on running until she caught the bus to her dad's.

She walked in, harangued, hot and confounded.

'I'm not busy by the way.' He followed her into the living room.

134

The low-ceilinged room was stacked with books, the curtains closed. The news playing on the television, a fan whirring by the sofa, a lamp lit in the corner.

Sara opened the windows, huffed at the curtains getting stuck, looked around the messy room and then, as if the entire enterprise had exhausted her, sat down. She glanced, reluctantly, at the screen where her image was being displayed once more.

Afzal took off her headphones and patted her cheek. 'Yes. I would be shocked too, but get yourself together, beta.'

Afzal went into the kitchen and returned with home-made lemonade and Victoria sponge. Sara watched her father cut two pieces of cake, his chin wobblier, his hair thinning, the bulk of him still strong and sturdy. She often wished that he had remarried, but he said love only happened once, if you were lucky, and however it turned out you had to stay loyal to it.

Sara supposed it had been harder for Lily to love Sara. How could she when Afzal had refused to acknowledge Lily's own need for a child so he could meet Sara's need for unconditional love?

The diaspora caused by Sara's abandonment had a knock-on effect in that sense.

'We can never know the consequences of our actions,' he said, eventually. 'Look at me bringing you here. How we struggled, hmm? Marrying Lily, divorcing Lily . . . Your father always said life is struggle, and it is the way we struggle that is the measure of us. He was very wise. Terrible temper though. We fight against the odds; sometimes they beat us and sometimes they make us.'

Her dad's calm elicited calm.

Just like rage elicited rage.

Words elicited words.

'You are fighting your own odds and it is very possible they will beat you, too,' he said quietly. 'Before you went silent did you ask yourself: what is the potential cost of this decision versus its gain?'

Who's to say which is more significant: loss or gain?

'*Beta*, you took a very unusual step. And it has taken a *very* unusual turn . . . Don't throw your arms around like this. You are feeling things, yes? You sit with it. Wasn't that a part of the point? I'm taking a guess.'

Sara stared into her lemonade. Eventually, she nodded.

'You have always been my unusual girl. See,' he added as he gestured towards the news.

'The impact on Britain's political landscape could be extraordinary. William Bac-clay, leader of the government's opposition, which suffered a huge defeat in the 2015 and 2020 elections, has spoken up.'

The camera cut to him in a red tie and charcoal grey suit, mics poised towards him, a friendly glint in his eye.

'In these tumultuous times, we must reflect upon who we are. We're suffering from the disastrous effects of the current government's policies. Ask small businesses, human rights attorneys . . . Harold Fernsby has failed to deliver on his 2020 election promises. Now is the time for him to understand what this grassroots movement, Non-Verbalism, means. To our followers, constituents, anyone in need of answers, we are here for you . . .'

He muted the channel.

'He is still here because this man has principle, you see. Even if sometimes he puts you to sleep. I told you the 2010 coalition would be a disaster and this current *panchod* party has had a majority vote in election after election because of it. Maybe *this* – Non-Verbalism – will change things . . .

'Anyway,' he continued. '*You* must focus.'

But Sara glanced at the television again:

BREAKING NEWS:
First hate crime towards a Non-Verbal, leaving woman hospitalised after attacker attempts to cut off her tongue.

Unedited: *The Movement . . .*

Claire Rumbold: **Member of Parliament for West Heath**
Colleague to Caitlin Harris, the first Non-Verbal MP
Verbal

Aadhi: Was Caitlin Harris' declaration of Non-Verbalism a shock?

Claire: Yes and no. She's been at the forefront of railing against austerity for years. I believe she read Javed's letter after journalist Joanna Marks' public conversion to Non-Verbalism. She called me in the middle of the night, telling me she couldn't stop thinking about its strength in the face of all this noise.

I told her to go back to sleep.

Then Lynda Taylor was attacked.

Aadhi: How will Harris, as a Non-Verbal MP, serve her constituents in Berriland?

Claire: That's what a lot of us have asked, but there was something about that moment on television. When she stood up in the House of Commons and read out Javed's letter to a baffled audience. Declaring her Non-Verbalism because of all the ways this government has failed us.

'We have spoken, and spoken, and spoken and it has fallen on deaf ears.'

The millions that watched, who've felt voiceless, related to it, which is why moments can be so misleading. They don't offer a broad enough view and, quite frankly I'm disappointed that the likes of George Hammond stood up and proclaimed, 'I declare the same.' Followed by Rosa Wood, Edmund Peak, Jaspreet Gill . . . one after the other.

Aadhi: Is there fear that Non-Verbalism will slow positive change?

Claire: Of course. We've never seen anything like it - it's a shocking thing to witness in many ways but . . . People watched and they were *moved*. Caitlin's never been busier. Silence is being integrated into her workspace. As a lettered Non-Verbal she communicates via emails and letters. She has a *mood board* in the office. The feedback I'm getting is that people feel heard. It's confounding and . . . fascinating, if I'm entirely honest.

Aadhi: Do you see yourself becoming a Non-Verbal?

Claire: After a lifetime of fighting just to be heard about the life and death impact of gender inequality, and the ever-urgent need for a fair and decent living wage? Absolutely not.

Attack on Non-Verbal Shakes the Nation

Jason Krueger, *The Daily*, July 2021

PM Harold Fernsby has come under scrutiny by the public for his lack of response to the violent attack on Non-Verbal Lynda Taylor. In a televised press conference last night Fernsby called for calm and compassion on both sides but has faced criticism for not taking a stronger stance against a hate crime, and particularly the issue of violence against women.

Leader of the opposition, William Bacclay, fully condemned the attack in a statement on the day and demands the Prime Minister follows suit.

Polls indicate Bacclay's popularity has increased by 14% in the South West of England and 8% in the North since the public declarations of vows on silence that sparked the growing popularity of Non-Verbalism . . .

There has been a further incline in people openly adopting Non-Verbalism since the attack on Lynda Taylor.

Ms. Taylor is said to be making a slow but steady recovery.

The attacker, who lost a finger during the attack, is in custody and awaiting trial.

Author Sara Javed was contacted for comment on the hate crime but has not responded.

For ongoing updates about *The Silent Movement* click <u>here</u>.

Grace

Manchester, July 2021

From: D.Hodgkin312
To: Grace.Jenkins55
Subject: RE: Hello

Grace,

I've tried calling several times but now the call's not going through. Not sure if it has anything to do with this Non-Verbal madness. I know I was in the wrong, but I am Benji's father and I want to try and make things right. This isn't about you and me, is it? It's about him.

Yours,
David

Grace sat in the semi-dark, watching the news about Lynda Taylor. There had been plenty of enjoyment at the poetic justice of the attacker losing his finger, but a loud minority was already highlighting what Non-Verbalism meant with regard to violence against women.

(Memes of a decapitated finger were being circulated nonetheless.)

As a mother, Grace had Benji to consider. As a woman, she had to consider her principles. As a person, she switched off the TV. She knew that fear was too primal a reason upon which to make a decision.

Grace read through David's emails again, listened to his voicemails. She had Googled him before he'd even come back into her life, gone through his Facebook (wife, two children and a dog). She had looked at these pictures of bike rides and birthdays and felt a pang at having lost something she'd convinced herself she didn't want. What would David coming into their lives now look like?

What if he believed the son he sought to know was unknowable? Was David the type of man to take time to understand the nuances of Benji's looks and manner? How would he understand their sign language? What if he got frustrated and gave up trying to build a relationship with Benji? Hadn't her son faced enough loss? And why should she reveal Benji's condition to a man who simply considered his abdication a mistake? A forgivable one at that.

She had been reading Sara Javed's books, listening to podcasts, radio interviews in an attempt to understand her more. To recognise something of Javed in herself.

Witnessing the attack on a Non-Verbal, Grace remembered how she used to help women similar to Lynda Taylor. A rebel with a cause when the cause wasn't her.

Grace had often told herself she'd get back on the ground one day: when she had less responsibility, more time, managing to lull herself into a false sense of eventual philanthropy. If the Taylor incident meant anything it was that the time to act was *now*. So, she Googled voluntary organisations that supported victims and survivors of male violence against women and girls. Before long she came across a local women's refuge where they required legal advice for occupants. How she would carry this off as a Non-Verbal, she didn't know, but in the stillness of her mind she was propelled into action.

★

Grace and Benji left the house to make their way to her meeting in the refuge. A leaflet flickered on the windshield of her car.

BREAK THE SILENCE

Don't be fooled by the government's ploy to silence the people.

Say **NO** to Non-Verbalism.

NO to injustice.

NO to propaganda.

DON'T LOSE YOUR VOICE

Grace screwed up the paper. They drove past live billboards with the hashtag #BewareTheBarrennessofaBusyLife, followed by people hugging, holding placards with #NonVerbal4Lynda. Walls graffitied with: *Down with capitalism.*

There was a mural of a woman who had protested against stolen elections – in Iran, was it? Face-to-face with police who had turned violent.

We will buy our freedom with silence.

The revolution is here.

The image was being graffitied around the world now, photographed and posted online on Pinterest and Instagram.

Grace had explained over email to the refuge that she was a 'lettered' Non-Verbal, but that she had practical strategies to help the women in their care. The refuge could update their website to make it more user friendly, for one. They had hesitated. In the end though, her expertise and their desperation meant overlooking the trivialities of speech. Grace grabbed Benji's hand as they walked into the centre. She felt the familiar sensation of purpose. Even that sense of belonging she had when she had been in Calais.

'We have accommodation for up to twelve women here, but also have a day walk-in centre. Lots of women who can't speak English so in that sense your being a *Non-Verbal* . . . Well, it won't matter much.'

Angie Davies, lead management, had the air of a woman who'd lived a life of inconsequence, quite in contrast with her reality. Her

142

face kind yet remarkably forgettable. Her tone, however, was to be reckoned with.

'I've been working in domestic violence for over thirty years,' said Angie, 'But I'd never thought I'd live to see a day like this. You understand we might have some Lynda Taylors come in?'

Grace nodded.

'With women's lives at stake, you'd think people would reconsider the implications of their Non-Verbalism,' she added, giving Grace a withering look.

Grace found herself bristling. It's not as if she wasn't used to prejudice. What was another to add to the list? Yet it felt galling, disappointing, not to be understood by a woman who claimed to comprehend the plight of women.

They walked through the office into the refuge, which had several bedrooms, a clean living area and kitchen.

'We need you three mornings and two afternoons a week. Mainly you'll be informing our women of their rights, helping with documentation, finances . . . And *how* will you do that?'

Grace handed Angie printouts of clear bullet points of what divorce proceedings involved, the different stages and potential outcomes. She had put together a fourteen-page document on optimising their digital awareness campaign, a how-to guide for women seeking financial independence and more.

'What about the ones who can't read or speak English?' asked Angie.

Grace had printed out various translations – Bengali, Polish, Chinese.

'Hmm.'

They were standing in the doorway of the living room. Three women were seated on a battered brown sofa. One of them was breast-feeding; she looked as young as Grace had been when she'd had Benji.

'That's Cara. Been here a few days . . . You must have questions? You're a lettered NV, obviously.'

To be silent was to become a passenger in the story of your own life and Grace was used to being a driving force, so, of course, she had questions. But she also had responsibilities.

She shook her head when she saw Benji walk over to the woman with the baby.

'You wanna hold her?' Cara asked him.

Grace watched in mild disbelief as her usually unwilling son nodded and settled into the sofa beside Cara.

'The top of babies' heads are like sponge, so you've got to support it, all right?' Cara smiled encouragingly.

He nodded again.

Grace sat next to him while he held the baby; he was staring at it as if trying to understand the concept of life itself.

'How old are you?' Cara asked.

Benji was too engrossed in the baby so Cara looked at Grace who held up nine fingers.

'You're a Non-Verbal?'

Grace nodded.

'Your son's a bit young for it, isn't he?'

Grace shook her head.

'Cat got your tongue, kid?'

The blood seemed to rush to Benji's face. Grace got up.

'I didn't mean any offence,' said Cara, confused.

She reached to get her baby, but Benji held on to it.

Grace noticed the bruises on Cara's arms.

She looked at Benji, pointed to the baby and then to Cara. But he put his finger on the baby's nose, its lips, its chin. He brought his face closer, their noses almost touching. Grace's heart beat faster, observing him. Entranced by his enchantment.

'He's all right,' Cara whispered.

The baby squirmed as her whimper transitioned into a sharp cry.

'Thanks, young man,' said Cara, taking her baby back into her arms. She glanced at Grace.

'You're volunteering here?'

Grace nodded.

'And Non-Verbal?

144

'Imagine that, Ada?' said Cara to her baby. 'Speaking up's got us here, hasn't it, baby girl? Not ideal, but at least we're free.'

Grace wanted to know Cara's story. She took out her card and handed it to her, indicating for her to call. But Grace would be able to say nothing. It seemed an empty gesture, in the end. Cara pocketed the card as Benji put his hand in Grace's, both of them watched Cara walk away.

Cara's words fed into Grace's brain on a loop as she drove home with Benji. As a distraction, Grace played the *Shrek* soundtrack and noticed Benji bop his head to 'Bad Reputation'. He was looking out of the window, smiling, shaking his head to the beat.

Then she saw him mouth the words.

She stopped at a red light, staring. Benji glanced at her and bounced his shoulders. 'I don't care about my bad reputation' pounding through the speakers. She couldn't remember him ever having mouthed words before.

Surely this was a step in the right direction? She had heard of cases of mute children doing this, or repeating questions and phrases which left parents feeling frustrated, but Grace had never seen *Benji* do this. It meant something surely.

Grace had to stop doubting her decision. She bounced her shoulders with Benji as they both drove home, smiling, mouthing the words together.

Approaching the flat's private parking lot, she noticed a figure outside the building. They walked towards the man who'd now turned around.

She stopped.

His hairline had receded; he was clean-shaven and had a stout body.

'You wouldn't return my calls.'

How the hell did David even know where she lived?

He paused, looking at Benji. 'Hi, little man.' He put out his hand, staring at her son, as if trying to identify his genetic pool.

Benji nestled into Grace's side.

She moved to walk past him.

'I've only come to talk.'

She swept around and gestured with her hands.

145

He looked confused. 'Five minutes, that's all.'

She opened the door, but stood there for several moments before David looked at Benji again. 'Is he OK?'

Grace put an arm around Benji and turned away.

'Grace, wait—'

But before he could step any closer, she slammed the door shut.

Silence is the New Self-Care

Underground/bus stop advertisement, summer 2021

Do you have social fatigue? Is your search for peace blocked by the incessant noise? The Yoga Rooms *is proud to launch an innovative new course,* Silent Waves. *Professional instructors will help you to navigate your Non-Verbal energy and discover an untapped source of spiritual nourishment.*

#JoinTheWave

Follow *Silent Waves* on Instagram @Silentwaves

Zainab

Glasgow, July 2021

'I want to say that I am staggered at Non-Verbals' commitment to silence,' said Harold Fernsby, in his second press conference. 'This country must continue to demonstrate how we can learn from one another. We must also remember that the tragic attack on Lynda Taylor was an isolated incident. I am delighted to say that she is now back home with her family, her recovery aided by our brilliant NHS staff.

'Together, we can create an atmosphere of cohesion and prosperity . . .'

The local imam was being problematic. Namely because, to him, self-knowledge came before social activism, and the younger crowd wasn't ready for it. Didn't people note, since Non-Verbalism, that there had been a steady decrease in homelessness? It seemed philanthropy was peaking. Who knew? There weren't as many media posts about it. The warmth of the imam's manner spread in the mosque, alongside collective indignation that a woman had been attacked for her silence. Kashif's friends, and Kashif by default, were feeling especially inspired.

Now he came home and kissed Zainab on the forehead. The first time had been perturbing. But it had become a regular occurrence and Zainab wasn't sure what to make of it.

'Imam Zahid says compassion and kindness are heightened through silence,' said Kashif at the dinner table.

Zainab felt that compassion as a learnt behaviour seemed to miss the point.

His dad ate the chicken.

'This imam speaks too much about modern life,' said Naz.

'Don't we deserve choices?'

'Ashraf's family has gone silent,' commented Iqbal.

'It's his *wife*,' replied Naz. 'This is what happens when men don't act like men.'

Iqbal nodded with solemnity.

'The imam suggested that we try Non-Verbalism,' said Kashif.

Zainab's heartbeat quickened.

'*Hai*. What will work say?'

'What does my job even *mean*, Mum? I'm taking some holiday and I'm their best employee. If they don't like it, well, we have to fight for our rights.'

'Say something.' Naz looked at Zainab. 'You're his wife.'

This theory only reared its head when it meant speaking up against something that didn't suit her mother-in-law. But Zainab's mind was racing. Would her husband's self-focus just mean further delay to her visa application?

'The imam says you can't know God unless you know yourself.'

Iqbal sighed. Spiritual notions had always baffled him.

Naz was so forlorn she spent the next half-hour giving a lecture on the Islamic obligation of obeying one's parents.

(There was no end to what she was tasked to do for her family. It had possibly come at the expense of her own self-knowledge.)

'Do you think I'm wrong?' Kashif asked when he and Zainab were in bed later that night.

Zainab had her back to him. She checked her phone, waiting for a response from Suleiman to her message:

Are you going silent too?

Kashif had been reading *Reflection on Silence* – about a man who'd taken a vow of silence several years ago, before it had become a phenomenon.

149

Similar books were being published – a niche market was now exploding into the mainstream.

'Zainab.' He put his arm on her shoulder, forcing her to turn around. 'Tell me.'

'What about my naturalisation?'

Kashif pushed back a lock of her hair. They hadn't had sex for a month now. But each day increased the trepidation of when he might hold her head against the wall.

'I'll finalise that before I do anything else.' He kissed her on the forehead. 'Good night.'

Eventually, he fell asleep. She lay there thinking; she was hardened against his words, but this softness of touch was confusing. She noticed the glow of her phone and breathed a sigh of relief.

No. I couldn't go a day without speaking to you.

Unedited: *The Movement . . .*

Elizabeth Beatty: Environmental Lawyer
Leader of The Silent Movement in North America
Non-Verbal

Aadhi: Thank you for going Verbal for this interview. I'll keep it concise.

Elizabeth puts her hand up. Reads from a paper.

Elizabeth: The Silent Movement is not a homogenous
one. We are from different walks of life and sets of
beliefs: young and old, rich and poor, but we all
seek contentment. We're tired of our leaders, our
employers, and even our own lives. The feeling that
we are slaves to a system - work, societal norms and,
yes, even family. We seek agency but also allyship.
Because we all have a right to choose, to not be
demonised for our choices. Isn't that the essence of
humanity? In holding back our tongue we believe we
are holding on to our dignity - one which has been
stripped to such a degree that we didn't even realise
it. Until now. Our needs were not met when we expressed
them using words - but we *will* be understood through
silence. Despite the action that is taken against
us - the trolling and bullying, the threats to our
lives and livelihoods - we are not, so easily, going
to give it up.

151

FACULTIES OF DISCERNMENT

Sara

London, 2014

'Aren't you bored of hearing me say the same thing?' Sara asked Roxy after one particular book event in Foyles' Charing Cross.

Roxy appearance at most of Sara's events had created an alarmingly gratifying sensation. *Woman in Waiting* had barely sold a thousand copies and her latest novel had very low pre-orders. The constant barrage of other authors' bestsellers, foreign rights, their this and that award, kept Sara awake and, crucially, at her laptop.

'Would it be weird if I bought you a coffee?' asked Roxy.

She reminded Sara of a time in life where there was the promise of everything and certainty of nothing – a state of freedom, in its own way – and so she replied with: 'No, I'm buying *you* coffee.'

'You've done what most women like us never manage,' said Roxy as they took a seat with their drinks in the café.

'What?'

'You're *published.*'

'According to people like Aadhi Sathar I shouldn't be.'

'Ugh. I wish he'd just, you know, *shut the fuck up.*'

Sara laughed.

'Men love the sound of their own voice,' continued Roxy. 'I'm so tired of being told what to say, who to *be.*'

'Who to be . . . The universal problem.'

Sara's eyes flitted from corner to corner, her mind trying to grasp something. She opened up Notes on her phone:

How does a universality of meaning distil itself into a single narrative?

'Society's always telling us how to behave,' added Roxy. 'But *you* . . . with your books. They subvert all of it.'

'Do they?'

'You're too modest for your own good. You need to own it.'

'Oh, well, ownership isn't a meritocratic business.'

Roxy looked at Sara, confused. 'Forget bloody Aadhi Sathar. You give me hope. And one day you're going to be *huge*. God, I'm such a cliché, fan-girling a writer who I basically want to be.'

Sara's cheeks flushed. To have affected a person she hardly knew felt as bizarre as the idea that anyone could give another hope. But there was something about Roxy's zeal that invigorated her.

Vigour, for Sara, was an elusive thing.

'You know, you inspired me to finally write . . . Anyway, enough of that.'

'No, go ahead.'

'It's just . . . I'm a gay Muslim. So, you can imagine the rest.'

'I see.'

'I mean, *whatever*. Plenty of people lead double lives. That's why your book meant so much.'

'Fuck my book,' said Sara, seeing the pained expression in Roxy's face. 'I'm sorry,' she added. 'About the difficulties. If it makes you feel any better my mum decided to abandon me altogether.'

Sara was not prone to spurting out information, but the sadness in Roxy's eyes had prompted her to speak. Even though she might later regret it. At least Sara hadn't cried. She would never have forgiven herself for such a public display of emotion.

'You don't want to write about it?'

'God, *no*. I just write *around* it.'

'Don't you think about her?' Roxy asked. 'I think about my parents all the time. And they only live in Hounslow.'

'I do think about her,' Sara admitted, eventually.

'And?'

'Once you start asking yourself questions, it never stops. So, I try not to. Sometimes I fail. Often, in fact,' she added.

'I want to do what you do.' There was a look of admiration and something Sara couldn't quite discern on Roxy's face. Envy? 'Take pain and pour it into creativity – my writing has to mean something, otherwise, it's so futile.'

'You're too young to believe in futility,' said Sara. 'Save that for your mid-thirties.'

'Oh, I know. It feels that way now and again but I know that I – *we* – have to change things. Through words.'

'Writers are just narcissists, I'm afraid.'

'Changing the world isn't narcissism.'

'Ego is a quiet, monstrous thing,' Sara said. 'It's why telling stories can sometimes be preferable to living. Containing it within the pages.'

There was a long pause before Roxy asked, 'Have you never wanted to look for her? Your mum?'

Sara wanted to say that she looked for her every day in her own actions and thoughts. Features. The words that she wrote. Instead, 'I've always wanted her to look for *me*.'

'That's—'

'Sad,' Sara finished. 'I know.'

But life also had unexpected moments like these. Ones that could be shared with strangers and, Sara laughed to herself, give one some hope.

'And yet, look,' she added. 'Here we are.'

Roxy raised her coffee to Sara. 'And whatever you say – we *will* change things.'

Grace

Manchester, 2014

Grace returned home from another gruelling day in the office. Initially, the sheer privilege of the corporate world, her very salary – even in a junior role – had made her nauseous. But material comfort was becoming necessary for her and Benji, even though her work hours felt relentless.

'Should I be doing this many hours?' Grace asked her mum as Dede took Grace's dinner out of the oven. 'I mean . . . Am I doing the right thing? Being away from home so much.'

'Like living in this place, do you?' replied Dede. 'With those kids out there, doing god knows what. You've almost saved enough money to get out of here. And if you leave work who's going to pay for Benji's specialist care?'

'I know, I know. You're doing all the exercises with him?' Grace asked.

'Of course. Don't worry, our boy's going to thrive.'

Dede showed Grace pictures she'd taken of them both that day. In the park. In the library, reading. He was safe with his grandmother. A thought Grace never imagined having.

'What if he speaks and I'm not here?' asked Grace.

'Focus on what *now*. Not, *what if*. *Now*, he needs to see a speech specialist. Waiting lists are ridiculous – you know money talks.'

'I just feel like I'm missing him growing up. Becoming a person, you know?'

'I know.'

But did she?

'I've done the shop for the week,' added Dede.

'Thanks.'

'I spent a little more than you'd given. Organic food makes a difference to their development.'

Grace handed Dede an extra twenty pound note.

'At the park he pointed to all the animals and objects I named,' said Dede as she set the table. 'He understands things.'

'I'm just the one who doesn't understand him,' said Grace, taking a seat.

'Grace. I never apologised to you.' Dede looked at her daughter. 'I wasn't there for you, I know. I missed so much, baby girl. I live every day knowing that. I won't ever forgive myself for it, but I hope you will. One day.'

'Mothers always feel like they've come up short.' Grace put her hand on her mother's. She recognised something in Dede's regretful look. The pull of genetics. Its capacity to dilute anger and dissolve particles of mistrust.

After dinner, before leaving to go home, Dede paused at the front door.

'Oh, I forgot, the plumbing in my bathroom's gone. I've found someone to take a look, but funds are low.'

'I'll transfer money into your account.'

'Never ending expenses,' Dede sighed. '*But*, we have the most important thing here. We have family.'

Grace buried her doubts and guilt.

For once, her mother was right.

Zainab

Glasgow, 2014

'Sometimes these women don't seem to have a life,' Tahera commented, giving Zainab the once over before taking a seat next to her at their latest chai party.

Zainab's increase in adornments since her affair with Suleiman began hadn't gone unnoticed. Even Kashif appreciated that although his wife was barren at least she was beautiful.

(Every time Suleiman looked at her, his guilt about betraying his friend diminished quite rapidly.)

Now, the wives clinked their teaspoons and ate their home-made cupcakes.

'Sorry,' said Tahera. 'I shouldn't backbite but *God*, I can see the boredom on your face.' She gave Zainab a playful nudge. Zainab managed a smile.

The doorbell rang and a few moments later Suleiman walked in with a box of sweetmeats.

'Ah, look at my little brother bringing *mithai*,' said his sister, who was hosting.

Zainab felt her heart race. They had done such things together she still blushed, a throb in her body. Guilt permeated her sleepless nights. Desire encompassed her days.

'If you want to stay, you're going to have to prove yourself worthy,' said Tahera to Suleiman.

'Oh, no one's worthy of *your* company,' he replied.

Zainab's cheeks burned. The problem with becoming the type who betrayed one's husband was that one began to see others as deceptive too. Kashif and Suleiman seemed to conflate in that moment – was her mind working? It couldn't start playing tricks on her; it was the most precious thing she had. The thing that made living bearable, because *she* owned it.

'Excuse me,' she rose, making her way to the bathroom.

She locked the door and leant against the sink, repulsed by her own image in the mirror. Muffled laughter came from downstairs. *What was she doing?* So much sin and for what? There was a knock on the door.

'Someone's in here,' she called.

The knocking continued. She tutted and opened the door. She'd hardly looked up when Suleiman strode in, pinning her against the wall. Before she could speak his hand brushed up her thigh and moved between her legs.

'God, I love you so much,' he whispered.

Even though she wanted to leave, she knew she would stay. She took his hand, pushing his fingers into her flesh.

'I love you too.'

Change could almost be palpable – if you reached out, you could touch the shift in your own life. Such was this moment for Zainab.

She could not let go of this feeling. And in holding on to it, she forgot all the ways in which she was deceiving others, as well as herself.

Unedited: *The Movement . . .*

Jane Pritchett: CoE Vicar
Inter-faith activist
Semi-perm Non-Verbal

Jane: Mondays, Wednesdays and Saturdays the church café is Non-Verbal. There's a certain energy those days. I'm in awe of how my congregation is more at peace with itself and the world. To be a part of something without being consumed by it - isn't that a modern-day miracle?

Aadhi: Is that how you view Non-Verbalism?

Jane: Look at how such frantic energy had drained us. This expectation to reach professional and personal heights. The need for more. Interfaith leaders are united in seeing current changes as positive.

Aadhi: You used to be in education. What do you make of the recent OFSTED report which suggests that Non-Verbal teenagers are undermining their chances of long-term employment?

Jane: We need an education system which develops creative thinkers, not corporate machines.

Aadhi: Unemployment around the world is continuing to rise.

Jane: Workforces are being made to adapt. It shows that power can still be with the people.

Aadhi: Do you think that one way of life is better than another?

Jane: No. When one *thinks* their way is better, that's when we're in trouble.

Aadhi: Smaller businesses are beginning to close due to less demand for non-essential goods. Verbals are finding it hard to adapt with the Non-Verbals' growing majority, which is polarising our society.

Jane: Do you fear being in the minority?

Aadhi: How did you feel about Dana Ingleberry, the woman who died in hospital because she wouldn't respond to doctors' or nurses' requests for critical information?

Jane: It was a tragedy. It *is* a tragedy. But there's also been a forty-two per cent increase in care home visits in England since July.

Aadhi: As a priest, aren't you worried about the lack of communication in families, threatening it as an institution?

Jane: Heaven forbid that I should consider personal contentment greater than any institution.

Aadhi: Are you concerned about people who already feel voiceless?

Jane: Look, injustice is a failure to comprehend a worldview outside our own.

Pause

Most of our volunteers at foodbanks, who have gone abroad, have chosen Non-Verbalism. Did you ever consider that when the privileged silence themselves, it's likelier for the ones who didn't have a voice, to be heard? If you've stripped yourself from a rich internal world - well, is it really any wonder the outside world is impoverished?

Pause.

Aadhi (off-camera): I guess that's the sermon over.

Sara

London, July 2021

Dad: Watch Hello, Britain. We're all going to hell in a handcart. Love you.

'We have Aadhi Sathar and Roxy Hussain joining us to talk about The Silent Movement that is sweeping the globe.'

Sara, sitting on a tartan blanket in her furniture-free living-room, felt a pang in her stomach. That stupid photo of her on stage was in the background *again*. She noticed Roxy glance at it.

Henry walked in and took one look. 'Can we *please* shut that off?'

Eventually, she heard the front door slam shut.

'Roxy, you were friends with Sara Javed?'

Roxy nodded, mouth straight, posture similar.

'Why do you think Non-Verbalism has become such a sensation?'

  'Let's not talk about it like that. As a feminist and person of colour, Sara Javed spoke to women like myself, but as a role model she's failed. Women have been silenced since time in memoriam and now Sara is consciously propagating that oppression . . . and she might very well be doing it, I don't know, just to stay relevant.'

Sara felt her heart sink. She considered the conversations she and Roxy had in quiet corners of darkening cafés, walks along the embankment, getting Ubers home at two in the morning. All those complex conversations, condensed.

Sara was becoming the victim of the grave injustice of soundbites.

At the hands of the person she had let in and called a friend.

'Aadhi?'

'People's reaction to both Javed and Munkin shows the need to lionise – or demonise – one person to perpetuate a skewed reflection of our society—'

God, he was a prick.

Whether he was right or not was hardly the point.

He carried on.

'There are two things that occur during key social moments. One, it is commercialised, as we saw with Munkin's show – and it's worth noting that the attacks on her reveal that the vulture culture lives on, even in Non-Verbalism. Businesses are using silence to motivate sales: just look at the production of Non-Verbal merchandise being sold as a means of displaying one's beliefs. Secondly, it is politicised. We have the opposition exploiting the situation to garner support for, let's face it – considering the previous two elections – an entirely ineffective party. All this has a significant impact on the social psyche.'

The presenter responded by reading out figures: people moving out of cities into towns and villages; the 24% decrease in crime (*surely this was just because fewer people were reporting?*), 17% reduction in GP-reported anxiety; the stats on increased (albeit self-reported) philanthropy, day-to-day efficiency in workplaces that allow Non-Verbalism . . . The benefits seemed immense. Had Sara's silence, really been the spark for all this?

She focused on the subtle movement of Roxy's brow, the almost imperceptible intake of breath as Aadhi continued.

'I'd like to know the source on—'

Roxy interrupted.

'Numbers don't tell us anything if we're not listening to the stories behind them. An Unveiling, my bestselling book about growing up gay in a Muslim household, is an example of a struggle that might be a statistic for any other purpose. If I, and others like me, went silent, our stories would be buried, and us with them.'
  'But Sara Javed has inspired people.'

The photo of Sara changed to one of her sitting in Waterstones Piccadilly, doing a signing. Then on a panel with Jyoti. A series of photos of her from various events, laughing, looking pensive, talking to readers. *Engaged.* Roxy was clearly pissed. Embroiled in the muddy waters of seeking validation. To be seen as the pioneer in *something.* Whatever it might be.
For a moment, Sara felt sorry for Roxy. Until she spoke again.

'A silent woman is regression.'

Sara's phone rang.
'Your friend is an opportunist, through and through,' came her dad's voice.

'I understand you're collaborating on a documentary revealing the truth about Sara Javed?'

Roxy and Aadhi exchanged a glance.
This was the same man Roxy hated.
Called him a misogynist!

'We're dismantling the idea of the woman behind the movement – Sara Javed – as a revolutionary or a saint, so people can understand the damage they're doing by following Non-Verbalism and these tools of historic oppression.'

167

Afzal let off a slew of swear words.

Sara's heart raced. What so-called *truths* would Roxy reveal? Which words they'd shared, if any, remained sacred?

People made detaching oneself from life really fucking difficult.

'Hold on to your conviction,' said Afzal. 'When it is strong, people try to break it.'

That night Sara replayed the interview.

Then again.

And again.

She would go to sleep with no other thought: *A silent woman is regression.*

The following morning Sara's arm slumped on to Henry's side of the bed and landed on a piece of paper.

Sara,

There was no point in telling you in person because it's not as if you'd respond.

I gave you everything. I loved you. Maybe you didn't see it. But then you've only ever seen what you wanted, only wanted what you didn't have. You're the reason the world is falling apart and still you're in your bubble. You emptied our house of everything we'd built, walked around wearing those fucking headphones as if I was the problem. But it's you. You're the problem.

Nothing was ever good enough. I'm not saying things were easy for you but did you ever consider others? Me? Because when you say no, come hell or high water, you mean it.

I want to say I wish you the best. One day, maybe I will. Until then I'll only hope that you're sorry, rather than believe that you are.

Henry

Sara read the letter several times. She patted the bed for missing pages, looked under the blanket. Nothing. She jumped out of bed and threw up in the toilet.

The inevitable had happened, but she didn't think it would happen this way.

Sara searched for a feeling.

Any would do.

She read the letter again.

Nothing seems to be good enough for you.

Sara crawled back into bed, the words in the letter foaming in her head. She slept until nightfall.

When she awoke she didn't know where she was. It was all she could do to remember *who* she was. But that had always been tricky. The letter was still in her hands. She was bewildered at her lack of emotion: if she didn't feel the devastation that should come from the failure of her marriage, a socially sanctioned state of happiness, then what did that mean?

There were several missed calls from her dad.

'Where have you been?' he exclaimed when she FaceTimed him. 'I was getting worried. You have called me back so you must be OK. Yes?'

She nodded. Why didn't she speak? But then her dad would probably respond with something unhelpful like 'a man with such a weak chin cannot bring about strong emotions'.

The worst part was that Henry was right. She wasn't sorry. And *shouldn't* she be? Yet, here she was, not a tear to be gleaned. Just the knowledge that abandonment was a way of life.

A tear finally surfaced.

Popular opinion was that to go through life in emotional stasis was not a life lived at all. Yet Sara's inward stagnation had led to an outward movement and she was still unable to fathom how removed she felt from it. Wasn't this detachment what she wanted?

In ordinary circumstances, Sara might've written a rebuttal to Roxy spouting shallow sentiment on national television, citing that movement isn't necessarily progress and to progress one needn't have a movement; knowledge was not understanding; and what was the point anyway, when it was all lost in perception?

Non-Verbals, Verbals, did they really *see* each other?

Instead, her argument ended up being with herself. It lasted well into the night.

Unedited: *The Movement* . . .

Afzal Javed: Retired
Sara Javed's father
Semi-perm Non-Verbal

Lily Thompson: Secondary School Teacher
Sara's ex-stepmother
Verbal

Roxy: Thank you for reaching out to us.
Afzal: Your documentary needs balance.
Lily: You have to understand, Sara's aim was never to be revolutionary. She's laughed at the very idea.
Roxy: What *did* she want?
Afzal: Loyal friends—
Lily: Let's stay focused, shall we?
Afzal: The world's too keen on keeping time without understanding the restriction of it as a social construct.
Lily: That argument didn't work when we missed our flight to Egypt, and it's not going to work now.
Afzal: Sara took after me - she wouldn't be told what to do or think, because she understood that our thoughts are never as free as we believe.
Roxy: What were Sara's last words to you, before she went silent?
Pause.

171

Afzal: *I am bored of the sound of my own voice.*

Roxy: Was she emotional?

Afzal: Sara was always very good at managing her emotions, but she was especially calm.

Roxy: Her biological mo—

Afzal: *Rukhsana* . . . be careful. Sara knows we're here, but there are limits.

Lily: She's trying to let go.

Roxy: Of what?

Afzal: Tst. What makes living so hard? When you try to hold on to things that are not yours. Nothing is. In the end.

Lily: Sara thrived in the quiet. She was always clever. Remember that time she asked whether we were real or if life was a dream?

Afzal: Only seven years old and interrogating simulation. She'd just started piano lessons.

Lily: Violin.

Afzal: Sara always had questions, very sharp with the tongue - but she was a dreamer.

Lily: Oh, yes. Sara had dreams. But we can tell you—

Afzal: She didn't want this.

Roxy: You know Sara best. What does she think *this* is?

Afzal: Oof. Chaos.

Roxy: One last thing: does it seem to you like she cares that there's chaos? That she, intentional or not, started it?

Long pause.

Lily: That's a question only Sara can answer.

People Deleting Social Media Accounts by the Millions

Nikki Mayhew, *The Snuff*, July 2021

Recent polls suggest an increase in levels of happiness due to a gradual reduction in the use of social media. Twitter has reported a 29.2% decline in global usage, a possible correlation with a newly reported 23% decrease in medication for depression and anxiety. Did we ever need to be so connected? However, Dr Richard Cunningham, a professor in Social Sciences at the University of Kirkland, says that these drastic changes are significantly impacting revenues of some of our biggest online platforms and retailers and could lead to significant economic upheaval . . .

Are you a Non-Verbal who wants to contribute to the world's leading Online News Forum? Email us with a bio.

Subscribe to *The Snuff.*

Grace

London, July 2021

By the time Grace opened her post Benji was asleep, the TV playing in the background.

Harold Fernsby came on screen, looking sweaty and dishevelled.

'The government is taking measures to show respect for different ways of life, particularly when it comes to employment policy. To Non-Verbals I ask: think of your country and fellow countrymen. We live in a world that's dependent on one another. This is how we flourish as a society.'

Recognising the pitfalls of individualism was all about timing.

The fringe movement had officially been absorbed by the mainstream and Grace almost felt sorry about it. She switched off the news.

Quiet in the household had now become synonymous with peace, not failure. A world of Non-Verbalism may be just the one her son needed. Even telling Benji off diluted the frustration in Grace's expression, if not feeling. He would furrow his brows. But whatever had happened to their words, emotions hadn't been muted.

What would Dede have made of it all?

Why did Grace even want to know?

Grace opened today's mail and out slipped an A4 letter.

She had to sit down.

Dear Ms Jenkins,

Re: Proposed Application for Child Arrangements Order

We act for David Hodgkin, who is seeking to make an application under S.8 of the Children Act for a variation to the current Child Arrangements Order insofar as it concerns arrangements for the residence of Benjamin Jenkins (D.O.B 02/06/2011).

My client has attempted for the last 4 months to contact you in order to arrange contact to his son but you have consistently refused to return his calls.

Our client is concerned, in light of Benjamin's documented and formally diagnosed medical non-verbalism, that your voluntary participation in social Non-Verbalism will have a negative impact on Benjamin's development. We have instructed an expert in the area who agrees that it is not in the best interests of the child to live in a household where the residential parent engages in no verbal communication at all.

We are prepared to enter into mediation in order to resolve matters but a pre-requisite to our client considering abandoning his proposed application would be for you to relinquish your Non-Verbalism.

We look forward to hearing from you within 7 days failing which we have been instructed to issue an application forthwith.

Yours, etc

Grace read in disbelief.

How on earth did he know about Benji's mutism? Had he followed them? Contacted the school?

And he couldn't abandon his child and then have the audacity to suggest *her* negligence.

The letter trembled in her hands. *Relinquish* Non-Verbalism? What would anti-Non-Verbalists know about silence without having experienced

175

its peace? Specialists who have no idea about the way Benji now looked her in the eye, mouthed words to songs, smiled more, slept better. Give it up? The hope, too, that she would hear him speak one day. A conviction she felt in her gut, the same place from which she had once nourished Benji. This was a mother's instinct and like hell would she let it go.

@RoxyHussainAuthor

#InstagramLive

Today I had my second panic attack. I visited the Silent Room *to understand why people have chosen Non-Verbalism, because how can I judge something without trying to understand it? That's my first responsibility as a writer and producer of the upcoming documentary:* The Movement that Silenced Us and the Woman Behind It. *To express truth in its purest form. In the room I felt myself blur as painful memories came flooding back. Like a caged bird. I was reminded of Maya Angelou:* 'There is no greater agony than bearing an untold story inside you.' *I couldn't breathe. I had to get out. The door wouldn't open. I had to bang on it repeatedly. When it finally opened, I ran out into the street, gasping for breath and words. Words to explain what had happened. Words to relate my experience. I'm still recovering from the trauma, trying to process it. How the experience brought me so much pain. But now I know that to protest Non-Verbalism is not just a passion, but a duty.*

If you believe your voice matters then it is your duty too.

We won't be silenced. Not by Sara Javed or society.

#Novoicenopeace #AnUnveiling #verballife #empathy #amresearching #silentrooms #documentary #themovement
5,346 likes
93 Comments . . .

sherbert_sweetie So sorry you went through this. Love and solidarity ♡

analogous We fight together. You're the VOICE of reason

trimbeard Attention seeking desperado.

paXi I had a similar exp and Im so glad someones had the courage to spk out. I don't understand how people dont c the damage its doing. Thank u 4 being brave 4 the rest of us.

sofie92 whatever happened to equality? Youre a joke.

Curlywurly Bitter bitch

Zainab

Glasgow, July 2021

Kashif, as promised, had completed her naturalisation form, but Home Office staff shortages (attributed to the increasing number of resignations of disaffected Non-Verbals) meant there was a huge backlog. It could take up to a year for a final decision to come through. Zainab found her anxiety compounded, and not just because of the delay. Kashif had been Non-Verbal for a month now. His workplace now held Non-Verbal mornings in the office. People were at their most productive, which felt like a no-brainer to Kashif's boss who had invested in silent cafés after he had read an article in *The New Yorker* about several opening in cities like New York, LA, London, Paris. Cities renowned for their bustle, and so naturally in need of an antidote.

Silence was proving lucrative.

The muted tension at home meant that Zainab was hardly required to speak, which suited her fine. Perhaps, in another life, she'd have taken up Non-Verbalism, but it didn't feel like a particularly marked difference.

All silences were not created equal.

She had come home after teaching to find Kashif praying in the living room. Her in-laws were out so she went into the bedroom to freshen up. After a few minutes Kashif entered. He closed the door behind him. Her heartbeat quickened. She went to leave but he took her by the hand.

'I have to get dinner ready,' she said.

He led her to the bed.

It had been inevitable. She might as well get it over with, so she began to unbutton her top. In some ways it would be easier now that she wouldn't have to listen to the incessant language of his self-delusion. But he stopped her, held her face in his hands before kissing her. Only this time, he didn't pull her hair and spit in her mouth – he laid her down on the bed. He ran his hands up her thighs. Zainab stared at the crack in the ceiling.

Instead of switching on the television, he looked at her, and its unfamiliarity unsettled her. Slowly, he unbuttoned her blouse, kissed her chest, her stomach, lifting up her skirt and peeling off her knickers. He softly stroked the inside of her thighs. Pulled her closer. The crack in the ceiling blurred as she found herself closing her eyes. She forgot that it was Kashif with her and surrendered to the sensations she never knew he could evoke, reaching that point of release she'd never experienced with him.

Breathless and dazed, when he came up to kiss her, she could not comprehend the way her body throbbed with the force of her own ecstasy.

The whole thing both confounded and disgusted Zainab. Her body had reacted to a man who repulsed her. Perhaps it was the memory of the love she thought she once had for him that was resurfacing, tricking her into believing that it still existed.

She couldn't bring herself to go home after class so she walked through the streets of Glasgow. She put in her earphones and listened to a pre-NV podcast with Sara Javed. They were all the rage – people analysing her words from the past to understand her silence in the present.

'I'm interested in how a singular experience can have a universality of meaning,' came Javed's voice.

Zainab walked past a series of shops with Sara's letter framed, thinking about Kashif's hot breath, the way he unbuttoned her shirt. Then Zainab came across a *Silent Room*. It claimed one could unearth what lay beneath the surface of their actions. Even thoughts. A therapy session in which you were your own therapist. And all for twenty pounds an hour.

Or fifty-five pounds a month, if you were a member, which Kashif was. Empowerment didn't have to mean poverty.

Zainab switched off the podcast and read the sign on the door.

> *This is a sanctuary for silence and peace. Please refrain from vocal communication.*
> *Our receptionist will provide non-verbal guidance.*
> <u>*Beware the Barrenness of a Busy Life.*</u>

The magnetic pull of peace led Zainab inside. The noise of the traffic ceased as the door shut behind her. On the opposite wall was a large glass frame with scrambled letters raining down. A small square plate next to it read:

> *Letters taken from Sara Javed's note. A reminder that what we say is only as powerful as the meaning we give to it. Let us rest our voice, so we can find our meaning.*

Did Kashif buy into this? Did *everyone*? The receptionist, wearing her *Permanent Non-Verbal* badge, smiled at Zainab and handed her a questionnaire. Zainab took a seat.

> *The* Silent Room *embraces Javed's ethos of cultivating the inner voice to transcend the barriers of noise and find the silence within.*
> *Please fill in the questionnaire and hand it back to our receptionist who will guide you towards the path of self-discovery.*

The appointments came in half-hour slots. Studies showed that anything less wouldn't reap silence's optimum results. A full two-hour session (recommended) could create new cells in the hippocampus, which was linked to learning, remembering, and emotions.

All necessary tools in leading one's best life.

Zainab read the questions set out for Verbals:

1. On a scale of 1–5 please state your level of daily verbosity, 1 being the least verbose, 5 being the most.

Zainab circled '1'.

2. How much of your daily speech takes place at work?
   a) 1–3 hours
   b) 4–6 hours
   c) 7–9 hours
   d) 10–12 hours
   e) 13 hours +

She circled 'b'.

3. How much time is spent talking about your work?
   a) 1–3 hours
   b) 4–6 hours
   c) 7–9 hours
   d) 10–12 hours
   e) 13 hours +

Zainab circled 'a', continuing until she came across the final one.

25. How do you envisage silence impacting you? (You may choose more than one.)
   a) Refocus priorities
   b) Think more about what I say and to whom
   c) A richer inner life
   d) A better relationship with other people
   e) A better relationship with myself

Zainab considered the impact of Kashif's silence. What had brought about the change in his bedroom manner? She had often allayed fears about leaving him; she would deal with the gossip, explain to her parents. It would be difficult but Suleiman would be the resultant ease.

But her slumbering dutiful nature was now awakening.

Zainab circled all options, surprised at how few hours she spent speaking about anything important. What had she been saying all her life? And what, in turn, did this say about her?

> Please indicate if you have any requirements (smells or colours you dislike). We wish you a transformative experience.
>
> *All information is confidential and is covered by the Data Protection Act.*

Zainab walked into a room with white-and-green cushions splayed in the middle. A scent of vanilla. She sat on the cushions.

What was she meant to do?

How many minutes had passed?

She had an impulse to pray.

She tried to expel the frenzied thoughts about Suleiman and Kashif but a yawn escaped her. A lethargy so strong washed over her that she lay on the cushions and drifted into sleep.

Where was she? *Who* was she? Zainab held on to herself, feeling the form of her body for long enough to understand that she still existed. The relief that she still had her body – defunct as it was – provoked gratitude. She felt tears on her face. A green light appeared above the door. Zainab walked out on to Calder Street. The light hurt her eyes. The noise felt at odds with her mind. It did not race. They had not been tears of grief.

THE RIGHT TO REMAIN SILENT

Sara

London, 2016

Sara's fourth book, *Rule-makers,* came out with less fanfare than her previous three. It was about a couple in the eighties, opening a school in north London. She had based it on her dad and Lily, who had taken their boldness of spirit and done exactly that. Neither had been prepared for the realities of running a school, where pupils decided what they wanted to learn and there was no timetable nor uniform. Students were the rule-makers in a school established by a pair of rule-breakers.

The school had failed in 1985. A tale of both comedy and tragedy.

By paperback publication there was the escalating need to *amplify* voices, harried commentary on *representation*. It led to Penelope and her sales team pioneering the times by picking Sara as the lucky recipient of their 'inclusion' strategy. Which, incidentally, led to Sara winning her first award.

Sara's publicist, new to the job, had pitched it, without Sara's knowledge, as a true story. Sara had mentioned to the publicist the real-life inspiration behind the book, but assumed that the conversation had been private. Her publicist hadn't considered such a concept.

With the help of extensive marketing and publicity campaigns, Sara's book tapped into the prevailing mood. The immigrant narrative, the working-class trials, the audacious characters who turned out to be *actual people.*

Now Sara's opinions were increasingly being sought out. It had been pleasing to begin with, but she had not fully considered that professional recognition would be in direct conflict with her innately quiet nature.

'You *did* write about it.' Henry was cat-cowing on his yoga mat.

'It's *fiction*. Personal things bleed into work, but you have to draw *some* lines. Fucking publicist,' she mumbled.

'Have her fired.'

'There's no need to be a dick.'

Henry stared at her while moving into happy-baby pose.

'Sorry.'

Sara *was* grateful for the success. Her previously published books were now being given brand new covers. But she could not shake the claustrophobia of having to now answer incessant *questions*. People insisting on dipping into her mind, which, quite frankly, she preferred to exhibit on the page. It's how her own thoughts were revealed to her.

She had written *Rule-Makers* to give her dad and Lily something of their past to treasure, but also to understand the necessity of their separation. She had spent hours with them, helping them to relive feelings, as a result of which, she witnessed joy on her dad's face.

Now she was being rewarded!

Actual sales.

'It'll be good for your brand,' said Henry.

'Why are you always so advertising?'

Henry wobbled into tree pose and lost his footing. 'Ow. *Shit*. Is that the time?'

He glugged coffee, darting between oiling his beard, coiling his man-bun – how long would this particular crisis of his last? – and gathering papers which never would be organised.

'*Where are my keys?*'

Henry looked at Sara. He stared at her for so long that she replied: 'Well, they're not on my face.'

His own face went a shade of red. 'You know, it's a big day today.'

Henry, witnessing Sara's professional ascent, had decided he wanted to quit his job and find his life's calling. They had savings and Sara, whose financial situation was improving, had supported this decision. That was two months ago. Every day was a big day that never transpired. So, more recently she had stopped offering words of encouragement because there was nothing more offensive than empty sentiment. Henry, however, found this level of honesty selfish and lacking in imagination.

'Not everyone has a dad like yours who blindly believes in them.'

'*Blindly?*'

Henry paused at the door, before saying he had to leave and that they'd talk about it tonight.

Agitated, Sara got up to make another coffee. *Blindly.* And why was he *always* losing his mind and keys? She reminded herself of Henry's support through rejections, bad reviews, industry indifference. *You are amazing*, he would say. Now that strangers told her this regularly, he seemed to have lost interest in reminding her of it.

Sara checked her Twitter, which now had a following of over 8K. She got lost in comments, opinion inciting opinion, heart buoyed at compliments, leaden by criticism. She looked at the time.

Bollocks.

She'd been scrolling for over an hour when she received an email from Roxy.

HOW DO YOU KEEP YOUR SANITY?

Sure you'll quote for my book? What if you HATE it? Sorry about shouty caps lock. Still on for coffee at yours?

Your needy mentee

Sara wrote back.

OF COURSE I'M SURE I CAN'T WAIT TO READ I DO NOT
COPE BUT THANKFULLY I HAVE A REASONABLE
DISPOSITION AND NOT MY FATHER'S SHOUTY NATURE.

Sara and Roxy were sitting on her brown, leather sofa in the living room
as she complained for a full thirteen minutes about all the personal features she'd had to do for *Rule-makers*.

'*No* is a word,' said Roxy. 'Though I don't know why you're being so
high-strung. What your dad and Lily did is so interesting.'

Sara was taken by how easily Roxy seemed to assert *no* in her life. She
had hardly considered it an option when trying to clamber her way up the
ladder of professional success.

'You're *right*.'

'Of course . . . Which bit am I right about?'

'Why can't I say no?'

'Because women are always taught to say *yes*,' replied Roxy.

'Hardly my dad's parenting style.'

'True. But if your parents don't fuck you up society will.'

Sara was staring at the wall.

'What are you thinking?' asked Roxy, as if it was a dangerous pastime
of Sara's.

'Oh, nothing.'

'*Sara.*'

'It's silly—'

'We've known each other for, what, two years now. You can tell me
shit.'

Sara hesitated. 'Every time I consider what I think, say or do, I can't
help but wonder whether I get it from my mum. As if I have no choice
over it. Stupid, I know.'

Roxy leant forward. 'Hardly.'

'What does all this mean when you don't . . .'

'When you don't?'

'Forget it. I hate this *finding yourself* narrative. It's so hackneyed.'

'But it makes sense,' replied Roxy. 'Listen – and don't go all Sara on me and make that face – I sometimes write letters to my family. You know. Say the things on paper that I can't in real life.'

Sara looked at Roxy, then let out a laugh.

Roxy's face went a shade of red. 'Fuck, Sara. That's worse than you making a face.'

'I'm not laughing at that.'

Sara got up and left the room, returning a few moments later with a shoe box.

'My journal of letters to my mum.'

'*No.*' Roxy raised her brows. 'Just when I think you have your shit together, I realise you're just as messed up as me.'

'I know.'

She put the box down. They both looked at it.

'Can I—? No. Sorry.'

'What?'

'I just wanted . . . to read one.'

Sara felt her heart race. *What a request.* Could she reveal such raw thoughts to someone else? Henry often said Sara was reticent about sharing things.

'Sorry. Total invasion of privacy,' added Roxy.

Sara hesitated. 'You won't laugh?'

'*Laugh?* Cry more likely.'

'Not in front of me, please.'

'It's weird, isn't it?' Roxy said, after a pause. 'That we both do the same thing.'

Sara had a rare case of understanding the impact of shared experience.

'I'm going to make another cup of tea,' she said. 'What's in the box is yours. Apart from the shoes.'

Sara went into the kitchen, feeling a knot of anxiety and relief at the same time. She did not want to witness Roxy's reactions as she read the letters. She managed to stay away for a full fifteen minutes. Such intimacy required distance.

191

When she walked back into the room, holding two mugs of tea, Roxy looked up at her, tears in her eyes, journal resting on her lap.

'*Sara,*' she whispered.

Sara felt her hands tremble. Roxy took the teas from Sara and set them down on the floor. Then Roxy did exactly what Sara didn't want. She hugged her.

'It's fine,' said Sara.

'No, it's not. You've got grit, you know.'

Sara's laugh came out muffled against Roxy's shoulder. 'You're one to talk. Sometimes I wish I had your conviction. That I wasn't always so fucking uncertain of things.'

Roxy hugged her closer.

'Honestly, I'm *fine.*' But even as Sara tried to pull away, her voice cracked.

'Accept the fucking hug, Sara.'

She felt such a wave of sadness come over her, she couldn't argue. Instead, they remained in an embrace until it had become quite uncomfortable. After which they sat on the sofa, for the rest of the evening, in companiable silence.

Sara stashed her Kindle away as she walked into BPH Studios. After Roxy had left a couple of evenings before, a surge of love – quite unexpected for Sara – prompted her to start reading Roxy's manuscript.

It had been a dispiriting move.

Upon finishing the manuscript, Sara could think of describing it as nothing but a veritable word salad of worthiness.

How had Roxy, in using her own words, lost her voice? Her vivacity was absent in reliving the misery of her past. Her family one-dimensional. Sara had introduced Roxy to Penelope, so sure was she of her friend's talent. Such were the pitfalls of unsubstantiated belief.

Now, Sara entered a green room of people who would be opining on identity politics and the future of Britain, while she'd be wondering how on earth she'd respond to Roxy without breaking her heart. Softness of manner was not Sara's forte.

She overheard someone say that we were headed towards a national reckoning, another commented on the canapés. Sara ate a biscuit.

When she had first entered this room four years ago, she recalled how her pulse quickened every time someone asked her a question. The excitement of new ideas. Thoughts. Now the people and chatter felt the same. How could one find inspiration in repetition?

She was sitting in a corner, thinking about Roxy's manuscript, when she saw Aadhi Sathar, head down, walking towards her.

'Oh.'

He looked up. 'Aadhi Sathar,' he said before sitting down.

Sara decided she would face this moment with grace and humility, showing him that *his* words hardly mattered. She would tell Roxy about it and it would no longer be a source of embarrassment but a moment of comedy.

'Sara Javed,' she replied.

'I know.' He scrolled through his phone. How was she meant to show grace and humility if he didn't look at her?

Eventually he spoke. 'You're here to talk about . . .?'

What a dick you are. 'My parents' school.'

'Oh, yes. Your latest book. Useful, for your purposes.'

'Sorry?'

'I suppose I should address the elephant in the room . . . I had been looking forward to your debut . . . but opinion is subjective. Professionally, you've done well.'

She ignored that. 'What do you mean, for *my purposes*?' As if Sara was the benefactress of her parents' history.

'Aadhi, Sara. Great, you've met.'

Neither had noticed the producer approach.

'It's not exactly been a pleasure,' said Sara, without thinking.

Aadhi, surprisingly, didn't look offended. 'Well, *this* should be interesting.'

The producer glanced between the two. 'Shall we do a mic test?'

'I'll give you a percentage of my book sales if you make sure *his* doesn't work,' whispered Sara. 'It might even get you a chocolate bar.'

The producer laughed. 'I don't think you should say that, what with the success of *Rule-makers*.'

Sara, despite often being told she was a success, was startled.

'To whisper effectively you might consider actually lowering your voice,' said Aadhi as they took their seats next to each other. 'Reviews aren't personal,' he added.

'No, just self-satisfied.'

'If we're talking about self-satisfied *A Wom*—' He broke off. They were on air.

Sara was asked about her parents' school; how it had shaped her views and writing. As Sara answered each question, she felt the boundaries of her personal and professional life blur.

'We live in an age of entitlement.' Aadhi's voice was exasperated. 'Where stories matter more than facts.

'I'm a journalist, so stories are the foundation of my career, of course. But there's a danger of looking to storytellers for opinions, which they give based on their experiences rather than objective knowledge – it all leads to a belief in the primacy of *feeling*.

'*I feel therefore I'm right.*'

Sara's face burned. It's not as if she *sought* giving opinions. And people like Roxy found solace in her words.

Aadhi continued to talk, talk, talk. When was the last time he had looked inwardly?

When was the last time *she* had?

When Sara got home, she was annoyed at some of the things she'd said; wished she'd phrased others differently. Aadhi had watched her speak, his look so condescending. She also felt bereft that she had not liked – let alone loved – her dear friend's work. That it was – and it pained her to say it – lacking in literary merit. Then Henry came home and began to splurge such a deluge of words about why he still hadn't told his boss he was leaving that she wished everyone would just shut the fuck up.

She found herself online, searching for something . . . *anything*, to quieten all the noise.

When the pair of noise-cancelling headphones arrived, Sara unpackaged them frantically, holding them up in the air, before finally placing them over her ears. She breathed a sigh of relief.

Even if all she had been offered was just the illusion of peace.

Grace

Manchester, 2016

Dede had come to Grace's to wave them off. She hugged Benji, then pinched her ear between her finger and thumb and winked at him. He winked back.

Grace suppressed her jealousy. The past few months she'd hardly seen Benji because of her workload, climbing the corporate ladder for that promotion so she could get him into a private school, specialising in children with mutism. A week off in the Lake District, just the two of them, was her way of making up for it.

Half an hour into the car journey, Grace glanced at Benji.

'Are you OK? Is this radio station boring? Shall we listen to your favourite music?'

She played the *Shrek* soundtrack, but Benji just stared out of the window.

By the time they reached the hotel all Grace wanted was to check her work emails.

She asked her son what he wanted to do the following day and he shrugged.

'I'm not a mind-reader, Benj,' Grace tried to say with a laugh.

She decided they'd go to the Beatrix Potter museum. It was crowded because of half-term. Children in groups, laughter inducing in Grace a panic to make Benji laugh. She told a joke but he just looked up at Peter Rabbit in the kitchen, surrounded by pots and pans.

Then Dede phoned.

'It's going great,' said Grace. 'We're going to get McDonald's . . . I know he likes the fish burger.'

She didn't.

'And get him the strawberry milkshake . . .'

'*Mum.* I know what I'm doing with my son.'

Grace glanced at Benji, but he was no longer next to her.

'Put him on the phone,' said Dede.

Grace looked around, her heart racing, but all she saw were crowds of strangers.

'I have to go.' She hung up. '*Benji.*'

She pushed through the throng, each face that wasn't Benji's filling her with a growing dread. It would serve her right to lose him. She couldn't even spend a day with him without counting the hours.

Grace stopped every person she passed, asking if they'd seen a mixed-heritage boy with curly black hair and light brown eyes, until she found a security guard.

'I've lost my son,' she said, now frantic.

'OK, madam—'

'You don't understand. He doesn't talk.'

It was ten minutes before they finally found Benji, in the gift shop, watching a baby in its pushchair.

'Benji.' Grace pulled him into a hug. 'Don't ever do that again. *You stay with me OK* ?'

That night she called Dede back. 'Can you join us? He misses you. *We* miss you.'

When Dede arrived, Grace confessed what had happened, barely able to contain her tears.

'Hush now,' said Dede, holding Grace. 'The only time you really lose a child is when you lose yourself. So, hold on to yourself, OK?'

Grace didn't know what that meant, but in the comfort of her mother's arms, she pretended she did.

Zainab

Glasgow, 2016

Zainab's first planned escape to Lahore, four years after she had left it, couldn't come soon enough. The relief that she would see her parents, witness the hustle of the rikshaws, the lights strewn up in celebration for Eid. To be among people who didn't watch the way she put the dishes back in the cupboards, the creaking of floorboards when she'd tip-toe to call Suleiman – to sit on the veranda with her mother.

Her humility (which many who were much less prone could have learnt from) had been conflated with subservience. To make demands, even for her right to have satisfying, or simply respectful, sex with her husband seemed to be transgressing wifely bounds.

Was this any way to live?

She had stopped her regular prayers, substituting one habit for another. Her self-reproach was supplanted by being in Suleiman's arms, when he would whisper in her ear about the future they would have. The guilt of her sin no longer lingered. Was this as unnatural as her womb?

She had to stop this thing with Suleiman.

She couldn't stop this thing with Suleiman.

To be back home would create some distance and clarity.

So, it came as a surprise when on her second day back in Lahore she went to Liberty Market and the push and shove, the noise felt like an attack on her. At each dinner party, the pitying looks about her lack of children were made only worse when Kashif was commended for his commitment to her. How had the place in which she had been born and raised, become so foreign?

But Lahore had reminded her of her drive, her love for her students: it was a thing to be unearthed again, surely?

Upon returning to Glasgow, in all its gloom and glory, Zainab realised that something had changed within her, and it would no longer accommodate the Pakistan that now existed without.

When she sat outside The Gardener on Ashton Lane with her laptop, there was satisfaction in knowing what she finally wanted.

'Would you like some company?'

She looked up to see a man who had approached her. 'No, thank you.'

'Where are you from?'

'Pakistan.'

'You're a very beautiful woman.'

'Thank you,' she replied. 'I have a very good brain too.'

He laughed, tipped an imaginary hat and walked away.

She looked at her laptop again. Teaching maths to a classroom of nine-year olds in a mosque wasn't as fulfilling as people told her it should be, so she began to put together a research proposal for a PhD application, her interest in sustainable energy. She had found several programmes for it.

For so many years, she had felt her marriage as four walls, closing in on her, and now she wondered whether the suffering may have been an opening for something better.

She felt the familiar flutter of excitement when Suleiman called.

When she arrived at the hotel, she wanted to tell him about the PhD, but he grabbed and kissed her before she could speak. In the throes of such passion, her other thoughts were swiftly forgotten.

Suleiman was her very own respite.

(She would come to find that respite could not be a way of life.)

Unedited: *The Movement . . .*

Neil Brigance: Leader of *Britain For You*
Anti-Non-Verbal activist
Verbal

Neil: Fernsby yo-yoing, Bacclay on the Non-Verbal bandwagon shows that both parties are criminally out of touch. The idea that we can live side-by-side . . . How's that possible when you don't know what someone's thinking? Non-Verbalism's become a cult and it just isn't the British way. We have to take back control of our country.
Aadhi: You'd lost 33% of members by the end of 2020, before Non-Verbalism, and after criticism to do with racism in the party, hadn't you?
Neil: Our increase in membership since shows that they're beginning to have faith again.
Aadhi: An increase of 18%, if I'm correct?
Neil: And growing. We want to hold Sara Javed to account. *She has incited hatred.* If she were white . . . Well, let's be honest, nowadays we are held to a higher standard than 'marginalised' people. First, we couldn't say a thing, right? And now we're being told we can't say anything at all.
Aadhi: By 'we', you mean?
Neil: People without Privilege. 72% of Non-Verbals come from affluent backgrounds. We want to ensure

that people on the periphery of society still have a voice. Britain For You plans to get our country back to the way it was . . .

Fade out.

Neil leaves.

Aadhi: Almost makes you want to become pro-Non-Verbal, doesn't it? Although he made a few salient points.

Roxy: Ugh. Sometimes I can't believe I'm working with you.

NON-VERBALS SAY NO TO BIG BROTHER AND THREATEN STATUS QUO

Matthew Barker, creator of *The Nonrhetorical Forum* Blog,
Aug 2021
25,000 Followers.

The sharp decline in social media engagement, bar Instagram, is a credible threat for many private companies. Insiders report that research has been ramped up to produce graphics-led content to entice NVs back to forums such as Twitter and Facebook. Being unable to track preferences via our online presence is having serious repercussions for current power structures as less data is available for sale and advertising revenues, which are increasingly drying up. Further, in the absence of traditional media advertising platforms, goods producers are struggling to connect with their markets.

There have been several high-profile legal cases against Non-Verbal discrimination in the workplace. Overall, a reported 4.7% rise in unemployment, due to the lack of its accommodation in professional spaces, reflects a shift in our attitudes towards a less consumer-led lifestyle. If things continue this way analysts suggest we could have as many as 4.3 million persons unemployed by the end of the year . . .

This all sounds doom and gloom but I for one am willing to say goodbye to all the algorithms, tempting us to buy things we don't need; to advertising that has been forcing us to compare our grey lives to the ones displayed on filtered banners; to the data collectors, exploiting us for political gain. Our actions and even thoughts can no longer be manipulated. We are the surveyors of silence, and we declare that it has won.

To subscribe to the freshest takes on world affairs click <u>here</u>.

Sara

London, August 2021

It had been a few days since Henry left. From the window of her flat, Sara watched someone leave a note at her doorstep. Crowds continued to gather outside during the day, leaving flowers and cards of support, burning candles. Silence for Sara had, quite accidentally, become a prison sentence.

It was almost midnight. Sara went down, opened the door and checked no one was looming around the corner. She stooped to pick up the note.

You have shown us all a new way to live. Thank you, thank you, thank you. Yours in silent solidarity.

Sara sat down on the doorstep and blew out the candles, picked up the flowers. If there had been cameras, they'd have caught her smiling, despite herself. It was ridiculous to be moved by people she did not know, by misplaced gestures. But here she was.

That morning, before the crowds had time to gather, Sara had left the house. She stared at the children playing in Clissold Park and wondered whether a different – and overly energetic, in her opinion – environment might elicit some feeling about motherhood, a subject Henry had never seemed able to let go of. Affection would be preferable. Disappointment acceptable. A maternal yearning provocative.

Still nothing.

Children would cry and some women would go red with frustration but not utter a word. Jyoti's voice rang in her ears. Why *were* women slipping into another historical phase of silence? It baffled Sara. Like a non-believer who, with all the luxuries of the world, converted to an institutional religion.

One person's oppression was another person's freedom.

How long would it take for the world to accept *that*.

'I suppose you're getting recognised a lot.'

Sara broke from her reverie. She was wearing sunglasses and a baseball cap but it hadn't stopped Aadhi Sathar from finding her.

He had all but sat next to her before she began to walk away.

'Wait, please.'

Sara stopped.

'Roxy told me you might be here.'

She started walking again. *What the hell was he doing here*? Actually, she didn't care. To think that *this* man had stolen countless nights of sleep during her career. And why? *Who was he* ultimately? What was the substance of him? Of Henry. Of Roxy. Of *anyone* caught up in the sham of life.

Sara, contrary to being a woman who wanted to be able to let go, was now caught up in despair.

'I know you don't want to see me and for very good reason—'

She walked faster.

'I stand by what I wrote about your books.'

Sara involuntarily opened her mouth. He watched for a moment before she pursed her lips.

'I'll get to the point. You must know that I'm making a documentary about The Silent Movement. With Roxy,' he added. 'We want you in it.'

Sara let out a laugh.

Aadhi was obviously taken aback.

The absurdity of art!

The self-reverence!

She continued to laugh as she made her way to her empty home. There was a swarm of people outside, waiting to read her facial expression and report back to media outlets on what it might mean.

Meaning was forever being extracted.

Someone noticed Sara. The throng began making its way towards her.

'Come on,' Aadhi said, grabbing her arm. 'I brought my car.'

She'd no choice but to follow. They broke into a run, eventually scrambling into Aadhi's black Volvo. There were flashes from the camera. Clicking. Smart phones swam in the air. Images of her would be all over the news.

'Fucking journos,' muttered Aadhi.

She looked at him pointedly, as she took off her cap.

'I'm not like *them*. Grabby bastards . . . Where can I take you? Put an address in the phone.'

Sara hesitated. Eventually, she tapped in her dad's address.

Aadhi drove past a silent sit-in – a circle of peace, people liked to call it, letting out energy to promote global well-being. There was no accounting for certain beliefs. Queues of people stretched out for what seemed like miles, outside a cluster of marquees. These were the fiscally accessible version of the Silent Room. Scattered around them were homeless people. It was an established fact that people were more willing to donate money after a silent session. Tranquillity towards the self often translated into tranquillity towards others.

'It's something, isn't it?' said Aadhi.

Now they drove past the flashing blue lights of an ambulance. The sirens respectfully switched off.

'This isn't a vanity project,' Aadhi said, his eyes still on the scenes outside. 'We wouldn't be doing our job if we didn't get your perspective – in some form or another.'

We.

'Roxy told me about the letters. To your mum.'

Sara whipped her head around. Why she was any longer surprised by Roxy was beyond her.

They approached her dad's house and Aadhi switched the engine off.

'It's a part of your story and the documentary needs to explore the most important aspects of your life.'

Sara undid her seatbelt, opening the door without looking. A car blared its horn as Aadhi yanked her back inside.

'*Jesus*, Sara. Don't get yourself killed.'

Why hadn't Roxy come? If she was going to betray Sara entirely, the least she could do was have the courage to face up to it. Sara couldn't believe what a cliché her supposed friend had turned out to be: someone who claimed to care about Things, but only so far as it affected her.

'I won't insult your intelligence,' he added. 'We're putting the spotlight on how damaging Non-Verbalism is, and like it or not, you're at the centre of it. There's no reason you should help us, but I know you are a woman of integrity.'

Sara scoffed at that.

'How is our documentary meant to be honest without the woman who instigated it all? But, listen, whatever happens, it *is* getting made. Will you be a part of it?'

Eventually, he spoke again: 'You created a spark and it's changing the world.'

She wanted to say that the world had always been on fire, so why should she be the one burnt at the stake? Metaphorically speaking.

Until the Victoria Park incident, she had trusted Roxy almost more than Henry. There was something between them which needed no explanation. Sara had shared those letters with Roxy, thinking she was safe handing over a part of herself, but in the end, all she had handed over was control.

'Look. I'll ask questions and you . . . find a way to answer?'

How could she ever, in good conscience, now extend this control to such a man?

She removed her sunglasses.

Aadhi looked at her, as if trying to gauge what she was thinking. The last time they had spoken he'd barely glanced her way.

She held his gaze, wielding all the power of her silence, feeling it coalesce in that moment.

When you say no, come hell or high water, you mean it.

Non-Verbals Assert Human Rights Across Globe

Julie Snow, *The Expert*, Aug 2021

Non-Verbals are facing increased discrimination within private companies and the public sector. Protesters around the world have taken to the streets, demanding that institutions do more to accommodate Non-Verbals. In a press conference last night, the British Prime Minister Harold Fernsby said:

'We respect all ways of life but we must discuss the necessary issues in order to maintain the foundation of democracy upon which this country is built.'

The PM came under attack in an open letter written by The Verbal Collective – a group advocating for Non–Verbal support – which stated:

'Harold Fernsby's assertion that the issues can "be discussed" when the people to be protected are silent shows he has no understanding of the actual issues.'

Many Verbals in the workplace are refusing to communicate with Non-Verbals; parents are calling for segregated teaching; there's been a 21.5% rise in divorce rates compared to the same time period last year and despite an initial decline, experts are warning that in the last two weeks hate crime reporting is once again on a seemingly steep rise . . .

Subscribe to *The Expert* for just £1 a week.

208

Grace

Manchester, August 2021

Grace emailed a copy of David's letter to the only person she still trusted, with the message: *I need help.*

'Hi,' said Graham as she opened the door to him that same evening.

His tie hung loose around his neck, a grey pocket square peeping out of his navy suit. A familiar sensation bloomed in Grace. Graham, entering her home, brought with him the unfortunate relief of familiarity.

'Hey, you must be Benji.'

Benji, sitting on his beanbag, looked up from his comic.

'Well,' Graham said. 'Not sure how we're meant to do this if you're still Non-Verbal.'

Grace's silence seemed to expand the space around her – that it disturbed others gave her an odd sense of power.

'It's a nice flat,' he continued. 'More cluttered than I'd have thought. But it's like you. Unexpected.'

Grace indicated for Benji to go to his room. She jutted out her cheek as Benji rolled his eyes. He came and, instead of the kiss she'd expected, gave her a zerbit, laughing as he walked away.

She caught Graham staring at her.

'I wish you'd told me more about him. I thought we were friends enough for that.'

To be pitied was indeed pitiable. She fixed her gaze on him, attempting to assert some control.

'Since you're asking, yes, I'll have a cup of tea, thanks.'

He was seated on the chaise-lounge when she returned with two teas.

'So, you don't plan to stop? Despite this letter.'

She brought her file to the table, taking out letters of doctor assessments, which he skimmed over.

'These predate your Non-Verbalism. Under normal circumstances David wouldn't stand a chance, but things have changed. He has some nerve though.'

Graham was staring at her. Now would've been the time where she'd have made some quip. Anything to prevent him looking at her that way.

'Am I making you uncomfortable?'

She shrugged as if to say: I won't be moved.

'Come back to work,' he said, surprising her. 'We accommodate Non-Verbals now you're everywhere. The lettered and semi-Non-Verbals, that is. Thirty-three per cent, according to our latest figures.' He paused. 'I advocated for integration . . . I mean, what would we do if we lost more lawyers like you? We've got employees using new speech pattern software that's been released. And given how many clients are Non-Verbal, it's working well . . . Though the whole thing's still bizarre.'

She raised her eyebrows.

'You'd be the first to say it if you weren't practising it yourself. Having financial security will help your case. And how long do you think you'll last without a voice? You, Grace Jenkins, who always says things worth hearing.'

Now, he leant so far forward he was in danger of falling off the sofa.

'At least it made you smile. Anyway,' he continued, standing up. Grace got up too. 'We'll file a cross-application, then there'll be a hearing. You know the drill. Everything's changed,' he said. 'But it's still the same, you know?'

He seemed to tower over her, making her feel diminutive without feeling obscure. Ten years of motherhood had blurred her being. To not witness what should be normal milestones for your child, to not know what these should be, all had had the effect of erasing a part of her. But she felt herself flickering, like a film about to begin.

She placed one hand on his arm, the other hand on her chest.

He paused before replying: 'You know you're welcome.'

'Ms Jenkins, this is Benji's school. As you know there are concerns about Verbal and Non-Verbal integration. We are holding a Verbal-friendly meeting to discuss Hillingdon's approach to demands for segregation in school. Rest assured we are committed to providing you and Benji with the necessary support at a time like this. Non-Verbals will be provided with a feedback form to highlight their concerns, should they wish to use it.'

Grace listened to the message, so angry she could barely contain herself. Did Verbals know how long it had taken Benji to integrate into this school? Now they wanted *segregation*.

When she got to the refuge, one of the women, Julie, was singing: '*We are family, I got all my sisters with me*'. She high-fived Grace.

Grace laughed. She raised her eyebrows as if to say, feeling good today?

Julie replied, 'My husband couldn't believe the letter you sent him.' She pulled Grace into a hug.

Grace felt calmer as she made her way to the kitchen. She would go to the school meeting and have her say. Via a form.

'I wish she'd just *speak*,' she overheard Angie say. 'Personal beliefs are one thing. Where you practice it another.'

Grace cleared her throat.

Angie looked up.

Despite the success of Julie's letter, the previous afternoon Grace had spent three hours emailing instructions to volunteers to make phone calls that she could have made herself. Angie had a point. David's application would mean nothing if she transitioned into Verbalism. But something stuck in her throat. Her silence was not only bringing her closer to Benji

211

but also creating a space in which the women who *needed* to speak (sometimes to save their own life) were given the space to do so.

Grace made her tea and was about to walk out when Angie spoke. 'I'm not sorry for my point of view.'

Grace knew that if a person didn't expect you to respond, they'd say whatever the hell they'd like.

'I've lived through enough phases of women's silence to have to witness this.'

To break now, just to tell Angie that she could be a sanctimonious bitch would have been a little anti-climactic. Which political and personal priorities was Grace meant to reckon with in any given moment?

'It's an opinion,' said Angie as Grace walked out. 'God knows I've earned the right to it.'

But Grace had had enough of those. If she ever witnessed a world that was truly ready to listen, maybe it would be a world worth saving.

That night, David's letter, Graham in her home, Angie's voice, all played over in Grace's mind. It made for fitful sleep. Others would not dictate what she should or shouldn't do with her voice.

The next morning, she kissed Benji at the school gates and went to the printers, then on to a frame-setters. She strode into the refuge with a hammer, nails and an A3 glass-framed poster. She ignored the looks as she hammered a nail to the wall. She placed the frame on it. Grace looked around the room, specifically at Angie who had appeared at the banging.

'You haven't got permission to do that,' she said.

Fuck permission.

The women had crowded around the frame. It was Sara's letter with one sentence enlarged: '*The world's always been falling apart, but that's not to say I should fall apart with it.*'

Grace walked up to Angie and pushed the hammer into her hands.

Then she heard the volume on the television increase and turned around. BPH News flashed with images of protestors wearing masks and flooding Tiananmen Square in Beijing.

'*Crowds gather to protest their right to silence. The government has banned Non-Verbalism following its use as a tool for resistance among students, who are refusing to respond to authority figures in connection to the dissemination of Non-Verbal news from around the world, and its banned literature.*'

Each protestor's mask printed with '*Silence condemns more than loud accusations*'.

The police came in with tear gas and armour, beating back the voluntarily voiceless, the crowd surging in its fight to move forward. People around the world were witnessing it in quiet dismay.

(It was the moment in which many Verbals wondered why they lived in such fear of deliberate silence. And when people in authority recognised its stark, violent power.)

Unedited: *The Movement . . .*

Colm Murphy: Civil Servant
Economist and political analyst
Verbal

Colm: I had been warning officials since May, they
should have been paying more attention to Non-
Verbalism. If they didn't prepare to take action
early on if it spread – which, as we now know it
has – it could have long-term economic ramifications.
We have been plotting business activity against the
rise of Non-Verbalism over a period of three months,
taking into account key periods of NV surges and are
now starting to see its very real economic impact on
financial markets. For the first time since May 2021
the S&P index has dipped below 4,000; this has been
led by a decline in retail and media stocks. Twitter
has fallen to below $40 a share. In May 2021, before
the era of Non-Verbalism, it was a $50bn company, now
it's $33bn. There are other signs that traders are
concerned about. Gold, the traditional haven in times
of uncertainty, has rallied 9% in the last 3 months.
The authorities are being forced to look into this,
as it's having an impact on consumer confidence. If
the government could announce more definitive public
policies, gaining people's trust, this could help

decrease Non-Verbalism and thus *increase* consumer confidence.

Aadhi: In your opinion, could Sara Javed potentially help to stop Non-Verbalism by breaking her silence?

Colm: Who? Oh, Javed, yes. There has been a negative impact in a short space of time, but there's an opportunity to turn things around. The government *has* to take into consideration the driving forces behind Non-Verbalism; political ennui; health – including, substantially, addressing our mental health crisis; celebrity trends and influencers. They should ensure that Non-Verbalism is accommodated in the workforce.

Pause

Nevertheless, yes, Javed breaking her silence could hold strong sway on the social psyche, which could significantly help avert the coming economic crisis.

Sept 2021

Government Proposes to Raise Taxes for Non-Verbals

Sunil Shah, *The Ward*, Sept 2021

Conflicting reports about the proposal to raise taxes on Non-Verbals has resulted in outrage and a complete lack of confidence in the government. Statistics from the recent leaked report: The Non-Verbal Papers, *stated that 69% of Non-Verbal households are in a high-earning bracket yet are contributing 53% less to the economy than Verbals – and using this reasoning, the government apparently feels justified in proposing a bill – one they will attempt to pass as quickly as possible while they still have a majority – to increase taxes on Non-Verbals based on the household's median income . . .*

Is such a discriminatory taxation truly the answer for our struggling economy?

For detailed political analysis, follow our live updates.

Zainab

Glasgow, September 2021

When Kashif came home after a session in the Silent Room, he took Zainab's hand and sat her down next to him on the bed.

'What is it?' she asked, eventually.

He squeezed her hand.

'I don't know what I'm meant to say.'

Nothing.

'I have to prepare dinner,' she said, finally, and went to get up but he pulled her back and touched her cheek.

Eventually, after some confusion, she found herself talking. She told him about school, which boy was pretending to not have a crush on which girl, which parent, in her opinion, deserved a place in hell, for a short period of time, at least.

'I like you a lot more now you're silent,' she said when he stood up.

It was a slip of the tongue.

'You never really listened before. And we never . . . *you* never . . . The way you are in bed now.'

He stared at the ground, his hands on his hips. He remained like that for a few moments before walking out of the room. Zainab's phone flashed. It was Suleiman.

'You know not to call me at this time,' she whispered. 'What if Kashif had seen?'

'I don't care. I need to see you again.'

'Not for a few days.'

'Please Zainu. I *need* you.'

'To forgive was to change, and vice versa,' Zainab had read in *Woman in Waiting*. That Zainab should be the perpetrator of pain was as confusing as it was unwholesome.

She insisted on meeting Suleiman in the car. Meeting in a hotel would lend itself to too much desire – she had become a slave to herself. And wasn't the exercise of restraint the ultimate freedom? She thought of her parents. What leaving her husband would do to them. Before she'd had a *cause*. But what about now? Kashif with his kinder manner. Was he finally understanding what it was to be a husband? Did he have regrets? Was it Zainab's responsibility to forgive? The lines were beginning to blur and she wasn't sure where the distinction between duty and sacrifice lay.

Suleiman had parked up on a side street a few minutes' walk away from this month's tea party location. The rain was pelting down for the ninth day in a row.

'Kashif hasn't changed just because he's silent.'

But what if Suleiman was wrong?

Zainab wasn't blameless with all the cheating and lying. Her redemption, unfortunately, began to feel intertwined with her husband's.

'I'm putting a deposit down on a house,' said Suleiman. 'Once you get your passport there'll be somewhere for us to go. It won't be easy, but nothing worth having ever is.'

After years of such protracted waiting, why did everything feel it was now moving too fast? Eventually the purity of the union would outgrow the shame and guilt from which it was created. Surely.

Zainab's conviction wavered. The abandoned prayer mat filled her with a latent dread. She began to fear a reckoning. She took her hand away from his.

'Why are you so distant lately?' Suleiman leant in closer, whispering in her ear. 'Has he been . . . touching you the way I do? Is that why?'

She had to force herself to move away from him. 'I have to go.'

'Hang on.' He grabbed her wrist. 'Answer my question.'

All these parts of her life and body to which people felt they had a right. God had been her one constant, and she had relinquished that in favour of her own desire. It had not been the liberation she sought.

'I have a right to know, don't I?' He gripped her wrist tighter.

What if Zainab had been *determined* to stop Kashif on their wedding night? What if she had not given into her own desire with Suleiman? Had her temperament – her personal brand of Non-Verbalism – written her destiny?

'Then ask it without attacking me,' she exclaimed.

Suleiman released her. Zainab never raised her voice.

'*Attacking* you?'

She held her wrist, disgusted now by her physical and moral weakness.

'I'm sorry. But men need reassurance too.'

'I'm late,' said Zainab, opening the car door.

She opened her umbrella and hurried towards the tea party. Suleiman followed her to the corner of the main road. He caught up, wet and dishevelled, and pulled her towards him. Her umbrella lowered. He kissed her and she was ashamed at how much it aroused her.

'You love me, don't you?' He grabbed her face. 'Don't you?'

'I need to be alone.'

His face contorted in confusion. 'Zainu . . . *I love you.*'

But what, after all, did that have to do with anything?

'Where's Saba?' Tahera sauntered over and sat next to Zainab.

'She's *actually* become a Non-Verbal,' cried one of the wives.

Tahera's laughter pierced Zainab's mind. 'That'll cut Glasgow's noise pollution in half. Every new Non-Verbal brings Fernsby closer to getting ousted. Thank God.'

'Silent weekends with the husbands is pretty great though,' said another wife.

'*Please,*' replied Tahera. 'Another reason to have no accountability. That bloody new age imam.

'Tell me I'm wrong,' said Tahera to Zainab.

'Zainab never says a bad word about anyone.'

'She might as well be a Non-Verbal.' Tahera leant into Zainab and lowered her voice. 'It'd make it easier to keep secrets.'

Zainab felt her face flush. She had to get home. She *should* tell Suleiman they were over. But how? She *should* believe that Kashif would never go back to who he had been. But why?

After the party Tahera insisted on dropping Zainab home, the car radio tuned to the news.

'*A petition against the discrimination of Non-Verbals in the UK workplace has garnered over 82,000 signatures—*'

'You must have an opinion on all of this, given Kashif's an NV,' said Tahera.

'My opinion doesn't change things.'

'You're wrong.' Tahera sighed. 'Everyone and their arse has an opinion, yes, but that doesn't mean it doesn't change things.'

She parked up outside Zainab's house.

'Thank you for the lift.'

'Wait,' said Tahera, holding her arm. 'I didn't drive twenty minutes out of my way to let you go that easily. I saw you. It was a stupid place to kiss a man you're not married to.'

Zainab's felt the bile rise.

'He's good looking,' said Tahera. 'Of course it's more than that. I mean, look at you: educated, self-effacing . . . compliant. Which makes the whole thing even more . . . Anyway.'

Zainab's heart thudded. An unravelling had begun, she couldn't even hear her own breathing.

'This is what you do,' Tahera continued. 'You go back to your husband and you *never* look back.'

Zainab should have nodded. 'Why should I settle for that?' she said instead.

'Look at that. Turns out there is a fire in there. Kashif's a decent guy. Basic, but you can't have it all.'

Tears welled up, Zainab's problem, among many other things, was that she cried too readily. An exemplifier of a soft heart. Or weak one. The memories were impossible to shed. They came back to her now like a bolt, inducing nausea and a healthy dose of misplaced self-hatred.

'What is it?' Tahera peered at her, as if trying to discern the meaning behind Zainab's look. 'He's been good to you, no?'

Zainab remembered the promise of life before her wedding night, how quickly things had changed. Sometimes, she would look back on it like a cold, hard fact and move on. Sometimes it would make her throw up. Forever pregnant with this humiliation.

'Let me go, please.'

Always seeking permission. Always waiting to receive it.

'Look at me, Zee. Tell me.'

Zainab shook her head, tears falling freely. The idea that someone might understand loosened something within her, but not her tongue. She could not stand the way Tahera stared. Zainab started to sob.

'Zee,' Tahera whispered, bringing her into a hug. 'What happened?'

Zainab's body heaved, her mouth unable to move, unable to speak.

How did one exorcise memories which clung like second skin?

'Did he do something?'

Zainab found herself nodding as the memories flashed through her mind. Experiences that turned her into someone she no longer recognised.

'He . . . he just . . .'

'What?' asked Tahera.

Zainab could not say the words. She did not know what they might be. 'I'm sorry,' said Zainab. 'I don't know how . . . but it was wrong. It was all wrong, but I—'

'You couldn't what? What couldn't you do?'

'I couldn't stop him,' sobbed Zainab.

Tahera held her until the sobs subsided.

Zainab eventually extricated herself. 'I didn't know *how*.'

'Are you saying—'

'Nothing. Don't worry. Ignore me.'

'Look at me . . . Did he hurt you?'

Zainab looked at her lap and nodded. Minutes passed between them. Tahera stared ahead, her eyes wet. 'Take this tissue. Wipe your eyes.'

'I didn't mea—'

'It's OK,' Tahera interrupted. 'Just tell me, so I don't get it mixed up. He made you do things you didn't want?'

There was a long pause.

Zainab nodded.

'OK, now tell me. What are your choices?'

Zainab must have looked confused.

'You can't leave him yet, you don't have your passport. But if you carry on like this then it won't end well.'

'Maybe I don't care how it ends.'

Tahera tapped her manicured fingertips on the steering wheel. 'Does anyone else know about it? Suleiman?'

Zainab shook her head.

'Here, look . . .' Tahera wiped the smudged kohl from under Zainab's eyes. For the first time, Zainab wondered who Tahera was. What secrets was she living with? Zainab had never taken the time to consider her as anything other than what she appeared to be.

'Now, I don't say this lightly – but you could go to the media. We could make a noise. Get you support—'

'Who am I, Tahera? Nobody.'

'Look at you,' replied Tahera. 'We could reach out to those die-hard feminists, hashtag me too . . . If you go public, you could get your stay and leave that fucker altogether.'

Zainab started at the way Tahera spoke about Kashif. She'd never use such language herself, but yes, that is *exactly* what he was. So why was she intent on forgiving him?

'No. *No*. To have to *tell* people . . .'

Tahera grabbed her hand. 'Sorry. I'm sorry. I know. I'm just . . . I'm reliving what I wish *I'd* done.'

'You—'

'Look at me.' Tahera took Zainab's face between her hands, made her meet her gaze. 'You understand this *isn't* your fault?'

Zainab barely nodded. Surely there was some accountability? Could she have forced him to stop? She could have told someone.

'No.' Tahera's tone was firm. 'You understand that this *is not your fault*? You will *not* spend the rest of your life blaming yourself. He won't take that away from you too.'

Zainab felt her tears resurface, but she nodded.

'You keep telling yourself that every single day. One day you'll believe it.' Tahera let out a small laugh, and not because she found something funny. 'Trust me when I tell you that when the time comes, you *will* care how it ends. Only, Zee, if you don't do something now, you might not have any choice in it.'

Unedited: *The Movement . . .*

Gerard Lincoln: Social Activist
Leader of Occupy Silence
Semi-perm Non-Verbal

Aadhi: What is Occupy Silence?
Gerard: A sub-movement of The Silent Movement. Engineered to consolidate Non-Verbalism, highlight inequality, bring the 1% to account - Non-Verbals are challenging meritocratic structures.
Aadhi: In what way?
Gerald: You want people to work? Well, we'll do it on *our* terms. This abundant consumerism was crushing our conscience.
Aadhi: What about the long-term economic effects?
Gerard: You think society is fair right now? We've been given a moment where we can actually *change* things. This government's incompetent and the proposed taxation on Non-Verbals is prejudice in action.
Aadhi: What alternative do you propose to the current structure?
Gerald: What people like me and members of Occupy Silence are fighting for: more healthcare funding, a rehabilitative justice system, a welfare state that doesn't leave people homeless.
Aadhi: How exactly will Non-Verbalism bring this about?

Gerald: Bacclay has been sidelined for his views for too long. People are finally paying attention. We can build on this momentum and finally have a nation for the people, by the people. We, and all our allies, are going to fight each obstacle put up against us, every single step of the way.

PART THREE

PART THREE

ULTIMATUMS

Sara

London, 2020

'Great news,' Kat exclaimed.

Sara started.

She took off her headphones. They were backstage at a student festival in Victoria Park. A turnout ranging from six hundred to a thousand people wanting to be inspired. She had been scrolling through her phone, following the event's hashtag.

Sara was now expected to speak about, but not limited to; race, gender, class, identity.

Was she a feminist? What kind?

Did she consider herself Muslim? Liberal? Secular?

Sara, quite frankly, considered herself exhausted.

Apparently, she had a social responsibility to speak for people without a voice.

So she had spoken about what everyone wanted.

Writing as a woman of colour.

Writing from a working-class background.

She spoke until she was moved by neither poem nor plight.

Until she had told Kat that she would no longer speak about such things.

When Sara told Roxy, sitting in a coffee shop, how she felt, Roxy looked at her in agitation.

'God, Sara, where's your *fire*?'

The question had been demoralising. Nevertheless, she replied, 'Sodden.'

Roxy ignored her. Since the publication and success of *An Unveiling*, Roxy talked a lot about purpose and self-care, triggers and 'changing the narrative'.

Sara wondered if Roxy would ever change hers. It had not been a generous thought.

Sara had, ultimately, warned Roxy against publishing the book.

'Did you hate it?' Roxy had asked, the colour rising to her cheeks.

'No . . . *Hate* is too ubiquitous a wor—'

'Sara. This is my *life* you're talking about.'

Sara placed her hand on Roxy's. 'And you have so much to say, I know. But I once wondered whether I should write about my mother. I'm glad I didn't. It could've defined me as a writer.'

She didn't add that she had had better sense and sensibilities, than to tailor her grief for public consumption.

'Maybe I don't want to write like you.'

Sara removed her hand. 'This isn't personal. I care about your career. *You.*'

'What could be more personal than a fucking memoir, Sara?'

'Yes. You're right. Of course. What I'm saying, very inarticulately, is that one story can define a person. Take away nuance. And *you* are nuanced. Life is long. Books are short.'

'*I'm reclaiming my narrative,*' said Roxy indignantly. 'Not everyone's as *mild-mannered* as you.'

'OK.' Sara pursed her lips. 'But just because you don't agree with my *mild-manner* doesn't mean it's flawed.'

'Yeah. Well. Same.'

Their goodbye that day had been stilted. It took Sara at least twenty-four hours to reason with herself that Roxy was young and Sara had, after all, by her comments, suggested she didn't like her book. Sara could understand that devastation, so she had called Roxy to apologise. That she hadn't put things very well, that she was imposing her own ideas of what one should write about upon Roxy.

That, of course, the book *should* be published.

Roxy, begrudgingly accepted, repeated how her story felt too pertinent to their time and too essential to her own healing to remain locked up in a drawer. She was heralded by friends and literary acquaintances as being so important that her self-importance – understandably, given how she had felt the lack of it her whole life – had ballooned. The book's success was proof that Sara had been wrong.

Sara had celebrated with Roxy, commended her on the features and interviews, but when Roxy asked questions like: *Did I come across OK?* Sara couldn't lie.

Roxy came across as a worthy bore. A relentless victim.

'Don't ask me,' Sara laughed. 'I'm useless and have to be dragged into doing those things.'

The laughter had fallen flat.

Sara was perhaps lacking in courage, but how would Roxy handle her telling her the truth? Honesty often turned a perfectly fine relationship on its head. Sara's new book – *The Stories We Told Ourselves* – was about the price of honesty. And, ultimately, its necessity.

When Sara was with Roxy's friends, she noted how they often talked about compassion, and then didn't seem to notice the irony of their collective outrage when someone dared to have an opinion contrary to theirs.

They'd look at her, expectantly. Where was *her* rage?

Her self-containment was a mark against her.

These people *thought* they had fire, but, to Sara, all they expelled was smoke.

Now, on this autumnal day, Sara looked out in to the crowd, splayed on the grass with their coffees and street food, for Roxy. She was worried about the inanity of her speech. Despite everything, Roxy's presence would fortify her.

'You always feel like this before an event,' said Kat, who knew her well enough by now, 'and it's always great.'

Which, to Sara's mind, increased the probability of the next one being a failure.

'Anyway, are you ready for *news*?'

'What?'

'You've been longlisted for The Mildred Aitken Award,' Kat exclaimed.

Sara stared at her. Kat laughed.

'*What?*'

'It's *true.*'

'Oh . . .' whispered Sara. '*Oh.*'

She had only ever imagined what she would feel upon hearing such news, but no imagining, in that moment, was equal to the reality. Sara threw herself upon Kat, hugging her, in such a fit of unusual emotion that it shocked both of them.

'Are you *sure*?' Sara asked.

'No, Sara, I made a mistake.'

How could she ever have doubted her speech? *Herself*? Sara found her eyes filling with tears.

'Penelope's coming to celebrate. Preparing the fireworks,' added Kat.

Kat took pictures of the swelling gathering and Sara. 'Hashtag exciting news to come . . .'

'Oh,' she said, 'Roxy's posted on Instagram that she's here.'

Sara had to tell Roxy. Despite the awkwardness between them, their difference of opinion that seemed to get more pronounced every day, Roxy was the one who'd understand what this meant.

Sara walked on to the stage to cheering and applause. The crowd no longer felt oppressive. Never had Sara felt such *fire*.

She read out her speech, ending with the final line that seemed to rouse people: 'Because your experience is not necessarily in line with the truth. In the end you own your words as much as you own yourself.'

Sara had read the line so many times that it had ceased to mean anything to her. But the audience burst into applause.

She took a seat for the Q&A, looking for Roxy. Hands shot up. A roving mic made its way to someone.

Sara tried to answer questions with a smile. Generally, her perspective was aligned enough with her audience's so as not to cause controversy, but they were *so* tiresome.

How did she get published?

What was her opinion on the rise of the right-wing?

Where did she get her inspiration?

What advice would she give new writers?

Here, she paused.

'Be good at listening. Lean out of what you know and try to understand others.'

This, inconveniently, made her realise that she had been living in opposition to what she was saying. That she had a mounting contempt for people. So acute that she wore her headphones all day. Wasn't writing meant to be a perpetual advocate for humanity?

Her own hypocrisy brought on a shortness of breath. She scanned the audience for Roxy, and just when she thought she might have to get off-stage, there was her friend, grabbing the mic.

'Sara,' Roxy began.

Here was the person who had settled Sara's nerves at her first public event, the re-enforcer of the belief that Sara had the right to be on stage. Some people in the crowd seemed to recognise Roxy. A few started recording.

Sara did not have contempt for humanity. Roxy *was* humanity. Just because they differed on what someone's voice should mean, it didn't mean neither deserved one.

'You know I've been a huge fan of your work, and you, having been my mentee and inspired my own bestseller – *An Unveiling* – in so many ways,' Roxy began. 'Since there are loads of students here, can you tell us about the struggles of being raised in a single-parent household, as well as from a working-class household and being a woman of colour?'

Roxy knew Sara no longer talked about these things. Had always generalised even when she did. To construct a narrative around her struggles was to diminish them. Which in turn diminished her. She had developed an especial distaste for that sort of thing and refused to do it anymore.

'I prefer to focus on the privilege of being in an environment that cultivated knowledge.'

This, she understood, was not rousing. Audiences demanded inspiration, not truth.

Roxy was still gripping the mic. It always had been hard for her to let go.

'Don't you think that you faced *specific* challenges which are worth talking about?'

'Not to five hundred people,' said Sara, attempting a laugh. *What was Roxy doing?* 'We've become too obsessed with our own experiences. Mistaken navel-gazing for critical analysis. We give opinion as if it were fact.'

'Our *experiences*,' Roxy emphasised, 'colour the lens through which we see our reality.'

There was scattered applause.

'I question the need for public catharsis.'

'The need for our stories to be heard?' questioned Roxy. 'People are *hungry* for new narratives.'

'People,' said Sara, trying to get it through to her dear friend, 'are hungry for attention.'

Had Sara never been guilty of the same?

'The commodification of victimhood from a certain group of people, even section of society, has fooled everyone into thinking they're activists; we should be careful about whether it's a cause we're passionate about, or simply serving one's own ego.'

There were disapproving murmurs.

'Are you saying that people from marginalised backgrounds who voice their pain are driven by ego?' asked Roxy.

Sara was so taken aback by the conflation that she had to take a moment. That moment, by any onlooker, might have read like guilt.

Sara stared at Roxy and her capacity for wilful misinterpretation. She never had been receptive to being cornered. Labelled. Defined.

'Don't you support them?' added Roxy.

Sara clenched her fists. 'Not when they have no talent.'

Instead of celebrating her longlisting with Penelope and Kat, they'd set-up a Zoom crisis management meeting.

'Ugh, your *headphones*,' said Henry, as soon as Sara entered the flat.

But she was scrolling through Twitter, Instagram, Facebook, the tagged pictures of her, vitriol and victimhood.

'How can people think it's a good idea to reduce storytelling to a *single* one, about *themselves*?'

'You're being shouty,' said Henry.

'Roxy's *questions*. She made it sound as if I don't care.'

'About?'

'*People*,' replied Sara.

'But do you? Really?'

'What?'

'Care. Caring isn't your brand.'

Did her husband really believe Sara to be lacking in empathy? *Was he right*?

'Can you *not* talk about me as if I'm an ad campaign,' she retaliated.

'But you are. For what a woman of colour with your background can achieve.'

If her mum hadn't given her up, Sara wouldn't have had to put up with this shit.

She looked at her phone.

@BoobBludgeon

Shocking words @Sara_Javed saying marginalised people have no talent! Shame a brown author wants to keep the success for herself. Abhorrent. #binherbooks #Victoriaparkgate

💬 6   ⬆ 56   ♡ 207

@LeenMal

@Vicparkbookfest do you allow your panellists to personally attack audience members?? @Sara_Javed

💬 24   ⬆ 27   ♡ 125

That was author @RoxyHuss @LeenMal! Bestselling author of An Unveiling, As a woman from a marginalised background buy her book to support her!

💬 28   ⬆ 212   ♡ 1,002

Sara's contemptuous scoffs punctuated the assassination of her person in 280 characters.

Abhorrent.

She had begun to worry that all she had felt recently, perhaps for years, had been a latent irritation. Today she had been forced to the point of feeling. It rattled her sense of self. Aadhi Sathar's words resonated: *Javed's work might have the intention of enlightening others, yet she can't even convince herself of her own claims.*

Sara checked her phone again. Roxy had *liked* the tweet. And liked or retweeted every subsequent one relating to Sara being a sell-out, apologist, privileged, a bully. There were demands of retraction. Explanation. Condemnation.

@RoxyHuss

Triggered by SJ's cruel comments today. Hurt and confused. The anger will come too that a mentor and friend could betray me and marginalised writers this way. #Victoriaparkgate

💬 23   ⬆ 41   ♡ 509

Sara's hands trembled. That's not what she had meant! Why didn't Roxy pick up the phone, instead of this *performative pain.* For a moment Sara considered calling Roxy, telling her she'd got it all wrong, but the way Roxy had pressed her . . .

Her phone rang.

'I watched you online . . . you really must be clear about where you stand on certain issues.'

It was Lily.

'How could she think I was talking about her? And she *knows* I'm private about things.'

'She was provocative. But Afzal's always told you to be careful of your tone when you're irritated. It comes across condescending.'

'*Lily.*'

'I know you didn't mean to be, but you're being called racist. Consider your father.'

'I didn't say anything against marginalised people. *I'm marginalised.*'

'Yes well, oh, look . . . Ah. I think perhaps it's a good idea to stay away from Twitter for a bit.'

Sara searched frantically through the Victoria Park Gate hashtags..

@RoxyHuss

Thanks @LeenMal. Support appreciated! This is how minorities thrive. SJ lost her roots and it saddens me #Victoriaparkgate

☐ 490   ⬆ 110   ♡ 1,996

'*Roots?*' Sara was confounded. 'Roxy knows I have no roots.'

There was a long pause.

'Darling. You're rooted to us.'

Sara's voice came out in a whisper. 'I know. I'm sorry.'

Lily said it was no matter. Then she instructed Sara to write a piece for *The Ward*, clarify her stance, by which time messages about Sara had been retweeted a hundred more times.

It took some effort to stop her voice from breaking.

'Why? Just to calm everyone's reactionary perspective?'

'That's your job,' said Lily.

'To pander?'

'To push the boundaries of thought.'

Had Sara's words ever done that?

Her stories had gone from elucidating ideas to mystifying them.

Thoughts had become impenetrable; arrogance sold as conviction. To be judged on one's words and not their actions seemed a bizarre betrayal of the human mind. She was living in a culture of reverse Show Don't Tell.

And no one really wanted to push the boundaries of their *own* thoughts. Which is why, right now, Sara felt like pushing people off a cliff.

As soon as she'd put the phone down, she called her dad.

'Don't grip so hard for control.'

'What *do* I grip?' she asked.

'Unfortunately your husband is white. That is a mark against you.'

'Thanks, Dad.' She looked around and realised that Henry had left the room.

'Dad . . .?'

'Yes?'

'I think it's time. Will you look for her?' There was a long pause. 'My mum.'

'You're sure?'

'Yes. I'm sure.'

She put the phone down, unsettled, as she clicked on the Zoom link.

'A storm in a teacup,' said Penelope.

'Only Kat knows how abhorrent I am,' said Sara, referring to the tweet.

Kat managed to laugh. 'I'll write out an apology for you.'

'But I didn't say anything wrong—'

'Next week, this'll all be forgotten,' interjected Penelope. 'But there's a certain expectation of authors—'

'You're up for the prize,' added Kat. 'Don't jeopardise it.'

'It could affect that?' Sara's heart sank.

'Your work is also you,' said Penelope.

Life's choices didn't seem to be as vast as Sara had once thought. To have such shiftable principles surely weren't deserving of that name.

Yet all actions had their consequences.

Grace

Manchester, 2020

Grace had been working later than usual on her Brexit divorces: couples whose love or sense of reconciliation wasn't strong enough to withstand their ideological differences. A political symptom of the cleaving of lives.

She came home to find her mum and Benji lying on top of his bed, reading a comic book.

'Is that the evil one then?' asked Dede

Benji nodded.

'*Jesus*, that face.'

Benji looked at Dede with such adoration that Grace's heart swelled.

'Let's go out for ice cream,' said Grace. 'It's the weekend.'

They both looked up. Dede glanced at her watch and then at Benji, raising her eyebrows. He nodded emphatically.

At the door Benji remembered to get Tigger from his bedroom.

'Maybe it's time for me to accept that he just might *never* speak,' said Grace, watching him. They had tried so many ways, it had been so many years.

'You need to start balancing home and work better.'

'What?'

'Late night with Graham again,' said Dede. 'He's a good-looking man, but haven't you learnt anything about men? What are you looking to get?'

It had come as a surprise, that her mother's opinion mattered. That Grace's reflex response, in her own head anyway, was *love*.

241

'And I won't hear such talk about Benji. What if he heard?'

Guilt bloomed and grew tentacles. Grace had engineered a life of emotional freedom from everything but her son, yet here she was, dependent in adulthood on the woman from whom she was independent growing up, on love from a man who she would not trust – it had always led to disappointment. Without Dede, Grace might have coped, but at what cost? Sometimes she was sorry for not having been brave enough to find out.

Dede handed Grace a Sainsbury's receipt. 'For today's shopping. I know you like to keep account.'

Grace paused. Of course that was about money Dede had asked to borrow.

'It's ten thousand pounds. I just need to know what it would be for,'

'After how I've looked after that boy—'

Dede turned around to see Benji standing in the hallway with Tigger, his little face anxious. For a moment her expression revealed regret.

She was particularly lively at Taste It and had made Benji laugh so hard at one point he spat out his hot chocolate. Dede had then raised her own mug.

'Here's to a hopeful outcome for tomorrow's election,' she called out, loud enough for others to hear, not so loud as to be offensive.

A cheer erupted from one table. What was money when her mother could bring this much goodwill? When she brought such a smile to her son's face?

When Grace got home and put Benji to bed, she kissed his forehead.

'You love Grandma, don't you?'

He clutched his hands to his chest, scrunched his eyes tight and gave a goofy grin.

Grace laughed. 'Me too, kid. Me too.'

The following day Grace transferred ten thousand pounds into Dede's account. A week later, Dede disappeared once more from Grace's life.

Zainab

Glasgow, 2020

Zainab's mother had called to tell her about another cousin getting married.

'She was very clever catching that one.'

Zainab had witnessed women using the art of manipulation to get what they wanted from their men. It was, apparently, their power.

'I'm running late, *Ammi*.'

'Where are you going?'

Zainab was able to lie with impressive measure to everyone except her mum. When the proposal from Kashif's family had come her mother had said: 'To be a wife will be to make many compromises, but it's always been in your nature to make life comfortable for others.

'As for love, that comes after marriage, but you must feel that there is the promise of happiness.'

That her mum's happiness seemed to lie in Zainab's married life was a compromise she had not imagined.

Today, they had to meet in Suleiman's car because his parents would be home and getting a hotel all the time was expensive. He scrolled through Instagram.

'Is this why we met? So you could be on your phone?' Zainab was agitated. Perhaps she was due on her period.

'I *hate* not having a place where I can be with you.' He flung the phone on the dashboard. 'Sorry. I'm so lucky you're not like other women.'

'What kind of woman am I?'

He stared at her. 'You don't let your beauty or intelligence get to your head. And you're not all fiery and angry, like Tahera.

'A woman shouldn't be fiery in case she burns in hell?'

'What? That's not what I meant. Zainu, why are you being like this?'

'I get tired, too.'

'I know.'

'And fed up.'

'You're human,' said Suleiman

But, when she thought about it, she realised that he'd probably rather she wasn't.

Sara

London, 2020

An Open Letter from Sara Javed

TheBookBuyer.com

1 Nov 2020

*I want to share my deepest regret for my comments at the Victoria Park Book Festival. Which, not least given my own background, were unforgivable.
I offer my sincerest apologies for the pain I have caused – specifically to fellow writers who already struggle and have fought hard to have their voices heard.
I trust in books as a way to open minds and hearts and believe that the power of words should lie with all people, regardless of background. I have been, and always will be, an advocate for open dialogue.*

Kat had written the apology and Sara took her and Penelope at their word that it had worked.

There had been pieces written about the fiasco. Sara had received Direct Messages, strangers offering views on her views, calling her a slew of alarming names, and even a death threat or two.

It was expected that Sara would reach out and personally apologise to Roxy. Sara had texted her after the statement had gone out, clarifying that she had categorically not meant Roxy was without talent.

Sure Sara. Backpeddling to maintain your profile

Sara responded, asking how Roxy could think such a thing. She received her reply.

Because I know you.

That, Sara could not deny, hurt. Coming from someone who had read her letters to her mother. That someone could misunderstand her after she had revealed herself in such a way.

It only confirmed that attaching herself to others led to nothing but pain and disappointment.

She had attempted to forget her public faux-statement, but could not overlook its wording nor forget Roxy's message. And, though it had only been a few weeks, she could not ignore the lack of news thus far about her mother's whereabouts. Today, of all days, as she and Henry watched the general election unfold, and she checked her phone repeatedly, waiting for news about the award's shortlist, she thought it had all better have been fucking worth it.

Henry scoffed as he scrolled through Twitter. Scroll and exclaim. That was the routine.

Sara paced the room.

I know you.

And as for *open dialogue*! People were too consumed with their own monologues.

'—how can we *still* have the same government? *Everyone* is pissed,' said Henry, referring to the election results. 'Except my parents.'

'Ssh,' she said, almost instinctively.

Henry pulled his head back. 'I can't believe you shushed me.'

Sara's mind felt scrambled. She paced faster.

Her phone rang and her heartbeat quickened. The award. It had to be Penelope. Being shortlisted would root Sara to something real. She picked up.

'You just *shushed* me,' Henry said.

'*Beta*?' It was her dad.

'Oh,' she said.

'*My jaan.*'

He called Sara 'his life' during moments of acute emotion.

'I know the news is shit,' said Sara. 'But I'm waiting to hear about the shortlist . . . Dad? *Hello*?'

She looked at Henry, hands on his hips, staring at her.

Sorry, she mouthed.

'*Dad*?'

There was another pause. 'I found your mother.'

'What?'

'I'm sorry my *jaan* . . . She's dead.'

The news in the background, Henry's hovering shape, the confines of the walls restricting.

'What?' said Henry. 'What is it?'

Dead? She couldn't have died. That wasn't how the story was meant to go.

'Sara?' said Henry.

'Sara?' said her dad.

Another call came through.

'Dad, I have to go.'

'*Be*—'

She hung up.

'What's happened?' said Henry again, as she tapped her phone.

It was Penelope.

'We did it! *You've made the shortlist.*'

Everything blurred. Sara looked at her hands as if to ensure she was still present.

She could hardly make out the lines.

She awoke in the middle of the night, her sleep, along with hope, extinguished. Death had rather put her shortlisting in perspective. Ignoring

Henry's snores, Sara went downstairs. She stared at the spaces made oppressive by items that she'd never needed: the ottoman in the corner – courtesy of rights sold to France; the smart TV – royalty payments from her debut; the rose-green velvet sofa; pretentious art. Things bought in lieu of answers.

Sara's inclinations had outlived her mother.

She got out a bin bag. The more she looked for extraneous items, the more she found. It wasn't long before the bin bag was full.

'What *are* you doing?' Henry emerged from the shadows, in his boxers, rubbing his eyes.

'Clearing shit out.'

'At three in the morning?'

'Couldn't sleep.'

He stood there for several moments. 'Are you OK?'

She nodded.

'Just come to bed.'

'Not sleepy.'

He hovered. Eventually, she heard him go up the stairs. She carried on until the flat was neat and, most importantly, comprehensible.

The following day, Sara was in their bedroom, rummaging through her wardrobe. She found the shoe box in which she hid her journal. She thought it might induce her to cry.

She felt nothing.

'We're meeting your dad and Lily in twenty minutes,' Henry said, observing the clothes, shoes, accessories now in labelled boxes. 'Jyoti's coming too. Said she needed a meet-up after this news . . . Listen, I know yesterday was a blow. Let's talk about it. When we get back.

'What's that?' he asked, looking at her journal.

'Nothing.'

Sara changed and followed Henry downstairs. The mural behind him caught her eye. A 40 x 28 cm water-coloured with large grey-blue leaves and pale oranges. She had bought it to bring warmth to the home. What a notion.

'Sara? . . . *Sara?*'

'You never liked that mural, did you?' she asked.

'Can we talk about it over brunch?'

Sara supposed she would have to pay for that.

'*Sara?*'

'Oh, stop waiting around for me,' said Sara. 'For *things*. Make a fucking decision.'

'A decision?' he repeated. 'A *decision*? Fucking hell, Sara.' But she was too busy observing the darkened wall behind the mural's edges.

The front door slammed shut after him.

Sara got out her phone, finger hovering over Roxy's number. She would understand this. Despite Victoria Park. Despite everything.

The phone rang.

And rang.

And rang.

Until the call disconnected.

A few minutes later, she received a message.

I need some time to understand how you, my supposed mentor and friend, failed me. I guess people change. Just this once I want to put my needs ahead of someone else's.

Sara laughed. *The age of self-indulgence.*

'People don't change.' She flung her phone on the floor. 'They *die*.'

Which is when she realised that, ultimately, that's what life hurtled towards from the moment people were born – not fame nor fortune, not even family – only they hardly ever paused to realise it.

'I see why Henry thought I should come,' said her dad, walking into the now half-empty flat. He pulled her into a hug, squeezing her the way he used to when she had hurt herself as a child. 'Fate, *beta*.'

Sara snorted as she extricated herself from him.

'It's an interesting experiment,' he said, looking around the flat.

'All those *things*. What do they matter? . . . Do you know if I have any brothers and sisters milling around?'

'Two brothers. Both married. Both in America. I can get their details.'

Sara, as usual, wasn't sure how to feel about it. 'You'd think Henry would be able to handle this without your help.'

'I can't comment on weak men. I have little experience of them.'

'Helpful.'

'You know that old Chinese poem?' said her dad.

'Oh yes, that old Chinese poem, of course.'

'*Sara.*'

'Sorry.'

'Now, let me remember: *A bird gives a cry – the mountains quiet all the more.*'

'Am I the bird or the mountain?'

'Perhaps you're both.'

She looked at her dad's sparse grey hair, the lines etched into his forehead. He should've been enough. To yearn for something when she should be grateful for what she had felt like an ingratitude equal to sin.

'Or perhaps you're neither,' he added. 'That's not the point.'

'Do you regret it?' she asked. 'The life you could have had if I wasn't around, hampering things?'

He laughed. 'You are the single best thing I have done in my life. Don't ask me this question again. It's like asking if it would've been better to live without a leg.' He paused. 'Or heart.'

'Dad . . . It's just, sometimes I think you and Lily would still be together if—'

'*Beta*, sometimes we are sad because maybe we didn't know our mother, and sometimes because we didn't know ourselves.

'One day I hope you understand that you are tethered to nothing and no one, that who your mother is, or was, is an element of you, but not the whole. That is your greatest freedom.'

Sara felt tears sting her eyes. The pervading rootlessness needed an anchor, surely. She had tried to hold on to words and stories, but what did they mean in the end?

'And when, even for a moment, you tether yourself to people – the ones of your choosing – like I did with you . . . Ah, my *jaan*,' he smiled, 'that is life itself.'

A NECESSARY EVIL

BPH BREAKING NEWS

Government accused of double-crossing the British people

Dec 2021

A leak from the Confederation of Business suggests that the government plans to give incentives to companies who employ Non-Verbals. The leaked <u>CoB report</u> shows that Non-Verbals are more productive and 46% less likely to create issues in the workplace. Therefore, companies who employ them will be provided with government incentives, effectively discriminating against Verbals.

Non-Verbals had previously been threatened with higher taxation, with government highlighting the negative effect of Non-Verbalism on the economy.

The Chancellor of Exchequer stated: 'We urge Non-Verbals to help the economy by investing in market goods, and the run up to Christmas is the perfect time to show your support for your community. In the New Year we will move forward with increasing taxation on Non-Verbals. Because in order to invest in yourself, you must invest in your country.'

The government's mixed messages and hypocrisy about their long-terms strategy for Non-Verbals and Verbals highlights the question of their ultimate motive.

In the meantime, it is reported that almost 65% of the population of the West Coast in the United States is now socially Non-Verbal. Private sectors, such as hospitality and food, have incorporated Non-Verbalism into their workplace after the threat of a collective mass resigning.

For live updates about *The Silent Movement* click <u>here</u>.

Sara

London, December 2021

Sara went from marvelling at Aadhi's audacity to making the mistake of reading one article online. Her fingers did the rest, clicking on link after link about the leak, gaining all this knowledge without understanding its purpose. A clusterfuck of information not even relieved by Henry coming and taking more things. He had barely said two words to her, which was to be expected.

When the buzzer rang at one in the morning, Sara had been lying awake, muttering responses to each accusation, each accolade, to herself. She switched on the lights, looking out of the window. Had Henry come back? The rain thundered down, obscuring her vision. She picked up the receiver only to see a hazy, hooded figure through the camera.

'It's me,' came a voice. 'I know it's late and this is weird, but it's pissing out here.'

Sara's finger hovered over the buzzer. What on earth could Roxy have to say for herself? They hadn't even spoken since Victoria Park.

'*Please*? I want to talk.'

A combination of lack of sleep, a certain level of self-defeat and curiosity weakened Sara's resolve.

Sara buzzed her in.

Roxy relieved herself of her wet paraphernalia before walking in. 'Jeez. Where do you guys sit?'

Sara folded her arms, looking at the dishevelled Roxy who had walked into her life with the vastness of her disapprovals.

'Where's Henry? Slept through the buzzer?' She paused. Waited. 'I never doubted that you'd stick it out. Once you decide something . . .'

Sara tapped her wrist.

'Sorry, but this news about the leak . . . I don't know what to think. I can't sleep. You're on my mind *all* the time. I . . . . No. I won't apologise for what happened. I was speaking *my* truth.'

Sara scoffed.

'*Why are you still silent?*'

She couldn't believe it. All the voices, the news, the articles, had somehow congealed and were manifested in Roxy. She was here, in Sara's *home*, in the *middle of the night*, telling her *who* she should be.

Sara's breathing became erratic. *Deep breath through your nose – 1, 2, 3 – out through your mouth – 1, 2, 3, 4, 5.*

'Do you know how many people you're hurting? *An Unveiling* being a bestseller gave me something and I fucking used it. But you have *more* reach—'

Breathe deeper.

Breathe better.

'And after Victoria Park. How painful that was for me . . . It's just so selfish.'

'*Uggghhhh,*' Sara exclaimed.

Roxy stepped back. Sara raised her hands as if to shake Roxy.

The *presumption* that Sara was a mouthpiece for anyone other than herself.

She circled the room, looking for something, *anything*, to throw but she'd fucking *given everything away*. How could a person whom she had once loved be so fucking *self-obsessed*? A full *year-and-a-half* after Victoria Park, Roxy was *still* gripping on to it as a marker of her own victimhood. Situating her story at the centre of everyone's universe. Sara wanted to scream.

Plates! She had *plates!*

Sara threw open a cupboard and grabbed a white, china bowl. Turning around she propelled it across the floor, smashing it to pieces.

'*What the fuck.*' Roxy jumped back.

Sara got out a glass and flung it across the floor, shattering it.

'*Sara.* Have you lost your fucking mind?'

She got out plate after plate, glass after glass, hurling them at the wall. Roxy backed herself into a corner as Sara continued to smash and break and grunt, until it wasn't enough and she let out a scream that must have pierced Roxy's ears. The blood pumped to Sara's face and she wished she'd at least had a fucking chair, so she could break it against the splintered surface of the floor. But she could only hold on to herself.

She pressed the palms of her hands against her eyes, feeling the wetness on her face.

She felt a hand on her arm and jerked it away.

'*Sara,*' whispered Roxy.

She realised she was sobbing. A hand rubbed her shoulder.

'I didn't . . .' whispered Roxy.

Sara's head snapped up. Roxy's face was alarmed, pathetic. Sara pointed towards the door.

'Let me help you clear up,' Roxy said.

Sara jerked her finger towards the door again, but Roxy had already opened the kitchen cupboard and found binbags, dustpan and brush.

'Don't move. You're barefoot.'

Glass crunched under Roxy's shoes as she brushed aside the broken pieces of glass and china. Sara felt the beating of her heart slow. Her eyes were now dry. All she wanted was to sleep. The clinking and crunching seemed to go on forever, until Roxy knotted up the binbags and vacuumed the floor.

'I don't know what just happened but it doesn't look like Non-Verbalism's working out for you.'

If Sara had the energy, she would've flung a plate directly at Roxy.

'I know Aadhi's tried to get you on the documentary but I wanted to tell you about it personally. It's not like I owe you anything, so why do I feel like I *do*? You know I can't lie about the problematic views you've shared with me . . . You can speak to me about it. *This is your chance.*'

Sara's mind raced.

'I won't tell anyone about today. I wouldn't do that. But some things are bigger than you and me.'

Sara had so much to say to Roxy – to tell her that she couldn't believe she had ever respected, let alone loved her. That, actually, Roxy couldn't write for shit. What would it mean though if she gave into her very basic desire to be heard?

Sara turned around, plucked her journal from the kitchen counter and brandished it in Roxy's face.

Roxy looked at it and back at Sara. Eventually, she spoke. 'People want to understand you. It's part of the narrative.'

As if life was a book.

Sara dropped the journal and pushed Roxy so hard she almost fell to the ground.

'What the *fuck*, Sara . . . Unlike you, *I* have a sense of responsibility.'

Sara pushed her again.

'Sara! You're fucking hurting me.'

She pushed her back into the hallway, opened the front door and shoved Roxy out, slamming the door in her face.

'You've lost your mind, you know. You've fucking *lost* it!'

She was right. Sara *had* lost something. But she wouldn't find it here, in this godforsaken place that the world called civilisation.

Unedited: *The Movement . . .*

Henry Green: Screenwriter
Sara Javed's estranged husband
Verbal

Roxy: For purposes of full disclosure, I met with Sara recently. It didn't go well.

Henry: No. It never does when you disagree with her. The thing you have to understand is her single-mindedness. It got her far in her career, but her inflexibility became hard to live with.

Roxy: We want to clarify that you are now officially separated.

Henry: Yes. But I don't want to come across as a bitter ex. Just someone who knows - *knew* - her.

Roxy: How did this single-mindedness impact you?

Henry: We never had children, at her insistence, but I don't want to dwell on that. I've had therapy to move past it.

Her dad always put her on a pedestal though; then later on the success almost hardened her. Validation can do that.

Roxy: Would you say Sara is steely or stubborn?

Henry: Listen, her biological mother had given her away, her stepmother left when she was twelve . . . but Sara and her dad had a very co-dependent relationship. And he influenced her thoughts. If he didn't

260

like someone, you can bet that impacted how she saw them. Eventually, she thought everyone was stupid or ill-informed, entitled or privileged.

I know what people say about her and this movement - what she's supposedly achieved. But if you know her, then you know she's not an inspiration at all. She's a warning sign.

Is Bacclay the Leader to Guide us Through The Silent Movement?

Roma Dreyford, *The Snuff,* Jan 2022

Love him or hate him, Bacclay has been consistent in his approach to Non-Verbalism since its rise in May 2021. Nine months on and Prime Minister, Harold Fernsby, is hanging on to his position by a thread. The party seems incapable of establishing a concise way forward in addressing the economic issues. What's the truth behind the CoB leak? Is the government pro or anti-Non-Verbalism? And how do they intend to bring the nation together when their policies are consistently driving us apart?

In a recent interview with BPH News, Bacclay said: 'Let the government be clear and show the public their exact steps towards integrating Non-Verbalism into everyday life. Do they think it's going to magically go away? It is here to stay and it is the government's job to plan for this brave new world. They are failing because theirs is the old way. Ours is the new.'

For live updates about *The Silent Movement* click <u>here</u>.

Grace

Manchester, January 2022

Grace glanced at the social worker who had come to evaluate Benji. Her phone rang. She ignored it.

The social worker had been here for two hours. Observing Benji, observing Grace. Looking around their home, scribbling notes. It was bad enough that David had been given supervised visitation rights, but Grace was now the subject of scrutiny. Every time David smiled at Benji, ruffled his hair, Grace wanted to shout: *get the fuck off him.*

Of course, she had her constraints.

'His last speech therapy session seems to have been seven months ago,' said the social worker.

Grace gestured with her hands.

'You haven't taken him?'

Grace shook her head.

The social worker scribbled more notes.

Grace sat with Benji as they ate lunch together, under the social worker's watchful eye. She pointed out of the window to comment on the weather; sometimes they'd tap their fingers on the table to a tune; often they would flick through catalogues, pointed to the things they liked, giving each other the thumbs up or down.

Her phone rang again, this time she picked up.

'Ms Jenkins? Tap once if this is she.'

263

Grace tapped once.

'My name's Rebecca Craig and I wanted to know if you'd like to comment, in writing of course, on an article I'm writing about Non-Verbalism in families. I've had David Hodgkin respond . . . Hello?

'You can tap once for yes.'

Grace hung up.

Such levels of verbosity made the idea of Non-Verbalism feel like a fiction. What on earth could David contribute and why? Grace wondered how Sara Javed had retreated – how she lived in probable peace. To think that Grace had thought she could achieve the same.

The social worker stayed for the entire day, her shadow hovering over Grace and Benji, who scrunched up his nose at her.

Eventually, she left and Graham came over.

'How did it go?'

Grace shrugged. She wrote a short note to tell Graham about the phone call.

'Don't worry,' said Graham. 'It's to be expected. You're going to be OK.'

She turned away from him in an attempt to compose herself.

'Grace.'

He touched her shoulder. Benji was asleep. She put her hand on top of his, his body moved closer behind her.

'*Grace*,' he whispered. 'You're going to be OK.'

She turned around.

He moved closer. 'I know your life's complicated but since when have I shied away from complication?'

Why did she find it so hard to believe people?

Grace touched Graham's face, running her finger down the line of his jaw. What would it mean to let him into her and Benji's life, just for him to abandon them? Even as Grace's body stirred, she couldn't help but think how easily Dede had left. How much grief was Benji meant to suffer?

Grace felt too much in need and too much at a loss, and they both made for conflicting cohabitants. She shook her head at her own weakness. Even as she put her arm around Graham's neck and kissed him.

Graham waited for her to speak afterwards.

'You could make a man feel really bad about himself, you know,' he said.

She laughed.

'*Ow*. I should leave before you brutalise me.'

She should not have gone so rigid at the thought of him leaving.

Eventually, hesitant, he did leave. It had always been the way of things.

Unedited: *The Movement . . .*

Jyoti Patel: Author and activist
Sara Javed's friend
Anti-Non-Verbal

Jyoti: I thought I was being interviewed by Aadhi Sathar.

Roxy: I'm a huge fan of yours, I wanted to take this one.

Pause.

Jyoti: Thank you. That's very nice of you. It's women like you who change the world.

I want to be clear about my stance: I told Sara women have been silenced their entire lives and she's set us back a hundred years – Non-Verbalism is reinforcing patriarchal structures. How many more years must we fight? In some ways this documentary is in itself problematic. It's giving Non-Verbalism importance when we should be prioritising the women who *don't* have a voice. I'm furious. *We should all be.* We should be raging against injustice. Refusing to capitulate to Non-Verbalism. I will be nothing but an advocate for women until we are all equals.

Roxy: You were an advocate for Sara too, weren't you?

Jyoti: When I met her at a literary festival, we were on a panel together. She said: *I don't think I should be here.*

You know how many times I've heard women express this?

Every. Single. Time.

When will women believe they have a right to a stage?

Sara's writing was always called feminist but I wished we'd seen that in her as a person, not just words on the page.

But I cared about her. She was always a good friend. She listened. Even if you called her at three in the morning.

Roxy: But now she refuses to respond to the crisis. Despite many people trying.

Jyoti: Precisely. We are at a catastrophic point in history. I am sick to the stomach, wondering about the women who are being forced further into silence.

Roxy: Do you want Sara to break hers?

Jyoti: *Want?* It's not about *want*. It is a colossal, imperative, urgent fucking *need*.

Protest!

Harold Fernsby MUST resign!

Meet outside Downing Street, 22 Jan, 12pm
Verbals and Non-Verbals Welcome!

Zainab

Glasgow, January 2022

Between Suleiman, Kashif and the mad world, Zainab didn't have time to *think*. She met Suleiman – no mention of Tahera knowing about them. It no longer mattered. She had steeled herself for it, or she would talk herself out of her own misery, which was hardly an honest way to live.

'You can't do this.' Suleiman brought his chair closer to her. They were in a crowded café. Zainab had anticipated a scene like this. 'I love you.'

'I just need some time,' she said. 'Before it was different—'

'For once can't you do something for yourself?'

'I don't know if I'll stay with him. But I have to do things the *right* way—'

'You belong to me.'

'Suleiman.' She looked up then, voice firm. 'I belong to no one.'

'You're wrong. You will always be mine.'

The certainty with which he spoke dismayed and comforted her. But despite that and what Tahera had said, she would no longer be able to justify leaving Kashif to her family. One had to think about others.

Her moral hardwiring, in that sense, was impossible to reconfigure.

Before she left him, she had made it clear that they could no longer see each other. She entered the house, burdened with loss and the heaviness of duty.

The family was sitting in the living room. The news quietly playing in the background.

Zainab glanced at the clock. It was 4.30 p.m. Why was Kashif home this early?

'Where have you been?' asked Naz.

'I had chai with a mosque friend.'

Kashif was staring at the ground.

Her father-in-law looked grave.

Zainab's heart beat faster.

'We have always given you freedom,' said Naz. 'But someone has said something very serious about you. And why would anyone lie about such a disgusting thing?'

At that point, the floor was in danger of collapsing under Zainab and all her hopes – which she realised, no matter how trapped she felt, still existed. A long pause ensued, Zainab's manner, her very silence, admitting the guilt of her own sin.

'Such a quiet daughter-in-law you have, people said to me. How simple and pretty and—' With each word Naz's face contorted in contempt.

'We have called your parents,' said Iqbal. 'They have a right to know.'

A Breaking News banner appeared on screen but Zainab was trying to catch her breath.

'My poor son. Still silent,' said Naz.

Kashif looked up at Zainab. His expression of distress reminded her of what she had cheated on.

A man capable of crimes against her person, yet incapable of being anything other than a victim.

BPH BREAKING NEWS

Prime Minister Resigns

Jan 2022

The Prime Minister, Harold Fernsby, has announced that he is standing down as leader of his party with immediate effect. He will be succeeded by the current Secretary of State for Education Ruth Baynham. She inherits a legacy of indecision after the catastrophic introduction of higher taxes for Non-Verbals and converse support for companies employing them.

William Bacclay says:

'Gandhi once said: "Silence is part of the spiritual votary of truth . . ."
'I want to live in a place that promotes co-existence. Nations like Sweden and New Zealand have had high success rates in accommodating Non-Verbalism. If the new Prime Minister is really interested in uniting our country then let us have a general election so that my party has the opportunity to lead the nation towards a better future. Let the people decide.'

PART FOUR

DAY OF JUDGEMENT

Unedited: *The Movement . . .*

William Bacclay: Politician
Leader of the Opposition
Pro-Non-Verbal

William: Fernsby used Non-Verbalism as an opportunity to push his own agenda, his party wanted to take advantage of people no longer using their voice, but his lack of action, their deceptive rhetoric, has increased the animosity between Verbals and NVs. Ruth Baynham is no different. She's going to sit on the fence for as long as necessary while she's in talks with the US, China, European leaders, India . . . This party has been in power for too long. It has lied to its people and its true colours are now visible for all to see.

Aadhi: What do you want for the country?

William: To address the mounting unrest, create change on a structural level. To allow our society and *all* its people to flourish. In the past fifteen years, we've seen a rise in employment but a low standard of living. We've had fourteen million people living in poverty - we're talking nurses and police officers having to use food banks. Non-Verbalism has lifted us out of our apathy.

Aadhi: Do you have a plan that is fiscally viable?

William: We continue to have our top experts working on it.

Aadhi: Do you feel that you can reverse all the economic damage Non-Verbalism has done?

William: My party will limit the negative impact that Non-Verbalism has had —

Aadhi: So, would you say it has had a negative impact?

William: Non-Verbalism is a way of life for millions. I believe that every person who has felt oppressed, devalued, subjugated - should fight for the right to live as they want. I, as the leader of a democratic party, intend to uphold my promise and *duty* to give people the right to their freedom.

Sara

London, February 2022

Sara had cut her hair short, wore over-sized sunglasses and a baseball cap to stop being recognised in public. Talk about oppression. No one railed against it when it included gossip. At the newsagent's she looked at the cover of one of the few magazines still in print, major magazines had attempted to rebrand to accommodate the world's changes but a startling number had not been successful.

Sara Javed Silent and Alone?

Has Javed's husband left her, proving that men <u>actually</u> like women who speak?

Sara bought the remaining copies of the magazine and threw them in the recycling bin. It was midday on a Saturday and the streets were hushed. The tooting of car horns was now wholly frowned upon. A petition against it was being raised. Silence kept creating hills upon which to die.

Sara didn't know what to think as she walked through the park. She had felt trapped indoors. Outside hardly felt better. The constant changes jolted her back into a world from which she still wanted to detach; for long enough to at least understand what her life had meant.

The pervasive quiet, she realised, was what she had craved for many years, but was this the correct way to live?

As she approached the high street, she saw her letter, laminated or framed, in most shop windows. She was now used to the live billboards with *Beware the Barrenness of a Busy Life*. A quote that had struck her at a particular time when she'd worked full-time as a data processor in order to pay off student loans and debt accumulated from having helped her dad out with mortgage payments and bills.

How far they had come.

But one dissatisfaction had merely replaced another. Professional success had not brought contentment. Being a wife had not suited her, becoming a mother was something for which she never yearned. And words, in the end, had turned out to be a misdirection. Now her private failings and public successes were being documented for the world to eventually see. It was absurd! Mediocrity was sensational. Silence was compounding talk.

It had started raining so she made her way home only to find Penelope and Kat waiting among the crowd of people and reporters, clicking cameras, taking selfies.

'Good grief, this is quite something,' Penelope said as Sara, feeling rather browbeaten now, led them through the front door.

Penelope shook her umbrella at Sara's door, water flicking on to Kat behind her. 'We did call. I suppose you didn't check your phone.'

Sara let them into the living room.

Kat pulled Sara into a hug. 'Brace yourself.'

Sara sat on the floor as Penelope looked around the empty room.

Eventually, she manoeuvred herself down in her pencil skirt and sat awkwardly, legs tucked under her.

'Sara,' she began. 'I've had the most extraordinary request and by God, if you don't comply, I shall categorically lose my shit . . .'

Sara glanced at Kat.

'I've had a call. From *Ruth Baynham.*'

There was a protracted pause.

'The *Prime Minister,* Sara. The new leader of our nation. Disaster though it is.'

'It's true,' confirmed Kat.

'*Of course, it's true.*'

Sara was under the impression that Penelope was a woman on the edge. Was this a joke? Sara put out her hands, waiting for the punchline.

Kat took a deep breath. 'She wants to meet with you.'

Silence and the Dangers of Generational Social Trauma

Rebecca Craig, *The Telegram*, Feb 2022

Women who have taken to silence as some form of inverse protest seem to be labouring under the misapprehension that families raise themselves. What will be the effect of Non-Verbalism on children? It's too soon to tell but the answer terrifies me. Will we have an entire generation unable to communicate? So-called progressives will decry my omission of men's responsibility towards child-rearing, but let's be honest, it's women who are children's primary carers and it's women who seem to be the Non-Verbal majority.

Speaking as a woman, Non-Verbalism is not empowering. It is not freedom. How will future generations, bearing the brunt of such misguidance, look back on the way in which we – the ones who refuse to give up their voice – stood by and did nothing?

Rebecca Craig is a journalist and social commentator.

Grace

Manchester, February 2022

A crowd had gathered outside Manchester Civil Justice Centre and Grace found herself caught in a barrage of reporters' questions.

'Ignore them, OK?' Graham walked close beside Grace. His tone was abrupt. Tone, it seemed, was everything and now the whole social orchestra was off.

She nodded.

David, for all the veneer of congeniality, hadn't changed, after all. The social thirst for stories about Non-Verbalism had provided an all-too-easy opening for him to speak to a friend – female, for purposes of credibility – about family values. His abscondment from these values arced towards a tale of redemption, such was the capacity for forgiveness for anyone who spoke about remorse in the correct way.

Grace, alternatively, having left social media months ago, was now getting messages of abuse from anonymous neighbours – and who knew who else – through her letterbox. Many of these focused upon the colour of her skin, which though not surprising, was nonetheless affecting. It reminded her of how base people could be. How, despite this, it shook her out of the world in which she thought she lived, forced her to reconsider the things she should do to help change it.

Then she saw him. David with a woman, presumably, his wife, looking pristine and approachable. They held hands.

'Stay focused.' Graham leant into her. 'That's a media display.'

Even so, it was the appearance of it that mattered.

The judge walked into the courtroom and everyone took their seat. Grace's mouth felt dry as the social worker who had assessed Benji stepped into the witness box.

'I understand that everyone's read the report, and you've observed the child?' asked the judge.

'Yes, your honour.'

'And it is your assessment that the child continues to display normal forms of cognitive development but that the respondent, Ms Jenkins', decision to stop the child's speech therapy session in May 2021can be considered negligent in this circumstance?'

'Yes, your honour. She continued with his art therapy and Benjamin is an attentive reader of comics but was very reticent about being left alone with me. After speaking to his teacher, it's clear he still has issues forming meaningful attachments in and out of the classroom. This can be detrimental to a child's emotional development and have a significant impact on his future relationships.'

Grace had encouraged him to make friends, but she'd also been told by therapists not to force him. She should promote an environment of conversation, but not make Benji feel manipulated into it; to love but not to smother; to understand but not to judge; to teeter on the edge, but not to fall.

'And is it your firm conclusion that the respondent's Non-Verbalism is holding back the child's development?' asked the judge.

Grace swallowed hard. She felt Graham tense beside her.

'Yes. Especially given her disregard for medical advice. Benjamin continues to need regular therapy and Ms Jenkins is creating an environment in which he is never challenged. Watching his mother live a life non-verbally acts as a perfectly acceptable example for him to aspire to.'

'If Ms Jenkins was still a Verbal, how would his development be any different?' asked Graham. 'Isn't there a limited amount of data that correlates between a verbal atmosphere and a Non-Verbal child, like Benjamin Jenkins, going on to speak in adulthood?'

'It's a unique case, yes, but in my professional opinion I can tell you that the likelihood of his eventually speaking decreases significantly.'

Grace felt her head throb as David's solicitor took over the questioning.

How would Benji function as an adult if he wasn't encouraged to speak? To try and overcome whatever emotional obstacle he faced?

But no one seemed to understand the positive changes in Benji's behaviour aside from Grace.

'Your honour, we have a statement here and ask for permission to call upon a new witness . . .'

Graham objected to this being brought in so late in the day.

'I am sorry your honour,' said David's solicitor, 'but it is the respondent's mother, Dede Jenkins . . .'

For a moment, Grace thought she had misheard.

Voices seemed to distort.

'OK,' replied the judge. 'Let's have a read of the statement. We'll adjourn until 2 p.m. and see whether we will allow the witness.'

Grace looked at Graham, the shuffling of chairs and muttering. The look of accusation on David's face. She needed some air.

'Grace,' whispered Graham. 'This is *not* going well.'

But Grace swept out of the room, only to come face-to-face with her own mother. The woman who gave her life and was now threatening to take it away from her.

Unedited: *The Movement . . .*

Stephen Cable: OFSTED Inspector
Member of the Teacher's Union
Verbal

Stephen: We needed a systematic approach to accommodate Non-Verbals, especially with the demand for segregated classes. Given its dark connotations, we want to avoid this *at all costs*. We investigated what technologies could be adapted so students can communicate non-verbally, wanted to implement a system whereby Non-Verbal teachers could speak in classes on a rota-basis. But we came across obstacles.

Aadhi: What kind?

Stephen: The former education secretary cut our funding. It was as simple as that. Councils have been similarly impacted. You can't adapt to a new lifestyle without financial support.

Aadhi: What do you plan to do if the agenda to segregate classes is pushed forward?

Pause.

Stephen: I've been appalled at the way some Non-Verbals are being treated. I can't say I believe in Non-Verbalism, but you have to understand, politics aside, as people who believe in the power of

286

knowledge and critical thinking, we must stand up for what's right.

Aadhi: What, to your mind, is right?

Stephen: Let's just say, given the way things are headed, the union is preparing itself.

Zainab

Glasgow, February 2022

Zainab had been up since six in the morning, watching the *Hodgkin vs Jenkins* case. It was meant to have been a distraction, but she was hooked. How were you meant to fight a battle of this magnitude without using your voice? Zainab watched Grace Jenkins being ushered by her lawyer into a car. She looked so composed, but the pain in her expression – yes, Zainab recognised that. Crowds of women surrounded Grace Jenkins, some supporting her, some protesting against her actions. The sporadic chanting by Verbals felt more wearisome than usual against the silence in the house and world.

The floorboards above Zainab creaked. Her mum had flown in from Pakistan as soon as she got her visa. Her father's had been denied. To stay with anyone in the family would have opened them up to too much gossip and Zainab refused (such was her audacity, considering) to subject herself to further humiliation. So, she got them an Air BnB. Her father paid for it, which was all he could do.

Her mum came downstairs and went straight into the kitchen.

'Shall I make you breakfast?' Zainab asked, following her.

Her mother shook her head. She was standing, drinking her tea because her knees were too sore to go back up, and the alternative would be sitting with Zainab.

Zainab wanted to say sorry, but the words felt deceptive. And there had been enough of that.

'*Ammi*, go and sit in the TV room. Please.'

Zainab's mother looked up at her.

'What will we say to people?'

'Plead Non-Verbalism,' replied Zainab.

'Zainu.' Her mother looked at her as if she didn't recognise her. 'You know the things I've had to hear from Kashif's *Ammi*?' Her mum stifled a cry. 'Wasn't he a good husband? You worked because you enjoyed it. He helped you pass your driving test, bought you a car. You go to chai parties and have friends—'

'*Friends,*' said Zainab, almost in a whisper.

'Just because you are too shy or stubborn to like them.'

Stubborn? Tahera had managed to comprehend something that had been unspeakable. How could her own mother – the maternal fabric from whom Zainab's will and feeling was woven – not understand her silence?

'You tell me *one* thing he did wrong?'

Zainab felt the blood rush to her face.

'He . . .'

Her mother waited. Zainab's mind was fraught.

'I can't . . .'

'Well?'

'Can you just give me a minute? I don't know how . . .'

If Zainab didn't say something now, to her own mother, she would never be able to say it to anyone.

Watching Grace Jenkins showed her something about bravery, at least.

'It started on the wedding night.'

She looked at her mum, the slow but distinct understanding dawning upon her face.

'It can be difficult, yes. But let's not talk about what happens between husband and wife.'

'Even if he hurts you?'

Her mother paused.

'We are not like these modern women. You were innocent and—'

Zainab didn't realise that to explain something was almost as degrading as the act itself. That humiliation and shame should be more powerful than truth. She had never had to understand courage. It was, after all, an active thing.

But she steeled her voice and began to tell her mother every detail of her life's indignities.

'You let me talk,' said her mother as they drove to Zainab's in-laws.

Zainab's voice had trembled at one point when she told her mother about her suffering, but she collected herself – emotions detracted from facts. Her mum had hugged her and even that hadn't induced tears. Words had expunged them.

Now, they were silent, and for the first time Zainab felt in control. She drove past protests taking place in the city centre, demands of a general election. Traffic had been redirected.

Her mum merely said: 'Lahore is also like this.'

The atmosphere was one of mourning when they entered Zainab's marital home. A suitable metaphor.

Naz looked at everyone. Kashif refused to look at anyone. Did he understand how it had all come to this?

Zainab's father-in-law, Iqbal, so-called man of the house, was obliged to speak first.

'We are very disappoi—'

'She has brought shame on us all,' Naz interrupted. 'My son . . .' Her tears burst forth. Proof of her own trauma.

'*Beta*,' began Zainab's mother. 'God loves the one who forgives . . .' Bringing God into it quietened Naz's demeanour. It was an expert move, in that sense. But why was she addressing Kashif as her son? 'Can you forgive Zainab?'

What was her mother saying?

Zainab had told her everything – the times she'd lie there while Kashif did as he pleased – the times she had asked him to stop, times she had begged, and it had just made it worse.

Forgiveness?

Zainab demanded a reprisal.

Having been a woman of equanimity for so long the force of this feeling surprised her.

'You know what God ordains for women who commit such crimes,' said Naz.

'Some crimes,' responded her mother, 'are seen more clearly than others, yes, Kashif?'

He looked up.

Zainab waited for her mother to bring Kashif's crimes to the fore, so that he too could be judged.

Instead, Naz nodded towards Iqbal who brought out papers.

'Our son only wants a divorce,' he said. 'Sign the papers and please leave.'

'No,' replied Zainab. 'This country is my home.'

'You only know how to break a home,' said Naz. 'Who will marry you now?'

Zainab let out a laugh. As if she wanted it without love. Without the promise of respect. Surely that was the least one could demand of the institution – of life itself. And she had left Suleiman, the one hope of her having it all.

Why was her mother not saying more? Why could Zainab not find the words herself? Kashif could not strip her of her sense of self, *and* her home.

'Silent all these months, Kashif,' said Zainab. 'And you still don't see it? I'm a fool. You haven't changed.'

'If your daughter doesn't finalise the divorce,' said Iqbal, glancing uncertainly at his wife. 'Then your family in Pakistan . . . Zainab was seen going into a hotel with Suleiman.'

'We can all imagine the rest,' added Naz.

And the imagination was apt to run wild.

The extent of Zainab's misdemeanours became apparent on her mother's face. 'You went into a *hotel?*' Her mother's pallor drained. 'Zainab . . .' She took her daughter to one side. 'You must sign the papers.'

'*Ammi*,' Zainab pleaded.

'If people find out how will we ever show our faces? Kashif was wrong, but you did the worst thing a woman can do.'

For a moment, Zainab thought of Sara Javed. The way people, women, were outraged by her silence, and here was Zainab, living with the outcome of voicing the truth, becoming the sum of her sin.

'*Ammi*, Sulieman—'

'You think he will want you?'

'*Yes*, he—'

'Zainab, I'm begging you. Your father's heart is weak. If he found out *this* much, God knows . . .'

'I can't think. I need to think.'

But her mother's look induced such pity and self-hatred, Zainab would have to leave everything behind. She would have to live in Pakistan, shackled by her parents' disapproval. Confined by her iniquity, never to walk the grounds in Kelvingrove again – look at *Christ the Redeemer*.

Redemption, it seemed, was only to be had in art.

She walked over and took the papers, picked up a pen, and signed away all hope that life could be anything other than an obligation.

Unedited: *The Movement* . . .

Fran Mensa-Bonsu: Human Rights Lawyer
Campaigner and pro-Non-Verbal activist
Verbal

Fran: Something fundamental is at stake right now. This is a call to *everyone*, no matter their beliefs, because powerful change is with the people. Solidarity spreads. Even ones who hate, or used to hate, Non-Verbalism are seeing the duplicitous government for what it is. And NVs are standing up for something we all ultimately want – control of our lives. People like myself and *you* have to decide, when push comes to shove, whether we will be allies or enemies.

Aadhi: Thank you for your time, Ms Mensa-Bonsu.

Fran leaves.

Roxy: Well . . .

Aadhi: Yep.

Roxy: Push came to shove, you wouldn't fight for my kind, would you? You'd be railing against us.

Pause.

Roxy: It's not a rhetorical question.

Pause.

Aadhi: I don't know about anyone else, Rox, but I'd fight for you.

Tensions Mount in Jenkins vs Hodgkin Case

Elsie Parveen, *The Woman*

March 2021

A straightforward custodial case has escalated into a national crisis about what being a mother should mean in a time of Non-Verbalism. Grace Jenkins – for whom there would have been no question of keeping custody had this case taken place a year ago – is facing a verdict on whether a transfer of residence will be granted to her son's dad, David Hodgkin. Accusations of negligence have called into question Ms Jenkins' ability to be the primary carer for her son. People are demanding to hear from Sara Javed: would she condemn or congratulate Grace Jenkins? Freedom of non-speech is in peril, which begs the question: how free have we ever been?

To subscribe to the magazine that backs women click *here*

#imwithher

Sara

London, March 2022

Sara had gone for a walk in the early morning and had seen them sauntering down the street. Henry and Jyoti had been holding hands. For a moment, Sara had started, but then . . . the irony!

By the time she had returned home she was too engrossed in rumours about what the government might be planning next to feel pain. Too strained about how she might respond to today's meeting with the new Prime Minister, Ruth Baynham. Too frazzled by the barrage of emails she was receiving, asking for comment on the Grace Jenkins' story. A written piece? An interview that would just require a nod or shake of the head? Anything in which her opinion might be known.

She read the Jenkins' story updates on her phone, now kept by her side. She watched Grace on the news on her laptop. Such dogged determination, gambling with her son's future . . . The argument that she wanted to create a comfortable environment for her son felt nebulous at best, given expert advice. Sara Javed would *condemn*, obviously. She knew too much about the consequences of parental abandonment to have any other view.

She had to tear her eyes away from the screen when the car arrived. She checked her face in the mirror, brushed down her white shirt and black cropped trousers. Checked again that her flat, gold buckled, black shoes were polished. She'd made do with the remaining items in her wardrobe. The Prime Minister was just another person, in the end.

'Well, this is unusual,' said Penelope as they drove towards Westminster. Kat sat in between Sara and Penelope, a blue file on her lap.

'You've been watching the Jenkins story?' asked Penelope.

Pause.

Penelope leant over Kat. 'You *are* watching the news, aren't you?'

Sara gave a reluctant nod. She couldn't pretend that it didn't feel personal to her – a mother, ready to lose her son. Yet there had to be more to the story. There always was.

'Then you know the whole thing is being used as a catalyst for the anti-NVs?'

The driver glanced at them from his rearview mirror.

'Non-Verbal or Verbal?' Kat asked him.

He gave Sara a reverent nod.

Penelope sighed. 'Things are changing fast. If we're to maintain the image of you being heroic—'

Heroic?

'—then we must do it *now.*'

Sara caught the driver's eye in the mirror. Why had he embraced silence? How did his loved ones react? She felt an urge to speak – and to someone she didn't know. Perhaps she did still care about people.

'This is the campaign we have in mind over the next few months.' Kat handed Sara two sheets of paper.

'FT, *The New York Times, L'Obs, La Repubblica,* BBC World Service, CNN, Bernama News . . .' Sara looked at Kat quizzically.

'Malaysia.'

'We're approaching the one-year anniversary of your Non-Verbalism,' said Penelope as they drove across London Bridge. Banners promoting Non-Verbalism, denouncing it, people with placards in support of Grace, in opposition. Signs demanding Sara to speak, that she keep silent.

People's passions against London's grey sky, the hazy light of the sun filtering through the clouds, were impossible to ignore. A fight broke out between two groups. Police intervened, barely able to contain the fierce indignation on one side, the verbal tirades on the other.

'Jesus,' said Penelope. 'It's obvious it'd be more than just a powerful statement if you . . . *broke* your silence.'

The car jolted.

'If you took this moment to say something against Grace Jenkins, pro-motherhood, I think you'd win a lot of favour.

'I know you're not a mother, but you're a woman and really that's what counts.

'I think it's what the Prime Minister will ask of you, and if you do break your silence . . . Well, look around you. You could help to calm all of this.'

Sara felt a panic rise. She glanced at the driver again, his lips pursed. Outside the swelling, restless crowds.

How could she strive towards facing victory and loss with equanimity with such choices?

'Baynham's full of shit,' said Kat. 'The *unity*. She never talks about *that*. It's all disaster, disaster, disaster.'

The driver raised his fist.

'Sara, if you don't take ownership of this narrative now, it'll be too late. You have no idea how quickly people can take away what you have built. Kat, iPad, please.'

Kat played Sky News: competing protests all over anti-Non-Verbal European cities. *Al Jazeera*: police heralding swathes of people in Japan. BBC: riots in Texas where Non-Verbals were threatening a mass exodus unless the state accommodated Non-Verbalism.

Was the violence *really* this ubiquitous? Where was the other side of the story?

Lily's name flashed up on her phone. Sara declined. How in the hell was *she* responsible for *rioting*?

'Speaking out against Grace Jenkins will preserve your reputation as both a feminist and proponent of peace,' continued Penelope. 'It's the right thing to do. Trust me. I'm a mother.'

Which seemed all the argument necessary to be correct on the matter.

The car pulled into Pall Mall. The crowds with their banners seemed to heave forth like a wave as someone threw eggs at the car.

'What *the*—' Kat yelled, as Lily's name flashed up again on Sara's phone. Cars beeped behind them. Sara declined the call once more.

They stopped outside No 10 Downing Street. Police officers guarded the main door and a crowd huddled nearby, armed with cameras. The NV driver opened the car on Sara's side. She put her hand on her chest and the driver stepped forward. Sara hugged him, gripping tight to this stranger about whom she suddenly wanted to know so much. She heard the clicking of cameras, the flashes drew closer.

People always did enjoy something unlikely.

Sara and the driver smiled for the cameras.

As Sara walked towards No 10, she reached for her phone and saw a WhatsApp from Lily. She knew Sara didn't read messages.

The clicking cameras and flashes seemed to dull.

In all the demands being made on her to comment on Grace Jenkins' story, preparing to meet the Prime Minister, she hadn't realised until now that her dad hadn't called.

Beware the Barrenness of a Busy Life.

Sara tapped on Lily's name:

Where are you?? Your dad's been taken to St James' Hospital. Heart attack. Come quick.

Unedited: *The Movement . . .*

David Hodgkin: Journalist
Benjamin Jenkins' biological father
Verbal

Aadhi: You've very recently entered Benji's life yourself, haven't you?
David: Yes, but my wife and I are already learning to communicate with him using our own sign language.
Aadhi: Could that not cause some upheaval for him?
David: Well, we don't want to be dependent on that long-term. Non-Verbalism is affecting already marginalised members of society. This is a direct result of the affluent going silent, quitting work, companies going under, taking away job opportunities for workers who cannot afford to be silent. And now it's taking away a little boy's right to try and thrive in an environment that is predisposed to being hostile to him, simply because of the colour of his skin. Without a voice, how will he navigate this world?
Aadhi: Don't you feel that Grace, given her ethnic background, her experience in raising Benjamin, might be better equipped to handle these challenges?
David: She hasn't succeeded thus far.
Aadhi: Right. Was it the first *ten* years of his upbringing you missed?

David: Are you a journalist or judge?

Pause.

Aadhi: I'm quite good at both.

David: Grace is acting emotionally, refusing expert opinion, so I have to do *something*.

Pause.

Aadhi: Mr Hodgkin, thank you. I think we're done with this interview.

David: I thought you were going to ask about my take on Non-Verbalism?

Aadhi: We're done.

Grace

Manchester, March 2022

Graham threw down the day's paper on Grace's coffee table. She picked it up. There was an image of Sara Javed hugging a man who, according to the article, had driven her to her meeting with the Prime Minister. People wanted to know the story behind the hug and Javed's sudden abscondment from the meeting, but without facts, there was only conjecture.

'It would be a really good time for Javed to break her silence in support of you,' said Graham.

Grace found herself wishing the same, despite people demanding Sara speak out against her.

'You OK?'

She barely nodded. She couldn't sleep after receiving the message that the judge had called them into court before his ruling. She ended up sitting in Benji's room, watching him in peaceful slumber. Her baby boy couldn't be taken away. The way her mother, on the stand, had painted Grace; pre-occupied; distracted; at times, negligent. Losing Benji in the Lake District.

Graham had dutifully objected. 'Is every mother who's lost a child in a crowd for a few minutes to be put on a stand?'

He had gone on to describe Dede as a grabby, incompetent woman – reducing hers into a one-dimensional narrative (to avoid doubt and therefore sympathy) – who had taken Grace's money and walked out of both their lives.

Until now.

Dede had explained that she had been ashamed of losing her daughter's money in a scam that promised her financial independence. She didn't want to live on Grace's handouts. How much degradation could a person take? Leaving Benji was an enormous mistake. She had come back for him because he needed her. *Someone* to speak up for him. Whatever her reasons, Dede had not lied.

Guilt came in unexpected floods. That Grace had ever complained about Benji, that she had often wished for a *normal* child. She was coming to understand that her obsession with perceived normality was in contrast with who she pretended to be when she was trying to help people – whether that was refugees or survivors of domestic violence. She had been unable to apply such openness to her own son. When she had expressed her wish for a normal son (she now shuddered at the memory) to a doctor he had commented: *be careful of the language you use.*

Of course she had replied. She was a lawyer – using the correct language could make or break a case and family.

Now, not using that language might do the same.

They reached the courthouse crowded with people and cameras. A woman spat at Grace.

Grace turned around but Graham grabbed her arm.

'Don't be the confrontational woman,' he murmured as he dragged her through the crowd. She skim-read some of the placards.

Dis-Grace

No words, no mother!

Speak up for children.

Accosted by so many voices Grace looked around, she didn't know why, for Sara. Instead, she caught a glimpse of her Non-Verbal supporters, standing, in their minority, side-by-side, holding placards.

Amazing Grace.

Tears stung her eyes. A camera flashed.

Grace stopped at the courtroom doors. Dede was talking to a man who looked familiar. He spotted Grace, handed Dede his business card, and fell in step with Grace and Graham.

'Ms Jenkins, my name's Aadhi Sathar and I've learnt about the work you do. It deserves to be highlighted, which is why I'd like you to be a part of the documentary I'm making about The Silent Movement. The public should have your perspective.'

Grace let out a laugh and pushed past him.

'They're making you into a monster, Ms Jenkins.'

She paused, looked at him and shook her head. She would not get sucked in to such drama – let people think what they want. Aadhi Sathar gave her such a perplexed, warm smile, it surprised her.

'Are you interested in supporting Grace?' asked Graham.

'Bias isn't my business.' Aadhi seemed to understand Grace's resolution. He was about to turn away but stopped. 'But I genuinely wish you luck, Ms Jenkins.'

'I have been considering this case with great care.' The judge looked harangued and cross, presumably because of the crowds outside.

Grace felt a wave of nausea. She glanced at David, holding his wife's hand. Didn't *he* deserve to be accosted on the street? Told some home truths? Hadn't Benji deserved a father? Grace could not allow another upheaval.

'In this case the applicant father has been absent for almost a decade from the child's life. Ordinarily an application for residence of the child in these circumstances would not stand much chance. Particularly when the respondent's mother has clearly raised the child with great care.

'I believe Ms Jenkins has tried to provide Benjamin with a loving home . . . However, I have considered the report from the social worker and I've also considered the evidence of Mrs Dede Jenkins. Despite the respondent highlighting her lack of credibility, she was one of Benjamin's primary caregivers and her description of his upbringing in light of our current climate has to be taken into account.'

Grace felt the bile rise to her throat.

'To be silent is as personal a choice as to speak. That much is clear though one wouldn't think it, considering levels of opinions on the matter.' He sighed and looked at Grace, as if trying to understand the entirety of her. Even if she had chosen to tell the court her side of the story, feeling and life were so often lost in explanation, and didn't she have her rights? Didn't Benji have the right to a mother who fought for him when she knew everyone was wrong?

'This court is concerned, not about the mother you *have* been, Ms Jenkins, but the mother you *will* be.'

Grace felt Graham inch closer to her.

'The interest of the child is paramount. The court's task is to ensure that Benjamin is in an environment in which he will not only get continued help, but in which he might flourish.

'A child who is medically Non-Verbal deserves to have a parent who will open up a world of words. Language – whatever your personal opinion – is the medium through which we communicate and understand – *or at least try to understand* – each other. Having a voice connects us to society. The child, Ms Jenkins, must be given the best chance to *feel* a part of this society. The court is guided by its expert's opinion.'

Grace's nausea gathered like a wave, rising, rising, rising . . .

'I do not want the child to suffer a separation from his mother and home, which is why, before I give my ruling I would like to tell the parties what I'm thinking. If the respondent relinquished her Non-Verbalism then there would be no questions that the child would remain with her.'

Graham seemed to breathe a sigh of relief. Grace held her breath to contain the mounting wave.

'Does your client understand this?'

'Yes, your honour,' replied Graham.

'Do you want to take instruction from your client?'

Graham turned to Grace, almost cursorily, clearly assuming he knew the answer before responding: 'My client is prepared to speak.'

She wouldn't be able to contain it – the nausea was too overwhelming. Grace gripped Graham's arm.

'Could you please say, in your own words, Ms Jenkins, that you will relinquish Non-Verbalism?

The court waited.

The last time she had felt like this she—

'*Grace,*' whispered Graham.

—when did she last have her period?

She had taken the morning after pill following that night with Graham. She needed to look at her diary. She needed to throw up. She needed to keep her son.

'If you do not speak officially, before the court, you understand what my verdict will be?'

Grace's breathing came in long, laboured beats.

'Grace, *what* are you doing?' whispered Graham.

She had missed her period, and in all the custodial chaos she hadn't even realised. She had bought the pill, put it in her bag. She now grabbed her bag and rummaged through it, finding the empty sachet. But she had a vague recollection that something – Benji – had distracted her just as she had been about to take the pill.

'Speak, Grace, for Christ's sake. Or you're going to lose Benji, and there won't be any going back.'

Something was trapped in her throat.

What would happen if she did break her silence? She'd have her son, but she'd get visits from so-called experts, social workers, be *surveilled* to check she was upholding her word. Disturbing Benji's peace, forcing him to retreat into himself – she knew what he was like around strangers. Her life with Benji before silence had felt like a diluted way of living for both of them. A woman of feeling numbed by the daily grind. Benji was beginning to thrive *now*. Grace's principles always had been a sticking point. The only time she had compromised them was when her mother came back into her life. The outside world had always been something to rail against. Why should it have the power to impose its rules upon a woman who knew better?

The judge waited. David waited. The whole room waited. Every instinct of Grace's to protect Benji came into force as she clutched her belly. She could not speak when her silence seemed to make him so much more at ease with her and the world.

The court, people, even Graham did not understand. And it was not beyond Grace to take drastic measures to ensure her son got what he needed . . .

'Ms Jenkins, are you refusing to give up Non-Verbalism, standing to lose your child?'

Benji will not suffer again.

She nodded.

A whimper came from across the room from David and his wife. There was no going back.

'In which case I can deliver my final ruling that transfer of residence be handed over to Mr Hodgkin and his wife.'

David and his wife hugged, clutching each other.

'*Grace, what have you done . . .*'

'I believe the applicant has agreed to sit down with the respondent to work out visitation rights amicably?'

'Absolutely, your honour.'

David seemed to get everything he wanted without even trying. It was clear that if women like her wanted something they had to use other means to take it. She knew what she had to do.

'Ms Jenkins, do you understand what's happening?'

She nodded.

'I suggest that the transfer happens with as little disruption caused to the young boy as possible.'

The judge's words muffled. Everything within her seemed to heave.

'I can't understand why you'd do this,' said Graham.

'Grace?' David stood before her, his wife standing back, looking nervous. 'I'm sorry it turned out this way.'

Grace didn't know why she let out a soft laugh. Why something like hope sprawled within her. David looked confused. Or repulsed. What did he think? That after the world had woken up to its own silent reckoning that it could take Benji away?

She could no longer hold it in. Her body pushed against her will, her form heaved, her shoulders hunched and a projectile of vomit escaped her, splashing all over David's shoes.

There was a kerfuffle. She hardly noticed.

Benji was about to have a brother or sister. And come hell or high water, Grace would hold on to the life outside of this room *and* the life growing within her.

Unedited: *The Movement . . .*

Philip Barnes: Politician
Former Home Secretary
Verbal

Aadhi: You were closest to Prime Minister Baynham before she took over the leadership.
Philip: Yes. She's a strong, sensible and battle-hardened leader. Even now she's fighting problems on all fronts. Internal power struggles, national discontent, transatlantic deals affected by the movement . . . She needs to demonstrate that she has a handle on the situation.
Aadhi: Does she have a handle on it?
Philip: I'm told she's focused on ensuring the best for the country. You know, Baynham practiced Non-Verbalism before she was elected.
Aadhi: Hasn't she been its opponent from the start?
Philip: She claimed she did it to understand the lifestyle so it could better inform her perspective, but the party didn't like that. The main thrust of it is that if we don't follow in the footsteps of our *superior* nations, who perhaps aren't as amenable to democratic means – then we will pay an even greater economic price. Baynham will be looking at the bigger picture. And the party will take its measures accordingly.

Aadhi: May I ask why you stepped down as Home Secretary only two weeks after Baynham came into power?

Pause

Philip: I believe I had done all I could in my position. It was time for a fresh perspective.

Aadhi: I'm sensing some hesitation here.

Philip: Listen . . . there has been lobbying in support of taking whatever measures necessary to manage Non-Verbalism.

Aadhi: What sort of measures?

Philip: I can't divulge that.

Aadhi: But you felt it was significant enough to leave your position?

Long pause.

Philip: I can no longer, in good conscience, be part of a system for whom people's rights have become secondary . . .

The Protection of Silence

Joanna Marks, *The Woman*, March 2022

I am a lettered Non-Verbal. I now have a specific practice of a) never writing anything when angry, and b) waiting 48 hours before filing a piece. This goes against journalistic best practice, which necessitates speed over contemplation. But how had society ever expected the human mind to absorb this volume of information, reflect upon it, when seconds later we'd be bombarded with another headline, a trending hashtag, people hitching themselves to one or the other bandwagon. What we said had become the sum of us. Silence has been an act of civil disobedience against society's conventions. But the case of Grace Jenkins has brought to light the question: what rights do Non-Verbal women have? Why is speech being enforced upon us? This loaded expectation upon women. Again.

Listen to what Grace Jenkins' silence says, not about her, but us. If we – specifically women – are not afforded the same rights as those who choose to speak then we are no better than the history we have spent a lifetime condemning.

Joanne Marks is an advocate for women to choose how to use their voice.

Follow her on <u>Instagram</u>.

Zainab

Glasgow, March 2022

After she signed her life away, Zainab drove, alone, to Suleiman's through the rain and blur of her future. She banged at his parents' front door. Suleiman's father answered, took one look at Zainab and closed the door.

'*I'm not leaving until I speak to Suleiman,*' she yelled through the glass frame.

The neighbours' lights came on. People peered through windows that were draped with *Non-Verbal and Proud* signs.

The door opened again. His mum dragged her inside.

'Have you no shame?'

Zainab had clearly become desensitised to it. And with it came a freedom in which she had a duty to no one but herself. Her signature, in that way, had been a release as well as a sentence.

'Get out of our house,' his mother said as Suleiman's footsteps came thumping down the stairs.

'Mum . . .'

His dad put his hand up to Suleiman. He had been Non-Verbal for weeks.

'We're divorced,' Zainab said, looking at Suleiman.

'Not now,' he replied.

Such conflict.

Such love.

'This is what you wanted,' whispered Zainab.

'You'd changed your mind. You said—'

'You promised *forever*,' Zainab interrupted.

Suleiman's mother was already dialling 999.

Zainab waited for him to speak. Her tears had dried up. A pool of rain water gathered around her on the floor.

It might have been a few seconds, or an eternity. Either way, the conclusion was the same.

His words had meant nothing.

Zainab had thirty days in which to voluntarily leave the country. She had collected her things from her in-laws when Kashif wasn't there – to save him the pain, his mother said, of seeing the woman to whom he had been so loyal. Zainab had gone alone to save her mother from facing further disrespect.

She was about to leave when her father-in-law spoke. 'Just so you know, we think Suleiman is just as much to blame as you—'

'*Iqbal*,' said Naz.

'He's not the one being forced to leave,' replied Zainab.

Naz looked perplexed by Zainab's lack of voluble repentance.

Zainab could have outlined her grief; the way life had felt like a series of events which she had never actively chosen. The way Kashif had been her first rude awakening. That when she visited Pakistan, it didn't live up to either memory or nostalgia. Her home now, however wrecked and duplicitous it was, had switched continents and roles, a place where she had almost died, metaphorically, at the hands of one man and been brought back to life by another.

Perhaps she would not have to shed the skin of who she was, just the memory of the skin that clung to her. In that sense her metamorphosis was not complete.

*

That evening, Zainab sat down and watched the news about Grace Jenkins' son being taken away. People were calling her cold, deserving of all she got, but all Zainab saw was the woman's look of resolve. Zainab understood what multitudes could lie beneath silence. In the end, people would absolve one of nothing. One had to find their own absolution.

The doorbell rang. Zainab rushed down the stairs. Perhaps Suleiman had changed his mind, but when she opened the door Kashif stood there.

'What are you doing here?'

Nothing.

'Still silent?'

Kashif handed over an envelope.

Zainab felt the bulk of it. 'What is this?'

There was no pity in his look, or apology. He opened his mouth and Zainab almost heard a noise of sorts. She looked inside: a wad of cash.

'My *mahar*?'

He nodded.

It was the money promised to every bride when she got married. The exact amount could be negotiated but she could ask for it at any time during her marriage. If that marriage ever led to divorce then that money was rightfully hers. Zainab supposed this was Kashif's last act of ostensible honour.

He pointed at her, then at himself and gestured with his hands as if they were now officially over. Kashif turned to leave.

'Don't you want to hear my side?' she asked.

He paused.

'That Suleiman was a *man*. A real one.'

She noticed the clenching of Kashif's jaw, the way he tightened his fists.

'And every single time we were together . . . I wanted it. I wasn't *forced*.'

Kashif's confusion morphed into something else, his movement so sudden that Zainab flinched. His hand had stopped mid-air, just inches from her face. She was transfixed by it. Yet he hardly seemed to know how it got there. She felt such a power in that moment, that she had revealed Kashif to himself.

313

'You're *deluded*,' he spat. 'Sick and deluded.'

She smiled. Unveiling him, forcing him to break his silence – to speak like the man he really was, the vitriol in his voice – felt like her single biggest achievement.

The night before her eviction from the country, Zainab took out the prayer mat for the first time in several years. She wept for all that had happened, all she had lost, the future that would never be. She asked God to forgive her sins, the ways in which she had abandoned Him, but He must understand that she had felt abandoned too. One day, perhaps prayer would diminish despair as well as the distance between her and her one constant.

Tahera visited while Zainab pretended to organise her toiletries.

'You'll be OK, Zee.'

'You never lie, Tahera. Don't start now.' She sat on the edge of the bed. 'The last ten years – what do I have to show for it? No husband or home, children or career—'

'You have a career.'

'I'll have a job, but I'll live with my parents and they'll monitor my every move. Where I go, who I see. I'm no longer the daughter they thought I was. And *Ammi*—'

'Parents can be as disappointing as children.'

Zainab let out a small laugh.

'I'm a thirty-five-year-old woman. I've been through a marriage, three miscarriages, an affair. Abuse.' She looked Tahera in the eye. 'Is that what I am? A victim? No one tells us do they, what that looks like? Feels like. Most of the time you just end up living in a state of bewilderment.'

'It's a conversation killer,' said Tahera. 'I should know.'

Zainab took her hand. 'I don't want to *be* a victim.'

'Who does? That's why it can take so long to understand what's happened. It turns you into a type,' Tahera added.

'You know, I never realised how stupid Suleiman looks when he's being indecisive.'

'Men are weak, in the end.'

'Then why do they have all the power?' asked Zainab.

'You just have to be patient.'

'*You're* telling me this?'

Tahera smiled. 'The irony isn't lost on me.'

'Why do *women* always have to be patient? Why are we always told to make the sacrifices? Why aren't *men* taken to the slaughterhouse?'

'I kno—'

'And when did patience change anything?' interrupted Zainab. 'You're patient until you die, having lived a life you can't stand.'

Tahera put her hand on Zainab's arm. 'Patience doesn't mean having to be a martyr.' She paused. 'How much was your *mahar*?'

'A thousand pounds.'

'It's not a huge amount, but it can last a person if they're clever. And you are. Everything else was joint?'

Zainab gave an ironic laugh. 'I never had to account for things.'

Tahera took her purse out and placed a credit card on the bed. She wrote down a four-digit number on a scrap of paper and handed it to Zainab. She closed Zainab's fist around the paper.

'Take advantage of the mess the world's in, Sara Javed not turning up to meet the PM, the Grace Jenkins madness. There's some talk about a parliamentary vote to allow companies to demand staff be Verbal.'

It was the first Zainab had heard of it. The news was all Grace Jenkins.

'I'm just saying that if a woman doesn't turn up for her deportation . . . I just don't think it'll be the biggest news story right now.'

'Tahera, I—'

'What I'm saying is, even martyrs take action.'

Sara

London, March 2022

Sara pushed through the hospital doors, following the signs for the hospital's Verbal admittances. She entered a lift, up five floors, her shoes clicking against the linoleum. She opened her mouth at reception when someone called her name.

It was Lily, hugging her, pulling her. She glanced at Lily's husband, Martin, in the background.

'Don't be shocked,' said Lily.

Before she could say any more, Sara had already strode into the room in which her dad was lying. She stopped. The father who taught her how to ride a bike, held her dangling legs from the monkey bars, was now pierced with wires, surrounded by beeping machines. He turned his head towards her as she grabbed his hand.

Afzal lowered the nebuliser fastened around his mouth. 'Sshh. Don't speak.'

Sara opened her mouth.

'*Please. Beta*, wait.'

With that, he put the nebuliser over his mouth and fell asleep.

As she stared at her father's sleeping face, Sara recalled when she was five-years old.

They had been sitting in their small living room, crowded with books, Lily beside Afzal. She was smiling at Sara encouragingly.

316

'Now,' Afzal had said. 'Don't be disturbed by this but I am not your father. In the traditional sense.'

Sara had looked at the two of them. 'Did you kidnap me?'

Afzal let out a laugh. 'Yes. Didn't like who you'd be growing up with.'

'*Afzal* . . . He didn't kidnap you, Sara. The woman who gave birth to you, your mother, felt that he'd be able to give you a better home.'

'Why?'

'Because I brought you to this country,' replied Afzal. 'You wouldn't have liked Pakistan. Goats on the street. People shouting. Dusty roads and loud trucks. Noise.'

For a moment something seemed to catch in Afzal's throat. Lily put her hand on his leg. 'It had been my home, but it wasn't for you.'

'I like goats.'

Afzal brought Sara on to his lap. 'Listen, a father and mother are people who love you no matter what. Like me and Lily do.'

'So my mum and dad didn't love me?'

'Oh no,' exclaimed Afzal. 'They loved you very much, but sometimes that isn't enough. Anyway, don't worry about that because my love, it will never end.'

'What about you?' Sara asked Lily.

'I'm with your dad on that.'

'So I still call you Dad?'

'If you don't, I'll put you in the farm with the goats,' Afzal said, poking Sara's plump belly.

'That's against the law,' she giggled.

'I can do what I want,' Afzal said. 'Just like you, my daughter, will do whatever *you* want when you grow up.'

Sara paused in contemplation. 'I think I'll go to Pakistan and make sure my real mummy and daddy don't miss me.'

Lily had to look away.

Afzal cupped Sara's face in his hands. 'Now. The other thing I want to tell you is that your father died.'

'*Afzal.*'

He ignored Lily. 'Do you understand what that means?'

'Mrs Church's grandmother died and she was sad.' Mrs Church was Sara's schoolteacher. 'Should I be sad?'

'You don't *have* to feel any way, darling,' Lily soothed. 'Mrs Church was probably close to her grandmother.'

'So you're only sad when it's someone you know?'

'Not always,' replied Afzal. 'Sometimes you can hear a story about someone you've never met and it will mean something to you—'

'Stay on track, Afzal.'

'She understands more than we realise.'

'Will *you* die?' asked Sara.

'Everyone will die, *beta*.'

'I really think—'

Afzal laid his hand on Lily's arm.

'Dying is a part of life,' Afzal continued. 'But you know what the most important thing is before you die?'

'What?'

'The most important thing is that you *live*.'

'We're lucky he wasn't at home, alone.' Lily explained that the heart attack happened at the local grocery store.

'He doesn't want you to break your silence. It's the only thing he kept repeating.' Lily shook her head. She patted Sara's hand, taking it in her own. 'You're OK?'

Sara gave a brief nod. Lily gripped her hand tighter.

Day turned to night. Sara gestured to Lily to go home to Martin, who had left a few hours ago, and get some rest. She felt faintly ridiculous. She'd had little need to communicate in the past year, but today she had to think of people other than herself. It came with a vague sense of embarrassment, even in the midst of her turmoil.

'No, I'll stay.' said Lily. Then, after some time, 'Do you want to tell Henry?'

Sara shook her head.

'It's good to have someone during times like these.'

This time Sara was the one who took Lily's hand.

Rumours about Sara's abscondment from her meeting with Ruth Baynham ranged from it being a publicity stunt, to the government's attempt to discredit Javed. The news features were in full presumptuous swing when Sara's publisher issued a statement declaring that Javed had a personal emergency. Which did nothing to allay either side's point.

The following day, Sara and Lily were waiting outside Afzal's room when the doctor came and announced that Afzal was improving. Sara's eyes scanned his ID. *Semi-permanent Non-Verbal.*

'Mr Javed is suffering from some complications though—'

Sara strode into her dad's room. She tried to hug him through the wires.

'Oof. Careful.' His eyes were half-open.

She sat back, opened her mouth—

'No, no, no. *No* speaking.'

She opened her mouth again.

'I know what you'll say.'

Oh, really?

'You'll say that you love me.'

Sara brought her dad's hand to her chest.

'That I am an extraordinary father.'

She put her hand out, flipping it from side-to-side.

'OK. Average.' He let out a small laugh.

'That you're grateful for all the ways I push you, even when you hate it. Hate me—'

She shook her head.

'—That the time we have spent together, all those memories would sustain you if I don't make it out of here.'

The lines of his face were blurring through her tears.

'That you forgive me for not talking you into finding your birth mother. I neglected what I knew you would one day want.'

How could she continue to let him speak such words in this moment?

One that seemed to be passing too quickly, with too much to grasp and too much to lose.

Before she could open her mouth, he said: 'You must see this through. That I am proud is obvious. But if I had to leave you, it'd piss me off. One day I will have to face my maker, though, and give Him answers. I have a lot to answer for. We all do, in the end.' He wouldn't seek Sara's forgiveness. Her silence would be his redemption.

Sara kissed her dad's hand. He would be fine. No one made speeches before they died. Life was not that neat.

Lily came and sat on the opposite side of the bed. She took Afzal's other hand and inhaled deeply, as if about to give him a lecture. Her voice only cracked once, when she said: 'I've organised someone to check on the house. There's a list of things you should *not* be eating . . .'

Afzal had barely left his bedroom just under thirty years ago, after Lily had gone. For weeks Sara had crept into his room and left him food, pretending she didn't notice that he had been crying as she tried to make a joke, only to be met with a weak smile. She had become accustomed to the feeling of guilt. It had been her own fault for having eavesdropped on their conversation before Lily left.

'I love Sara but—' Lily had said.

'*But*? There is no *but*.'

'You never listen to what I mean.'

'Then *say* what you mean.'

'She would love a brother or a sister.'

'No. Having a child is a grave decision.'

'*Afzal*. How am I meant to bear this much *hopelessness*.'

'Lillu . . . *Lillu*.' Her dad had pulled her into a hug. 'We are enough, aren't we?' The answer had lain in Lily's absence.

'You're going to be fine,' Lily said now. 'Isn't he, darling?'

Sara nodded.

'Liars,' Afzal murmured, as he drifted into sleep.

*

It was on the third day that the doctors and nurses rushed into his room. Machines beeping faster, bodies weaving in and out of each other's way. It was all Sara could do to shout at them to *do something*. Lily had dragged her out of the room.

'It's OK,' Lily whispered in Sara's ear firmly. 'It's going to be OK.'

But Sara hadn't told her dad all the reasons that *she* loved *him*.

She just needed one moment. She had to explain that he had been the very thing that set her adrift and anchored her; that he had armed her against loneliness; that her words hadn't been a solace for not having a mother, but a homage to *him*, and now keeping her silence . . . that would be one too.

She wasn't sure how long she and Lily stood there, suspended in time, when the doctor came out of the room.

'I'm sorry.' A semi-permanent Non-Verbal.

In that moment Sara felt the intense, morbid insignificance of life. What had she done with hers other than strive for significance, then reject it, only to reach this point where she couldn't even tell her father the one thing she needed him to know?

The irrational way that she had tried to grapple with life through words, and then through their absence.

Nothing seemed to work.

The absurdity of pain and joy and . . . she looked at the TV screen above the reception. It was on mute. There were crowds gathered outside the hospital.

'—His heart was under a lot of strain—'

Sara looked up and down the hallway, at the people staring into space or on their phone, those with closed eyes, meditating, trying to find silence in the Verbal ICU ward. The Non-Verbal ICU ward was further down the hall. She watched the doctor's lips move, slow and steady. His glasses falling down the bridge of his nose.

'Ms Javed—'

She stared at his large pores.

'—I understand this is a shock.'

He glanced at the TV screen. 'There's a private entrance for staff that you can use.'

'Thank you, Doctor,' came Lily's shaky voice.

He cupped Sara's hands between his, looking at her with what she supposed might be respect. Then she saw a figure, rushing down the hallway, so familiar Sara felt the force of her own body move towards it, her eyes filling with tears.

Sara fell into Roxy's arms, weeping for her dad. For all the things she had lost. For the utter barrenness of her silent life.

Roxy had told a semi-disapproving Lily to go home and rest, that she would take Sara back to her own flat. There would be too many people crowding Sara's house.

'You can sleep in my room. I'll take the sofa,' said Roxy when they entered her home.

She made Sara tea and toast, which Sara picked at, staring at the kitchen wall. 'You should eat.'

Something to sustain the body if not the soul.

In that moment, the outlines of Roxy's body seemed to contain something which Sara did not comprehend. Where did it all go, after death?

Roxy came and sat next to her.

'Sara. I'm so sorry. I mean . . . I know how much you meant to each other.'

Sara's head was heavy from all the crying, her eyes sore, body exhausted.

She hardly realised how many hours had passed until the following day when Roxy had come home to find her sitting in exactly the same place that she had left her in. Sara was famished but didn't have the energy to eat.

Roxy made her soup, fed it to her, and for a moment Sara felt such a yearning for who they had once been. This only made her want to discuss it with her dad, and the knowledge that she would never again be able to do so, made her throw up.

She had lost all this time to silence. Time she could have used to savour her dad's every word, which of course had been fewer due to the lack of her own.

'Do you want to sleep?'

Sara shook her head. Still, Roxy took her into the bedroom, tucked Sara into the covers and stroked her hair until she fell asleep.

Her dad's funeral had been in a mosque. A man of quiet religion and contradiction, he would sometimes pray and sometimes have a whiskey.

'I love your selective Islam,' Sara had once said.

'We're all hypocrites,' he'd replied. 'Selective in our religion, selective in our humanity.'

Crowds had gathered outside the mosque and, inevitably, Sara was followed back to Roxy's.

Everywhere she looked there were gatherings, stalls with people handing out Non-Verbal literature. Banners inciting everyone to unite against the government. But all Sara remembered was her dad's serene face and inert body, before he was buried. What truly mattered in the face of eventual non-existence?

Roxy stepped around Sara, talking to herself, peering out of the window at the now substantial gathering, carrying placards urging Sara to remain true to her Non-Verbalism.

When they sat for dinner that night, the news playing quietly in the background, Roxy spoke. 'First time I met your dad he was too busy picking out a cake to listen to me. *"Now, if I have the lemon drizzle, Sara, you can share your chocolate cake with me."*'

Afterwards he had said to Sara: *'Roxy is what someone might call a pill. Lots of side effects.'*

'He was one of the good ones. I wish you'd tell me how you feel. You just *lost* something.' Roxy took their dishes to the sink. 'You have all these feelings but you won't *talk* about them. Tell me in a letter. *A note.* Use sign language.' Roxy's gaze turned to the television. *'What the . . .'*

But Sara saw Roxy's phone on the table flash with a message from Aadhi.

Think you'll get her to talk?

'Look at this,' Roxy said, turning around, then she saw Sara staring at her phone. She strode over, grabbing it, looking at the message. 'The thing is—'

Roxy blurted out a stream of sentences, but Sara hardly heard. Her dad was gone and Roxy had snatched the phone as if anything still mattered. *Make your documentary. Try to convince people of your own importance. Be known by strangers to make up for not being known by your family.*

But if she said it now, she would only be doing it to prove her own point: that words could move a person to tears, to joy and heartbreak, and reveal how base we really are. She shook her head at Roxy, not in anger, but in pity.

'I'm sorry. He's not as bad as you think—'

Sara put her hand up and began to gather her things.

'You don't want to be alone,' said Roxy. She gestured towards the television. More breaking news – *Grace Jenkins Kidnaps Own Son.*

Sara took a deep breath.

The world would not stop. She would not be dragged into its meaningless preoccupations.

To be alone was exactly what she wanted.

After all this time, it was the ultimate silence of death that had taught her this.

Unedited: *The Movement . . .*

Sara Javed: Author
First Non-Verbal and woman behind The Silent Movement
Non-Verbal
(Audio-description available for visually impaired.)

Roxy: Sara, thanks for doing this, especially considering the loss of your father.
Sara: *No expressive response.*
Roxy: Is silence an act of protest?
Sara: *No expressive response.*
Roxy: Are you trying to gain some control after everything that happened with your mother?
Sara: *No expressive response.*
Aadhi: Sara, have you been following the Grace Jenkins story?
Sara: *No expressive response.*
Aadhi: Were you in favour of the verdict?
Sara: *No expressive response.*
Aadhi: Do you believe you've played a part in Jenkins' 'kidnapping' of her own son?
Sara: *No expressive response.*
Aadhi: Do you see the damage Non-Verbalism is doing?
Sara: *No expressive response.*
Aadhi: Do you believe you have a responsibility to stop it?

325

Sara: *No expressive response.*

Roxy: Sara, why did you agree to this interview?

Sara: *No expressive response.*

Roxy: So you won't speak out against Non-Verbalism, even when it threatens lives?

Sara: *Shakes her head in bewilderment, ostensibly, over the question.*

Aadhi: You don't have to answer to anyone, do you?

Sara: *Reaches out a hand, as if he's got it.*

Roxy: No. She wants to *show* that she has to answer to no one.

Pause.

Sara: *Looks down and nods, slowly. Looks back up at camera.*

Sara Javed stands. Removes her mic, drops it on the floor and walks out of shot.

A door is heard closing behind her.

Trending #WhereisSaraJaved

When I lost my dad a few years ago I didn't need to disappear cos I know what responsibilities are #WhereisSaraJaved

💬 ⬆ ♡

I'm no fan of Javed but so what if she hasn't been seen for two weeks? Let the woman grieve #WhereisSaraJaved

💬 ⬆ ♡

Javed dont have to answr to noone #WhereisSaraJaved #fuckthisshit #nonverbalforevs

💬 ⬆ ♡

#SearchforJaved Get this trending and post any sightings so we can bring her home #Love #grief #Sarajaved #whereissarajaved #together #nolongersilent #breakthesilence

💬 ⬆ ♡

May 2022

The world knew that Ruth Baynham's address would indicate what leaders across the world would also decide. People in Australia had set their alarms, the US President, refusing to be second in anything, had timed his speech to coincide with Prime Minister Baynham's. The British people gathered in bars and pubs, in friends' and families' homes, geographical distances bridged via Zoom and Skype. As cameras began to roll and Ruth Baynham appeared on television, standing calmly behind her podium, viewers held their collective breath. This moment was proof that one person could change everything.

Specifically, if others followed.

INTERNATIONAL ADDRESS FROM
THE PRIME MINISTER OF THE UNITED KINDOM

In recent days leaders of the world's greatest nations met to discuss solutions for the unprecedented scale of Non-Verbalism that has impacted our globe. There have been concerted efforts to accommodate this so-called freedom of choice. But we must think about what we are saying – what it is we mean – when we say nothing . . .

Today we must look in the mirror and ask ourselves: who do we want to be?

I think of the women who gave their lives in the name of equality and thanks to whom I am standing here today. Did they do this in silence?

The men and women who have fought, and continue to fight, for our freedom – if they do not raise their voice, what becomes of us?

Unlike Sara Javed and Non-Verbal leaders, they did not abandon duty. They thought not of themselves, but of their communities and people.

Part of the immense burden and privilege of leadership is making difficult decisions for the benefit of the nation. And in this – what has become a global issue – we must not think of our nation as standing alone, but as part of a unified whole.

As such, after intense discussions, it is with a sober conviction I declare that there has been a majority parliamentary vote, and as of 4 August this year, Non-Verbalism will no longer be permitted in professional and public spaces.

You must not be silent.

Institutional legislation in the private and public sector will revert to pre-Non-Verbal standards, so our teachers, doctors, nurses and our emergency services can uphold their oath to serve.

In public spaces all Non-Verbal technologies are to be dismantled to, once again, unite us through the power of speech.

Non-Verbal spaces are to be reintegrated into verbal spaces to promote unity.

Upholding our country's tradition of liberty, people will be free to practice Non-Verbalism in their homes. However, given recent events – as the Jenkins' case and its aftermath has demonstrated – we cannot underestimate the potential threat of silence to our children. Therefore, families with children under the age of sixteen will be prohibited from Non-Verbalism. As will all children under the age of sixteen.

A full and comprehensive list of countries joining the United Kingdom will be available on the FCO site. But I can tell you that it includes our friends in the United States, China, India, Italy, France, Canada and many more.

To the Non-Verbals listening . . . You are an integral part of our global community. As your leader, it is my duty to create a safe and prosperous environment. I ask that you abide by the laws being set down. For the good of your family, your nation and the world.

PART FIVE

THE GREAT REFUSAL

The Prime Minister delivered her speech to a speechless nation.

The live camera cut to news anchors across the channels – famous faces, such as Peter Mercier, Rajini Amaradivakara, Natalie Judd, staring into the nation's eyes with all the gravity that such a speech warranted.

Verbals and Non-Verbals in restaurants, cafés and pubs stared back.

What parliamentary vote?

There had been many grave deceptions but this was the ultimate. Lies had morphed into the government's attempt for total control.

Peter Mercier opened his mouth then closed it again on *BPH News*.

Rajini Amaradivakara of *Channel 8 Live* interlaced her fingers.

Natalie Judd's stare on *TNC* was implacable.

And then Peter unclipped the mic on his lapel, removed his earpiece and laid it on his desk. He gave one more look to the nation and walked out of shot.

Rajini Amaradivakara touched her earpiece, looked momentarily confused then nodded. She stood up and followed Peter Mercier's example.

A moment later, Natalie Judd did the same.

'*Fuck*. Cut to President's speech!' the controller of *BPH News*, Susan Banbridge, cried out. '*Sam*. The fucking President.'

But Samuel Marshall, whose fifteen-year-old son was a Non-Verbal, stood up.

'What the . . .? *Sam*.'

But he had already left the control room.

'*Am I the only professional here?*' She rushed over and cut to the President's speech herself.

335

'—*To speak is a beautiful thing. Right? It's us and them. If you're Non-Verbal then you're non-existent and our great nation will always exist*—'

'Lucy, *are you there?*' exclaimed Susan into her earpiece. 'Bring Akari on ASAP. I don't care that her make-up's not done.'

No response.

'Lucy? *Lucy* . . .'

Susan needn't have worried. She was not the only one in a state of frenzied professionalism that moment. Employers, directors, CEOs were not watching their screens. They were watching in horror as Non-Verbal doctors and nurses marched out of hospitals. Office workers powered down their computers and left their buildings. Police officers on duty set down their equipment, took off their badges and walked away from their livelihoods. Notifications had pinged on parents' phones across the country that teachers, Verbal and Non-Verbals, were now on strike.

The very essence of freedom was being taken away.

Each Non-Verbal and, every Verbal in support of silence, knew that there comes a time when one must pick a side. Put conviction to the test.

The right to choose was being taken away.

Today was the day to unite in opinion and dare to disobey.

Graham Nash sat on his sofa at home, nursing a whiskey at precisely 7.36 p.m. He switched from blank screen to blank screen, until he could not stay indoors any longer. Outside he heard a glass smash. A group of men and women were tipsy, tripping over themselves until they passed him, putting their fingers to their lips.

He nodded to them as they pumped their fists in the air.

How would Grace be coping with this? What on earth was happening? He tried to call her again.

This number is no longer in use.

Now there wasn't even the hope of reaching her. He recalled the final hour they had spent together. He had expected her to break her silence when they arrived home to explain to Benji what would happen. He'd asked how she was feeling and whether she needed a doctor, but she had just brushed him away, hurrying towards the kitchen, kneeling on the floor, looking for something.

'What are you doing?'

She had got up. Her fist clenched.

'Are you OK?'

She had stared at him, opened her mouth.

'I don't understand why you chose silence over your son,' he eventually added.

The look, whatever it had been, passed.

Classic Grace.

He probably should've kept his opinion to himself. Then, perhaps she would have stayed.

One thing was certain, through their self-focused actions, she and Javed had given the government the moral authority to ban Non-Verbalism.

In that sense, they were to blame.

St John's Wood High Street was empty. Wherever he looked there were posters in support of Non-Verbalism. He noticed a flag with 'NV' on it, billowing over the local library.

Bring Sara Home.
Lock up Grace Jenkins.

Signs and posters demanding, searching, pleading, condemning.

If and when Grace got caught, she might never see her son again. She certainly wouldn't be allowed to practice the law. How could she have done something so *thoughtless*. Not even left Graham a note? (In moments of social despair, one could never forget the damage done to one, person-ally.) Graham always had caught himself in love with difficult women, and

Grace was no different. Her taking Benji being a case in point. He hoped she was safe. That she had what she needed. And wanted. Even if it meant she didn't want him.

Tahera Rashid and her husband, Kamran Khan, flicked through channel after channel, all blank, holding pages popping up. She scrolled through her social media. Every page with the same notice:

Owing to the UK's declaration to ban Non-Verbalism, we have taken the decision to stand in solidarity with Non-Verbals. We know how much staying connected means to our users. Today we will be connected through our shared values. We will be back when our Non-Verbal brothers and sisters are free to live the way they choose.

Tahera refreshed each page several times. *What on earth.*
Kamran stared at BPH Channel's screen:

We are committed to serving the British public with the most dynamic programmes and latest news. We apologise for the current inconvenience and are working hard to come back to you.
  In solidarity,
  The British Production House team

At 8.04 p.m. Tahera FaceTimed her mum in Islamabad, whose usual no-nonsense demeanour was rather more pronounced today. There was not the standard kerfuffle of her dad's face popping up behind her mum while she asked whether Tahera's youngest had learnt his seven times table, or giving details of her latest blood sugar levels. Instead her dad came and sat beside her mum, putting his arm around her and one finger to his lips.

Tahera nodded.

Her mum nodded.

338

Eventually, Tahera disconnected the call.

Their children were asleep. This is when she'd slide under Kamran's arm and appreciate the quiet. Tonight's speech, however, somewhat disturbed the routine.

An injustice dressed up as social unity would have an adverse effect on anyone.

Kamran, eventually, placed a piece of paper on to her lap.

It was a bank statement.

He pointed at the cost of £380 on her credit card for an Air BnB ten days ago.

Shit.

Tahera gave her best defiant look.

She wore it often and wore it well.

Kamran waited.

He waited often and waited well.

She wanted to say that she supposed she should start locking the drawers now, but to speak felt like a violation.

She put her hand on his chest and went to kiss him but he pulled back.

Tahera stood up, hands on her hips, searching for the words – knowing how wrong it would feel use them. She wanted to say that he should know her well enough to not ask for explanations. Being entirely honest with one's partner, in her view, was a naïve move in seeking marital bliss.

If she told him that she was funding Zainab's escape from the family and law, he would make her do what he thought was right. But for thoughts to be correct they needed all the information and she couldn't give Zainab's secret away without permission.

All Kamran would understand is that when Zainab's mum had called Tahera in a panic after Zainab had gone missing, Tahera had lied to her. When Kashif's family had asked Tahera every detail of what Zainab had said the night before she left, Kamran would know she'd lied then too.

'*The scandal*,' Kashif's mum had exclaimed. '*We* told the police she had gone missing and they took *Kashi* in for questioning.'

339

Tahera had laughed. Kamran had found it disconcerting.

Now, she could see his patience waning, his temper rising as he got up.

She took his hand, looking up at him. His features softened.

It was all Tahera could do *not* to tell every single person they knew what Kashif had done to Zainab. That his sin was such that even God wouldn't absolve. She believed this with all the conviction of her faith.

She took Kamran's face in her hands.

He put his hands on her wrists.

What was it that prevented *her* from speaking? As the evening unfolded, she was indignant, as she always had been, at the prospect of being dictated to. Pissed off that Javed had apparently decided to go on a jolly, leaving behind a trail of silent destruction. She was sorry for her dad's death but people needed to get their shit together.

Tahera stroked Kamran's bottom lip with her thumb.

He looked forlorn. Whatever her personal feelings about Non-Verbalism (a barrel full of bullshit), she could not help but be affected by her parents' silence. And she knew her husband. That it suited his spirit to reflect and observe others. Take the children, one of whom wasn't biologically his, and watch them play in the park.

Non-Verbalism had been a tonic for Kamran in this verbally indulgent world and now it was being taken away.

She kissed him.

Like many others she knew, they wouldn't give up without a fight. They didn't when his parents objected to him marrying the loud divorcée with a child – they weren't about to start now.

At 6.30 a.m. Penelope Pembrooke was hunched over her laptop, still attempting to decipher the blank email Sara had sent just after the PM's speech. Was it a message of remorse? An accident?

It was characteristically annoying.

You have been added to the group: Together in Silence.

'Ugh,' said Penelope.

WhatsApp groups such as Mothers 4 Silence; Non-Verbals Unite; Silent

Nights (which was particularly grating) etc. had been set-up. Penelope was being added to them with all the verve and passion that couldn't be expressed in words. Since no one was actually writing anything, the groups were considered to be more symbolic in nature.

Penelope was desperate to leave each one, but that gesture held its own symbolism and she had her professional standing to maintain.

An image popped up in the new group. The cover of Sara's first edition of *Rule-makers*.

'You've always cared too much about your authors,' said her husband, coming up behind her. 'I can tell you the feeling's probably not mutual.'

Penelope paused. 'Maybe not, but I believed in her books. In *her*.'

'I know.'

'And this year's turnover's been quite something.'

'Pen . . .'

'No one person should bear the responsibility of a whole people. But Sara must know . . .' Penelope paused. 'She *has* to come back.'

At 7.08 a.m. after a very late night and fitful sleep, for obvious reasons, Roxy searched frantically for her CBD oil. The figure next to her in bed rolled over. She went into the living room and looked outside the window, catching her neighbour's eye. He put his finger to his lips.

Roxy moved away.

She squirted a few drops of oil on her tongue as she checked Twitter.

It was dead.

Barren.

Had Sara planned to disappear after they interviewed her? Was her dad's death just a convenient excuse to vanish? It had been over a month and, despite her anger and resentment, Roxy still wondered: was Sara OK?

Roxy checked every social media platform but it was impossible to find global outrage. She was not used to such a lack of display of sentiment.

Her bedroom door opened as the dishevelled figure of Lauren sat next to Roxy on the sofa.

'There's nothing here,' cried Roxy. '*How are we meant to know what's going on?*'

Lauren reached for her bag and took out a piece of paper.

It was Sara's letter, printed and worn. Even now, a year later, Roxy felt affronted at the way people thought they knew Sara. As if they understood her obsession with questioning *herself* rather than the people around her. How positively archaic it all was.

It took Roxy at least ten minutes – so involved was she in her own outrage – to realise Lauren hadn't spoken.

'Don't you have an opinion?'

Lauren shook her head.

'You have to be shitting me. You are *not* Non-Verbal.'

To which Lauren gave a decided nod.

'You're being fucking stupid.' Roxy instantly regretted the words.

Lauren's face went red.

The doorbell rang and Aadhi strode in. 'Oh, I should've called . . .' He watched Lauren march into Roxy's bedroom. She came back out in a black mini-skirt and cheetah-printed top.

'Listen, I'm sorry but—'

Lauren held up her hand.

'So what? We're done?'

Lauren stuck her neck out as if to say *obviously* before she walked out, slamming the door behind her.

Roxy slumped down on the sofa. Aadhi, clearly agitated, paced up and down.

'She's just following everyone like a lemming,' murmured Roxy, still staring at the door.

Aadhi stopped. 'You *agree* with the ban?'

'You *don't*?' said Roxy.

'We should find Zainab Aalam,' he said, decisively.

'Who?'

'The email we got yesterday.'

'Focus, Aadhs. The documentary's more important now than ever.'

Roxy had been so focused on finishing the documentary, by turns so elated and anxious about her family's reaction to witnessing her be a part of something *significant* – how could she possibly think of anything else?

Aadhi took the remote and switched on Roxy's MoodBox, flicking from blank channel to blank channel. 'Without *this*, there is no documentary.'

48 Hours Later . . .

'It's confirmed. The production company's halted all works,' said Aadhi who had made a habit of turning up outside Roxy's door now. It was 11.30 in the morning and she was still in her dressing gown. She refused to try and find Zainab and so he had told her he'd do it without her help. But this particular piece of information, for Roxy, was a jolt.

She slumped on the sofa and put her head in her hands.

'There aren't enough people willing to complete their job without their rights.' Aadhi rubbed the back of his neck. 'And the channels can't broadcast anything new right now.'

Roxy felt the panic rise to her chest. Lauren had left her, and now the thing for which she had dedicated the past year of her life was being taken away.

He looked her up and down. 'Have you been out at all?'

She shook her head. Her only focus had been this documentary, and once that was in place, she could face the rest. Because, for perhaps the third time in Roxy's life, without anything else to hold on to, if she went outside she was afraid to know what she might find. All the indications pointed towards disappointment at best, devastation at worst.

'Get changed, Roxy.'

She reluctantly acquiesced. Aadhi grabbed her hand and they left the house. They walked down to the high street in Dalston.

Roxy stared at the usually bustling road with markets, people shopping and gathering to sit outside the Costa. Now, it was completely quiet. Most shops were closed. Boots was open, a security guard standing at the door, looking up and down the street until he saw Aadhi and Roxy. He waved and put his hand to his chest.

'Is this it?' whispered Roxy. 'Is this the end of the world?'

Without any access to news, there was no certainty on the matter.

There was the stomping of feet, a distant shuffle. A sea of walking bodies emerged, banners flying high.

Roxy squinted, discerning the writing:

We Refuse.

'Fucking people.' Aadhi grabbed Roxy and turned into Gillet Road. Music permeated the empty square through the jazz club's door. Gone were the groups of people usually smoking and drinking, the crackling barbeques. All that remained was the faint smell of urine and the frenzied thrum of a trumpet. They watched as a crowd walked past. Their faces indignant, resolute. Aadhi and Roxy followed.

The crowd swelled as it walked through Hoxton, down past the Barbican. People peered through windows, came out of their homes into the street, joined in, hands on their chests. A hardened mix of anxiety and resolve. They marched down the embankment, London's grey skies threatening rain, banners splayed on windows: *Beware The Barrenness of a Busy Life.*

Roxy could not speak: despite her beliefs, she could not help but be moved by the mass, made obscure and insignificant in its mix, yet somehow undeniably powerful.

After two hours of walking, they reached 10 Downing Street. A lectern had been set up with mics. The crowd, now large, gathered outside, banging their placards on the ground.

How could a democratic leader dictate to the people what their voice should mean? *It would not do.*

Soon, Prime Minister Ruth Baynham walked out, hair frizzing at the sides. She stepped up to the lectern and began speaking, 'Two days ago,

I stood in allegiance with leadership all over the world. We took a collective stance because we believe in the voice of the people.'

Furious faces stared back. Discontent. More banging of placards.

Baynham paused. 'We could not support a movement that steals the voice, the very thing that has given rise to such momentous occasions in history.' She swallowed hard. 'We paid the price. We woke up to a world we do not recognise. This past year has been tumultuous for us all and, despite what I inherited four months ago, I have served the nation with full heart and vigour.'

The sound of the placards hitting the ground was now deafening. Accountability must be had.

'*But*—'

She raised both her hands, asking for quiet. It took several minutes before it came.

'—You must have confidence in your leaders. We recognise your need to be heard. Even in your silence. And so, it is agreed that there will be a general election on 4 August—'

Cheering erupted, so loud Roxy covered her ears.

Baynham waited for the noise to die down.

'—In light of this, and to navigate this government towards ultimate victory—'

There were jeers at the very notion.

'—I have formally offered my resignation as leader of the party to Her Majesty the Queen. Through democratic means we have voted John Kipple in as the interim leader of the party, and of the country.

'I have served you to the best of my ability—' Here, her voice cracked. 'It is now up to you to use your vote wisely and make the *right* choice.'

Finally, Baynham stacked her papers and walked back into Downing Street.

The people of the nation were now asked to decide on 4 August 2022: *Vote for Choice* or *Vote for a Voice*. The two, by an electoral turn of events, became quite mutually exclusive.

24 Hours Later . . .

Speak for Change

Rolling Statement on True News

The government is offering grants and a career package to the game-changers of society. We seek innovative thinkers who are committed to progress and free speech. For further information please call 0300 478 478 and speak directly to our head of culture and communications. Verbalism is essential for this role.

Please note that for the safety of our staff against Non-Verbal extremists, we will be broadcasting via rolling statements only. We will endeavour to deliver the highest quality journalism and hope to return, verbally, to your screens as soon as it is safe to do so.

'You must be the change you wish to see in the world' – Mahatma Gandhi.

VOTE FOR A VOICE

12 Hours Later . . .

The Great Refusal

Rolling Statement on The Refusal channel

This is a live image stream of news from around the world. We believe in Non-Verbalism and the stand against an authoritarian government, but we also believe in the power of knowledge.

To stay united we must know what is happening around us. Our team is working hard to develop strategies to honour Non-Verbalism and keep us connected and updated about #TheGreatRefusal.

We are being pitted against one another. This channel is here to help us to fight the good fight.

VOTE FOR CHOICE

'Seen this police notice?' said Aadhi to Roxy, showing her a screenshot of a leaflet that had been put up in Glasgow.

Police are searching for a woman of Pakistani origin, 35, 5ft 6, in Glasgow. Zainab Aalam – a Verbal – has been reported to have absconded her ex-marital home to avoid deportation. If you have any information regarding this issue, please contact your local police immediately.

'It's been doing the rounds,' he added.

He was, once again, in Roxy's flat, trying to fathom the changes of the past 72 hours. The rallying silence was perforated by True News. A channel seemingly committed to disseminating information via rolling statements, attempting to rouse people out of their silent indignation.

The statement on The Refusal had been followed by images from around the world of quiet streets, banners in New York and Delhi, Saudi Arabia and Israel, Scotland and Japan, presumably in an attempt to ensure people held on to their conviction.

Instagram had rebranded itself overnight as Hushes, its algorithms reconfigured to display images of people coming together, globally, in unified silence, at the top of people's feeds. Images of Sara's books were displayed on the platform far and wide. Aadhi tried to get Roxy to understand that even though she and the government might want the same thing, it was, ultimately, unjust to all.

'Oh my God,' Roxy exclaimed, whose particular variety of suffering injustice was different to his. 'This Zainab thing's interesting, but can we just focus on at least *trying* to get the documentary out?'

'*Where?*' Aadhi asked. 'There's no chance. And look at the bigger picture. You're acting worse than Sara.'

Roxy called him a coward.

Aadhi called her selfish.

Over the next few minutes, each offered up various accusations about the other's professionalism and personal agendas. Eventually, Aadhi swept out of the flat, slamming the door behind him.

When he returned home, he spent hours thinking of ways to find Zainab Aalam. He had replied to the email they'd initially received but he still had no response.

Aadhi remembered how much he had looked forward to meeting Sara; what a woman with her upbringing might offer in terms of intellectual diversity. All he had found though was mediocrity. He would come across online conversations from the beginning of her career, fans outraged at her lack of literary fame – believing she wasn't given the same chances because she was a brown woman.

Sometimes it's not that you're brown, it's that you're average, he had once tweeted. This resulted in him being blocked and unfollowed by hundreds, as well as the closing in of options to write opinion pieces. Instead of raising people of colour, he was accused of attempting to diminish them. But Aadhi believed himself to be an egalitarian and, the truth was, idiocy didn't discriminate.

Then Sara got her literary fame. And more besides.

But she was no idiot.

Only, *where was she?* He could not help but feel an increasing sense of foreboding about her absence.

He wasn't sure how long he'd been lost in this reverie when a New York friend of his FaceTimed. She gazed at Aadhi through the camera, her husband next to her in the car, her two children behind them. A *Vote for Choice* sign at the back of their car, was just about visible. The two slogans were being adopted in most democratic nations.

'How are you guys?' Aadhi asked.

There was a collective thumbs up.

'Where are you going?'

Where the hell was anyone going?

'Grandma and Grandpa's,' shouted one of the children.

That was in Virginia.

'New York silent?' he asked.

His friend nodded.

'And Virginia?'

She shrugged.

'What is it *like*?'

Aadhi was left to decipher his friend and her husband's expressions. The President's power had waned by virtue of lack of dissemination of his views, according to another friend of his – still Verbal – in the US.

'Honestly guys, I thought better of you.'

His friend stuck her finger up at him.

With not much more conversation to be had, Aadhi disconnected the call. He had been against silence for so long that he had refused to acknowledge the possibility of living in a reality that was so opposed to his beliefs.

The feeling was hardly particular to him.

The following day he went to see his dad who was now living with Aadhi's sister. She was a selective Non-Verbal, and only spoke to their father.

'Hey, Pops,' Aadhi greeted.

He seemed to have aged a year in the space of a week. 'Your mother left the heating on again.'

Aadhi's mother had been dead for several years.

'I'll switch it off.'

'No, no. You know how cold she gets.' His dad leant forward and whispered: 'Happy wife, happy life.'

Aadhi attempted a smile. He told his father about what was happening in the world. There was little point, his dad would forget again tomorrow, but Aadhi had many problems, and accepting defeat was one of them.

'So, they've put a stop to my documentary.'

'But you're studying medicine.'

'That was twenty years ago, Dad.'

His dad nodded thoughtfully. 'Shall we have tea? Why is it so hot in here? Your mother's left the heating on again.'

Aadhi struggled not to well up. Today, he needed the father who used to have all his mental faculties intact. He needed his mother, who would have sat him down and written out a pros and cons list of this ban. Told him not to be swayed by public opinion.

Aadhi's phone rang. It was Roxy.

'I just got a phone call,' she said. 'From Zainab Aalam.' Her voice was subdued. 'Fine, you have a point. I'm trying to look at the bigger picture. And there is more to tell.'

Aadhi and Roxy, it would transpire, were still on the same side.

Since the Prime Minister's speech a week ago, Angie had taken to staying at the refuge to ensure that the precarity of the outside world didn't make the women's lives in the refuge even more precarious. When there was no spare room, she slept on the floor.

With a general election now on the horizon, people had begun to go back to work, but no one had forgotten their commitment to #Refuse. The rallying must continue if equality and justice were to prevail.

The Work Continues was a commonly shared slogan on Hushes.

It was one o'clock in the morning and Angie was transfixed by the television. She was wondering who exactly was funding True News, what had become of Grace and where Sara Javed had gone – would she come back and *do* something – when there was a knock on the door. She slipped into her gown and peered through the peephole. It was a woman, dishevelled and fraught. Angie, as was her rule, opened the door.

For a moment, the woman just stared.

'I'm Verbal.'

Angie, who was now, on principle, a Non-Verbal, let her in, putting a finger to her lips. She had never believed in the movement, but she believed in the ban even less. Her ideas always were based on an assessment of the

situation rather than a pervasive need to follow a rule. As with most reasoned ideas, hers was not a popular one.

The woman – who Angie observed was no ordinary looking lady, and
possibly Indian or Pakistani – looked around, as if searching for something. The whimsy of Angie's own lost youth flickered as she put a hand
on the woman's arm. She sat her in the living room and brought her a
cup of tea.

The woman shook her leg, tapped her feet, looking tired, yet enchanting.

Angie inhaled deeply, exhaling for five seconds, indicating for the
woman to do the same. She obliged. After several of these, Angie nodded
as if for her to speak.

'I . . .'

Angie gestured for her to continue.

'I'm looking for Grace Jenkins.'

Angie felt a pang of regret. She and Grace never had been on good
terms but whatever might be said about her, Angie couldn't countenance
a man who, after such a long absence, claimed to have any rights. Everyone had them, of course. But some more than others.

It almost made her ashamed of the colour of her own skin. She knew
how these things worked. The deep prejudice of perception.

'Is she here? Grace?'

Angie shook her head.

The woman put her head in her hands. 'She never came back?'

Did you know her? Angie wrote on a piece of paper.

The woman shook her head.

Then?

'I've followed her story.' The woman paused. 'I found out she used to
work here and I just thought . . . I don't know what I thought. But I had to
leave my marriage and needed somewhere safe to stay but wherever I go
there's no sound. It's driving me crazy. The one friend I have is also Non-
Verbal now, which I understand, but I just *need* someone. *Anyone.* I need a
place to stay.'

Educated. That was clear from the fluidity of her speech. The elegance of her manner. No ordinary woman. And yet, here, with nowhere else to go, she was ordinary enough.

Aadhi and Roxy drove up the M6, past billboard after billboard with the same incentives plastered in uninventive ways; live, multicoloured, flashing: *Vote for a Voice*. The government was injecting millions into initiatives that might 'rebuild the fractured nation'. If nothing changed then it was suggested through this propaganda that one would only have themselves to blame.

Ads celebrating the Non-Verbal lifestyle had evolved into #VoteFor-Choice rhetoric. Refreshing the narrative, moving away from stalwart Non-Verbalism – in this way, the opposition might get die-hard Verbals to tick the correct box on the ballot.

Every time a new graffiti emerged in support of Non-Verbalism, some-one was clearly being paid to paint over it. People needed to put food on the table after all, however reluctant they might be about the means in which to do so. It was, as was often the case, survival of the fittest.

'I don't understand why she called you,' said Aadhi.

'She said a friend of hers – Tahera Rashid, reluctant Non-Verbal – wrote to her about having emailed us. That she knew Zainab needed support. So Zainab Googled us.' Roxy shook her head. 'She came across the quote Sara gave me for my book. She told me the connection gave her confidence.'

'What does she want?'

'To stay in the country.'

It appealed to Roxy's sense of drama that she was willing to drive for hours to listen to a Verbal woman in these Non-Verbal times.

Zainab, it turned out, was in Manchester, for reasons she hadn't explained. Roxy followed the SatNav to the green where she'd be waiting. In a red coat. They drove through the town centre, where restaurants and shops were open again. #Refuse, plastered everywhere. Staff wore T-shirts or face masks declaring #VoteForChoice. Verbalism, in public, was met with censure and even, upon occasion, eviction.

They saw her from afar; sitting on a bench, hands tucked into her red coat pockets as she stared into the distance.

'Zainab?'

She looked up and eventually made room on the bench where Roxy took a seat. Aadhi chose to stand. He glanced around, checking others couldn't witness them speaking.

'Thanks for meeting us.' Roxy's voice low. 'Can we record this?'

Zainab considered it for a moment before nodding.

'Why did you call us?'

She paused. 'I don't know. Tahera – the one who told me to get in touch – she once said I should go public with my story.' Zainab let out a small laugh. 'As if it might help my case.'

'What is your story?' asked Aadhi.

Zainab looked at him. Even Aadhi, man of the world, felt an acute discomfort at her beauty. If she were a news story, she would make a compelling one. Illegal immigrants weren't meant to look like her. Nor were they meant to speak like her.

'I'm not sure yet,' replied Zainab

'What is it you want from us?' asked Roxy.

'I don't know that either. I just don't want to feel like I'm alone anymore.' She paused. '*Unheard.*'

'Where do you stand on Non-Verbalism?' asked Roxy.

'I don't care,' replied Zainab. 'Speak, don't speak, it's your life. Even though it changed so many things for me.'

'Does Sara Javed's disappearance anger you?' added Roxy.

'Anger me? I was *disappointed*, yes, but the way people had been hounding her. So much expectation from one woman. No wonder she disappeared.'

'Do you agree with the ban?' asked Roxy, heart thudding.

'I just want to be able to choose my life. Let others choose theirs.'

Zainab Alam's eyes grew watery. 'Is that on?' She gestured to Roxy's recorder.

'Yes.'

Zainab began to speak. As Aadhi and Roxy listened, captivated by Zainab's soft tones, Roxy imagined what the blurb of a book of her story might be: *A woman, brought to a foreign land, suffering in silence, abandons duty for freedom, only to be stripped of her identity* . . . Roxy was a creature of habit, after all.

As Zainab finished telling her story Roxy felt all the dismay one woman could for another. The cumulation of shame and disappointment; the quiet indignities; the not-so-quiet demand for reprisal. Aadhi had to hand Roxy a tissue.

She was a creature of feeling, too.

June 2022

David Hodgkin was so used to good luck that when it didn't come his way, it felt especially traumatic. Nevertheless, his son being kidnapped and then the world going categorically silent were unique circumstances for anyone.

Weeks had passed, which could have been years, could have been minutes. People were maintaining their stance, each day, and would do so it appeared until the day of truth. In workplaces, colleagues had begun to understand each other through sign and shorthand notes. Team meetings were certainly more efficient, though few people now went into the office. Working from home was both prevalent and a preferred mode in order to maintain Non-Verbalism.

People had taken to walking in the park, nodding at one another, fortified by unity of opinion while, sometimes, also quite uncertain of it.

Online search engines were being used again. But anyone who suffered was doing so in silence.

Food drives, helping those in financial insecurity, were being organised. Celebrities were funding soup kitchens. People were checking on their elderly neighbours. Despair and defiance had coalesced into a sense of duty.

The dissolution of the top, it seemed, began at the bottom. It was hardly ideal but then what was?

David, Helen, family and friends had been posting leaflets with Benji and Grace's photos on them, going door-to-door in Grace's neighbour-hood, but it was futile: they could be *anywhere*.

Without social media platforms, news anchors probably fearful of the repercussion should they go on television, David felt voiceless.

'That fucking Sara Javed,' said David. 'Are the Smiths speaking?'

'Behind closed doors, you can count on it,' replied his wife, Helen.

Some even boldly employed *Vote for a Voice* posters in their front windows.

Aside from the ones who now lived in fear of speaking, there were the *allies*, standing shoulder-to-shoulder with Non-Verbals. But it was quite trying to practise conviction so consistently. For a cause they hadn't even considered until it became a phenomenon. They satisfied themselves by practicing it when convenient and buying much of Javed's backlist to edu-cate themselves. Uploading all pictorial evidence on Hushes. Constantly sharing and resharing #WhereIsSara. It made defending slipping into Ver-balism now and then justifiable to themselves, and, crucially, others.

'How are we going to get him back?' he asked.

Helen kissed him on the head. 'Darling, you get whatever you put your mind to. This time will be no different.'

As was her daily practice, Kat flicked through the channels to check if anything new had come up. Another connection, however small, to *some-thing* outside her neighbourhood. Sometimes she'd travel to north London and hover outside Sara's flat, wondering if she might turn up there. The front brimmed with flowers and messages. Someone had set up a book in which to write messages of support for Sara. The inspiration she'd been. Someone else thought it acceptable to throw eggs at her door. Graffiti her wall with *Fuck You, Bitch*. Kat painted over it.

True News was peddling a 'Sara Javed abandoned everyone' narrative, and Kat only hoped that Sara hadn't seen it. She understood that many people held her accountable, but Kat believed in a person's right to retreat when they wished. The more onus put upon one person, the less responsibility was put upon the very leaders who'd ultimately got them here. If Kat was more hive-minded, she might wear a T-shirt that relayed something to that effect.

Kat had gladly given up her voice in unity with the masses, but she now found herself restless and, oddly, resentful. Of course, she'd have supported all Non-Verbals, but this silence felt as enforced as speech had. She, and Kat was sure there were others like her, felt that to speak at all right now could spark hate crimes, and this sort of hypocrisy, quite frankly, was trying.

Still sacrifices had to be made. What she wanted and what was needed might be at odds with one another but some things were greater than the individual. Her wisdom and self-restraint in this sense was more honed than that of many self-congratulatory Non-Verbals.

When her doorbell rang, it was almost a relief. She opened it to a harassed looking Roxy who didn't wait for an invitation before she marched in.

'All right, Kat. I'm not apologising about whatever's happened but the truth is . . . Aadhi and I need your help.'

Roxy went through her post, eyes flicking from her laptop to the TV, alert for any changes in written statements.

The government's desperation to turn people Verbal was unseemly. She watched the endless adverts to 'Serve Your Voice,' and the letters that now came through the post – telling Roxy about various schemes and grants to recreate a vocal society.

'*Fuck off*!' she shouted, to no one but herself.

All her friends were now Non-Verbal – partaking in various forms of spiritual retreat, social protest, personal development. Roxy found it particularly confusing since so many of them had been staunchly anti-the movement until recently. Her sister, Halimah, had deleted all her social media accounts. Roxy wasn't sure whether everyone's reaction was a rebellion or conformity.

Sometimes it was very hard to tell the difference.

Roxy changed the channel and her heart almost skipped a beat as Zainab's picture appeared on the screen.

Silent For Zainab

Rolling Statement on The Refusal channel

While the government is bribing us into Verbalism, we must all stand together and recognise that to be silent is not only a right but, for Zainab Aalam, a necessity. She is a woman who has been in this country for ten years and is now being forced to leave with an unfair notice for deportation. She was reported to the police by members of the marital home in which she was subjugated, and now there are calls to contact local police should anyone see her. Do not capitulate. We must continue our silence both for Non-Verbals and Zainab Aalam.

She called Aadhi who was still half-asleep. 'Switch on The Refusal channel.'

A few moments passed. 'Well, look at that.'

She could hear the smile in his voice.

'Will it work?' asked Roxy.

'I don't know.'

'I wish she'd let us tell her *whole* story,' said Roxy. 'Not this cherry-picked version.'

'It'll have to do,' replied Aadhi. 'And everyone loves a cause. You included.'

'You were just as taken with her story . . . Or her.'

'They both become one and the same after a while. You know what we're doing is in direct opposition to what we set out?' added Aadhi.

'Yeah, well . . .'

Zainab hadn't changed Roxy's opinion. Or the principle of the matter. But something snagged for Roxy, so significantly, it began to unravel her

363

prejudices. If a woman like Zainab could look upon Non-Verbalism without vitriol, then surely Roxy could consider a ban on silence a form of censorship.

'So, what's next?' she asked.

'This'll be playing on a loop, yes?'

'For at least the next week, every hour,' confirmed Roxy.

'Good. The Hushes account?'

'Done.'

'Emailed all Non-Verbal MPs?' asked Aadhi.

'Yeah. Which, by the way, begs the question, what exactly are *you* doing?'

He paused. 'I'm looking for Sara.'

Open Doors, Closed Mouths

Protect Zainab Aalam

The message had been graffitied on Bridgwater Canal, alongside Deansgate, on the upper beam of Salford Quays' Millennium Bridge. To vote for choice was to vote for freedom, and Manchester was the proud proponent of liberty.

Within a week *Silent for Zainab* posters were, indeed, all over the country. Images posted on Hushes. The Scottish had taken to the cause with fervour. Wherever Zainab was, it was every citizen's duty to hide her from this unjust, out-of-touch government. She had been oppressed in her marital home, rejected by her family and was now facing deportation. She wasn't an *illegal* immigrant, usurping the UK's natives' rights. She had been a model citizen. She *paid her taxes* (which is more than could be said for many). She had been a *regular* at Kelvingrove Park Gallery.

White liberal women felt a renewed purpose by the idea of this dutiful woman, suffering oppression. Brown liberal women couldn't help but feel ownership over Zainab and the cultural mores that continued to persecute their kind. That the former group was able to fortify their own

Western ideals and offer unstinting support, and the latter could use the story as a reason for blanket condemnation of the traditional South Asian community, was a much-needed distraction from all this refusal.

Fingers fidgeted, mouths twitched. People were being forced to sit with their feelings, ideas and opinions. Silence had never felt so trying.

But no matter the temptation to speak, or even wish to concede to governmental bribes – and there was plenty of temptation – here was a beautiful Asian woman who was being publicly wronged by that very government. It cemented Non-Verbals, and its supporters' conviction, that this government had to be ousted in the election on 4 August.

To show that silence was now tantamount to justice, *Free Zainab* badges were being eagerly produced and even more eagerly worn.

Angie was certainly wearing hers. She bought Zainab a cup of tea. *Thank you*, Zainab mouthed.

Angie noticed Zainab staring at Javed's letter in the frame that Grace had put up all those months ago. Zainab had now become a very recognisable woman since her photo was being televised: a prisoner in the name of social freedom. So Angie went out for anything Zainab needed. She walked passed the quiet shops that were open; restaurants with signs: *No Verbals. Eat Your Words*. If Javed's letter was not visible, if there was no #Refuse sign conspicuously hung in sight, then that business could bet no customer was walking through *their* door. But recently, shops with *Vote for a Voice* posters were becoming increasingly visible.

Angie stopped in front of a brick wall, lined with posters of Zainab and carrying the hashtags of the moment.

#VoteForChoice
#SaraComeHome
#SilentForZainab
#JailGrace

She took a photo of the posters to show Zainab when she returned to the refuge. It might do her some good, to see that she had garnered the type of support from strangers that she had failed to receive from her own family.

Vote for Choice

Rolling Statement on The Refusal channel

Leader of the Opposition Bacclay vows to save Zainab Aalam from deportation. Vote for everyone's right to choose their words and home.
#VoteForChoice on 4 August
#SilentfortheSilenced

Who the hell was Zainab Aalam and why was *she* all over the few channels available? If any story should be going viral, it should be the case of the kidnapped son. David supposed it was easy to pity a beautiful woman.

(Which it was – especially one as fair-skinned as her.)

The intense interest from the press that David had had during the court case had since all but disappeared. He *must* jog the nation's memory.

'I'll be annihilated if I speak out,' David said to Helen now.

'I think it's time to risk annihilation.'

July 2022

'This is not easy for me to do . . .'

Aadhi: Are you watching True News?

Of course Roxy was watching. A mass mailout of leaflets posted through the letterbox of thousands of households was photographed by almost every recipient and then forwarded to friends and family. It had eventually gone viral. Someone was going to *speak* on national television.

'My family and I have the utmost respect for Non-Verbals and Verbals – ourselves included – standing in solidarity. But . . .'

David Hodgkin looked at the camera. His wife, presumably, standing behind him.

'We cannot be silent about our medically Non-Verbal son. His biological mother, Grace Jenkins, took up Non-Verbalism, and for anyone who followed our public court case you'll know it's been confirmed by every expert that it is having a serious psychological impact on our son. His mother is not fit to care for him.'

There were tears in his eyes.

'*Forgive the desperation of a father who wants to be reunited with his boy, but anyone with a child who's vulnerable . . .*'

His voice broke.

'*Whose life and future depends on their parent, please help us find our baby. And please, look at us and remember to vote for a voice.*'

A picture of Grace and Benji appeared on screen.

Roxy's mobile rang.

'As speeches go that was pretty effective,' said Aadhi. 'He was more likeable than he is in person.'

'I guess that's all that matters.' Roxy continued to look at the screen filled with Grace and her son's picture. 'It's sickening what that woman is putting her son through.'

'Ever with the compassion, Roxy.'

'I have plenty for people who deserve it.'

Roxy took a few more drops of her CBD oil.

Angie was woken up by a noise in the front hall. She squinted at her phone. It was 3 a.m.

Her heart thudded. Angie got a knife from the kitchen and crept into the passage. She had been faced before with discontented partners tracking down their supposedly anonymous address and turning up, threatening violence. Her nerves tensed as the handle turned and the door sprung open, keys jangling from the lock.

A figure emerged, round and slow.

A smaller one beside it.

What in the . . .?

Angie smacked her hand over her mouth.

Grace Jenkins and Benji stared at Angie in her pink gown, rollers in her hair and knife in hand. Angie pulled both of them indoors, checking that no one had seen them.

She had, like everyone across the country, watched the appeal. The very first time anyone had spoken on screen since the day of refusal. Who could miss it? Once inside, it took a moment for Angie's eye to catch Grace's hand resting over a significant bump.

Angie had always looked upon Grace as a mystery. But when she had watched her, pre-Refusal, on television, her mother turning up to testify *against* her, Angie felt a maternal instinct to hold her. It had alarmed Angie that her otherwise empathetic nature had not always extended to Grace, that it had not emerged sooner.

She had seen posters of Grace below Zainab's in the town centre. When she turned a corner. A live advert on a billboard. The side of a bus.

Raise Your Voice for Family.

#VoteforaVoice.

Now, Grace sat at the kitchen table, Benji staring at his mum. Angie got out some bedsheets, an air mattress and made it up for them on the other side of the living room. She looked at Grace, gesturing to her that it was all she could do.

Grace put Benji to sleep as Angie made her tea. They both sat at the kitchen table.

Had she seen the appeal? Did she think the place she used to work was safe, considering there was a nationwide hunt for her? Grace gave Angie a small smile, gesturing for her to speak. Angie grabbed her Non-Verbal badge and showed it to her. Grace let out a laugh. *Here we are,* she seemed to say, as she held out her arms.

Angie didn't believe that Grace was doing what was best for her son. *But* – and sometimes a but was necessary – if she was keeping Zainab from the police, then there was no reason not to do the same for Grace.

The following morning Angie observed Benji looking at Grace's belly. He then made Grace a cup of tea, put his hand on her bump, smile radiant when, clearly, the baby kicked. Angie could see a distinct difference in his behaviour – he didn't flush red, for example, when Angie smiled at him now. Perhaps the experts had been wrong.

When Zainab came into the common area and saw Grace, she strode towards her. Zainab seemed momentarily taken aback by Grace's bulging belly. Then she hugged her. Grace was obviously perplexed and then seemed to catch the look in Angie's eye. Eventually she hugged Zainab back as if they were long-lost friends, even though, of course, they were strangers.

One could love a person without liking them but Lily DeSouza was surprised that she should feel such conflict towards Sara. That, until recently, been reserved for Afzal.

Lily had taken to staying indoors since the events of 'The Refusal'. The outside world looked too much as if it was on the brink of an apocalypse, which in Lily's view, was rather dramatic. She hated that she dreamt of Afzal every night, the look of sympathy that Martin gave her, mistaking heartache for insomnia. She had to actively stop herself from thinking about Sara. The one who used to regularly call for updates, ask about Lily's husband and children. Lily had always considered Sara to be a grounded individual based on these facts.

But her rebellion had taken things *too* far. Afzal had centred his life around her – and now Lily needed someone with whom she could mourn his loss, someone who knew him, every grace and foible.

She couldn't help but feel that when she saw that man, David Hodgkin, appeal to the world, Sara had been the cause; that the woman – Zainab Aalam – who was being threatened by deportation – was a victim of Sara's ideas and ideals. And now that Afzal was gone she found it hard to recall what she had disliked. Which meant she was only left with its alternative.

Sara had not thought of anyone but herself. Other than that one email she had sent. *I'm safe*. Along with one word on her location. So, when Roxy and Aadhi had turned up at Lily's doorstep, she had let them in.

'We're going to speak,' said Roxy. 'You have to let us. Please.'

They both sat down, Roxy tapping her finger on her knees. Aadhi put his hand on her arm. Martin came in and shook their hands. He was Non-Verbal. When he took a seat, Lily gave him a meaningful look. He hesitated before he got up and left.

'We need to know where Sara is,' said Roxy.

Lily pursed her lips.

'Sara needs to face up to what she has done. We're worried that people won't . . .' Roxy used air quotes. '"*Vote for Choice.*"'

'You've changed your minds,' said Lily.

'Yes. *No*,' replied Roxy. 'Just that . . . well, I'm not a fascist.'

'Anymore,' added Aadhi.

Roxy gave him a sarcastic smile.

'We haven't changed our minds,' said Aadhi. 'Just, the alternative is rather bleak.'

'I don't see what Sara can do,' replied Lily.

'We think she can rouse the masses. Help to vote against the ban,' explained Roxy.

Lily sighed. She had lived a lifetime of fighting, losing, one step forward, two steps back. In the end all she could say about life is that it wrought what it did, and it was probably best not to yearn for more.

'You know, in the end, nothing changes.'

'You're wrong. This is it.' Surprisingly, Roxy spoke with all the hope and vivacity of youth that Lily had once employed. 'It can. It *will*.'

Silent for the Silenced

Rolling Statement on The Refusal Channel

*Protect Zainab Aalam from being deported. Divided in silence,
united for Zainab.
#VoteForChoice
#SilentfortheSilenced*

The hashtag was specifically rousing for Kashif and Suleiman when they came across it on Tahera's Hushes account. There was a selfie of her with Zainab, Tahera laughing, Zainab smiling – beautiful, understated, irreverent. Always the embodiment of winning combinations.

#Sister

#Truthsyoudontknow

#SilentfortheSilenced

Tahera's playfulness and sharp tongue, which Kashif and Suleiman had enjoyed in the past, now felt like tailored trolling.

Suleiman had thought of Zainab every day since she had disappeared, and now the nation's call for her protection reignited his need to protect her too.

Kashif felt hard done by. What about *his* suffering? Betrayed by his friend. Loyal to a wife unable to bear children.

All his life Kashif had been told he was a *good man*. The sexual desires which he imposed upon his wife were simply man's nature. (He surrounded himself with enough like-minded individuals to give credence to this belief.) She hadn't even appreciated the conscious changes he'd made post Non-Verbalism when they slept together.

He had never restricted her freedoms. Such was the magnanimity of his nature and concept of liberty. Now, to watch *her* be painted as a victim was too much.

He had watched David Hodgkin's appeal on True News while The Refusal was doing nothing but promoting Zainab's crime. He had written to The Refusal, effused respect for their ethos and asked for a chance to tell his side of the story.

He had received a response:

We are sorry that we cannot accommodate your request. We are focused on ensuring the correct outcome on 4 August. As a committed Non-Verbal, we know you will understand.

Yours,
The Refusal Team

Where was the equality? Kashif had been forced into writing to True News, detailing his version of events. That the pedestal upon which NVs had put Zainab, in reality, belonged to him.

He had got a response.

We are interested in your story if you are willing to break your
Non-Verbalism for a live interview?

Kashif had stared at the question for an hour.

He had been reasonable, but he could only live through so much
humiliation.

So, he wrote back with all the self-importance that came so naturally to him.

Yes, I am.

Graham, who had never been a fan of badge-wearing, wore one now. It
was the only way he could show support for the woman he loved. He had
watched the interview with Zainab Aalam's ex-husband. Kashif Taufiq
had a sort of pathetic face in some respects, and it had induced pity.

Perhaps Zainab was just another beautiful woman taking advantage of
an unimpressive man.

Graham continued to go into the office. People at their desk, clicking at
their keyboards, mouths pressed shut. It had been a particularly trying day
with a colleague refusing to represent her client who was anti-Non-Verbal.
The client was filing a suit for discrimination as a result. Graham had
wanted to get rid of both but his hands as well as his tongue were tied.

On his way home he paused in front of the billboard:

Unite Voices, Unite a Family

A single slogan with two pictures side-by-side: David and his wife, Helen,
and a separate picture of Benji, who by his expression, also looked keen to
be united. They were all over Manchester and the nation. Notices demanding information on Grace's whereabouts.

Graham began ripping the posters from the walls. Then he turned the
corner.

A woman was doing *exactly* the same.

She caught his eye and stopped. Paper in hand. She looked familiar. She was wearing big sunglass. Baggy white T-shirt and loose paisley trousers. Where had he seen her? She swung around and strode away. He wanted to call out to her, but he took his badge seriously. Instead, he followed her. She looked over her shoulder, picked up her pace.

Why was she scared? He was wearing a suit.

He broke into a jog. Then she halted and turned around.

'*Don't* follow me,' she called out.

Her voice pierced the quiet summer day.

He put up his hands.

The form of her face began to come together. The angular jaw, high cheekbones . . .

Another step forward.

'*Stop.*'

A few people on the other side of the road were staring. She turned around and broke into a run.

There was no denying it was Zainab Aalam. And she was here, in Manchester. Now he understood her reaction.

What remained bewildering was why she was taking down the posters of Grace.

Angie had stood in front of the door to try and stop her.

Zainab had showed Angie each and every post on Hushes calling Grace all sorts of offensive and alarming things. She was *furious*. But Angie had understood it was agitation after having watched her ex-husband make her out to be a liar.

Grace had switched the TV off, much to all the women's annoyance. She had stuck her finger up at the screen. She had then crouched in front of Zainab, taken both her hands, pressing down all but both middle fingers and forced Zainab to stick them up at the screen too. It was now ritual to employ this gesture whenever walking past the television.

Zainab was raging about the trending posters of Grace. Angie had always considered Zainab of a serene disposition so her stubbornness came at the most trying time. Had she absorbed it through osmosis, sharing a room with Grace? What were the words that Zainab whispered to Grace in the quiet of the night?

Zainab was the only one at whom Benji would smile. She spoke to him in such gentle, low tones, laughed with him so readily, reading comic books with him, letting him help her cook in the kitchen, that any onlooker might forget the boy never spoke. Angie supposed that beauty always had its draw, for children and cynics alike.

Now, Zainab returned, breathless and almost in tears.

'I'm sorry,' she whispered to Angie. She looked up to see Grace coming down the stairs. 'I saw your lawyer,' she said. 'He caught me taking down the posters. He ran after me.'

Grace put her hand on her belly.

'What if he reports me?' said Zainab. 'He was wearing a Non-Verbal badge.'

A smile escaped Grace.

'I should leave.'

Grace came down and caught Zainab by the shoulders.

'What if someone else recognised me? What if they're Verbal?'

If only Angie could record this moment . . . two outlaws, different sides of the verbal coin, holding on to each other. It was a provocative image.

Grace shook her head.

'But – Ow.' Grace had flicked Zainab's arm.

Zainab looked over Grace's shoulder at Benji, standing at the end of the passage.

She smiled at him, then looked at Grace's bump. Of course Zainab wouldn't leave.

Angie only wished the opposition had come up with a better tagline. *Choice* was such a lukewarm sentiment. It was, after all, only in extremity of feeling that people were roused.

★

375

Roxy insisted on going to find Sara on her own when Aadhi demanded he accompany her. He said that her relationship with Sara was too precarious. She retorted that at least the relationship was strong enough to have come to a point of precarity.

Would he know what to do if Sara refused to engage?

If she were angry?

Depressed and lonely?

And, in all likelihood, she would be all of the above.

Aadhi had conceded defeat.

Roxy had borrowed his car to drive to a town in the south of England that none of them – until Sara's four-word email to Lily – had heard of. She observed increasing signs for #RaiseYourVoice until she arrived at her destination.

Welcome to Pennington:
Proudly Non-Verbal.
#Refuse

She passed fields of yellow and green, before reaching a roundabout and heading towards the town's centre. That was as good a place to begin as any. The town, much to Roxy's consternation, was bustling. Election billboards were everywhere:

#VoteforChoice
#Silentforthesilenced
#Refuse

Shops were open. People sitting outside a big Morrison's next to Shipley's Shopping Centre, drinking iced tea and coffees. An Odeon played films with subtitles only.

She parked and walked towards the hub, where streams of people were basking in the sunshine in silence. Orchestral music played but Roxy wasn't sure where it was coming from. A live mime artist performed to a small crowd. She went into a Café Nero. The slurping of coffees. A baby crying and a mother shushing it. She walked up to the barista who gestured towards the iPad where Roxy placed her order. A sign indicated where she should wait.

She grabbed her drink and went to sit down when her phone rang. Everyone stopped, eyes narrowing at her. She put her hand up in way of apology and declined Aadhi's call. When she looked up a barista pointed at the sign: no mobiles. She looked around. Not a device to be seen. Roxy immediately wanted to take a photo, share the image, *tell* someone. Anyone. Unable to do so, Roxy left the café.

There were notices of protests being organised against the ban. *Support groups being formed*. Billboards here hadn't been co-opted by governmental incentives. *Beware the Barrenness of a Busy Life* was written across every other one. She saw Sara's letter, bigger than any other billboard she'd come across. Roxy went to take a photo but her phone rang again. Before she could answer it a whistle blew. Roxy whipped her head around to find two police officers striding towards her. The officer gestured that it wasn't allowed.

'What I—'

A crowd began to gather as one of the police officer's held up a finger to Roxy.

'Bu—'

The officer held up two fingers.

'Third time and I'm arrested?' said Roxy, letting out a laugh.

The officer scribbled something on a piece of paper and handed it to her. Roxy's laughter promptly converted to outrage. '*What?*'

The officer began to write out another note. She was being fined for disturbing the peace. Roxy shook the piece of paper in the officer's face before ripping it up. The officer simply wrote out another one.

How was Roxy meant to argue this injustice?

The crowd got bigger.

Roxy typed violently on her phone: *How exactly did I disturb the peace???*

The officer gestured around the small town, apparently very invested in the outcome of this altercation. Then the crowd seemed to part, and Roxy saw a figure emerge. Both officers now looked behind them only to see Sara Javed, in the flesh, walking towards them. She had clearly been curious about the crowd. The words from the billboard, *I have decided to shut the fuck up*, hovered over Sara's head.

Sara raised her eyebrows at Roxy before taking the fine from her and handing it to the officer. The officer shook her head. Sara sighed. Waited. Expectantly. After a few minutes the officer snatched the fine, screwed it up and walked away.

Roxy watched it all, thinking of how they had left things, that her friend was *here*. And, surprisingly, she felt intense relief that Sara looked OK. She edged towards Sara, the crowd still watching.

Roxy put her hand on her chest.

Eventually Sara stepped forward, putting her arms around Roxy as everyone stared, an image they would all describe to people for years to come.

Sara led Roxy into a café on a side street. She waved to the barista behind the bar who bowed to Sara in mock reverence. Roxy had been glancing furtively at Sara, watching her smile at people who stopped and shook her hand.

What was this place?

The barista brought them two coffees. Roxy observed the exposed brick walls, wooden tables covered in gingham cloth, various posters; a woman with her hair wrapped in a blue scarf, flexing her arm, *Proud Non-Verbal;* a picture of Buddha; a soldier, pointing his finger – *Ban the Ban.* VOTE FOR CHOICE.

Sara had never looked so serene and Roxy wasn't sure what to do with such quietude.

Eventually they finished their coffees. Sara didn't pay but left a ten pound note in the tip jar. Roxy followed Sara in her car until ten minutes later they pulled up in front of a tall terraced building. It was a small space. Kitchen and living room conjoined with a bedroom at the end of the hallway. There was no television. No radio.

A black leather sofa was pushed against a red wall. Books lined a mahogany bookcase. Sara's laptop rested on the kitchen counter. She realised she hadn't seen Sara with a phone.

'Wha—'

Sara raised a hand, shook her head. How was Roxy to convey *anything* without words? She went to open Sara's laptop. There was no Wi-Fi. Sara was living in a vacuum. *Of course* she was serene. Roxy got her phone out, but Sara shook her head at that too.

It occurred to Roxy how helpless it all was. How was she meant to rouse Sara into some kind of *connection* with the real world when she was ignoring it entirely?

It didn't occur to Roxy that perhaps Sara *was* living in the real world. She left the flat every day. Sat in coffee shops. Dined in silence, watching others do the same. *And she read.* Practically a book a day. She volunteered at the local pet shelter. On weekends, she volunteered at the soup kitchen. Three days a week she worked at the café in which they'd had coffee. Sara was in the enviable position of being cut off from this so-called real world, yet very much a part of it. And what did participation mean in the end? To be aware of global events? Subscribe to the prevailing opinion or live in opposition to it? Were those the only choices? Sara, and others like her, were proving otherwise.

Roxy sat down next to her. They both stared at the wall in front. Eventually Roxy looked at her. Sara looked back. Roxy couldn't read her expression, but there was a smile on her lips, however subtle. Roxy began to Google news stories about Zainab Aalam and Grace Jenkins but Sara gently took the phone from her.

'Bu—'

This time Roxy stopped herself. The world was shape-shifting and here Sara sat, in wilful ignorance. As if she was immune to its effects.

After a while Sara got up and walked out of the house.

Sara,

I left when you didn't come back after an hour. I didn't see any point staying, which I suppose was your intention all along. I came to convince you to come back to London, at least try to unite people against the ban. But you're living in your Pennington bubble and I can't even try to talk you out of it.

So, instead, I've left you something on your laptop. I hope that it explains in pictures what I was unable to say in words.

You know I've never been an advocate for silence. You know how much I've hated it my entire life, and that hasn't changed. But if you can do something good, because it's right, even if you don't agree with it, then surely that's something?

Isn't that what you've always said?

Roxy xx

Roxy left the letter on Sara's laptop. She'd cobbled together a video of Grace and Zainab's stories, news clippings, headlines, pictures – a collage of their separate lives intertwining under an umbrella of silence. She had hoped it would evoke something in Sara. How could Sara refuse to act once she truly understood what was at stake?

PART SIX

THE GATHERING

Official HM Government Notice

July 2022

Dear Mr Sathar,

We understand that a mass gathering is being organised the day of the general election on 4 August. Please be advised that you are strongly urged to stay home. There will be strict reprisals on persons involved in any conflict, which a crowd such as this might elicit.

Vote for us, and we will come back stronger and better.

I hope I may rely on you to do your part for your friends, your family, and your country.

Yours,
Prime Minster John Kipple

#StayHome
#SpeakUp

Aadhi was not without a sense of pride when he read the letter that had been circulated around the country. Roxy was mobilising the masses, organising a gathering the scale of which, he believed, hadn't yet been seen.

Strict reprisal.

If anything, that would serve as a catalyst for more people to attend.

Since she'd got back from her unsuccessful trip to see Sara, they hadn't spoken. *She* hadn't spoken. Whether she'd become a Non-Verbal was anyone's guess, but after she had ignored his calls, Aadhi had gone to her flat to ask questions. She'd just looked at him.

'What happened there? Rox. Give me *something*.'

She had hesitated and then showed him a post she was waiting to share on Hushes.

VOTE FOR CHOICE
and join
THE SILENT GATHERING
4 August, 9 a.m. onwards
Hyde Park

Roxy was now spearheading a retaliation against the very ideas in which she still believed. Acting on principle rather than prejudice.

Aadhi felt that perhaps there was hope for future generations, after all.

David trusted that the interim Prime Minister's letter would convince people into staying home. Fear was an important component in exercising some sort of order. Once Non-Verbalism was banned it was only a matter of time before Grace would have to come out of hiding. He sat at his computer, Googling Grace Jenkins, just as he had been doing for weeks on end.

All her social media accounts had been deleted. Then he saw a comment made by a Grace Jenkins posted on a Facebook page for a voluntary organisation. There were no details other than her name because the account had been deleted but it *had* to be her.

Of course, the organisation seemed to be a kind of women's refuge. Just the sort of thing Grace would be involved in.

Why hadn't he thought about it before? He noted the address and grabbed his car keys to try and find answers.

Penelope had paid for the promoted post on Hushes and, quite frankly, even if she hadn't the platform probably would have promoted it anyway. (Hushes had attempted to advertise pro-Verbal posts and it had resulted in so many people closing their accounts they were forced to renege.)

Roxy, Aadhi and Kat sat around Penelope's kitchen island. The television in the background, Kat switching between The Refusal and True News. They stared at Roxy's iPad, her Hushes post, garnering increasing likes, gaining momentum until #TheSilentGathering was finally trending. The ticking of the clock. The quiet whooshing of cars outside. The constant flicking of channels.

Penelope cleared her throat.

Kat folded her arms.

Roxy let out a long sigh.

Kat flicked the channel and grabbed Roxy's arm.

They all looked at the screen. A banner ran at the bottom:

SOUTENIR LE CHOIX et rejoindre **LE RASSAMBLEMENT SILENCIEUX** *4 Août, 10 heures a partir de, Champs-Élysées, Paris, France.*

A few minutes later another appeared.

SUPPORTA LA SCELTA e unisciti al **LA RIUNIONE SILENZIOSA** *4 Agosto 10 a.m. in poi, Piazza del Poppolo, Rome, Italy.*

Followed by another . . .

SUPPORT THE CHOICE and join **THE SILENT GATHERING,** *4 August, 2 p.m. onwards, Central Park, New York, USA.*

支持选择参加8月5日下午5点在北京天安门广场举行的无声派对

4 بجے، 5 اگست، الیکشن کی حمایت کریں، اور خاموش اجتماع میں شامل ہوں، اسلام آباد، پاکستان

поддержать выбор **и присоединяйтесь к молчаливому собранию,**
4 августа, 12 часов, г. Москва, Россия

Banners continued to show from languages across the world. Japan, India, Switzerland, New Zealand, Cuba . . .

Penelope pushed a notepad and pen towards Roxy.

She looked up at her.

'If this isn't something to write about, I don't know what is,' Penelope said.

Kat rolled her eyes.

Roxy, with all the earnestness of someone who had found inspiration, grabbed the pen.

Angie looked through the peephole. Her heartbeat quickened. There were three police officers. She ran up the stairs as fast as possible, clapping her hands.

Everyone knew this meant to get in their rooms.

She opened Zainab and Grace's door. They were standing by the window, Grace's hand on the arc of her back, the other over her mouth. They had seen the officers arrive.

Angie indicated for them to lock the door.

The doorbell rang, urgently.

She waited to hear the lock turn before going downstairs and greeting the officers with a smile.

The one in front glanced at Angie's Non-Verbal badge. He gave a curt nod and pointed inside, holding up a picture of Grace and Benji. Was there to be no safety for anyone? If she let them in, not only would they find Grace, but they'd find Zainab too.

The officer tried to step inside but Angie blocked his way. He indicated for her to move aside. She stood firm.

The officers behind him clearly impatient. Angie grabbed a piece of paper and pen – all now usefully dotted around the place – and wrote: *Warrant?*

She showed it to the officer. He looked at his colleagues.

Neighbours were peering out of windows. A few had stopped on the street. And then she saw him. David Hodgkin, looking up at the windows as if he might catch a glimpse of Grace.

He stepped forward, but before he could do or say anything Angie turned around and slammed the door shut behind her.

Angie watched from the doorway as Grace began putting things in her bags, slowly, considerately. Benji had put down his maths workbook as Zainab, rather emphatically, began taking the clothes out of the bag.

David stood outside, refusing to move. A crowd was gathering.

'You can't leave,' said Zainab.

Grace pointed outside. Eventually, clearly tired, she manoeuvred herself on to the edge of the bed, hand resting on her abdomen. Zainab stared at her bump.

Grace had to do the sensible, and therefore, correct thing. It was only a matter of time before the police came with their warrant. She would lose Benji. And they would find Zainab. Two for one. Quite the deal, in the end.

She wrapped her arms around Benji, kissing his head over and over. She had not done him justice. And when he squeezed her tighter, she thought she might break.

'If you go, I'm coming out with you,' said Zainab.

Grace looked over at Angie as if Zainab had lost her mind. If she did that then she could say goodbye to her country too.

Zainab continued to unpack Grace's case.

Angie and Grace could only continue to watch.

Aadhi surveyed the ballot that had come through the post. A lifetime of railing against an ideology only to be the person who was now helping to bring it back into being. The triumph of principle felt decidedly unvictorious.

More channels had started up, displaying banners from various countries, towns, villages around the world which were standing in solidarity with the right to choose.

Had people truly stopped loving the sound of their own voice? Had their curiosities dwindled to the point of extinction? After all this time, he still didn't understand Non-Verbalism.

The most disconcerting thing was that he now lived in a world with such stark, binary perspectives. This so-called refusal had served as a global anaesthetic, but the diagnosis for the source of the problem – that nuance had been lost – had been somewhat sidelined.

Yet to ban silence altogether was a different sort of tyranny.

He noticed a light come from his TV screen and looked up from his sofa. An image of interim Prime Minister John Kipple appeared. Aadhi turned up the volume.

'As a nation, you have the right to understand exactly what you will be voting for on 4 August . . .'

It had been a long speech. Aadhi waited for the opposition's response. Surely, they would retaliate? He flicked between channels. Eventually, all that came up was a statement from Bacclay:

> My party is here to serve, not to manipulate with speeches. Power is with the people. On 4 August vote for freedom. Vote for choice.

A low mist covered Hyde Park, which was to be expected at six o'clock in the morning. It was five days before the election. The Prime Minister wasn't the only one capable of national manipulation. Roxy and Kat, groups united for the cause, just had to be more inventive. They both looked up at the workers, connecting the wires to the 50-foot TV screen. Similar screens were dotted around the park.

In town halls and squares around the country. Goodwill was manifest with companies providing free toilet cubicles, celebrity donations, people setting up food stalls, red, blue, rainbow-coloured Non-Verbal badges being handed out. Aadhi and his cameramen were already filming. Police officers had volunteered to keep order. Councils had signed off blanket permits to all Non-Verbals and their supporters.

Observing such camaraderie was hopeful, and clearly unifying, but it was layered with a social anxiety that it could all be for nothing. This thought had propelled people to focus. More door-to-door visits to hand out literature – specifically targeting households that did not have *Vote for Choice* posters in their windows – fundraisers in the workplace, neighbourhood WhatsApp groups relaying friends and families' voting proclivities.

Roxy now had a following of over nine-hundred thousand on Hushes. By the end of the day she'd be sure to reach a million. Every now and then her eyes would linger, looking out for Sara.

She live streamed the workers fixing the wires and then clicked on the list of her new followers. Her heart rate quickened. It was her sister, Halimah, who had clearly reactivated her account.

Roxy wrote in her notebook: *A single action meant more than any words could capture.*

Angie had wanted to volunteer at the Town Hall to set up the day before the election but refused to leave Grace or Zainab. At the refuge, they still waited for the police. It was just a matter of time yet Zainab's obstinance was confounding. Especially since the crowds outside continued to grow, accompanied by journalists with their cameras.

Benji was resting his head on Grace's bump. Zainab glancing over at them every few minutes, a strange longing apparent in her expression. Grace shifted, struggling to get to her feet. She took Benji's hand and waddled from one end of the room to another as he copied her gait. They both laughed when Angie heard a sharp intake of breath. Grace was staring down at the rug. A look of panic. Angie's gaze followed to a wet patch, stained a mild pink. She rushed over to the calendar on the fridge. Grace had marked her due date for 27 August. It was too soon.

Grace took a deep breath, seemed to gather herself as she cupped Benji's face in her hands and patted her belly. When Benji burst into an excited grin, a tear ran down Grace's cheek.

'*OK*,' said Zainab, getting up. 'The baby's got a sense of timing, hasn't it, Benji?'

He pumped his fist in the air.

Even through her first contraction, Grace, looking at Benji, did the same.

4 AUGUST 2022

#THESILENTMOVEMENT

Sara

The gathering had already begun in Pennington's main green where, much like elsewhere up and down the country, screens had been erected. Sara hardly believed that turning up in Hyde Park would instigate some sort of victory. The alleged power of her presence was a glitch in people's ability to reason. It was not her: it was the idea of her. And what had been the point of slipping into obscurity if she were just to make a dramatic appearance at the exact moment that she was guaranteed to get the most attention? She had an especial distaste towards spectacles.

If she could speak, she would say that Non-Verbalism had clearly not been enough, because had people changed for the better? Had *she*? Such charged opinion suggested not.

Then perhaps she was wrong. Perhaps things would be different, calmer, moving forward. Perhaps voting for choice could restore this hope.

She stopped next to her closed laptop with her morning coffee. She had watched Roxy's clip an unseemly number of times. Her letter sat on the kitchen tabletop, covered in coffee stains. Sara hesitated, opened up her MacBook and clicked on Roxy's link again.

What truth lay behind Grace Jenkins' stony face as she pushed past cameras into Manchester's crown court? What had provoked Zainab Aalam to escape a marriage and then the law?

Sara pushed away the idea that she, like them, was in hiding. Although being sought after, looked to as some kind of solution to the world's problems, had turned her into a fugitive of sorts. But Grace and Zainab had real issues at stake. Sara could not plead the same. Image after image rolled on, from Grace's son, to Hushes hashtags, to Zainab's photo, pictures of Sara hugging the driver outside 10 Downing Street – Roxy's usual sense of subtlety.

Headline after headline.

A kidnapping.

An abscondment.

A society working to dehumanise and disempower the people who publicly, unequivocally, flout the norms.

Grace's story was the one though that Sara couldn't quite extricate from her thoughts. Her judgement of her, perhaps, had been premature. Had Sara learnt nothing? Perhaps one's life was just a series of events, punctuated with the certainty of one's own fallibility. The trick was to recognise and correct it.

She had dreamt about these women, their faces merging into each other, transforming into her mother. She had started awake several times, reaching for her phone to call her dad, only to remember. Then she would cry.

It would take a while to climb out of this dungeon of self-pity.

She blamed Roxy. Roxy and her storming into Pennington with a voice Sara could hear even without her having to speak. Roxy telling others what they should do, think, feel. The entire thing was an attack on the integrity of autonomy.

And yet.

And yet . . .

Sara looked out of her window, watching people making their way towards the town centre, parks and cafés. United.

She reread the quote by Emerson that Roxy had left.

'. . . the great man is he who in the midst of the crowd keeps with perfect sweetness the independence of solitude.'

Bloody Roxy.

★

Grace clutched her belly. 11.23 a.m. She took deep breaths.

Zainab had stuffed things into a bag: slippers, night suit, nappies, baby-grows. The pain eased and Grace's heart raced. After a reassuring embrace, Angie had taken Benji into the next room. What if she lost the baby *and* Benji? Why had she not told Graham about her pregnancy? Why, when Zainab had told her all the smaller details of her life, her wants and their abandonment, would Grace think: *Maybe I still have a chance?*

That chance was now coming too early. Would she lose everything in the process?

Zainab grabbed Grace's hand, pulling her towards the bedroom door.

Grace grabbed the bag from Zainab and pushed past her, as well as her burgeoning body could allow. She pointed outside. The crowds had dispersed, presumably to go and vote and there were now only a handful of journalists left. Once Grace left the refuge it would be over. But she would not put Zainab at risk.

Neither would she give up Benji, nor this baby, without another fight.

Another contraction ripped through her. *Oh God,* how time had dulled her memory. To undergo this kind of acute pain again and again, must be some sort of madness. Zainab rushed over to hold her hand.

11.45 a.m.

She shuffled into the next room and pulled Benji into one last hug, signing 'I love you.' He signed the same. She looked up at Angie taking Benji's hand into her own. Grace would have to trust in her. This is what life at its precipice must hold on to: trust in others. Independence was the lie people told themselves for the illusion of control.

Grace hobbled towards the front door, bracing herself to refuse Zainab's relentless humanity.

Something seemed to be coming to an end and Grace just prayed that the baby that had bloomed within her would have the chance to bloom before her eyes.

★

Zainab was used to Grace shaking her head at her. Whether in disagreement, annoyance or affectionate laughter. When Zainab's insignificant life had ended up on screen, she wondered whether her family had also watched Kashif detail her loose morality? Had Suleiman? Were either living with regret, and if so, of the two, who did she resent the most? She was not beyond resentment.

But she was beyond the need for approbation.

Telling Grace, piecemeal, the details of her life had somehow weakened the stronghold on Zainab's shame. It had not been like when she had told her mother. This had been an ablution of sorts and had cleansed her. That words could do that had Zainab almost praying for the ban on Non-Verbalism.

She saw the distorted shapes of journalists outside. People had abandoned their placards to vote and cast their judgement elsewhere. She pulled the door handle, then stopped as Grace dropped her bag, bent over, suppressed a groan.

Zainab rubbed her back. 'It's OK. I'm here.'

Eventually Grace put both hands in front of her, begging Zainab, presumably, to stay indoors.

A small laugh escaped Zainab. Did Grace think that hers was some kind of sacrifice? That she was relinquishing her freedom for Grace? She had neither freedom nor fate in mind.

She took Grace's hands. 'You *will* let me help you bring life into this world.' Then she pushed open the door.

The cameras flashed, capturing the moment Zainab and Grace came out of the house, hoping to bring into the world a miracle.

It was 12 p.m. Sara wore a burqa she borrowed from someone in Pennington, complete with nikab. Religious freedoms had their uses. She drove back to her local church polling station and handed her ID to the man behind the desk. He looked up and then back at the identification. She lifted her veil. He opened his mouth but then clamped it shut. Beaming. It elicited a warmth in Sara. She crossed the square on the ballot before making her way to the tube station.

Sara weaved through the clumps of people gathering in Hyde Park and grabbed a bunch of multi-coloured badges. She stuck them on her burqa in an attempt to blend in. Around her meats sizzled on barbeques and the sun beat down on people lounging on blankets, sipping iced coffees, beers, Cokes. Hope was manifest on their faces and the subtle movement of their otherwise quiet selves. Her face veil was trying but it was the only way she wouldn't be recognised.

She looked up at the giant screen, displaying images from the past year from around world. Speeches by leaders muted, so that only their expressions were telling. The no longer barren hashtag, news headings, images of the gatherings and protests, of shops and cafés with Verbal and Non-Verbal signs. Of Mimi Munkin.

A row of police swayed towards an incoming group. A group was chanting: *Vote for a Voice.* They were kept at an acceptable distance but nearby Non-Verbals watched, as if appalled by people who were still slaves to their own opinion.

The screen paused on Sara's letter.

She thought back to the feelings that had moved her to pen such a thing. None of her words relayed the truth of her heartbreak at finding out she would never know her mother, that the things she sought, for which she fought, were in the end, a misguidance.

And wasn't the same true of people?

A notification pinged on her phone. An image of Grace Jenkins and Zainab Aalam entering Brentley Hospital. Zainab's hand on the small of Grace's back.

Sara stared at it for a few moments.

How did they know each other?

Did it matter?

Was knowing the entirety of a person the measure of love? Yet Sara had hardly known herself, and standing here now, looking at that image, among the crowd, she felt ashamed of her own apathy. She had spent the past year avoiding feeling, denigrating people's opinions – the very thing that had led them all here.

The crowds watched the screens intently, rereading Sara's words, which over a year later and given the gravity of events, felt rather narrow in scope to her now. Sara's self-indulgence had taken things too far. She'd felt that the world had owed her something but, in truth, it had not even owed her a mother.

And then she saw Roxy standing on the grass, her body dwarfed by the screen she was looking up at.

Sara had been holding on to the idea that she did not owe her voice, words, or even an explanation to people. But if today's crowd was evidence of anything, it was that one has a debt to the world in which they live, and there comes a time when it must be paid.

That was just good manners.

Grace pointed towards the Non-Verbal maternity ward. Zainab hesitated but Grace could not deal with her argument on that matter too. The receptionist, unsurprisingly, stared at the two. Eventually, she handed Grace a form, indicating that she fill it in.

Grace wrote down she was four weeks early, at which point the receptionist rang the bell three times and a nurse appeared. She paused, also staring at Grace in the wheelchair and Zainab behind her.

Grace caught sight of the television on which there were images of gatherings in Birmingham, Sheffield, Cornwall, Portsmouth . . . all congregating in local parks and town halls.

She wondered if Graham was in any of the crowds. Why had she kept this secret from him? Self-preservation? Preservation from what? Feelings, pride, guilt? The entire spectrum of human emotion, which one called life?

Then she saw a figure walking towards her. The slight limp detectable from afar. The heavy gait. Hair pulled back. Her mother.

It might have made for a satisfying conclusion to let Dede into the room with her. Open arms, forgiveness, all those notions that were meant to give life meaning. Grace put her hand up.

'*Grace*,' her mother whispered.

'Ssh,' exclaimed the nurse, pointing at the Non-Verbal sign.

Grace looked her mother in the eye, ignoring the sharp stab in her rib. When she shook her head, it was not with contempt: it was a final goodbye.

A shooting pain pulsated through her, her insides contracted.

She heard the stomping of feet. Grace looked around to see two, three, four police officers. The receptionist strode towards them, stopping them in their path.

She gave Dede a final look as Zainab pushed Grace into her room and helped her out of the wheelchair. Grace gripped Zainab's arm as she clutched her belly again. The cramps beating at her back.

Grace eventually recovered and lay on the bed. She had to remember that her body had been built to house this pain. The nurse checked Grace's temperature, pulse, blood pressure. She checked the baby. The door opened again and Grace glimpsed a police officer, waiting outside.

And then she heard it. The soft beat of her baby's heart, thrumming in the silent room.

5.44 p.m.

They had been in the room for almost six hours.

The contractions were now six minutes apart.

Zainab put a cold flannel on Grace's forehead, watched her take gas and air, throw up afterwards. Mucus being wiped from the bedsheets. Every time a contraction would come Grace would throw her hand over her mouth.

Was this silence or punishment? And if the latter then punishment for what?

Grace pointed to Zainab's phone. Zainab handed it to her, watching as Grace wiped the sweat from her brow, put on a smile and FaceTimed Angie.

Benji appeared on the screen. Grace put two thumbs up, smiling widely, even as Zainab saw the tears in her eyes. Zainab took the phone, holding it high to show Benji the bump. He beamed, sticking two thumbs back up.

A nurse walked in, pushing a television into the room on a trolley. She strode towards Zainab, bringing her into a hug. She then looked at Grace, clasped both hands together as if in prayer. She looked mildly deranged. Everyone turned to the screen, watching images of gathering crowds and rolling statements from around the world in various languages.

Watching Grace's resolve, Zainab almost felt her own body pulsate.

By 9 p.m. Hyde Park had filled with tens of thousands of people wearing an 'I Voted for Choice' badge. A sea of bodies, awaiting the final hour in which the fate of society's need for contemplation rested.

People meditated, smoked, drank, prayed. It was co-existence at its finest. For one moment Sara felt a prevailing peace – obscure in the midst of such certainty, and in awe of such passions.

Some groups entered the park with their anti-NV placards.

Silence is the enemy of progress.

They claimed that the ban would restore the world they once knew. But no one considered the tools necessary for such a restoration. Who needed to be told what the measure of success was? When to speak and what to say?

Surely we had discovered that tradition could not make way for a new way to live.

At 10 p.m. BST candles would be lit. It had been Roxy's idea. The kind of symbolic action that meant nothing, other than the fact that everyone performed this meaningless act together. Naturally, Sara bought a candle and lighter.

She had been following Roxy, watching her gesture at Kat, nudge Aadhi, ply Penelope with bottles of water. She had seen her look in surprise at a young woman, wearing a hijab. They had hugged for a long time. It looked like her estranged sister.

Two other figures approached Roxy. Lily and Martin. Hand-in-hand.

Henry would not have come.

What would her dad have said? *The presence of weakness weakens us all.*

Then she noticed that Kat was carrying a pair of noise-cancelling headphones. Sara laughed to herself.

The clock struck 10 p.m.

The screens switched to pictures of colour-blocked maps and graphs.

The nation watched, every being composed of conviction and hope.

And then there was a wobbly shot of a semi-detached house. A woman lighting a candle and resting it on the front garden wall. Seeing the camera and waving. Ex-Prime Minister Ruth Baynham.

In the park, and around the country, the scratch of lighters and scraping of matches lit the night in millions of glorious flames.

The TV screen had gone dark. Flames flickered.

The nurse at the foot of the bed looked at Grace and put up ten fingers. *It was time.*

Grace clasped Zainab's hand.

She would not break her silence; she did not need to make an exhibition of her pain. She would never be told when to speak and certainly not *what* to say.

Her silence, in that sense, was as miscalculated as it was courageous.

Zainab tore her eyes away from the TV as the nurse tapped on the bed and Grace pushed.

Sweat pouring down her temples, face clenched, mouth clamped.

Breathe. Breathe. Breathe.

Zainab stepped towards the foot of the bed.

A nurse replaced the dirty sheet with a new one.

The baby's head crowned. Clotted blood, matted hair.

Tears stung Zainab's eyes. She rushed to Grace. Brushed her hair back. Gripped her hand.

The nurse tapped the bed again.

*

Light and shadows wavered under the starry night as votes were being counted, the flickering flames obscuring everyone's face.

Sara inched closer to Roxy and Lily. They stood at the end of a path at the bottom of which was a stage, a screen erected upon it. A row of candles illuminating it.

Sara, under the refuge of the night felt able, *willing*, even, to remove her veil. As garments go, it felt faintly ridiculous, but revealing in its own way.

Candle in one hand, Sara held out the other and touched Lily's arm. Lily looked up.

'*Oh,*' she let out, almost blowing out her candle. That would've taken symbolism too far.

She reached out and hugged Sara.

Sara stretched out the hand in which she held her candle to prevent setting Lily on fire. The world had been enough.

Sara felt the tears falling down her face. Not of grief, but relief.

Kat, realising what was happening, came and hugged her now.

Aadhi shook her hand, something like kindness in his manner, which was both surprising and not altogether displeasing.

Penelope opened up a file on her iPhone and tried to show Sara her latest sales figures.

And then came Roxy who took the candle from Sara, so she could embrace everyone properly.

Roxy stood with both hands full, holding on. Always refusing to let things go. Until they all looked up at the screen.

The first exit polls result were in. But it was too close to call.

The nurse tapped twice.

Where was Graham? Grace *needed* him. She could not push again.

She shook her head at Zainab. She'd tell the nurse to leave her alone.

But her baby had other ideas.

Head light, body heavy, Grace pushed through the contracting of her limbs, the burning between her legs.

Someone stroked her forehead.

She saw Zainab through her blurred vision and wanted to cry.

Where was Benji?

What had she done?

Two taps.

She looked into Zainab's eyes. No more pushing. *Please*.

Two taps, only louder.

Zainab gripped her hand.

Grace had been here before, but this time was different. Her baby would not wait. Grace pushed, past the burning, past the stabbing pain, past the dizziness of her own mind.

'*Oh*,' Zainab exhaled.

Grace fell back, breath caught in her throat, body limp.

The nurses held up the baby, clotted with mucus and blood.

A girl.

Zainab cut the umbilical cord and a few seconds later came a stilted cry, puncturing the silence. Grace cried tears of relief. The nurse handed her the baby, wrinkled and slight. Outside, Grace caught the shadow of police officers. She looked at Zainab who sniffled, stroking the new-born's cheek.

Grace looked down at her miracle. It would be a story to tell her little girl when she grew up. How she had been born into silence – how she had pierced it with a cry.

And without thinking, Grace whispered: 'Hello, baby.'

Zainab sat with Grace who had fallen asleep. Her baby had been taken to be monitored. She knew what was waiting for her outside the room. The nurses were detaining the police, making up God know what excuse for Zainab, just for a few more minutes of freedom.

Going back to Pakistan had felt like an oppression, but she might be just as oppressed here, if she stayed. Having seen the birth of a baby, the glory of God – and woman, when push came to shove – she had witnessed the inevitability of a voice. The way needed a will, and Zainab felt that hers was stronger now. She had gone from family home to marital home and had been ready to repeat the process, but what about the home she could make for herself, *by* herself?

Looking at Grace, she understood this.

Zainab, after so much had not been said, and so little had been done, felt equal to the task.

The election result reports continued to come in. See-sawing between hope and its abandonment.

She did not want to wake Grace and she was not ready to walk away just yet, so she sat, watching the television, mesmerised by the flames that continued to burn. Savouring this moment of peace.

The hours passed. People slept in their tents by turn. Some out, watching the stars and screen with numbers coming in from all over the country. No social commentary, no projections, assertions, run-on sentences packed with platitudes and repetition. Just the colours of the nation before them; the soft sighs of hope dwindling; the anxious expressions covered by the night.

By 4 a.m. the flames, inevitably, began to die, as daylight started to break. The hope for choice, according to incoming results, had been misplaced. The balance was tipping in Verbals' direction. Sara had been sitting on the ground with the others, heads bent low, faces forlorn. In times of grief, words don't work anyway.

The stark reality of this moment filled Sara.

She had come too late.

Roxy looked at Sara with tired eyes and then glanced towards the stage. The group watched her. Even Aadhi looked at her as if in need of some kind of answer. The orange and pink sky lit their pale faces.

Sara stood up.

As she made her way towards the stage, people began to come out of their tents, bleary-eyed, shaken awake by friends.

They looked, pointed, prodded others, started clapping.

They got to their feet, clapped louder, cheered.

People on the other side of the park, started clapping too, although unsure why.

The applause, cheers, whistles, got louder and louder as Sara approached the stage.

Sara might not have deserved this particular stage, but it was hers, and this time, without any hesitation, to rapturous noise, she took it.

When Grace awoke daylight filtered in through the blind's slats. She started at the figure before her.

'Hi,' whispered Graham.

'Where's Benji?'

'He's safe.'

'Where? *How?*'

'I've got all the information you need.'

Graham told Grace he had been keeping track of David's whereabouts until he turned up at the refuge. Judges were tired of everyone's voice, or lack of, and getting a warrant, based on a hunch, in order to barge into a place of safety for women was quite a demand. In the meantime, Graham had been working to convince David to drop the charges.

'While at the same time,' he continued. 'I was getting an injunction against him.'

'*What?*'

'I needed to buy some time for us to appeal. I put in writing to the judge that if Benji was taken away, considering all the negative media attention, it'd put your mental and physical health, and his, and the new baby's, in jeopardy.'

The judge hadn't needed much convincing. The man whose job it was to hand out judgement was far more willing to offer mercy.

Hopefully, the masses had learnt something similar.

Grace let her head fall back on the pillow. 'What about Zainab?'

'She's gone.'

'*Where?* Why didn't she wake me? Did the police take her?'

Graham put his hand on her shoulder, reassuringly.

'Don't worry. We're going to do whatever we can to help her, OK? But perhaps first, you want to tell me about my baby?'

407

Grace collapsed back into bed.

'I'm sorry. Jesus, Graham, I'm so sorry.'

'Can I see her?' he asked.

'She's in NICU. But you can go in later . . . You know the most absurd thing?' Grace said.

'What?'

'I don't even think it matters if Benji speaks or not. I want him to, of course. I've spent so long trying to just be *normal*.'

'Who would want that?' Graham teased.

'Someone who's never had it,' she replied, pointedly, to the man who'd never needed to fit in by virtue of being privileged. 'I just want him to be comfortable in the world he's in. That's all. To belong. He has to figure that out on his own though, doesn't he? And I just have to stand by and help wherever I can. Christ,' she added. 'Good luck to me.'

'Grace Jenkins, are you learning to let go?'

She laughed. 'Not of everything.'

He came closer. Kissed her. And Grace realised that when things came together, there was a moment in which everything was shockingly, unnervingly perfect.

She pulled away.

'Oh, God! Who *won*?'

Zainab had walked into the hospital amid a silent world and came out into one trying to find its voice again.

She had been taken out of the hospital in handcuffs, which should have been a source of embarrassment. Instead it was defining moment: she had never felt freer. Especially when the smattering of people outside, applauded. Zainab, a lifelong poster child for dutiful woman, had become the poster child for freedom.

A man stepped out of the crowd. Suleiman, beseeching and contrite.

Such was Zainab's current state of contentment, she did not need to search for any feeling upon seeing him.

She had just enough feeling for herself not to have to expend it on any-one else.

'Mrs Taufiq—'

'Ms Aalam,' she corrected as she sat in the detention room. 'I refused to change my name even when I married.'

Graham rested his briefcase on the table. She noticed he was still wear-ing a Non-Verbal badge.

'Grace ordered me to come as soon as possible. She's found her voice all right.'

Zainab laughed.

Graham, Grace's lawyer, colleague, lover, had rushed into the hospital room.

Glancing at Grace, Zainab had put her finger to her lips, stepping for-ward to whisper: 'Are the police still outside?'

He'd nodded.

'When she wakes up, tell her I'm OK. That I'll be *fine*. But I'm going to expect to see her and the baby before I leave the country.'

She hadn't even given him a chance to stop her.

'You might've gathered the baby's mine,' he said now.

Why Zainab felt the need to cry she didn't know. Perhaps it was seeing a love story come to fruition. Grace had two of the things that Zainab had coveted her entire life. But she didn't feel envy – just satisfaction that these things still existed. Sometimes that must be enough.

'Where's Benji?'.

'Ms Aalam, you understand what's going to happen, don't you?'

'Just tell me they're not taking him away from her.'

'It's too soon to tell. Even if Grace is Verbal now.'

'He couldn't wait to meet the baby.'

'How would anyone know?' Graham asked.

'You can't hide joy,' replied Zainab. 'If we spoke less and observed more, we'd see things clearer.'

'Yes, well . . . Listen, I'm sorry, but you're being sent back to Pakistan tomorrow.'

Zainab's breath caught in her throat.

'Tomorrow?'

'Your mother's here with a friend of yours. Tahera. And someone by the name of Suleiman.'

'Oh.'

'Do you want to see him?'

'Yes, but you have to tell me. What was Grace's reaction when you told her who won the election?'

Sara's quiet disbelief at the results should not have quickened the beating of her heart this way.

The Prime Minister, John Kipple, appeared on the screen behind her and around the nation. Some cheers from pro-Verbals erupted on the fringes of Hyde Park. Kipple's mouth moved, but here, at least, the sound was muted.

Just over half the country had decided that *choice* was not as fundamental a right as one would have hoped. And after over a year of silence, surely in this moment of palpable mass disappointment, Sara must say something profound.

She had been sitting on the stage, but now stood up.

Everyone looked to her. How would Sara Javed perforate the pervasive peace? With which words would she – *they* – accept defeat?

(The etiquette of how others should have broken their silence would be discussed extensively in months to come.)

Sara promised herself that this would be the *last time* she took the stage for others. No matter how hard one tried to push against expectation, to lean into one's own whims, one never was free to do as they pleased. Neither silence nor speech could hide the fact.

She opened her mouth, ready, but the image on the screen behind her switched. Bodies sitting on the grass shuffled, tired vision adjusted to the change. The soft intake of breath at the gathering of a crowd in . . . the sign on placards:

New Zealand Chooses.

The image then swept to another.

Bangladesh Chooses.

Sweden Chooses.

Crowds from around the world were declaring themselves on placards, holding up their thumbs, smiling into the cameras.

What did this mean?

Brazil Chooses.

Countries making a declaration: celebrating the now legally mandated right to choose. The crowd in Hyde Park, in each city and town hall around the country, in every single home, watched. Their hope perhaps had not been entirely misplaced. There were other countries from whom they could learn – take inspiration. Sara looked through the placards that had been stacked up near her. She found the one she wanted.

This, honestly, truly, *would* be the last time.

She held up the sign.

#REFUSE

The crowd rose.

They did not clap or cheer.

They stood, still, calm.

Silence had been called many things: a subtraction; a bewitchment; an oppression; a reflection. But, in the unravelling of the self and of lives, one could not deny that it had, to so many, been a revelation.

AFTER THE SILENCE

Are We Happier Post-Ban?

Ian Brent, *The Daily*, Sept 2022

Results from a survey taken of voters who cast their ballots in favour of the Silent Ban show that many had not anticipated its adverse effects on their day-to-day life.

'No one told us that we'd be forced to share our opinions on everything. In the office and out. And now we even have to fill out questionnaire's at work about what we think . . . It could affect who's promoted! I miss the silent corners in restaurants and cafés . . .'

Expert, Dr Susan Dooley, says that the loss of Non-Verbal measures such as silent workspaces, reflection corners in public, may reverse all the positive changes that Non-Verbalism wrought for people's mental health. There had been a 39% decline in prescribed medication for anxiety and depression. This, however, is good news for pharmaceutical companies whose stocks are rising again . . .

Mimi Munkin's live appearance on Pixie Plus, two months after the ban in the UK (and the USA), was streamed and watched, naturally, around the globe.

'You suffered a lot of backlash after your exposure as a Verbal,' spoke the host.

'I guess I was struggling with wanting to be Non-Verbal, but not being able to live up to my own expectations about how to be true to it. It taught me that we all make mistakes. It was a humbling experience, but what matters is what we learn on the journey.

She looked at the audience, who clapped.

'I want to apologise to everyone who felt I had lied to them. You have to understand, I was lying to myself too. I apologise to Sara Javed, who was such an inspiration for me. If Non-Verbalism's taught us anything it's that we should all try to be better. That's why I'm making a new documentary. To learn from others and their experiences with Non-Verbalism. I want my life to be about other people's stories . . .'

'Well done,' said Roxy to Aadhi. '*This* is the kind of shit we're going to have to watch now.'

They sat on his sofa, looking at the screen.

'You don't have to watch it. *Your* choice.'

Roxy scoffed. 'Hashtag get me a placard.

'I tried to use my powers for good,' added Roxy. 'But you . . .'

It had been a grave moment for Aadhi, watching Sara, to be quite honest, in an act of distinct ridiculousness, with that placard in hand. And yet, it had moved him.

He could not stop thinking about both Grace and Sara in the face of such outrage and expectation – how they had held on to their conviction. This could do nothing else but elicit his respect. Invoke Aadhi to carry on and do the same.

He felt he had been missing something in the documentary. Perhaps even in life. But he wasn't sure what. In fact, it had meant him going silent for a while. Just to think things through.

He later spoke to Roxy about his discomfort. That Non-Verbalism, in the end, had lost. Should Sara's perceived ambivalence, her refusal to do the 'right' thing in the documentary, considering her later actions, be revealed?

Many were already arguing that had she appeared sooner, the results could have been different.

And the memory of that moment when she stood on stage might be lost over time, as might the documentary – but what if it wasn't? What if they had not done justice to their portrayal of Sara?

He realised that truth, of which he was such a big fan, did not come in one big burst. It must, by the insidious nature of deception, take a while. Trickle through time and space. If the woman who had become the centre of the movement should want her story told, then she should be the one to tell it. Didn't Roxy agree?

In the end, it was impossible for her not to.

When they had talked to the production company about a revised documentary, without the parts about Sara, there were arguments about breaking the terms of the contract, losing the deal, being unprofessional. Unfortunately, Aadhi and Roxy were led by their feelings and maintained their ground. As a result of this they had to accept a revised, and some-what disappointing, monetary agreement. The price of passion and conscience.

In the end, the company chose not to broadcast the documentary at all. Now *Day Break* was working on a script with Sara Javed's ex-husband, Henry Green, and former friend, Jyoti Patel. An announcement had been made and some press was involved.

'Look at what we've made room for,' said Roxy. 'Fucking Mimi Munkin, trotting around the world, story-seeking with her long blonde hair.'

Roxy had rewatched their documentary, convincing herself of each positive aspect. The sources they'd found! The personal stories! She had almost felt the BAFTA in her hands. But the interviews about and with Sara kept Roxy in an argument with herself about propriety, of all things.

She knew that the documentary made Sara seem like an enemy of free speech: now Roxy wondered whether she had in fact been its caretaker.

'What's going to happen now you're poor?' she asked Aadhi.

'Cardboard box.'

'Write a book,' Roxy suggested. '*Memoirs of a Converted Commentator.*'

'I'll leave that kind of thing to you.'

'I got another offer today from Tailor Books,' she replied.

And it would not be the last for Roxy.

Aadhi, incidentally, *would* end up writing a book and it would pay off some of the debt. Work would come to him in abundance, although he'd still have to downsize. He'd be moving into a one bedroom in Catford, with his belongings and principles. The latter making the move less painful, at least. The book would, eventually, be lost in a deluge of others being published at the same time.

'I hope you're happy, Rox.'

'I think I am. Maybe it was seeing my sister at the protest. Some family's better than no family.'

She looked at her watch and took a deep breath.

'It was never going to be easy,' he said. 'But meeting with Sara, passing over the interview files about her, is the thing we have to do.'

Even as Aadhi said it he felt his muscles tense.

'I don't know why,' Roxy began, 'but I feel sad. Like I lost her again, even though I'd never got her back. I didn't even want her back, really, but still. For a while she had meant something. At one point, everything.'

'Maybe that was the problem,' he said. 'Come on. We'll be late. I booked it ten days ago. If Sara had just let me use her name—'

'You've been in contact?'

'Yes. On and off.'

He acknowledged that he had spent many years in mild contempt of her because he hadn't found her books worthy of their accolade. He still didn't. But he realised that hardly signified. Why should his expectations of her have been any greater than of others?

Aadhi did not relay to Roxy that since then, their talking to one another was becoming increasingly regular. That he found Sara was not lacking in humour. That her measured, quiet way of deconstructing her own silence, was almost mesmerising.

Any restaurant, bar, shop, supporting Non-Verbalism was getting generously fined and, so, understandably those establishments were where everyone wanted to visit. People felt vastly satisfied about paying for a lovely meal and supporting the industries that were still taking a stand against the ban.

It was a convenient sort of activism.

Aadhi and Roxy made their way to Covent Garden where Sara was to meet them outside *Shhhhh* . . . They could not speak once inside, which seemed to defeat the point of Aadhi's attempt to officially apologise.

Images from the global protest were now shared, blown up, exhibited, posted all over the world. Someone had caught an image of Sara with the #Refuse placard, behind her the clip of Baynham lighting the candle.

Baynham had commented, for the papers, that it had been a matter of respect for one way of life.

A series of photos were exhibited in the National Portrait Gallery, the Guggenheim, the Uffizi, the Louvre, of which this particular image became a prominent part. It had prompted tentative conversations, which provoked opinions, which incited debate.

Some came to simply observe and absorb.

#Refuse posters abounded. Though people were paying less and less attention to them.

Side streets had been marked as Non-Verbal. But sometimes passers-by didn't notice and would fall into speech.

Billboards to *Beware the Barrenness of a Busy Life* were displayed, side-by-side with adverts for one of the new, post-silence social media apps, *All Ears*. Where one was only allowed to write a maximum of three posts a day; reply to the same post once; and had to go through a series of questions before allowing any post to go public:

Is your language harmful?

Is the information true?

Will your words matter?

Eventually there would be quarrels about what was harmful to one might be useful to another; what is true is based on perception; and as for words that matter?

All words matter, surely?

The Silent Rooms continued to thrive.

Countries in which Non-Verbalism was still legal saw a significant influx in tourism and immigration.

Shops, bars, restaurants had put up banners encouraging resistance – some more clearly than others.

For most, rage was turning into indignation, would morph into dissatisfaction, and eventually turn into mild irritation. Until, that is, it would barely warrant a feeling at all.

It would have turned into a memory. Too long ago to elicit anything other than nostalgia.

As for what happened to Grace Jenkins and Zainab Aalam, their stories were repeated in several different ways – an independent film, a three-part drama and one theatrical production in Shoreditch – so much so that eventually, their lives weren't even recognisable to the women who had lived them.

Perceived facts would become truth, which would, ultimately, become history.

Until someone might find new facts, have other ideas and prepare themselves to reveal the untold reality; by starting again, from the beginning.

TWENTY YEARS LATER

The Channel 8 News

'Addressing the crises ravaging our planet are of paramount importance, and I believe that by reassessing The Silent Movement we can understand better the mechanics of how, as a society, we were, and are still, being manipulated by our leaders. The movement created an extraordinary moment in history in which billions across the world were united. We must take it as inspiration. We must not repeat our mistakes and let corruption win. . . .'

'That was emerging content creator and producer Cara Jenkins-Nash, who is developing a series of programmes and films about Non-Verbalism from her unique perspective as the daughter of one of its central figures. The Silent Movement, which took place between May 2021 and July 2022, was sabotaged due to governmental corruption. Reports of officials being bribed to lobby for legislation to set the ban in law materialised in 2024, along with evidence that private data was illegally obtained for targeted advertising.

'Funding for True News, a channel that was dedicated to anti non-verbalism, had been traced back to private companies linked to entrepreneur Anthony Stoppard who stood to lose billions if Non-Verbalism had continued its stronghold. Pro-non-verbal channel, The Refusal, was spearheaded by media mogul and social progressive, Christoff Anderson, in a bid to support Non-Verbals and best Stoppard, a long-term rival of Anderson's.

'Jenkins-Nash added, "My production team and I are committed to raising funds for areas suffering the most from lack of food production and water supply issues. We want people to realise that their political choices – allowing authoritarian governments to stay in power because of fearmongering – only worsen an already critical situation. We must focus on hope and shared solutions. The Silent Movement shows that we did it once before, and, it's our firm belief, that through increased awareness, this time the right side will prevail . . ."'

Sara Javed heard the news with as much intrigue as could be expected from a woman who had lived through so much. In the first five to ten years post Non-Verbalism, there had been appropriate uproar about whatever new revelation came to light in regard to the movement, without the appropriate sense of reflection.

Mastery over the self, it seemed, was going to take longer than anticipated.

But what if Non-Verbalism hadn't been banned? Would a less materialistic way of life have prevailed? Would contemplation, rather than judgement, be the norm?

Would it have meant a world that was not now on the brink of destruction?

Sara made some notes about her next book on her PalmPad.

Nothing changes.

Her dad had always been right.

She had lost Lily in a car accident, five years after the ban took effect. Sara was glad to have savoured those years, speaking to Lily about all the mistakes they had made, about Afzal, all the good they had done for each other.

Over the years she had received messages from Roxy (now a motivational speaker with several bestselling books on how to personally thrive in a crumbling world, a long-term partner, and regular reunions with her sister) suggesting Sara write a book about the movement.

An opinion piece.

Maybe an interview.

Sara had done none of the above.

She could not say she still loved Roxy, but Sara could certainly see the shift in her own life's trajectory as a result of Roxy's presence.

This was perhaps stronger than love.

Some things do change.

For a while, after the ban, there had been fervent interest in both Grace Jenkins and Zainab Aalam. Grace had continued her work in women's refuges, specialised in human rights law while juggling motherhood, but despite her history, she had not said or done anything significant enough after the silence to warrant being remembered.

Zainab had completed a PhD at Columbia and then moved back to Pakistan. There, she led a team that specialised in sustainable energy in the global south, which was of little note since she had never bothered to bring her expertise to the global north. The esteem with which she was regarded, the accolade and prizes she had won, the story of the woman who adopted four children without ever marrying again, were confined to interviews and profile pieces in Pakistan. A mother of the nation.

Soon these women were written over, forgotten, replaced with more urgent stories and apparently pressing ideas.

It made the sensation of watching them now – in a special, unedited edition gifted to Sara by Cara Jenkins-Nash (daughter of Grace Jenkins and Graham Nash) – far more pleasant.

That Grace should not be globally acknowledged – just as individuals without status or power around the world were still not recognised – for the key part she played in The Silent Movement was unimaginable to a life like Cara's, which demanded recognition. That Zainab, a woman who had helped her mother through Cara's birth, should have been cast into the shadows, just as other women were still being cast, was *unjust* to a life that demanded justice.

In that way, Grace's story had lived on in her daughter so that when new facts came to light, Cara brought colour to fading memory.

Sara watched Roxy – who had taken part in the new documentary series – with nostalgia and the usual sense of loss.

But *the candles.* Aesthetically they'd certainly had a filmic quality.

And then Aadhi came on screen.

'God knows the various ways she'll fuck it up,' had been Aadhi's exact words when they had learnt of Cara Jenkins-Nash's series. Still, Roxy had convinced him to be a part of the fuck-up. Did he not see that younger generations should be allowed the hope that they can change things?

So, reluctantly, he handed over their dated transcripts, their old footage, which had to be converted and adapted for current technology.

425

Aadhi had asked Sara's opinion about his taking part.

'It's Grace's *daughter*,' she said. 'Where's your sense of poetry?'

'She *speaks!*'

Sara had laughed.

'Why do you still live in obscurity?' he had asked at their most recent dinner date. 'You could've had all the comfort imaginable. Profile pieces, private cruises—'

'Ostentation is a bugbear of mine.'

She had chosen to hold on to the parts of the documentary that had pertained to her.

Still, Sara smiled as Aadhi came on screen. He had aged well, as had Sara's feelings for him. He had been surprised when she had turned up at his father's funeral, a few months after the ban.

'I'm assuming you don't want to be alone. Feel free to tell me to piss off,' she said, helping him clear up the food at the mosque where the funeral took place. Roxy had had to leave to catch a plane for a meeting with a publisher in New York.

Sara had often acknowledged in her later books that Aadhi had made her a better writer. Her own ideas were often crystallised after she had interrogated his misplaced ones. There had been some remarks about her deference to him. No one liked the idea of a man improving a woman's talents, especially one who had won such honours for herself (including a Mildred Aitken Award several years after the ban, which Sara, this time, graciously accepted). So, ultimately, it was largely ignored.

She lit a cigarette. She was dying anyway, so why not?

Perhaps her final book would be about the ultimate capitulation: Death.

It could be a posthumous publication.

Her publisher would probably quite like that.

Sara had watched entire towns destroyed by hurricanes, children suffering from acute poverty, and often cringed at her own self-importance in her youth. The profits from her books now went straight to organisations fighting against the climate crisis. She wrote copy for political campaigns and organised food drives.

She insisted on doing all of this under a pseudonym.

Sara had been asked to take part in the interview with Zainab and Grace. Cara and the producers envisaged a long-awaited union, which would be ripe for viewing. So emotive it'd be the only thing people talked about, for a while, at least.

Sara had obviously declined.

She had continued to receive so many requests to comment on their stories that she had been forced, out of particular irritation one day, to respond with: *'This is not about me. Don't ruin the freshness of these women's stories with my tired, old, stale one.'*

The world remained to her both a comfort and agitation.

Then the camera switched to Zainab.

'Why did you never return to the UK?' asks Cara.

'Glasgow. My once home. The people – are they still as pleasant? I remember roaming the Lochs and feeling this wonderful sense of belonging. I had the chance to go back. The man with whom I'd had the affair wanted to marry me. The clerics here hate me admitting my affair – they say I shouldn't publicise my sins. And Western feminists – they hate my feeling guilt about it. Yet it was a shameful act so I should feel it – do not tell me when to speak and do not tell me what to feel . . .'

Sara laughed. She hesitated and then typed a message to Roxy:

That Zainab is something. Also, how are you?

She turned her attention back to the TV screen.

'Your mother. She taught me that. How is Benji?'

'A very good brother.'

'I knew he would be. I used to watch the way he'd look at Grace's belly. He had been waiting for you. Anyway, I came back to Pakistan, adopted my four children, carried out work that has, I hope, made a difference to domestic policy. And I spoke

427

about all those things we're not supposed to speak about. Things that were actually worth saying . . .'

Zainab's interview followed an emotional on-screen reunion between her and Grace who relayed her journey of silence with her son.

'I realised I had sought to change my son when I was the one who needed to change. My only job was to help him navigate the world so he could find his place. Not force him into a mould that didn't suit him.'

Grace continued to tell the camera that upon Cara's birth, just when she had stopped yearning for Benji to talk, he had started quietly, slowly, to speak.

Now he taught art therapy to selectively mute children. Benji had, ultimately, decided he did not want a relationship with his biological father. His stepfather, Graham Nash, was enough.

Sara, rather affected by all this talk of motherhood, paused the documentary and took out her old journals. She long ago stopped looking upon her mum as someone with whom she was so intricately bound, but, instead, simply as a person in her own flawed right. A subject to be explored.

For a moment Sara felt a panic that her life was going to be too short to be able to write about all the things she wanted. That there wasn't enough time to understand all the things she wanted to understand. The book would have to be about death *and* mothers. The power that lies between birth and that final destination.

Yes, the book would be about power.

And she would, after all was said and done, dedicate it to Roxy.

Sara let the panic subside and played the documentary again. Perhaps she would ask her publicist to get in touch with Grace and Zainab, to meet them.

A deathbed request.

She settled back into the sofa, knowing she would see Aadhi later, to

428

discuss all that had been documented and lived, everything they continued to live through. Until then, she listened to the women who had rewritten tales of tragedy and turned them into a living philosophy.

(And it all made, essentially, very good viewing.)

Sara Javed declined to take part in Remembering Silence: The Truth and the Legacy.
Panels will be taking place around the UK to discuss Javed's integral role. Book your tickets via PingPlan below.
For extended interview features, press 'Next'*

* *Beware the Barrenness of a Busy Life.*

Acknowledgements

As much as I appreciate the art of shutting the fuck up, there are some people to whom I'm very grateful for not doing so. To my agent, Nelle Andrew, who, each year, becomes increasingly brilliant and never wavers in her support and wisdom. People tell me I have the best agent in town and they're right. To this book's editor, Eleanor Dryden, who worked so hard I began to feel sorry for her by draft number two-thousand-and-fifty-six. Am pretty sure we'll notice something we should've changed even after it's published. I'll always be grateful for everything you've done for 'The Movement', me, and my writing. There was no way not to dedicate this book to you.

Thank you to the Red Hot Chilli Writer boys: Amit Dhand, Alex Khan, Vaseem Khan, Imran Mahmood and Abir Mukherjee, for your ongoing support and bakwas. You boys make me glad I never had any brothers. Special appreciation to Imran and, I suppose, Vaseem, for reading early proofs. I love you idiots. But not equally, because Alex is the best one.

For my dearest, long-suffering friends who have all leant their support over the years: Amber Ahmed, Sadaf Sethi, Jas Kundi, Clara Nelson, Yasir Mirza, Ailah Ahmed, Alicia, Kristel Pous, and the dynamic duo, Remona Aly and Onjali Rauf. A special acknowledgement to Simon Cauchemez for his patience in me writing that scientist character into a novel. The next book will be the charm, I promise. Huge thanks to Daisy Buchanan for her early read of the proof and generally being incredibly generous with both her time and praise. Thank you also to Bradford Literature Festival director, Syima Aslam, who has been so supportive of my career ever since *Sofia Khan*, and for all the incredible work she does at BLF. Thank you to Nafeesa Yusuf, always an early (and fast) reader, and Shaista Chishty, another early reader and to whom this book is also dedicated – because you piece together my puzzled brain, and sometimes my most puzzling actions.

To Nadeem Dean, for getting me through the worst of lockdowns. Your dogged persistence these past eleven years finally worked out for me (imagine, another eleven years and we'll have served life!). I'll never look at a bucket of chicken, or a pole, in the same way again. Thank you for over a decade of laughter. It has been singular.

This book required dreaded levels of research and so thank you to everyone who took their time to help. I'm especially thankful to Helen Clydesdale for all her insight into mutism. There are some great resources out there on children with mutism and I'm grateful to everyone whose stories I read online to help get a better understanding of the condition. Thanks to Sharaz Hussain for helping me to comprehend enough economics to wing those tricky documentary sections, and to poor Ben who picked up the phone when I called an immigration lawyers' office and who offered advice on the ins and outs of indefinite leave, deportation and that kind of thing. Must mention Imran Mahmood again here for re-writing the lawyer's letter for me after telling me it was, and I quote, 'The most moronic thing I've ever read.'

Huge thanks to the Headline crew, including but not limited to, Frankie Edwards, Lou Swannell, Lucy Hall, and especially Rosanna Hildyard whose patience with all my to-ing and fro-ing has been exemplary. It takes an incredible team of people and planning to publish a book, without which it simply would not exist. I'm very thankful to the people who are forcing anyone and everyone to read my words.

Thank you to my family. My mum, who's still only ever read *Sofia Khan is Not Obliged* (and even that took her a year. She blamed the font size) my sister, Nadia Malik, who keeps saying I write good books but only ever asks when I'm going to write another 'Sofia Khan' story, my brother in-law, Shazza, who is our fruit-ka-pot. And of course my babies, Zayyan and Saffah Adam, who are both simultaneously the reason I never want children, and the reason I'm eternally grateful that people continue to have them. I love you both the most.

Finally, thanks to God for all of the above, and the ones who are yet to come.